Praise for *West for the Black Hills*

"Leavell has spun a nicely textured narrative with complex main characters . . . There's enough here to keep western fans awaiting the next installment, with faith elements nicely woven in. This absorbing read is a good counterweight to the West as it is often envisioned by inspirational romance writers."
—**PUBLISHERS WEEKLY**

"Peter Leavell writes a compelling story of coming to terms with the past in western style. Research for the time and setting is blended in nicely to deliver a story of one man's search for justice."
—**TRACIE PETERSON**, award winning, best-selling author of over 100 books, including The Lonestar Bride series.

"Peter Leavell brings a historical setting to life with relevance, intrigue and adventure. In *West for the Black Hills*, fans of Louis L'Amour will love the elements of faith."
—**HILAREY JOHNSON**, author of *Sovereign Ground*

"In the tradition of *Shane* by Jack Schaefer, author Peter Leavell has given readers an unforgettable story of a reluctant hero in a tale brimming with everything that makes a great western."
—**NANCY KIMBALL**, award-winning author of *Chasing the Lion*

"With its perfect balance of fast-paced action and tender love story, this new spin on the classic western made me want to strap on a gun-belt and head for the Black Hills. Peter Leavell's reluctant gunslinger is guaranteed to steal reader's hearts."
—**KAREN BARNETT**, award-winning author of The Golden Gate Chronicles and *Mistaken*

West for the Black Hills

WEST FOR THE
BLACK
HILLS

Peter Leavell

Mountainview Books, LLC

For Tonya, Jost & Kade.

My wife, son & daughter.

Thanks for letting me play Philip Anderson when we circled Devil's Tower.

Acknowledgments

This book, the first in a series, is indebted to several people.

The historical society in Mitchell, South Dakota, sent me material almost ten years ago when I started writing a western. The manuscript only made it through a first draft before I put it away to tackle my history degree and then historical fiction novels. They were eager to help, and now that I have worked with historical societies across the country, they are one of the best I've ever worked with.

Thanks to Trisha Brown who read the first draft before I learned a thing or two about writing. Your comments sent a fledgling writer down the road to success.

Chip MacGregor, thanks for your belief in westerns. Holly Lorincz as well.

Terrie Todd edited *God & Gun*, the first edition of *West for the Black Hills*. Your friendship means the world to me.

Becky Lyles is, once again, indispensable. A Peter Leavell novel is not readable without her editing expertise. And thanks to her husband, Steve, who had a hand in the project as well. He should be writing a novel of his own.

The crew at Mountainview Books have been incredible. They are skilled and thorough. I've learned so much from their edits, and in the end, they do nothing to get in the way of the story. Instead, they enhance it.

Thank you to my wife, Tonya, who let me grow a beard while writing *West for the Black Hills*. And to my children, who put up with fuzzy goodnight kisses.

1

Spring 1873

Terror froze my soul as I peered from under a bush. Through the darkness, I could just make out the rider. His moccasin tapped the side of his horse and he rode toward me, moonlight reflecting off the horse's white blaze.

Despite the cool spring night, sweat dripped into my eyes. I bit my tongue to keep from crying out. My breath came in involuntary heaves, and I shivered so that the leaves of the bush shook.

I stared at the bow and quiver full of arrows tied to his naked back.

His horse stopped beside the bush. He hefted his lance and poked just past my arm.

Should I attack him? At ten years old, I was a small target for his arrows.

In the distance our wagon burned, my parents' bodies lying nearby. I choked back a sob. Outlaws had killed them, and I had run. Only to face Indians.

The warrior swung his lance hard and hit my side. I couldn't control the surge of panic, and before I could think my legs darted from the bush, taking me with them.

The Indian swerved his horse to cut off my escape, and I veered to the left. He was quicker. I spun, but he thrust his long spear at my feet, and I slammed into the grass.

I backed away, crawling as he approached. He looked down and pointed the weapon's tip at me. "*Ta ha na dah pe.*"

I shook my head.

"Come here."

Trembling, I stepped forward.

He lowered the lance and pointed toward the river. "Go."

Silhouettes of four more Indians on horseback appeared like ghosts in the soft, silver light. I walked toward them.

They would scalp me, then roast me over a fire. Everyone at home in West Virginia knew the savages in the West enjoyed torture, children their favorite target. My parents' death by bullet seemed easy and painless in comparison.

Perhaps the outlaws who had just killed my mother and father would fight these natives. And then I could escape.

They led me away from the river, out from the bushes and trees, and into the open prairie back toward the wagon.

Its orange glow filled the night. Flames leapt from the canvas into the dark sky. The fire reached to the stars.

The wagon had been my home from West Virginia to the Dakota Territory.

As we approached, heat singed my skin. Blacksmith tools lay strewn about the campsite, and I knew my father would be angry that his tools had been left out. If he were alive.

A wooden maul lay at my feet. I picked it up, took a deep breath, and dove into the inferno of the burning wagon. The fire above roared like an angry bear, and the flames licked my body. At the other end of the wagon, the wood crackled and flung sparks, burning flour, blankets, and clothing.

I lifted the maul and swung it at the floor. The hammer bounced off the planks and stung my fingers. I reached back and slammed it down again. A crack split along the middle. Heat washed over me and I felt like a wilted plant about to burst into flames. I fought the rising terror, and with a few more blows the floorboard shattered. I reached into the family hiding spot and pulled out our red wooden box.

The furious heat nearly melted me. I backed out of the wagon, choking from the dense smoke that swirled over me. Strong hands wrapped around my arms and pulled me from the sweltering blaze.

One axle gave way, and the wagon tipped. After a few moments, it collapsed into a fiery heap. The frame crumpled in a shower of sparks.

I sat with my fingers over my face. A numbness filled me, and the shakes stopped.

The Indians knelt over my parents' bodies.

"Stop!" I jumped up. "Stop it. Don't take their scalps." I made a dash for them.

A lance butt struck me from behind, and I crashed to the ground.

"They look for sign." The Indian who'd found me pulled back the weapon.

I stared up at him. "Sign?"

His waved his arm over the campsite. "Track those who have done this."

The four Indians with rifles got to their feet and approached us. They spoke to each other. The one who'd found me and knew English signaled, and then the four men disappeared into the darkness like ghosts. My guard stayed behind.

I reached for the red box and clutched it close. What was I to do? All I wanted was for this Indian to go away so I could do something, anything. I couldn't think with him so close.

He reached down, picked up a shovel, and hefted it in his hand. He considered the tool for a moment then gazed at me. He held it out, motioning toward his heart with his other hand. "Dig. Help you."

I didn't dare disobey. I set the box on a rock, took the shovel, and near a small pine sapling that only reached my hip, I drove the shovel through the thick grass. I wiggled the handle to drive the tip deeper, then lifted a small amount of grass roots and red dirt. In the firelight, I could see the tiny branches of the tree shake as I worked.

The Indian dropped to one knee beside me, and with a

chisel he'd found near the burning wagon, broke up the ground.

After digging for some time in the waning firelight, a rustle in the grass caught my attention. The other Indians stepped back into the light from the glowing embers. They spoke to the lancer. I leaned against my shovel to study them, waiting. They were discussing how to kill me. Glances my way told me all I needed to know.

The fire died as they talked late into the night. I tossed dirt into a pile at the foot of the hole, shovelful after shovelful, until the wagon's firelight died and darkness covered us.

I felt the warrior's presence and glanced up at his shadow, outlined by stars.

"It is deep enough," he said. "Come, gather what you need."

I dropped the shovel.

He held out a large leather pouch. I slid the box inside and then looked for anything else that could be of value.

I turned, and my parents' bodies were gone. Two of the men were pushing dirt into the hole. I took a step toward them, but the Indian stepped in my way.

He motioned to his chest. "Running Deer."

I tried to rush past the English-speaking Indian, and he grasped me with strong hands. I struggled, until I saw they were burying my parents. I sagged. "Philip. Philip Anderson. Are you going to murder me?"

"No."

"Then let me go." I wanted revenge, to kill those outlaws, all of them. Every bad man in the whole world.

Running Deer picked up his lance and straightened. "You are brave." In the darkness, I could barely make out his gesture toward the other Indians. "Those who did this have escaped. Too much head start."

My knees buckled, and I crumpled to the ground. No tears came.

I would get them. Somehow, somewhere, I would kill them all. Every one of those outlaws—their faces seared into my mind—would die by my hand.

What better way to learn to kill than from an Indian? Maybe they would teach me.

Despite my exhaustion, I rolled over and got up. It felt like a dream as I picked up a hammer and chisel from my father's blacksmithing tools, and in the shallow light chipped a rough cross into the rock beside my parents' grave. I looked up, and the morning light shone on a towering stone column in the distance. It thrust itself into the sky like a single bright flare, higher than anything I'd ever seen before. The top touched the clouds. I glanced at my parents' grave and the giant monument in the distance.

The tower burned itself into my brain.

2

Somehow I'd always believed west was the direction all Indians traveled, away from the Mississippi River, away from the cities toward the open, untamed lands the savages fought vigorously to defend. But with me on an extra pony they'd found in a nearby rancher's barn, these Indians pressed toward the settled east on their horses.

"Eat." Running Deer held out a dried piece of meat.

I squeezed my knees tightly on the pony's bare back, reached out, and took the food. It tasted like deer.

The riders traveled without a word, but I couldn't help questioning them. "Why east? Won't you be shot and killed?"

They rode on in silence.

"I won't join your tribe."

Other than the beat of the horses' hooves as we crossed the wide prairie, quiet cloaked our passage. The wind bent the grass, blowing around my hair and chilling me. My mother's smiling face appeared in my mind, and I burst into tears.

The sun crossed the sky, and I rode in miserable silence. As evening turned into night, my eyes closed to the soft rhythm of the pony's steady gait. I almost fell asleep.

The pony stopped. I looked up, saw the Indians dismounting in darkness, and rolled off my beast.

"Sleep," Running Deer said. "Tomorrow I tell you story."

I did sleep, utterly spent. In the morning after a breakfast of more dried venison, we mounted and he talked of his tribe. They were Minniconjou, a Lakota Sioux group that had banded with another Sioux tribe, Hunkpapa. He motioned to the West. "Sitting Bull, great warrior of Hunkpapa, asked us to talk to agent in East so white man will stay away from Paha Sapa, our hunting grounds."

"Why take me? Am I going to be an Indian?"

For the first time, a smile cracked the thick exterior of the savage. "You will not be harmed, *Miya Ca*."

"What's *Miya Ca*?"

"Wolf. Prairie Wolf." He motioned toward my eyes.

While people had often mentioned my intense, slate-gray eyes, it was the first time I'd been named for them. I lowered my head.

He spoke of his tribe and talked throughout the day while the others rode along without speaking. I found his tone comforting. He taught me several Lakota words.

For three weeks we traveled. Sometimes north, other times east. One day I realized I liked Running Deer, even his friends. This somber warrior filled a void that was left by my father's and mother's death. His sinewy arms, long hair, and dark eyes filled my thoughts, and I stayed close to him. It was no wonder I picked up the warriors' language, learned their ways of hunting and fishing, and respected their ideas of warfare. These men had become all I had in the entire world.

Running Deer told me his men believed my wolf eyes gave them extra power when hunting and fishing. I watched his hands, quick and powerful. I knew if my hands could be as fast, revenge for my parents' death someday would be easier.

Every night I dreamed about their murder. And wondered if I could have stopped it.

The flat prairies turned to rolling hills, and we crossed them without seeing another person. Soon farmhouses dotted the wide expanse, tiny hovels made of sod or planks, boasting of the home my father wanted but would never have. A small town was nestled between two hills, a swollen stream flowing nearby. We rode down the wide street that divided two rows of businesses. Townsfolk paused to watch the small group of Indians wearing a single feather in their hair, rifles in their scabbards, bows on their backs. A few men with hands on pistols stepped forward. But no one stopped us.

Running Deer paused, looked at me, and reached into a leather satchel. From it he withdrew a faded paper. He sniffed. "Where is this?"

I took the paper and could barely make out an address. "I'm not sure." I glanced around and saw a round man in a white shirt stained with sweat. "Sir, could you tell me where this is?"

The man snatched the slip and held it up so sunlight touched the page. "Could have guessed. Blasted Indian agent. Always getting this kind in town," he said, motioning toward Running Deer. "The agent's back on Third. Turn 'round, take a right, fifth house on the left." He looked at me. "Boy, you gotta leave these Indians. They'll kill you."

I ignored him and he dropped the paper, spun around and returned to his shop, mumbling as he went.

Leaving the paper on the ground, I looked up at my traveling companions. "Follow me."

I walked, my pony trudging along as I led him by the thin leather reins. We crossed the street, found Third, and I counted the houses until we arrived at the fifth house. A small sense of pride filled me as the Indians trailed behind. They needed me.

A porch wrapped around the front of the house, and I stepped onto it. "Should I knock?"

Running Deer gave a single nod.

I rapped my knuckles on the wood panel.

A man opened the door and peered out. His bald head shone in the sun. I could see my reflection in his tiny spectacles, which he adjusted. He licked his lips. "Y . . . yes?" The man was almost as small as me.

Running Deer stepped onto the porch, his moccasins

making no noise on the wooden planks. His naked chest looked out of place in the civilized town. "We come to see Mr. Preston."

"Of course, of course, come in. Yes, come in. I'll see if he's available."

The tiny man left the door open for us and disappeared down a long hallway. Running Deer and I stepped inside and entered the parlor. The others waited outside. Rather trusting, I thought, leaving an Indian and a small boy alone in the parlor.

After weeks of sleeping under the night sky, the confines of the papered walls felt suffocating. I stepped closer to Running Deer and brushed against his buffalo skin leggings.

The sound of boots pounded down the hallway, and the small man stepped around the corner. "He will see you now."

Running Deer looked down at me. "Wait." He followed the man.

After a moment the small man returned, a mug in his hand. "You've been living with the Philistines. You need milk. Drink up."

How living with Indians made milk necessary I didn't know. But the mug was cool in my hands, and the milk white and thick on my tongue. I stood in a corner facing the man, a small fireplace to my right, an elegant red chair to my left. The sweet perfumes of the house made me aware of my own outdoor smell.

"The horrors you must have seen, boy. What's your name?"

The horrors? Running Deer had begun teaching me to track animals, fire a bow, throw a hatchet, skin a deer, speak his language, and a hundred other bits of life on the prairie. I shrugged.

"Soon you'll be safe." He smiled and licked his lips again.

I set my mug on the hardwood floor and shook my head. I didn't want to be safe. Running Deer was my life now.

I was about to scamper by the small man when Running Deer stepped around the corner. He leveled his dark eyes at me. "Agent Preston. Speak to him."

"I don't want to talk."

"You must. Go. I wait here."

The long hallway stretched before me, an open door at the end. After a few strides, I turned and looked back toward my friend. He motioned his hand toward the room, as if impatient for me to finish what he'd begun. After a deep breath, I walked into the Indian agent's office.

A wide, dark desk stretched across the floor. Behind it, a large man studied a map that spread over his desktop. I peered at the lines drawn on the yellow paper. It was a map of the United States.

The Indian agent looked up. Despite his wide waistline, he dashed across the room and grabbed my elbow. "Sit down here, boy." His voice was gruff but his grip crueler. He threw me into a chair. "Tell me everything. Leave nothing out."

I hesitated.

He drew up his bulk and hovered over me. "Tell me. Now."

During my time with the Indians, I'd pressed the past to the back of my mind, far from my thoughts, only remembering my family in my dreams. But this man forced the memories to flood back.

"My parents bought land near Yankton. We're from West Virginia and my father, he was a blacksmith. Thought he would make a go of it in the West." The long wagon ride crossed my mind—the dust, the hunger and thirst, the agonizing boredom. And that night beside the river, a quiet night. My father read his Bible while I helped mother cook over the fire.

They came out of the darkness into the firelight with guns drawn.

"We've no money," my father said.

"Wrong answer." The gunman's pistol flashed with a blast that reverberated off the trees along the river.

My father fell back, grasping his belly. With a scream, my mother, sizzling pan in hand, charged the man. Another explosion rocked the night and she fell.

When she didn't move, I slipped away, toward the river.

I wiped tears from my cheek with a sleeve. "If Running Deer hadn't found me, I would still be out there. Dead."

The man looked at me for a moment, as if considering my story. With a deep sigh, he stepped behind his desk and opened a drawer. He pulled out a Bible and held it out. "Swear to me all you have said is true. If you lie your eternal soul will rot in hell, and the demons will make sure you never see your parents again."

I choked. With shaking hand I touched the Bible. "I swear. I'm not a liar."

He pulled the Bible back and nodded as if satisfied. "Very well." His tone softened. "Are you sure it wasn't the Indians who killed your family?"

I reached for the Bible again. "It wasn't Running Deer."

He held the black Word of God against his chest. "No need to swear. I believe you." He sighed. "You see, Congress has said the Black Hills were to remain Indian land." He leaned against the desk and motioned toward the front of the house. "These Sioux say settlers are looking for gold in the hills."

I shrugged and with some effort tried to put forward my opinion. "Running Deer is not a farmer. He needs land to hunt on."

A slight smile crossed the man's face. "But if there is gold in the Black Hills . . ." his voice trailed. "I was about to send Lieutenant Colonel Custer into the hills to find out if the rumors were true." He leaned forward. "You didn't see any gold, did you?"

I shook my head. We hadn't been in the Black Hills. Yankton was on the east side of the Dakota Territory, the Black Hills on the west.

"Well, it seems you've been well treated, in any case." He returned the Bible to the drawer. "We've an orphanage in Fort Madison where you will learn a trade, become a contributor to society."

My future, I'd taken for granted, was with Running Deer. "No, thank you. I better be going now." I stood.

"Sit down." He placed both hands on the desk. "There's nowhere for you to go. I will care for you here."

I took a step toward the door. "Running Deer will take me where I want to go."

"You will blacksmith for me."

I scratched the side of my head, thinking. What family could I go to? All I knew of was an uncle in Sioux City. "I have somewhere I can go. Running Deer will take me."

"The second you're out of this office and away from my protection, you will die." He snapped his fingers. "They will kill you now that you've served their purpose. You were simply a token of goodwill. An indication they can behave civilized. But now that your usefulness is over . . ."

I reached for the door handle. "I'll take my chances."

"My place has two meals a day. With your blacksmithing, you can make it three."

"Your place?"

A grin crossed his wide face. "That's right. I own the orphanage."

"You can't just own an orphanage." I pulled on the door-knob. Locked.

"This is for your own good." He stepped around his desk and reached for me. I jerked away, but he grasped my arm. With a grunt, he hauled me away from the door toward a side window. He threw open the lock and slid the glass up the tracks.

"No. Leave me be."

"You'll thank me for this later, boy."

"Running Deer, help!"

I fought against the man, his grip like a blacksmith's vice. He thrust a leg through the window.

"Quiet, now. No need informing the whole town."

The knob on the door rattled, and in less than a second it flew open. Running Deer stood in the doorway, his dark gaze locked on the Indian agent.

"He's trying to take me to become his blacksmith." I tugged hard, loosened his grip on my arm, and rushed toward the Indian. "He wants to take me to his orphanage."

The man crawled back through the window and lunged at me. Running Deer lifted his arm and threatened to bring his brown hand down on the agent's head.

The agent backed away.

We left town. Surrounded by Sioux warriors, I reached up and took Running Deer's hand. I smiled at him, and even though he showed no emotion, I believed he was pleased. Life with him would be perfect, and the tightness in my chest rolled away. I would be an Indian forever.

3

One week later, I entered Sioux City alone. Running Deer and the others stayed outside of town. Waiting.

I asked storekeepers if they knew of any Andersons in town, anyone who might know my uncle, but it seemed he did not exist. Relieved, I returned to Running Deer.

"He doesn't live here." I reached for my pony's reins. "I'll have to stay with you."

Running Deer gazed into the branches of the cottonwood that shaded us from the sun. He took a deep breath, his chest rising and falling. He reached up and took from his neck a leather strap with a single bear claw dangling from the end. I watched him drop to one knee so that I looked down on him.

"*Miya Ca*. You are brave. And you have proven you are a warrior. But we must part ways. I go to war. You go to learn. Come, let us go to orphanage. It will not be like the other. You will be safe there."

"But—"

"I am firm in this."

Running Deer's stern look left no room for argument.

I motioned to the others good-bye, and I cried as we entered town again.

"Here, take this." He handed me the necklace as we neared a tall, brick building. "Learn what you can. Find your uncle or find your way."

I held the claw. "This is your medicine."

"*Miya Ca*, you need good medicine. This is to make you happy during sad times."

A sob caught in my throat. "But you make me happy." I bit my lip when he put a hand on my shoulder, and I looked into his eyes. "I will find you some day. I will repay you for saving me."

Life at the orphanage in Sioux City could have been worse. At least an Indian agent didn't own it. Instead it was run by a nice elderly woman who was paid by the community.

I studied in the mornings. Afternoons I found work with a single man who owned a blacksmith shop. Terry Feather, half French and half Cherokee, needed a boy like me who could do menial tasks around the shop. His business had picked up due to the railroad coming to town.

Soon I was hammering nails, horseshoes, and doing other light work. He paid well, fifty percent of the job. As I took on more domestic chores such as sharpening axes, plows, hoes, fixing wheels and then eventually making them, Terry Feather was free for the heavier jobs from the railroad. After hours, I would sometimes stay late and pound out kettles, pots, and ladles to sell on my own time.

The years were kind. I grew tall and my muscles hardened. Before long, I was helping with the heavy work. Sometimes we were paid in cash, other times railroad bonds that quickly grew in value.

My father's image standing before his killers still returned to my mind often. He couldn't pull his revolver fast enough. His slowness killed him, my mother, and almost me. So I purchased a Smith and Wesson .44. Every day at lunch and some evenings I practiced at the edge of town.

An old man from Arizona heard me shooting and joined in. "Reckon if you wanna learn t'shoot, I better learn you t'shoot right. Back in my day, we was learning t'hit a nickel at a hundred yard, but nobody taught us aiming at people ain't right. Gonna pound that into your head."

One day I was faster drawing from the hip and more accurate than my friend. He paused, bowing his head. "Now I reckon you'll be bent on revenge. But when it's over someone'll be after you, and you'll be needing that gun the rest of your life, 'til you run into someone faster and more accurate than you." He looked into my eyes. "Dead's mighty permanent."

I shivered, and my wish for revenge waned. The idea of killing someone revolted me. Instead of looking forward to revenge as I honed my skills, I thought back on that night and pictured myself defending my parents.

I read newspapers about the American West. Custer, the name thrown at me years before by the Indian agent, indeed found gold in the Black Hills. Later, he was killed at a place called Little Bighorn. Had Running Deer been there?

By the age of seventeen, the lust for revenge failed me. I still found that pulling my gun and shooting at a target was relaxing and continued to practice for sport long after my shooting friend died. My thoughts of the future created more questions than answers. I knew as a man I would have to make my way in the world. Slowly a plan formed in my mind.

I dreamed of the Dakota Territory. As Terry Feather and I shaped and bent metal, I talked about the crops I could grow after taming the grassy expanse.

But another love came into my life.

"She's beautiful." I set the hammer on the anvil, wiped my forehead, and looked at Terry. "Nothing like I've ever seen before. Small ankles and not very tall. But she's strong. And fast. I talked to her owner. She comes from Arabia. Can carry a man one hundred miles a day, even a man as tall as I am."

Terry Feather didn't look up from his work, just shook his head and chuckled.

So began my love of horses, especially this rare breed called Arabian. They were more beautiful than any woman I'd ever seen.

The Homestead Act gave 160 acres to anyone over twenty-one who could work the land for five years. No charge. Orphans could apply at age eighteen. I was counting the days.

I wanted to breed Arabians, maybe even train and sell them to Army officers. It took some doing by the large livery stable in town, but they contacted a dealer in Virginia who knew someone in Germany with a friend in Egypt who bred Arabian horses. When enough cash had passed from my bank account through Virginia and Germany to Egypt, a stud and three mares were put on a ship that crossed the ocean and traveled up the Mississippi River. After the vessel turned onto the Missouri, the horses were unloaded and shipped to a new town blossoming in the Dakota Territory, Mitchell.

But I couldn't resist buying a Belgian draft horse in addition to the Arabians. I named him Franklin. His enormous body dwarfed mine. He and I would walk the hundred fifty miles from Sioux City to our new home near Mitchell.

With a heavy heart, I visited the grave of my gunman friend from Arizona and said good-bye to Terry Feather. I thought about strapping on my Smith and Wesson but decided against it and tossed it into my pack. Thankfully, where I was going there would be no need for guns.

4

Five Years Later
Spring 1887

I couldn't wait for the land assessor any longer. There was work to be done.

Franklin stomped his hoof impatiently as I checked the straps stretching from his harness to the gnarled stump. I kicked the shovel from the deep gouge in the earth and tossed the pick to the side.

With spring came planting, and after pulling weeds in the wheat and the garden, it was time to pull stumps and roots to clear more land. From the moment I stepped foot on the homestead I hadn't run out of projects.

The fierce Dakota sun cooked the freshly-dug soil around me. Bright rays penetrated my straw hat. I wiped sweat from my eyes with a sleeve, crawled out of the hole, and gave the stump a final kick, to no effect. I walked around a pile of roots I'd cut earlier and took my position in front of Franklin.

"We've pulled many a stump like this one before. You ready, boy?"

He nodded his huge head as if he agreed.

I pulled him forward until the ropes between the horse and the roots were taut.

"Boy, step up."

He pressed ahead. Roots snapped and popped. The stump groaned.

"C'mon, boy."

His massive feet grabbed at the earth. I strained, pulling on his noseband.

The ropes snapped. Franklin lurched forward and I fell, his giant frame flying over me. His back hoof slammed against my forehead and the world spun.

An animal scream filled the air, and I struggled through the fog in my mind. Franklin lay on his side, his head trapped by a huge root against the ground. I tried to rise, but nausea rose in my gut. I crawled to his side.

The root was stuck between his noseband and his face, pinning his head to the earth. He writhed.

"Easy, easy." I touched his nose. Only a scratch where the branch had rubbed against his skin.

I pulled a knife from my pocket, opened it, cut through the leather of the noseband and the ropes behind him. He jerked back and heaved himself to his feet. With a whinny, he darted a few feet into the clearing and paused. His flanks quivered.

I leaned back, closed my eyes, and let the heat fight with a cool breeze against my cheek. After a few minutes the world righted itself, as did my stomach. I opened my eyes and Franklin stood over me. He shook his coat, and dust rained on my head.

"Hello. Mr. Anderson? Are you Philip Anderson?"

Surprised, I crawled to my feet, but the dizziness returned. I touched my head gingerly. "You know who I am, Mr. Halliday."

He patted the horse's back and thrust a thumb through his suspender. "You look terrible. What happened?"

"Just one of my many farm accidents." I took a deep breath, reached down, and picked up my hat. I inspected it for damage, found none, and carefully set it back on my head. "You ready to look the place over?"

He waved his hand. "Mere formality. Your horses, log

cabin, barn, fields . . ." He shook his head. "Mere formality. Hard to believe you've lived here five years already."

I nodded. "Thanks. Where do I sign?"

"No time for that."

"No time? What do you mean?"

"Marshal Stone has asked for you to come to town right quick."

"The marshal? Why?"

He shrugged. "There's a savage woman downtown he needs help with."

"What savage woman?"

"Sioux squaw in town causing trouble. Stone wants you to translate."

I cleared my throat and shook the dirt from my clothes. "I doubt she's a savage."

Halliday frowned.

"I suppose I can head to town." I studied him for a moment. "You came twenty minutes from Mitchell just to tell me the marshal wants me?" I stiffened. I hadn't told anyone I could speak their language. Where had he gotten the idea I spoke Lakota?

Halliday looked away. "I overheard Marshal Stone telling his deputies he knew you talked savage."

Since leaving Running Deer, I'd done my best to remember the Lakota Sioux dialect. I'd even practiced it to myself. But I had told no one of my time with him or anything about my childhood, not even my closest friends in town, Leroy and Scott. That part of me died a long time ago and was privileged information.

"I need to saddle Raven, and then I'll join you."

"I'll head to town now. Come by the office to sign the deed when you're done."

With a nod, I made my way to Franklin. I led him toward the James River that bordered the eastern side of my land. We skirted the wheat field. I saw Halliday mount his horse and ride up the lane that divided my two fields in half and then up the ravine that enclosed the western side.

Franklin and I passed the house and stopped at the barn.

I opened the corral, led him inside, took off what was left of the harness, and let him wander into the pasture. I let loose a whistle.

Over a small knoll in the center of the sixty-acre pasture loped Raven, my barren mare born in Egypt. Her inky-black coat simmered in the morning sun. The rest of the herd, a stud, two mares, a pair of three-year-olds, and the yearlings crested the hill but slowed and paused when they saw I only wanted Raven and had no oats. They returned to their grazing.

My wallet was in the house, so I grabbed it and snatched the riding tack from the barn. I hefted Raven's saddle onto her back and mounted. I maneuvered my horse and closed the corral gate, tugged my straw hat tight on my head, and thrust my heels into Raven's sides.

It may take most folks twenty minutes to travel from my farm to Mitchell, but Raven and I could easily halve that time. If there was trouble in town, I wanted to get there as soon as possible to help.

I passed Halliday on the way and waved behind me. He called my name, but I pressed on, eager to see the marshal.

Two ruts stretched to the north high above the James River. I glanced to the right, over the deep valley and the slow-moving water below. Trees created dense thickets in some areas, breaking up the fields freshly plowed with wheat and corn. To my left was a flat stretch of farmland where cows and horses grazed.

The sky, filled with tall white clouds, seemed to stretch forever. I closed my eyes and felt the spring wind on my face. The fresh smell of flowers tickled my nose. Raven's smooth gait gave me the sensation I was flying with the billows above. Several minutes of riding and the ravine to the right flattened as the trees closed in on the road. I pressed on, past the forest and into the populated outskirts of town.

Riding through Mitchell made me feel good to be a part of the hustle and bustle. With its sudden growth, I was considered a founder of the area, a long-term resident.

In 1880, two years before I staked my claim along the James River, Mitchell was home to fewer than 400 residents.

In just seven years, the town had blossomed to over 3,000 individuals and served as the Davidson County seat.

The reason for the population explosion was the same for many towns in the Dakota Territory—the railroad.

As the Chicago, Milwaukee, and St. Paul Railway Company laid its tracks across the endless expanse of grass, someone decided the best place for a town was on the western side of the bridge that would cross the James River. A piece of driftwood was found several hundred yards west of the river, and it was guessed the flood plain ended there. Just off the flood plain a town was started. Named Mitchell, after the president of the railroad, the burgeoning village soon became a major depot.

Mitchell had every business I could imagine. A lumberyard, several general markets, dry goods, four banks, restaurants and saloons, blacksmiths, tack shops, millinery shops, textiles, law offices, barber shops, hotels, and three newspapers. There was a lovely cemetery on the edge of town, with tall cottonwood trees standing guard over the gravestones. City Marshal Stone made sure people ended up in the graveyard of natural causes, and the Dakota Wesleyan University strived to make people smart enough to stay out of the cemetery as long as possible.

I was pleased with my growing town.

But I had noticed a change in the last two years. Summers came with blinding heat, and the winters were cold and dry. Spring storms scurried across the plains weekly but never carried enough rain to sufficiently satisfy the thirsty crops. Crop prices steadily declined. No area was left unclaimed around the city under the Homestead Act, so the price to expand a farm was high.

With the land in private hands, new settlers became rare. Every now and again a business would close its doors, and the building would remain empty for months. But despite the slowing economics, Mitchell was enormous compared to its county neighbors.

As I neared Main Street, people nodded my direction in recognition. Carriages passed, as did horses and riders.

Shoppers on the boardwalks all seemed pleased and happy until I pulled up at the marshal's office where a deputy waited.

"Marshal Stone's been waiting for you." He mounted his horse. "Out front of Gale's Market."

I nodded and followed him, barely glancing at the long rows of businesses connected by a single front. Mitchell was a one-gun type of town, and Marshal Stone carried that gun. I saw him leaning against the hitching rail, his bulldog face red under a wide-brimmed hat. A crowd surrounded him, but no one stood too close to the marshal.

Under Gale's shop overhang huddled a dark-skinned family. Three small children with tear-stained faces watched as their mother argued with Gale. The argument must have been going on for over half an hour by now based on when Halliday came to get me.

I followed the deputy as he rode into the throng. A dusty cloud settled on the people, and they turned to look at me. I swallowed my rising discomfort and dismounted a few feet away, tied Raven to the hitch in front of Jon's Leather and Tack, and walked toward the children. I knelt before the youngest and touched her wet tears. I stepped back to the edge of the crowd.

The woman's words reached my ears as she spoke with the marshal. Her noble accent and pronunciation excited me. It had been a long time since I'd heard Lakota.

I tried to gather the reason for the fight. Gale was upset she took a flour sack but did not pay for it. She claimed she gave him the money. Neither one understood the other. The flour sack was on the ground beside the children.

Gale kept glancing up. I followed his gaze and saw he was looking at Jacob Wilkes. Jacob, who leaned against the porch rail of a nearby store, shook his head.

Why would a banker's son be involved in this dispute?

"Where's Anderson? He was here a minute ago." I heard the deputy's voice over the murmuring crowd.

With a sigh, I stepped toward Marshal Stone. He was nearly three inches shorter than me, but so were the rest of the men in the crowd.

"About blasted time." Marshal Stone stepped forward. "You speak Sioux. See if you can tell what she's getting at. She hasn't paid for that flour, and she's not about to."

I frowned. "What makes you think I can speak her language?"

"I'm not addle-headed. Get over there."

"How did you know—?"

"Now's not the time." His dark eyes flashed, and he nodded toward Gale and the Indian woman.

I crossed my arms. I didn't want to get involved in a conflict. I took a few tentative steps in their direction, the marshal by my side, and paused when the Sioux woman looked up. I took a deep breath. *"Hilhe 'iciya po. O'wakiyin kte."*

Her eyes widened.

The grocer brought the bottom of his white apron to his forehead and wiped away dust and sweat. He wiggled his thin mustache. "What was that? What did you say to her?"

I faced him. "I told her to take courage. I will help."

"You're going to help this squaw? She's lucky I let her into my store. I doubt anyone else would."

I ignored him and glanced at Jacob, who had straightened and was taking in the scene with interest. He looked so out of place with his white suit and cane.

I turned to the woman. The words slipped smoothly from my lips as I asked her what tribe she was a part of.

"Hunkpapa."

"What are you doing here?" I waved a hand behind me, motioning at Main Street.

"I am buying food for my family."

"This far away from your home?"

Her head drooped, and she spoke so fast it took a moment to comprehend what she said. "My husband works for a white trader. My husband wants to be as whites. My husband sends me to buy food."

Out of the corner of my eye, I saw Jacob raise an eyebrow at the grocer.

Gale growled. "I don't like them talking like that, as if they was plotting something."

I glared at the grocer then turned back to the woman. "They are saying you didn't pay."

She exploded into a tirade. I stepped back. "I did pay him," she insisted. "I gave him a full dollar and ten cents."

The crowd hushed as I changed to English. "She says she paid you for the flour."

Gale's teeth clenched, and he spoke with forced restraint. "She paid me a fraction of what the price is."

Jacob gave a nod.

I tried to smile and hoped he would accept the explanation. "Flour's a dollar ten for twenty-five pounds. She says that's what she paid you."

"Flour's two-fifty." The grocer crossed his arms.

"Two-fifty? When did flour get so high?"

"That's the price for *her* flour. I'm the only one who will sell to her, and if people find out I let a savage in, they won't shop with me. Risk management."

I balled my fists, ready to hit the man.

Jacob had taken a step closer, and many in the crowd backed away from him. He motioned toward Marshal Stone.

I glanced at the marshal. His face was unreadable, but he did nothing to intervene. The crowd remained quiet, expectant. I spotted Scott, my friend who was my age, and Leroy, a Civil War veteran. Neither moved, only stared at me.

Grumbling, I shoved past Gale and stormed into the store. I pulled out my wallet, snatched two coins, and held them up. As Gale entered behind me, I faced him. "Two dollars more." I slammed them on the counter. One dropped to the floor, rolling across the wooden planks and under a shelf of canned peaches.

I pocketed my wallet and hefted a bag of flour. A jar of peppermints lay open on the counter and I reached in and snatched a few. "The goods are mine. Who I give them to is my affair. And you still make money." I brushed by him onto the porch, picked up the woman's other bag of flour, and headed for her wagon. The crowd parted ahead of me.

With a heave, I lifted both bags over the side and into the bed. When I turned, I saw the Indian family follow, the children's eyes wide. My heart softened, and I dropped to a knee and held out the peppermints. The children hesitated, looked up at their mother, and after she nodded grabbed the candies from my palm.

The Indian woman stepped forward, ignoring the crowd. I stood and faced her. "*Tanyan.*" All was well.

"*Hi, hi*," she said, thanking me.

I glanced at Marshal Stone, who frowned but backed away and left. The crowd around us began to disperse. Gale didn't emerge from his shop again.

Jacob stared at me. He gripped his cane as if he were strangling it. He turned and walked down the street.

My hands shook.

As the woman loaded her children beside the flour, I directed questions at her. Where was she from, what she was doing? Knowing that members of the same tribe knew one another intimately, I asked the most important question. "Do you know Running Deer?"

She hefted the last child into the wagon and nodded. "I know Running Deer."

My heart leapt. "Where is he?"

"West at Grizzly Bear Lodge, where sometimes we winter."

I shook my head. "Where is that?"

"Paha Sapa, past the mountains, lies a tall rock that reaches to the clouds. Under the rock is the lodge."

"Paha Sapa, the Black Hills? And the rock, what is the rock?"

Her voice softened, as if telling a child a fairytale. "Children played. A bear chased them in hopes to eat them. But the earth knew the bear was greedy and told the children to jump onto a rock. The rock grew tall above the bear. The bear, more greedy than ever, grew to reach the children, but the rock sprouted in size so quickly the children were launched into the stars."

Her eyes turned toward the West. "The bear's claws scraped the edges of the rock, making great grooves in the sides. And the children became stars."

I reeled backward and put a hand to my head. Images of my past forced themselves forward—the high column towering into the clouds, that dreadful morning, the light hitting the massive stone. I'd seen that rock when I etched the cross into the stone grave marker, but I always thought it had been in Iowa or Nebraska. I had no idea my parents could've died in the Dakota Territory.

"Devil's Tower?" I asked.

She shrugged. "That's what white man call it."

I cradled my head in my hands. Memories assaulted my brain. I backed away. In the corner of my vision, I saw the woman climb into the wagon, flick the reins, and turn the corner.

I rested against the hitching rail, trying to think. The tall column of rock, Devil's Tower. And the Black Hills. Both lay close to one another. Why had I not remembered that fact?

Because I didn't want to.

My parents' homestead was south of Mitchell at Yankton. They had passed by their land and continued west for the Black Hills. They were killed hundreds of miles beyond their destination. And I didn't know why.

5

I stood on the rough-hewn boards, watching the woman and her wagon drive away.

The crowd was gone and Marshal Stone mounted his horse.

I approached him and folded my arms. "How did you know I spoke Lakota?"

He glanced down at me and picked up the reins. "I know your past."

"How?"

"It's my job to know everyone's past. Thanks for your help." He tapped his horse's sides and rode off.

My friends Scott and Leroy leaned against the porch rails of Caroline's Kitchen across the way, looking at me with confused expressions.

I would have to think through the implications of recent revelations later. I untied Raven and led her across the ruts in the street.

Scott took off his hat and brushed back his bright red hair. His face, youthful despite being in his early twenties like me, was nearly as enflamed as his mane. "Just when you think you know a guy," he muttered to Leroy.

Leroy turned his grizzled face upward. "He speaks Indian? Never knew that about him."

Scott tugged on Leroy's arm. "C'mon, let's go back inside, where we know the people."

The two spun on their heels, crossed the front porch, and disappeared inside the the restaurant.

I glanced side to side, prepared to follow them but paused. Standing alone was a woman I'd not seen before. Her dark hair was tied with a ribbon behind her head, her skin fair. She wore riding pants. I took a second look. Women in pants were rare in the city.

She was staring at me. I knew what she saw. Everyone noticed my cold, gray eyes. When I first met a person, sometimes they would shift nervously, unable to look directly at me.

I tipped my hat, turned, and ducked into Caroline's.

Two small windows at the front illuminated the interior. It took a moment for my eyes to adjust. I passed several empty tables and saw Scott and Leroy at our usual table.

The aroma of freshly-baked bread wafted from the kitchen. My stomach rumbled. Yes, food. That's what I needed. Hot vittles that I didn't have to cook.

I stepped toward my friends, avoiding their gazes. Instead, I looked at the bare plank walls.

Leroy grunted. "I'm not sure you should sit with us." He squinted up at me. "Don't know if you'll go savage."

I settled next to Scott and took off my hat. "So, what happened? Town meeting and everyone decided to call Indians savages today?"

Scott smiled, his teeth perfectly white. "Mosquito bite?"

I reached up and felt a knot on my forehead. "I was pulling stumps with Franklin when the rope snapped. Took us both down."

Leroy took a quick sip from his mug. "You don't learn to speak that language just by wantin' to." He peered at me through squinted eyes. "You gotta live with them."

Information was a privilege, and while I enjoyed my friends, I was loath to tell them about my past. Everyone thought I'd traveled here as an adventurer, leaving my parents in West Virginia. Which was true. Everything in between that time had ceased to be.

"A head for languages." I thumped my forehead with a finger and winced. "Lakota is one I chose to learn. I enjoy it." I hated lying to my friends, but it was for the best. I clenched a fist as guilt washed over me.

The furrows in Leroy's brow relaxed. "I knew you was smart." He leaned back.

Scott gave me a shove. "Of course he's smart. He and I are the best catches in town."

"Then how come neither of you are married?"

Caroline, owner of Caroline's Kitchen, grabbed a chair and set it at the end of our table. With a groan, she dropped her bulk into the seat and smoothed her apron across her legs. "You boys need to marry."

Scott flashed a smile. "With your cooking, we've no need."

She flung the rag on her shoulder at him. "No excuse. Time you two be getting married." She smiled. "You, too, Leroy." Her eyes opened wide, revealing deep brown, and her ample face glowed as she looked at the older man.

Leroy grunted.

I decided to change the subject. "Five years ago this year I came to the Territory. Land assessor just approved me. The land is mine."

Leroy slapped the table. "Well, now, that's something to celebrate. You live in the best place in the country." He sat up. "I was just saying to Scott that Mitchell should be capital of the Dakota Territory, not Bismarck. Too far away. And I know more bad stories about Bismarck than I know of President Cleveland. And he's a Democrat."

Scott smiled. "And Yankton's too far south. Mitchell's perfect."

"What about Becky?" Caroline lifted an eyebrow.

Scott turned his head toward her. "Becky?"

"She's pretty. And just turned nineteen." She sighed and her hand touched her heart.

Scott drummed his thumbs on the table and lowered his head. He looked past thick brows. "I heard marrying is bad for your liver." He pointed at my hat. "There's the reason you're not married. That straw hat."

"It stays."

Caroline sighed again. "Love is wasted on the young."

I thought of the woman watching me from the end of the porch. She was beautiful. Could I marry someone so stunning someday?

Anna Johnston lifted her boot and set her foot in the stirrup. She swung her leg over the saddle and settled in the seat.

The man with the funny eyes had looked at her riding pants. Twice.

Fair is fair. She turned in the saddle and saw through the window the tall man walking through the restaurant. She glanced at his pants. Dirty. As if he'd rolled around in the dirt. A farmer.

But a farmer with an Arabian black? She'd read a lot about horses, and black for that breed was rare.

With a soft flick of her wrist her horse, Alita, trotted down the street.

She wouldn't think about the tall stranger with the funny eyes and the knot on his forehead. Men were too . . . what was the word?

"Welcome to Mitchell."

She pulled back on the reins as a blond man in a white suit stepped in front of Alita. His hand rested on a cane.

"You are the most beautiful woman this town has ever seen."

She opened her mouth to speak, but nothing came.

"Would you do me the honor of having dinner with me tonight?"

How could Jacob Wilkes find her attractive in her riding gear? Avoiding men was the point, not attracting them. She looked at him again. His smooth skin was pale, his lips dark and thin, yet his dimpled jaw held a strange appeal for her.

But if she said yes, would she find herself in the same predicament that had caused her father to move here from Missouri?

She meant to say no, but instead found herself saying yes.

"Excellent. The Alexander Mitchell at, say, seven o'clock?"

What had she done?

"What is your name?"

"Anna."

"Anna, if you like, I can call for you at your home. Just tell me where you live."

His deep, mellow voice eased her worries. It was simply supper, right? "I will meet you there."

Alita snorted and pawed at the dirt.

"I look forward to it with all my heart." His smile was charming as he stepped to the side, a slight limp making his movement slow.

Her cheeks tingled. She squeezed her calves and Alita took her past him.

As she explored the countryside to the south of Mitchell on the well-trodden lane, her mind wandered. The first man's kindness to the Indian woman was intriguing. His ability to speak her language seemed to surprise everyone in the crowd. What other surprises did Mr. Eyes have?

But the second man's manner was winning as well. Charming and sophisticated.

She lifted her hand to shade her eyes and took in the vast plains that spread to her right.

An animal screech under Alita's heels made the horse jump. Anna grasped the saddle horn with both hands as another shriek made her horse bolt to the left. A narrow path stretched through a thicket, and Alita thundered through, the branches and leaves slapping at her rider.

Anna leaned back and pulled trying to slow her but couldn't. The horse galloped into a clearing, and near the edge the path turned. Alita cut to the left, but Anna didn't. She flew through the air, the sensation of weightlessness exhilarating if she didn't know the end result.

She cleared a boulder with a log balanced atop it and hit a tree. Alita's leg bumped the log, and it fell on top of Anna's leg.

Wide-eyed, Anna stared at the log wedged between the tree and boulder. It pressed heavy against her thigh but had stopped just before crushing her bone. She tried to slide her leg out, but a sharp pain made her scream.

She lay back and looked through the branches to the sky overhead. "Alita!"

The horse was gone.

While I enjoyed the company of my two buddies and wasted many an afternoon with them, I was eager to spend some time alone thinking. How many times had I dreamed of that night, of the shooter pulling his pistol on my father and mother? The image of Devil's Tower in the distance loomed in my mind. I had completely buried the memory of the rock somewhere in the recesses of my brain all these years.

I'd seen the old deed to my father's land when I registered for mine. The Homestead Act demanded 160 acres be developed in five years or the land defaulted to the government to be cycled through the Homestead Act again. My parents' death had prevented the development from happening.

For some reason, they had rolled us and our wagon right over their land on our journey west and continued another five hundred miles. Why?

Since I was already in town, I decided to run a few errands. Town chores involved a deposit at the bank and a canned peaches roundup at the market. Not Gale's grocery, though. I loaded the cans in my saddlebag and watered Raven. She twitched and shook her head as I rubbed her ears.

Raven and I headed for the bank. I dismounted and stepped onto the boardwalk at Main and First Street.

The Indian woman had said Running Deer was camped at Devil's Tower. I'd promised to reward him someday for saving me and taking care of me. A visit was in order to give him one of my horses . . . and to search for my parents' graves.

I stepped up to the Wilkes Bank. The door burst open, and a man slammed into me. We flew backwards in a tangle and landed in the dusty street.

I scrambled to my feet and gasped for air. A quick look down and I saw it was Jacob Wilkes.

"Here, let me help." I spotted his cane lying nearby and reached for the long stick. It was heavy.

His face was red and knotted, but he didn't say a word.

I reached down to help him up. "I'm sorry."

He slapped away my hand.

I shook the sting from my skin. "Now, see here—"

He snatched the cane from me and righted himself. Dirt smudged his white suit. He took a step forward, leaning close to me. In a calm voice he whispered in my ear, "Touch me again, I'll kill you."

Pulling back, he wore a smile, but his eyes were squinted and filled with fire. He turned and shuffled down the street. A small group of men stood talking in front of him, and he shoved through them, pushing them to the side.

I tried to shake off the episode as I cleaned the dust from my clothes. Jacob felt like a burr under my saddle. All the loans and businesses he controlled should have made him a happier man. But he ruled them with an iron fist. Not just farmers and ranchers like myself, but important businessmen as well.

Biting back a few remarks, I entered the building. Stairs rose to the left leading to a balcony where offices with closed doors housed the internal workings of the bank. Ahead, a row of bars crossed the room, their presence a reminder of the bygone days of bandits and bank robbers. I approached an open station.

Evening sunlight streamed through the single window on the western side of the building, shining off the clerk's bald head. With a smile, I pulled my wallet from my pocket, scanned the contents, and pulled out a few bills. I slid them through an opening in the metal bars.

He wet his thumb with his tongue and counted the money so quickly I could barely keep up.

"Blacksmith work."

He nodded without a word.

"This bank ever been robbed?"

He glanced up at me, a questioning look on his face. "No, sir, not to my knowledge." He eyed my straw hat.

"Just curious. These bars are good blacksmithing."

He nodded, scribbled out a receipt, and handed it to me. "Good day, sir."

As I turned to leave, a figure stood on the stairs, masked by the light from the western window. He motioned to me and I took a few steps closer, recognizing Mr. Wilkes, the bank's owner.

"Mr. Anderson, would you join me in my office?"

Surprised, I nodded. "Yes, sir."

He took a few steps up the stairs, crossed the balcony, and entered the far door. I followed, removing my hat. Every step felt heavier as I climbed, as if marching to my doom.

His office was a hodgepodge of knickknacks with seemingly little thought to organization. A longhorn skull hung on one wall. There was an assortment of bows and arrows and on the far wall a painting of two nuns digging a grave. I pointed to the picture. "Interesting."

"Belonged to my wife. She bought it just before she died. Don't ask what it means. I have no idea."

I scratched my late-afternoon stubble.

He pointed to an upholstered wingback chair. "Sit." He sat behind his desk, reached down, and brought up two small glasses. A small decanter of brown liquor sat at the end of his desk. He poured some into the two shot glasses and held one up to me.

I settled into the seat. "I don't drink."

He frowned, looked through the glass, and then in one swift motion tossed the contents down his throat. "Better." He turned his complete attention on me. "You've been here . . . five years?"

"That's correct."

He shook his head. "Where does the time go? You've been a faithful customer. You interested in a loan?"

"No. No loan is needed." I couldn't keep the wary tone out of my voice.

"I'm sorry. For my son's behavior, I mean. He's sometimes

PETER LEAVELL

irrational, hot-headed." He sighed. "I saw him through the front window."

So the man was offering me a loan as an apology? "No harm done."

He looked down at his drink, as if embarrassed. "Jacob and I were talking about you, you see."

"About me?"

He drank the second shot. After a few coughs, he continued. "Ambition. Ambition tied with competence. You've made a positive influence on this community. Your blacksmithing is second to none."

"I do my best."

"You're raising horses, training them to be sold to officers of the Army."

I sat up. I hadn't told many people of my plans. Privileged information.

"Modest attempts to make a living." He refilled both glasses. "You won't get rich, but I suspect that's not your aim."

I wished he would stop this pointless interview. "Mr. Wilkes, I'm not sure where this is going."

"To the point. I like that." A grin spread across his round cheeks. He leaned forward. "Up-and-coming men like yourself are needed in this community. My son is one and his ambitions are satisfactory, but his methods are, shall we say, overly aggressive. He could use your calming influence."

I scratched my head. "I don't understand."

"I'd like you to keep an eye out for my son."

I turned away and tried to hold back a groan. Jacob, a partner in his father's bank, already employed two men to do his bidding, Jeb and Ryan. The coincidence that Marshal Stone had two deputies and Jacob hired two thugs—as I saw them—was lost on no one. If men were not able to pay their loans, Jacob, Jeb, and Ryan would show up at their door to either extract the money by force or take possession of the business and land.

"I've got plenty to do."

"I'm willing to pay."

I stood. "Mr. Wilkes, I appreciate your confidence in me, but I think I will pass."

47

He rose to his feet as well. "The Dakota Territory will be split into two states soon. Mitchell has every chance of becoming the capital of the lower half. A party is being planned in hopes of garnering support for the Republican effort. It'll be in Yankton at the end of the year. Your name is on the invitation list."

I shuffled my feet. "An honor." I tried to say it with feeling.

"I hope you reconsider about my son." He leaned against the desk. "Also, be at that party. We need men like you."

I raised an eyebrow but didn't ask any questions.

After leaving his office, I stood outside in the late evening sun, breathing in the cool air and trying to push the conversation from my mind. I looked up at his window. I chafed at being told what to do. Watch Jacob? It felt like a job for a nurse. Besides, I had problems of my own.

As Raven and I headed home, my thoughts drifted to my parents and what mysteries lay in the ruins of their wagon under the shadow of Devil's Tower.

6

Night closed in on the Dakota landscape. The moon shone brightly above, casting a silver gleam over the flat fields along the road. I let Raven have the reins. She knew the way home.

Rummaging through my brain, I found my mind returning to the childhood memories of Running Deer and the events surrounding my parents' murder. Too many questions, far more than answers. There seemed to be only one solution—head west, find the grave, and see if something, anything, might give me a clue as to why they'd pressed past their homestead.

A soft voice cut through the night air, and I jolted to full alert. The lingering cries seemed to come from the woods on the left. I whispered a *whoa*, and Raven halted. The murmur of the James River and the chirping of crickets filled my ears.

The cry came again, this time more distinct. Without a second thought, I turned Raven and urged her into the undergrowth.

The full moon illuminated each leaf with a soft glow as the brush gave way to tall cottonwoods, leaving me in a world of shadows made by ancient trees. Despite Raven crashing through the vegetation, I could still hear the voice. Soon the brambles were so thick she couldn't press through, so I slipped off her back and continued on foot.

The cries of a woman calling for help came from close by. I hurried forward until I felt a splash, and cold water seeped into my boot.

I retraced my steps, paused, heard the voice coming from upriver, and followed it. A shrub barred my way, but I burst through into a small clearing. In the center I could just make out the dim outline of a person beside a boulder. I dashed forward.

She moaned.

I'd been working on keeping the latest expression *are you okay* out of my vocabulary. It wasn't easy. "How bad?"

"Not broken." She gasped. "The log wedged my leg against the rock. I can't get it out."

Pain etched the woman's voice, and she shivered violently. The chill this close to the river cooled even me. I had no blanket other than the one under Raven's saddle.

"I'll be back." I put a hand on her shoulder and realized she was the woman with the riding pants I'd seen earlier in town.

"Please don't go." She held tightly to my arm.

I squeezed. "Right back." Her fear touched something inside me. I would do anything to save her.

It took only a moment to find Raven. Together we pushed through the brush, back into the clearing. I undid her cinch, pulled off the saddle, and took the horse's blanket. I wrapped the woman in it. "Sorry about the smell. But Raven's warm back . . ."

"Oh, thank you." She closed her eyes.

The boulder had wedged a massive log against a tree so the only way to get her leg out was to lift it. It would take several men to boost it high enough for her to escape, but the closest help was in Mitchell. It might take half an hour, even longer, to get them. And the way the girl seemed to be wilting under the pain and shaking from the cold, I knew time was growing short before she would surely pass out or worse.

"How long have you been here?"

"Well before the sun went down." She trembled. "Can you get me out?"

"Let me try something. When I lift, see if you can move." She nodded.

I wrapped my arms around the behemoth log. "Ready?"

In the darkness, I could just make her out, biting her lip. She nodded again.

"Lifting." With all my strength, I heaved upward and felt my biceps bulge with the strain.

"Ouch!" she cried, almost screamed. "It won't budge."

"Letting go." I released the log. It hadn't moved. I wiped my hands on my pants and took a moment to catch my breath. "What's your name?"

"Anna."

"Philip's mine. Do you have a horse?"

"She bolted upriver."

"Don't go anywhere. I'll be back."

She inhaled quickly. "I'm not going anywhere."

I crashed through the thicket. It didn't take long to find Anna's horse, her reins tangled in the brush. She thrashed wildly until I whispered a few kind words and she let me pull her free and lead her back to the clearing.

We stopped close to Anna.

"Alita," she whispered. "Is she injured?"

"No, not a scratch." I quickly looked over the mare to make sure I hadn't lied. Assured Alita was unharmed, I returned to Raven and pulled rope out of the saddlebag. I smiled to myself at the ancient proverb. *Rope. Rope. Always carry rope.* Now I knew why.

I threw Raven's saddle over her back and cinched it tight, then tied one end of the rope to the saddle horn. She stomped and shook her mane as if eager to escape the tiny clearing surrounded by shadows. I wrapped the rope twice around the log, leveraged it over a thick branch overhead, and attached the other end to Alita's saddle. Anna's horse stood patiently, as if she knew what I was planning. The horses' flanks touched, and Raven reared. I patted her muzzle.

I spoke to Anna as I worked. "Morgan horse. Beautiful."

She took a deep breath. "Her name means *winged*."

"Lovely." I checked the knots. "I have a Belgian Draft at home. But it would take too long to get him."

I felt her eyes watching me as I checked the ropes. I wanted her to keep talking. "How did you get yourself into this predicament?"

She leaned back onto the ground and sighed. "We went for a ride, Alita and I. A raccoon darted out from under us, Alita bucked me off, and I fell. She kicked a log that was leaning on the top of the rock, and now I'm trapped here."

The ropes were tight. I paused and looked at her profile in the moonlight. She was beautiful. I shook my head. Not the best moment to ogle a pretty girl.

"Are you ready?"

She nodded.

I cleared my throat. "I'll slap the horses, and as they pull, I'll lift. Raven's never pulled before, and I think she'll be flighty, so I don't know what will happen. When you can, get your leg out."

"I'll try."

This had to work. I grabbed a long branch, motioned to Anna, and she lifted her body with her arms. I hated to strike my horse like this, but I was out of ideas.

Her voice was firm. "Do it."

I swung the branch at Raven's rump. She jumped and strained at the rope. Alita followed my horse's lead.

I dropped the stick, wrapped my arms around the log, and lifted with all my might. A groan escaped my lips.

Anna's voice was soft and gentle. "A little more, almost there."

A bead of sweat trickled down my cheek. The sound of horses grunting and hooves churning the earth punctuated the night air.

"I'm free!"

With care, I let go of the log and rushed to both horses, backing them up until the log settled to the ground. I stroked their soft shoulders.

"Sorry about that, girls."

Raven snorted.

I scratched between her ears. "Good girl."

Assured the horses were uninjured, I returned to Anna's side, lowering myself to one knee. She rested her back against the tree trunk. With shaking hands, she rubbed her leg.

"Are you hurt?"

She bit her lip and after a moment put a hand on my shoulder and struggled to her feet. Standing, she tentatively put weight on her leg. A careful step forward, then another, and soon with a noticeable limp she reached Alita's side and wrapped her arms around the horse's neck.

Her horse was jumpy but soon settled down as she talked to her. My heart beat faster. She adored her horse as much as I loved mine. The spooky moonlit scene made me smile.

I waited, listening to the soft nicker of her horse, until Anna broke the embrace and turned to me. "Thank you. You saved me from a cold, miserable night."

I approached Raven and reached up to untie the rope. The knot had crimped tight, too tight to loosen. I dug around in my pocket, pulled out my knife, and opened it. "You live near here?"

"In Mitchell."

I touched the sharp end against the knot, and it easily sliced through. The rope fell limp.

"I'll ride with you back to town."

She brought a hand to her head. "Return to your family. I can make it by myself."

As I cut the rope attached to Alita's saddle, I glimpsed my ringless finger. Hadn't she noticed? "I've no family." I'd checked earlier and had seen that she wore no band, although why I had thought to look I didn't know. I put away the knife and pulled the ropes free. With a smile, I looked down at her. "The Dakota Territory's safe. But not that safe."

She bit her lip again then nodded.

An owl hooted overhead and she jumped and cried out. It startled me. My heartbeat thudded from the scare, and suddenly the night seemed filled with evils, imagined witches, and hags.

I thought of my pistols, hidden in my cabin, and wished for their comforting presence against my hip. "Let's get out of here."

"Let's."

I took the reins of both horses and led them through the bramble, Anna close behind. We broke from the bushes and onto the open lane. I brushed dirt and old leaves off my clothes. She did the same. The soft smell of spring mixed with her lilac perfume touched my senses.

She took Alita's reins from me, and I watched her mount, her movements stiff. She winced as she dropped into the saddle.

I climbed on Raven's back and leaned forward. "Shall we?"

Anna gave a tired smile and clicked her tongue. Her horse started toward Mitchell as if she knew the way.

I followed. I was no longer thinking about my parents, only Anna.

That couldn't be good.

7

Thank you for helping me." Her voice had turned mono-
tone, and she slouched in the saddle. "You're a hero."

I grunted. "I'm no hero." We rode to the rhythmic creaking of our saddles. "I'm no hero."

"You can say it three times, but I still appreciate what you
did. You're a hero to me."

My mind churned. Heroes were men who saved people
from oppression, fought against evil.

Stopped outlaws from killing parents.

"I'm no hero."

I was sure I heard her sigh. "Your horse is beautiful, what
I can see of her."

"She's a good horse. Fast." I patted Raven's withers and
looked at Anna's form in the darkness. "New to town?"

She shifted in her saddle and gasped. "Ow. My father
bought the flour mill."

I'd heard someone had purchased the mill from Mr. White
a month ago. Her father. How old was she, twenty? Old to be
unmarried still. Her beauty must surely have garnered many a
man's attention.

Silence carried our journey for a few moments, yet the gentle rustle of grass felt comfortable. I took a deep breath. "Where are you from?"

Instead of answering, she nodded toward my horse. "What is she?"

"Arabian."

Quiet again. Smells of plowed earth mixed with a wood fire drifted in the breeze. Stars shone brilliantly at the edges of the earth, only to be muffled overhead by the moon.

I decided to offer more conversation. "She's from Egypt, really. I've more Arabians at my place. I'm breeding them, training them for officers in the cavalry." Quiet. Privileged information.

She seemed unimpressed, riding on without a word.

We rode over a small rise, and Mitchell spread out below us. Kerosene lamps lined the streets, casting a yellow glow over the town. We rode onto Main Street, where the lights shone against the business fronts and reflected in the windows. Several saloons along the way were filled with raucous crowds. The rest of the town seemed to be asleep.

Anna turned Alita down Fourth Street beyond a lawyer's office on the left and past several houses. No lamps lit our way here, and darkness regained its dominance.

When she pulled Alita to a halt, she turned to me. "I'm not a bad rider, really." I could hear the hesitation in her voice.

"I can tell." I fumbled for words. I'd done this before, in the orphanage. Gotten idiot nervous around a girl. "What I mean is, someday I may put that to a test." What was I saying? I felt a strong urge to force the issue, make her promise to see me again.

I stared at a nearby house with a stone facade, the rocks basking in the cool night after the heat of the day. In the distance, an owl hooted. Raven shook her head, impatient for her pasture.

Anna flashed a weary smile. "Our home isn't far. I better say goodnight, Philip. In case there are more girls for you to save." She waved. "Thank you." With a kick of her heel, she and her horse continued down the dark road.

I turned Raven left and rode out of town, alone. I had a feeling Anna would be another person to add to the list of acquaintances I'd never really get to know.

Regretful, that.

The bright sunlight splashed against my face as I stepped out of the cabin onto the front porch. The wind scurried through the thick grass as a gray mist rolled off the river and across the edge of the fenced prairie. My horses wandered, heads down, around the pasture. The gentle gurgle of the slow-moving James River behind the house urged me to cross the yard to the outhouse.

Was it natural for me to find Anna so attractive? We'd hardly met. Her manner with me was short and abrupt. I suppose from her point of view, meeting a man at night in a thick forest would be unnerving, no doubt. She'd given no indication she recognized me from the episode in town with the Sioux woman.

After I visited the outhouse, I returned to the cabin. To the left of the large front room was the kitchen, where I snatched a metal cup. To the right stood a small dining table and my rocking chair, both next to the fire where my coffee warmed. I poured a cup of the thick, black mixture and took a sip. Satisfied, I walked down the hallway, glanced into my bedroom, and turned to my storage room on the right. I found a fresh, oiled blacksmithing apron. I'd burned the last one a week ago.

With coffee in one hand and apron in the other, I managed to lift the latch on the front door again and cross the worn path to the barn. Using my foot, I slid open the barn door. Stalls lined both sides of the barn. Overhead was the hayloft. Where one stall should be on the immediate left waited the forge, anvil, and tools.

I set my cup down and put on the stiff apron.

After visiting Scott and Leroy in town one day, I'd noticed a mobile furnace, the round top rising up out of the long grass.

The owner said the oven was from the Civil War. The lumber that had hauled it from battle to battle had rotted, leaving the heavy anvil and furnace to rust. But Franklin made light work of hauling it home.

The coal was gritty and quickly turned my gloves black. I lit the furnace and once it was hot, the odorless embers glowed bright. Smoke drifted up through the small chimney. After putting on dark glasses and a thick, asbestos glove, I snatched the long, metal tongs and thrust a horseshoe into the fire.

While the metal heated, I turned and watched through the door. The horses were busily grazing, tearing tender morsels of grass with their teeth. I couldn't hold back a smile. Their nimble Arabian feet always needed a shoe smaller than the ones available in the local tack shops. Lucky I could forge my own.

The metal, now white-hot, was ready, and I hefted the tongs and set the horseshoe on the anvil. The hammer felt heavy in my hand, and I lifted it high and brought it down, the weight strong and in need of control. I crashed the hammer into the metal, hammering the shoe into shape. The swing wasn't from my strength. I let the hammer's fall do the work.

Sparks showered the dirt floor. I pounded until the shoe was the right size and smoothed out sharp and lumpy areas. Then with an awl I punched holes for nails. The scent of hay and horses was gone, the pungent odor of the hot metal overpowering.

God worked the same way, I'd always felt, pounding the impurities out of us. I'd taken quite a hammering when I was orphaned as a youth and had to make my own way through life. Now God had given me everything I'd ever wanted—a home and barn and horses that were my family. An image of Anna's face flashed in my mind just as a shadow crossed the anvil.

I spun to see the silhouette of a man standing at the door in the sunlight. Nothing was as conspicuous as the shape of a holster at his side. I thought of my gun, sitting over the fireplace.

The man stepped into the shadow. His red hair came into view.

"Scott, don't sneak up on me."

My friend smiled his wide, lopsided grin. "Was hoping to target practice. You look busy though."

I glanced over the strewn tools and heated forge. "Raven threw a shoe last night."

"Bad luck."

I motioned to his revolver. "I hope you brought your rifle. You can't hit anything with that."

"Exactly why I'm here. You mind if I get started?"

"Soon as I'm done here, I'll join you." I thought for a moment about the small range I'd built on the edge of the pasture by the river and added, "Scott, don't shoot any horses while you're out there."

He grunted.

I could tell something was wrong. "You okay?" I kicked myself for using the slang I hated. I refused to sound like the young boys in Mitchell.

"I can't find work. Ever since the tanner left town, I just can't find anything."

"You will."

"My savings has almost run out." He rubbed his chest. "I think I've got a condition. My heart can't handle the pressure." He stuck out his tongue. "Ith my 'ongue white?"

"Pink. Pink as ever."

He closed his mouth, and with a sigh of what I thought was resignation he spun on the heel of his boot and slammed into a man stepping into the barn behind him.

"Hello there." The voice was deep and filled the barn.

The stranger strode in where I could get a closer look at his face and leveled his gaze at Scott. "Do I have the pleasure of addressing Philip Anderson?"

Scott shook his head and motioned toward me.

The man tapped Scott's chest. "I overheard what you just said. I'll talk to you about a job in a moment." He turned to me with his hands on his hips, his jaw clenched. "My name is Calvin Johnston. I believe you met my daughter last night."

8

His thick arms hung loosely by his side, muscles bulging out of his long sleeves. A narrow puff of hair ran around the edge of his scalp. A thick mustache covered narrow lips.

Despite my height and my own bulk from blacksmith work, I felt small.

Mr. Johnston pointed his thumb over his shoulder toward the corral. "Talk there?" His manner was casual but firm.

I glanced at Scott, whose eyes were wide. With a nod, I stripped off the gloves, pulled the apron over my head, and set them to the side.

Mr. Johnston eyed the cooling horseshoe. His eyebrow rose, and I wondered what he thought.

We walked out into the bright morning and leaned against the split rail, both of us facing the pasture and my herd. Scott stayed inside the barn, and I could only guess what he was doing, probably trying to listen. Maybe loading his rifle to defend me from this stranger. What did Johnston think happened last night? I rubbed my hands together.

He nodded toward the field. "Your horses?"

"Yes, sir."

"You buy this spread?" He motioned toward the cabin.

"I built it."

"With your father?"

"No." I waited a moment. "Just me."

"Wife? Kids?"

"Just me . . . alone."

He turned his eyes back toward the barn door. "That boy your friend?"

I didn't like the way he said *that boy*. I found my intimidation turning to irritation. I faced him directly. "*Best* friend."

"He a hard worker?"

"He is." When fretting didn't get the better of him.

"How long have you lived here?"

"Five years. Yesterday." I decided to try a question myself. "You new here?"

He ignored the question. "Your parents live nearby?"

Privileged information. And he wasn't privileged. I crossed my arms and couldn't keep my foot from tapping. "No parents. No wife or kids. A few friends, dozens of acquaintances. I have plans for life. And nothing happened between your daughter and me last night other than me helping her out from under a fallen tree."

He studied me for a moment then broke into a wide grin. In an instant his demeanor changed, and he slapped me on the back. "I appreciate you helping Anna. You did a mighty fine job. Your quick thinking saved her from disaster." He held out his hand. "I'd like to thank you."

Off balance, I grabbed his hand, which was as calloused as mine, and we shook.

He thrust his thumbs behind his suspenders. "I'd like to invite you over to our place tomorrow for dinner, after church." He frowned and his brows closed in on each other. "You do go to church."

"I do. Pastor Humphrey's church."

His countenance relaxed. "After church, then? As a thank you."

"How is Anna? She was limping pretty bad."

"Feeling better. Sore, but no damage done." He paused, as if wondering what to say next or if he should say it. He brushed his nose with the back of his hand. "She would have ridden out here with me today if she'd been up for it."

I found myself wishing she had come with him. "Is there anything I can bring tomorrow?"

"Mrs. Johnston would be insulted if you did."

"Then let's not insult Mrs. Johnston."

The corner of his mouth turned up in a smile. "Wise man." The grin turned to a frown. He leaned toward me and lowered his voice. "That boy in there?"

"Scott Ladd."

"Yes, Mr. Ladd. I overheard he was looking for employment."

"Let's just say he's looking over several opportunities."

"Does he always venture out so heavily armed?"

My mind flashed to the pistol and rifle Scott brought for target practice. "He's going to kill a few cans." I nodded toward a sharp rise on the other side of the river where I'd set up a few targets. "Sometimes fancies himself a gunslinger."

Johnston grunted and faced the barn door. "Scott. You can come out now."

The redhead jumped into view. I had to admit, he looked ready to join a posse and hunt down the Maxwell Gang roaming the Black Hills. He slowed as he approached us. His shoulders sagged. "Am I in trouble?"

Johnston shot his hand out and Scott returned the handshake.

"Mr. Ladd," Johnston said. "I've acquired the flour mill up river from Mr. White and am looking for workers. I understand you're without employment at the moment." He paused. "I'm offering you a job which requires heavy lifting and long hours, especially around harvest. Forty dollars a month."

I raised an eyebrow. At least the wages were decent.

Scott rubbed his hands together. "I'll take it."

Johnston nodded. "Fine. I'll see you at the mill, sunup Monday morning." He turned to me. "I'll see you tomorrow."

We watched the man mount his horse, turn its head

toward the lane, and ride out of the ravine. Dust puffed gently behind them as the horse broke into a trot.

I turned to my friend. "You get talked into something you didn't want to do?"

He shrugged. "I need a job. Why, did you?"

I rubbed my jaw. "I think I did."

While Scott shot at cans I trained my horses, something I tried to do every other day.

The growing bellies of the mares had me focusing more on training my gelding, Tucker, and his half-sister Princess. Although I'd taught him the finer art of verbal commands in the round pen, I'd been thrown more than once trying to get Tucker under saddle.

Arabians were smart. Smart and feisty. Luckily we'd progressed beyond the bucking stage and Tucker was nearly finished. Princess could be sold anytime now.

I brought them into the corral while their mothers, Desert Sand and Sheba, watched from behind the closed gate. Their sire, Solomon, a beautiful black with a touch of red in the sunlight, stood atop a small knoll in the pasture, watching. His head was distinctly Arabian, a thick, wide forehead and dish-shaped face.

He was also Raven's sire, and where her beautiful jet-black coat came from. Tucker and Princess were born on my homestead the second year I was here, both chestnut like their mothers. With two more foals on the way, my Arabian herd was growing.

I whistled and Princess trotted toward me, while Tucker pranced from one side of the corral to the next, as if he didn't hear. I whistled again, this time louder.

He snorted and with slow, deliberate steps came close. I led him into the smaller round pen adjacent to the corral to wait his turn and keep him out of the way while I worked Princess first.

Who needed children when I had these?

I slipped a bridle over Princess's head, fitting the snaffle bit easily into her mouth. I rode her around the corral, circling this way and that, halting, walking, trotting. Dust filled the air as Tucker pranced around the pen eager to be next.

Finally I mounted Tucker. He wanted to break into a long, full gallop, his muscles under me desperate to work. But I got his attention with lots of changing direction, one-rein stops, stepping backward, and side passing.

Then I gave the whistle he loved. Low pitched then high, and he reared then twisted. I slammed onto the ground.

He whinnied as if full of joy. The other horses, including Raven, joined him.

Good. It hurt, but it was good. He was coming along nicely. Several other whistle combinations when I was on the ground, and he ran away or came close, depending on the call.

After a few more commands, it was time to reward Tucker.

I opened the gate, re-mounted, then touched his sides with my heels.

He didn't need to be told twice. He burst by Princess, through the gate and around the other horses, and we thundered down the pasture trail cut by the animals themselves. Wind flew into my face as the ground whirled by in a blur. I couldn't help myself. "Yippee!"

As I dressed for Sunday morning church, I could barely get my black jacket on without groaning after being dumped by Tucker. And when I tightened Raven's cinch, my back muscles cramped. I rubbed my shoulder, snatched my black dress hat off the saddle horn where I'd left it, and mounted. A quick glance in the cabin window at my reflection showed me my silver-gray eyes stood out in contrast to all the black I had on.

Mitchell's streets were mostly empty except for a few who were late for church like myself. Bells pealed, their percussion loud in the humid morning air. At the edge of town, I stopped near the church and tied Raven between two buggies.

The building's tall, white steeple reached higher than the surrounding cottonwood trees, and the doors were already closed. I took a deep breath. Nothing to be nervous about. Just a Sunday service, something I did every week, and then a meal with folks I didn't know. I'd be all right.

Singing voices through the thick doors didn't drown out the pounding of my boots as I walked up the wooden steps or quiet the creaking of the hinges as I opened the door. From inside burst the voices of men and women singing to God.

My regular pew, third from the back, was half empty and I slipped in. I took a moment to appreciate the mingled perfumes, lilac the strongest, and old rotten wood from a roof leak somewhere.

The men were suited as I was, but the display of clothing the women wore always took my breath away. The colors, mostly vibrant blues, reds, and yellows marched up and down every row. White, it seemed, was going out of fashion.

While the hymn "I Am from Sin Set Free" continued, I searched for and saw Scott three rows ahead of me, sitting in the row with older ladies. On the other side of the aisle sat Becky Hall, her curly blonde hair not quite hiding the green eyes that ventured Scott's way every now and again.

A little more searching and I discovered the back of Anna's head. My heart began to throb in my ears. Why was I so nervous?

Her cream-colored hat hid most of her black hair, except for a few waves that cascaded around her shoulders. Her blue dress showed off her complexion perfectly.

The song ended and Pastor Humphrey took the stage. The floorboards groaned under his massive frame, a body made up mostly of hours studying God's Word and the fine cooking of many widows. The Good Book asked for the church to care for those whose husbands had gone on before, but in this church, they took care of the pastor.

As the message progressed, my heart saddened for Caroline and Leroy, the old war vet I called friend. No matter what Scott and I tried, the two never set foot through the church doors. I reminded myself it didn't mean they didn't believe.

I saw Mr. Wilkes, bank owner, and Jacob sitting nearby. Jacob's eyes lingered on Anna. I shifted in my pew.

Pastor Humphrey's deep baritone rattled the windows. "Love is not pointing fingers at men in saloons, calling them evil because they drink to forget their troubles and their Maker. No, love does not condemn. Instead, love is bringing them into God's fold."

After the service, Jacob Wilkes rushed toward the front and cornered Anna. I bit down on my jealousy and felt a sense of relief when she looked at me and smiled.

Restless, I slipped out the door and into the bright afternoon.

People filed out of the building, and I turned to see Mr. Johnston approach me. "Dinner will be served in a few minutes. Follow us."

I nodded, untied Raven, and mounted.

Mr. Johnston helped a woman with pinned up brown hair into the wagon and a younger girl into the back.

Something tugged at my emotions, but I couldn't place it. The feeling grew stronger, and I closed my eyes. My mother and father, with me in the back of the wagon, on the way to church. I'd forgotten the memory but it flooded back now, and West Virginia sunshine and trees surrounded me. I rubbed my eyes, took a few deep breaths, and the sentiment cleared.

Anna and Jacob stepped out of the church, side by side, laughing. His blond hair ruffled in the breeze, and I noticed Anna glance at it. The two parted, and she watched him walk away, his cane clicking against the stones in the gravel.

Why couldn't I ride home now? If I hadn't given Mr. Johnston my word, I would have turned Raven and headed back right then.

9

I arrived at the Johnston home after the family. With dread, I halted Raven at the front gate. A white fence surrounded a neatly-trimmed lawn, and a stone walkway led toward the large home.

The door swung open and the young girl with brown eyes and hair I'd seen at church smiled up at me. "I'm Elizabeth, Anna's sister," she called. "Everyone calls me Beth, even though I like Elizabeth. I'm not the only Elizabeth. There was a queen in England by that name."

She paused for air then said, "Bring your horse around back." She pointed to a path outside the yard. "There's a pasture you can use to turn her loose."

I didn't know much about little girls, but I decided I should at least try to be friends with Beth. "Do you like horses, Elizabeth?" I said as we walked beside the house.

She tossed her ponytail. "I'm ten. All girls my age like horses." She smiled. "You saved my sister in the woods."

"Ah, yes, well . . ."

"That's wonderful."

I decided to remove the saddle and bridle, and then I did

as Beth suggested and turned Raven loose in the pasture. Instead of mingling with the three other horses, she stood at the gate, looking at me. I turned to Beth. "I hope I'm not late."

She led me back to the front of the house. "We can't use the back door to get inside. It's Anna's fault. She put bookshelves over it."

The front door swung wide, revealing the lady I assumed to be Mrs. Johnston. Her grin was wide and welcoming. "Philip, come in." She gave Beth a glance. "Kitchen."

Beth scurried away.

Anna was just coming down the stairs. She looked startled as she stopped and stared at me.

I knew what she was looking at. She'd not seen them in the daylight up close. My eyes. My wolf eyes.

Normally I didn't care what people thought of my eyes. The way she stared, though, almost as if they frightened her, made me hate them.

She blinked and drifted down the stairs, gripping the banister until she reached the bottom. She seemed to recover quickly, but her face had paled. "Hello, Philip."

Unable to dispel the quivering in my stomach, I bowed my head and muttered, "Anna."

"Thank you for coming."

Why did I have the feeling this dinner was an obligation for her? I dug deep and pulled out a wagonload of courage. "How's your leg? Better?"

Her smile, to her credit, was warm. "Much better, thanks to you. She motioned toward the room immediately to the right. "Please come in. Dinner's almost ready."

As I observed her arranging the table and helping her mother, I couldn't help but watch her hands as she set a pitcher here, a bowl of gravy there, and lifted a heavy plate of roast. Her family talked with one another, but I didn't participate in the conversation.

I just stood, waiting for the invitation to sit and wondering what would change if a woman moved into my cabin. I kept it clean, sparse, and comfortable, but it was nothing special. This kitchen and dining room, luxurious compared to mine, was filled with beautiful things. Would a woman do that to my place? I gathered my thoughts and tucked them away. Ridiculous.

The family found their seats, and Anna motioned to a chair at the end of the table opposite her father. Anna sat on my right, Beth to my left next to her mother. When was the last time I sat down with a family? Scott, Leroy, and Caroline were the closest to family I'd had since I left Running Deer.

Mr. Johnston sat, cleared his throat, and bowed his head. "Heavenly Father, we give thanks for all the provisions You've given us. Bless this food. Bless our friend who's come to dine with us today. Amen."

He reached immediately for the potatoes. "You've some nice horses. What are you planning to do with them? They don't look like work animals."

The aroma drifting from the table made my stomach rumble. I reached for a roll and pulled off a quick bite before the hunger turned loud enough to be heard. "I'm training the younger ones for the military. I was hoping the officers could spend a few dollars more on a decent mount. How's business with the mill?"

"Slow until harvest."

The meat was passed around, and he talked more about wheat, volume, and flour, and I found myself wishing I could talk with Anna alone. She kept glancing at me out of the corner of her eye, and I wasn't sure if she liked the way I looked or if I was part of a freak show and she was trying to figure out my eyes. I wanted to find out.

I finished filling my plate. "I've planted wheat this year." Mr. and Mrs. Johnston along with Beth, all listening intently, made me uncomfortable.

"I'll buy your crop, and we can include harvesting for a fee. If you're interested."

I shrugged. "Hope it grows. I'm better with horses than I am with crops, I think."

Mrs. Johnston turned her full attention on me. "Where are you from, Philip?"

"Sioux City. And West Virginia. Did you tell me you were from Missouri?"

"Branson." Mr. Johnston took a bite and spoke from the side of his mouth. "We had a mill there. My boy, John, is still in Branson. Runs it now."

"Boy." Anna laughed. "He's about Philip's age."

Beth dropped her fork and looked at me. "How old are you?"

Mrs. Johnston put a hand on her daughter's arm. "Now, Beth, that's not polite."

"Twenty-three." I tried to give her a reassuring smile to show I wasn't offended.

"I'm ten, Anna's nineteen, and mother's—"

"That's enough." Mr. Johnston gave Beth a stern look. "Eat up." He glanced over at me, pointing his fork. "I've heard Anna's story about how you saved her life. I'd like to hear your version."

While silverware clanked against porcelain plates interspersed with interruptions and questions, I told the story of wading through the thicket and finding Anna. They seemed to find it funny.

After so many years of solitude, sitting with a family at a meal felt strange. But the Johnstons seemed comfortable in each other's presence.

My plate was empty long before I was full. I glanced through the lace curtains on the window. The sunny day reminded me I should go home and tend my animals.

Or something.

"Pie?"

I turned to Mrs. Johnston, trying to hide a frown. "Pie?"

"Of course." Mr. Johnston pushed away his plate. "It's why we eat dinner, to get to the pie. Bring it out, Emily."

Being more of a cake man, I usually left pies to the less discriminating tastes, or so I believed. And of all the pies she could have made, it was rhubarb. To me, the sullen plant tasted more like celery with a tang than anything that should be put in a pie.

I didn't want to hurt their feelings, so I cut a small piece and shoveled it onto my fork. They stared at me, waiting for me to taste the first bite. Despite my misgivings, my brain

PETER LEAVELL

seemed to have no control over my hand, which forced the bite into my mouth.

It tasted horrible.

I smiled a grim, puckered smile and nodded.

They attacked their pie, laughing and telling stories. Grateful they were no longer focused on me, I shoved one small bite after another into my mouth. I was the last to finish, but finish I did.

A silence settled over the dining room. To break the awkward moment, I said the first thing that came to mind. "I'll help with the dishes."

Anna smiled at me. Her brilliant, stunning smile penetrated my mind and riveted my attention, as if she and I were the only ones in the room. "Do you like to read, Philip?"

There it was again. She'd spoken my name, and I liked it.

I rubbed my temple and told myself to stop being such a colt. "I can't sleep at night without reading a few pages of something. And, of course, my Bible."

Mr. Johnston stood. "You show him the reading room, Anna. I'm going to go take a nap." He tipped his head. "Thanks for coming over, Philip. I'm sure we'll see each other soon."

I nodded his way.

"Thanks for coming, Philip." Mrs. Johnston's kind eyes wrinkled and warmed me with her honest appreciation of my visit.

Anna motioned toward the kitchen, as if beckoning me to follow. I trailed her through the long, narrow kitchen filled with dirty pots and pans. An area at the end, which would normally lead outdoors, was closed off by a red curtain. Anna pushed it aside to reveal a small room that had probably been added on after the house was built.

Light streamed from an octagon-shaped window and illuminated hundreds of books. The shelves spanned from floor to ceiling including across the back door. In the center of the room was a short table atop a carpet that reminded me of stories in *A Thousand and One Arabian Nights*. Dust and a wholesome bookbinding odor tickled my nose. "You've collected all these?"

She bit her lip and nodded. I liked it when she bit her lip.

I stepped over to a shelf and perused the titles. I attempted to focus on the books instead of her. From Roman history to books about John Adams, science books and stories, the library was complete.

"Amazing."

"You like it?"

I crossed my arms and leaned toward her. "Secret?"

She pursed her lips and pinched them together with her fingers.

"I read a lot more than I let on. But finding books isn't all that easy out here."

Her head turned, and I studied her profile as she looked out the window. "You are welcome to borrow a book any-time." She glanced back at me. "Would you like to go for a walk?"

"With you?"

She looked around the room in mock surprise. "Anyone else want to go with us?"

I grinned and offered her my arm.

A cottonwood tree towered over the dirt path leading away from their house. As we walked underneath it, the leaves shook and birds burst from their perches.

She jumped and brushed against my shoulder but backed away quickly. "Sorry. Scared me." Her face turned red.

The spring wind whipped at her hair and her dress.

"Missouri," I said. "Do you miss it?"

She nodded. "Not that the Dakota Territory doesn't have its charm."

The narrow path wound its way through tall, spring grass. The long strands rustled in the breeze and brushed against us as we walked.

Her blue eyes lit up. "I want to thank you for saving me the other night. I haven't done it properly, so thank you." Again, the smile melted my heart.

I bowed my head. "Anyone would have done the same."

She frowned. "Maybe." She stopped and I paused. She tucked a strand of hair behind her ear. "I didn't know . . . I mean . . ." She took a deep breath, visibly gathering herself. "I didn't trust you, but I do now." And she looked directly into my eyes.

My eyes. Perhaps she didn't hate them after all.

She flashed a lopsided grin. "Now you think I'm silly. Well, I stand by my words." With mock solemnness, she marched down the path.

"Wait. I don't think you're silly. I just . . ." What? Do I admit I know nothing about women? Even how to talk to one? Especially one so beautiful. As I caught up with her, I decided to be honest but to match her playfulness. "I've not saved a lot of women in the woods, so I don't know how this goes."

She laughed. "We start by introducing ourselves. I'm Anna Johnston, and I believe you're—"

"Philip Anderson." I couldn't help but notice she leaned closer to me.

"I must tell you." She swallowed, as if gaining courage. "I thought you might not have all the best intentions that night."

I paused, and she took a few steps, stopped, and looked back at me.

"I understand," I said, shaking my head. "People's intentions . . ."

She lifted a hand toward the wide prairie around us. "What I mean is, we were alone. And now I recognize you. You helped the Indian woman and her children. And then you helped me."

Never before had I felt a blush creep into my face. I could do nothing about it, so I started walking again in hopes she wouldn't notice my embarrassment. "So, why didn't you stay in Branson?" The moment I said the words I guessed they were a mistake. I was prying.

"Business." She didn't hesitate.

We arrived at the bank of the James River. A thick green canopy of trees lined the muddy water, the reflection of the sky and the foliage on the river a poor attempt but still beautiful. A cloud blocked the sun, darkening the shadows in the woods. She led me along the river until White's Mill came into view. The three-story plank building edged a spillway that held back the slow-moving water, a paddlewheel under the mill locked for the day.

We rounded the mill. The building blocked the never-ending wind, a blessed relief.

Anna sat on the sandy, manmade beach, and I joined her.

With her head cocked to the side so that her dark hair draped over one shoulder, she fixed her gaze on me. "Tell me, Philip, how do you come to speak Sioux?"

I couldn't hold back a scowl as memories of violence touched the edge of my consciousness, dreams I'd long repressed. "Tell me the reason you left Missouri."

"I told you."

"The real reason." Why was I digging so deep? Was I deflecting her questions or did I really want to know? I decided to stop and just let the conversation go where it would.

She sucked in a deep breath, brushed hair from her face, and looked toward the opposite shore. I studied her profile. Her lips were soundlessly moving, as if she was pondering how much she really wanted me to know and if she could trust this stranger with wolf eyes.

A tear trickled down her cheek.

My tone had been too harsh. And I'd pried. Now she was crying. I knew I couldn't talk to women. I blew out a long stream of air. "I'm sorry." I held a hand to my head. "Forget I mentioned it."

She sniffed. "Philip, I . . . I want to tell you. Bad memories. I want to trust you. Look at me." She wiped her eyes.

How to make this right? I couldn't believe I made her cry. "What if I tell you something about myself that no one knows?"

She turned back and folded her arms in her lap. "Sure." She pressed her lips together as she smiled.

I squinted toward the sun and then back at her. "All right. Um, I hate pie." My chest fluttered, surprised how difficult even that little bit of truth was to tell.

She laughed. "I noticed."

"I hope your mother didn't."

"I doubt it. She doesn't notice those types of things. Philip . . ."

I smiled at her, and she seemed to warm. A strange sensation washed over me and I felt close to Anna, as if I'd known her forever. But it had been just moments. It didn't make sense.

"You don't have to tell me." I boldly took her hand, surprising myself. "Nothing I must know, I'm sure. I'll tell you one more thing."

She looked at me, waiting.

Why was this so hard for me? "I, uh, I think you hate my eyes." I looked away, up the slow-moving river.

Instead of pulling away, she gripped my hand. Her fingers were smooth, and her moist palm rubbed against mine. "What if I promise to tell you about your eyes later? Don't worry, I like them." She hesitated. "A lot."

A fly tickled my chin, and I chased it away with my thumb. "All right."

It was her turn to take a deep breath, and she didn't let go of my hand as she spoke. Instead, the clasp grew tighter. "He was a customer. And taught in our church, Sunday School. Thirty-nine years old." She shuddered. "His wife died."

She didn't look at me. Instead, I could tell by her gaze that pierced the river she was looking into the past. "He asked my father if he could court me. Father told the man to ask me. I had no reason to say no, so I agreed."

My heart sunk. I already didn't like where this was going.

"He owned a large business, a grain cooperative, and to combine Father's business with his was smart. So he discussed marriage immediately. If married, both families would be in excellent financial standing.

"I asked if he could give me two weeks to think his marriage proposal over. He refused. His business could not wait, would take him away for several months, and I needed to go with him. I told him if I could not have the time, the answer was no."

Her voice tightened. "He was angry, said he and I had made a deal, that I had ruined his plans. The next several days were horrible. He stood outside our house, watching me. But it didn't end there. His grain co-op tried to put Father out of business."

She turned to me, her lip quivering. "He spread rumors about me. Things I would never do. I ran to a friend's house, and on the way home he confronted me in the street and I called him a liar." The tears flowed now. "He hit me and then stomped away, leaving my lying on the ground."

She touched her cheek as if remembering.

I squeezed her hand.

"Father wanted to kill him. I asked if we could move, and why not? The business was failing, and I could never marry now, not with my reputation in shambles." She gripped my hand tightly but then let go. "You need to know this about me. I'm innocent of all charges, yet the rumors still sting and may follow me here to Mitchell."

She took a few deep breaths and looked into my eyes. "There's my secret. Now yours."

I meant to tell her, had every intention of giving her a quick idea of my past. I wanted to say the words *I'm an orphan. Spent time with the Sioux. After that I learned to blacksmith, learned to love horses.*

I opened my mouth to speak but no words came out. I tried again, but I couldn't make a sound. Never before had I told anyone my story. Even the orphanage and Terry Feather, my former employer, knew little of what happened the night my parents were murdered.

With a choke, I muttered a few words. "Spent a while with Sioux warriors when I was young."

The image of my parents' bodies lying in their shallow graves was too much. When was the last time I'd thought about them enough to recreate what happened? My stomach churned and threatened to dislodge the rhubarb pie. Please God, no. Not in front of Anna.

I felt her hand on my shoulder, and then she touched my back. "I'm sorry, Philip." She stood.

I looked up at her and saw sympathy in her eyes.

She held out a hand. "I'm sorry. In your time, you'll tell me. Let's get back."

I took her hand and got up. I knew at that moment that I was falling in love with her.

10

My fingers shook as I broke my Smith and Wesson in the center, exposing the loading end of the chamber. I took a calming breath and thumbed six cartridges into the slots. Then I snapped the gun closed and hefted the belt that rested on my rocking chair.

A quick peek out the front window showed Scott's back as he waited for me on the porch.

I strapped on the belt, holstered the revolver, and retrieved my rifle from the rack above the fireplace. Cradling it under one arm, I snatched a box of ammunition with a free hand.

I thumped across the planked floor, giving Scott notice I was coming out the front door.

He eyed my hat. "You wore that ratty ol' straw thing around her?"

I stepped off the porch and headed for the pasture, calling over my shoulder, "Who's her?"

Scott caught up with me. "You know who I'm talking about."

It was *her* who made me need target practice. After our walk, the memories of the burning wagon and Running Deer finding me—all had come back to me in my dreams last night. When Scott showed up in the morning, I eagerly readied myself to join him.

"I wore my Sunday hat. You saw it."

He shifted his belt and switched his rifle to his other hand. "That straw hat is the ugliest thing I've ever seen."

"I'll burn it the day you switch from Colt to Smith and Wesson."

"I can't shoot a single action, and you know it."

I smiled, understanding his dilemma. I'd trained on a single action, cocking the hammer back with my other hand, then firing. His Colt did both with a pull of the trigger. The truth was, I owned a Colt double action but couldn't keep myself from pulling the hammer back. It was too ingrained in me. I'd hidden the gun in my bedroom so Scott would never know.

Over the fence we climbed, because I was too lazy to open the gate, and into the pasture we strode. The horses lifted their heads, saw we carried our rifles, and drifted away from the river and our shooting range. Raven stayed close though, the morning sun shimmering on her flank. I had trained her not to fear gunfire. We walked to the edge of the field, facing away from the horses toward our targets.

"Can we start with rifles?" Scott motioned to a rock near the top of the small knoll in the horse pasture. "I'd love to beat you at something."

I desperately needed to use the Smith and Wesson but agreed.

He dropped his bag of cartridges, quickly lifted his rifle, and fired. A can from across the river rattled.

"Nice shot."

He leaned back and crossed his arms. "Let's see you do that."

I could. But the rifle was his world. I pulled the trigger and felt the kickback on my shoulder, and I knew I'd missed. Barely.

He pointed at me, a grin on his face. "Told you."

We shot without speaking, taking turns, and I began to remember.

As we closed into revolver range, I let the night of the

murders wash over me. Inside my head, I stood under a cloudless night sky.

A man stepped into our camp. Only I was no longer a ten-year-old but a man with hands that could easily grip a revolver.

Targets lined the river. I faced them like I would the would-be murderers. They challenged my father, asking for money.

He denied having any.

The men pulled their guns.

The cans became men. I pulled my pistol and fired once, twice, three times. All three men fell in crumpled heaps. And my parents lived.

Dust drifted over the cans.

"What . . . what was that?"

I came back to the present, catching my breath. I dropped in the grass, curled up in a ball. A headache washed over me, and I held my head in my hands.

Scott stood over me. "Philip." His voice was urgent. "Philip, are you okay?"

I turned to him, dazed. "That was a remedy to an ailment."

"What happened?"

I tried to calm my breathing. "Scott, I can't talk about it. It's privileged information."

Scott whistled. "Never seen anyone shoot that fast—or be that accurate."

My shooting teacher's lessons popped into my head. *There'll always be someone quicker, better than you.* I shook my head. Time to change the subject. I sat up and put as much enthusiasm into my voice as I could. "Hey, you going to ask Becky to the social? Chicken Dinner Social's coming up."

Scott brushed his red hair from his eyes. "I'll never admit I told you this, but I do find Becky attractive."

"Then what's the problem?"

"She likes me. Too much. If I asked her today, she'd marry me tomorrow. You sure you're okay?"

I held a hand to my head and nodded. I wanted to argue with him about Becky, but it was true. She wore her affections on her sleeve. "There may be more to her than just her likin' you."

"Well, if you ask me, love should be fought for."

Anna was like a peppermint. One taste and you only want more. I thought about her all week. She haunted me almost as much as my parents and their inexplicable journey beyond their destination.

The next Sunday I decided it was time to take Princess into town. She was almost ready to sell, so I would take her for a ride after the morning service. I rode to church, and as I left my little valley for the prairie, Raven stood at the fence, her accusing eyes watching me leave on another horse.

Anna was beautiful in a red-and-cream dress. I couldn't hold back a smile. She nodded as she passed and started for the front row, and my week-long hunger for her attention began to satiate. I slipped her a note, asking for her company on my afternoon ride.

She bowed her head for a moment, as if truly praying during Pastor Humphrey's prayer, but I guessed she might have been reading. My hope was confirmed when she turned, looked out from under the side of her bonnet, and nodded with a grin.

My heart soared.

After the service, she met me beside Princess. "Different horse. She's beautiful."

I watched her run her hand over Princess's chestnut muzzle. "I promise to have you home before dark if you'll join me on my ride this afternoon."

"Of course. Who would save me if I didn't go with you?"

"I need to eat at Caroline's first. You're welcome to join me and Scott. And I could introduce you to Leroy and Caroline."

"I'll not make Caroline's today, but maybe next week."

I loved the way she smiled at me, tilted her head to the side, and gave a friendly wink as she started for her parents and their wagon.

I stood in the middle of the road staring after her until I heard snickers and looked away. A group of children listened from a nearby tree.

What on God's earth was wrong with me? I was pathetic.

With a sigh, I turned for the saddle and thought it best to check Princess's back left shoe before riding on. She seemed to favor it as she stood. As I lowered to one knee between two horses, I overheard Jacob Wilkes talking. Eavesdropping wasn't a habit of mine, but the callous man spoke such few words, I had to listen.

His voice was smooth and mellow. "Beauty in this city is rare, and you've given me the rare gift of observing the most striking object ever created. Please, have dinner with me at the Alexander Mitchell. I won't accept no."

"Thank you for the invitation." Anna's voice sounded cheerful. "But I'm taken for the afternoon."

"Perhaps tomorrow then?"

I held my breath.

"I'm sorry, Jacob. I have engagements the rest of the week."

His voice lowered, and I sensed menace behind the tone. "May I ask with whom?"

"Must you?"

"If you have no other reason than you do not like me, just say so."

She hesitated. "Philip . . . Philip Anderson."

I heard a snort and then footsteps.

I turned back to my work, lifting Princess's leg. The shoe was tightly in place.

Anna's acceptance of me into her life slowly dawned on me. She had rejected Jacob, the handsome, successful business-man who always got what he asked for—because of me.

I felt my cheeks strain with a grin.

Jacob passed by and looked at me.

"What are you laughing at?" His eyes narrowed. He stepped between the privacy of the two horses and pointed his finger at me. "You need to understand something, Anderson. My father likes you. Anna likes you. The whole town likes you."

I wasn't aware of the town's feelings. But there was no objection from me. I stood and faced him.

He continued. "You can have my father. Maybe even parts of this town. But Anna is mine. Leave her alone."

He had my attention now. "She can make up her own mind."

His lips curled into a thin smile. "There's nothing a poor dirt farmer like you can do about it."

I drew myself to my full height, towering several inches over his blond head. "Since I'm the one riding with her today, looks like I've done something about it already."

With a flick of his wrist, he swung his cane around and jammed the round end forward into my gut.

I doubled over as air exploded from my lungs.

Out of the corner of my eye, I saw him flip the cane around again and swing the stick at my back.

It felt like a slice across my skin. The slapping sound sickened me as I crashed to the ground. The horses jumped and sidestepped away from the weapon.

I couldn't breathe and couldn't move. He leaned so close to my ear I could feel his breath. He whispered. "You talk to her again, there's more in store for you."

From the ground, all I could see was his boots. As he walked away, a cloud of dust hovered in the small space. I struggled to fill my lungs, and after a few moments another pair of boots stepped close.

"Philip, what happened?" Scott's arms surrounded me, sending a fresh attack of pain through my back.

I swallowed a shout.

"Sorry. Sorry." He held up his hands. "What happened?"

"Jacob."

"Jacob Wilkes did this?"

I struggled to my knees and watched from under the horse as Scott dashed after Jacob.

I tried to stand but couldn't.

Scott returned as quickly as he'd left. "He's gone. C'mon, you look pretty bad. Let's get you to Caroline's. Get you cleaned up."

"Was going to . . . I was going to ride . . . with Anna this afternoon."

He grunted and leaned close. "You can borrow some of my clothes."

Pain was nothing new to me, but my back didn't feel right. "Help me take off my jacket."

Once I was on my feet, he tugged it off. Pain seared as the coat slid across my back.

"Philip, don't move."

I gripped Princess's saddle horn as Scott examined my back. "You're bleeding, bad. We've got to get you to the doctor. You got a good caning."

Scott always exaggerated. "You can't bleed from a caning."

"I've heard of it happening. C'mon, let's get you to a doctor."

"Just get me to Caroline's place."

The ride through town was excruciating, Scott leading the way. I couldn't sit up straight and sat hunched over like an old man. Through the fog of pain I was thankful most of the church folk had left before the beating.

Why hadn't I defended myself against Jacob? Did it happen too fast for me? Or was I just someone life happened to instead of fighting for what was right? Some hero I ended up being.

The streets were nearly deserted except for a few families strolling along window shopping.

Scott led Princess to the back door of Caroline's Kitchen. "Wait here."

He disappeared into the wooden lean-to porch on the back of the building. The sun beat down on me. I pulled my hat down over my eyes and slumped.

Why would Jacob beat me just because a girl rejected him? Anna's image crossed my mind, and I knew the answer.

She wasn't just any girl.

Caroline was probably busy. She ran the only reputable restaurant open on Sundays. But I couldn't wait any longer. I had to get off Princess. I pulled my feet out of the stirrups and hanging onto the saddle horn slid down, tumbling to the ground. A jolt of pain shot through my back.

My face was in the dirt when Scott returned. He growled, "Told you not to move." He gripped my arm.

I looked up to see Leroy's crotchety old face inches from mine. He squinted at me. "Why didn't you git Jacob some what-for?"

Leroy took my other arm. I grunted, feeling every stiff, swollen muscle in my back.

"Caroline said to take him to her house." Scott led me toward her small shack behind the restaurant.

I shrugged away their grasps and stumbled forward, trying to ignore the spasms in my back. Leroy hobbled ahead and opened the door.

Inside the sparse room stood a table. I crossed the floor and leaned against it.

Scott threw open the curtains and a ray of light hit the floor at the foot of a nearby bed. "Help him take his shirt off. I'll get clean clothes from my place." Scott paused at the door and looked back at me. The sun caught his red hair. "I knew something like this was going to happen. I knew it. I could feel it."

"Scott." Leroy's shaky voice sounded weary. "You always got a feeling. Now, go get some clothes for the man."

The coat, draped over my shoulders, slipped off. Leroy whistled. "That Jacob Wilkes. Knew he was good for nothing."

With unsteady fingers, he worked the buttons of my white shirt and brushed away my hands when I tried to help. "Scott said Jacob used a cane. Good thing I'm around. Saw many a wound in the war. One man deserted and got a caning with a tiny rod, and it sliced open his skin with every swing. Tighter the skin is, the more it cuts. Poor man died."

"Leroy, you're not helping. He only got me once."

"Come here. Turn your back. I want to see it in the light." He snorted. "Got a few wounds in the war myself."

I slipped the shirt over my shoulders and it peeled slowly away from my skin, the drying blood pulling. I couldn't hold back a moan.

"Oh, Philip!"

I turned and saw Caroline step into the room. She

dropped a cloth she'd been holding and pressed her fingers to her lips.

The late morning air felt strange against my naked chest. I looked down at my stomach and saw the knot where he'd punched me. I glanced up. "I got the worst of that confrontation."

Leroy touched my back. I could barely feel his fingers, only a burning as they pressed from my left shoulder blade to my right kidney. "A long stripe. But I don't think you'll need sewed up." Leroy stepped in front of me. "Couple o' thick bandages will do."

Caroline sniffed. "You'll find clean strips of cloth in a basket under the bed."

I looked up and saw tears brimming in her eyes. "Thanks, Caroline."

"Jacob's got to be stopped." Her tears were angry.

Leroy squinted at me. "He's gonna run all over you till you stand up for yourself."

Caroline looked toward the restaurant and then back at me, as if deciding something. Finally, she wiped her hands on her wide apron. "Anna is a beautiful girl, Philip. I like her. You two are a good match. But . . ." Her voice trailed off.

"Out with it." I winced as I rolled my shoulders, testing my ability to move.

Concern shown in Caroline's eyes. "You know Jacob's reputation around town. What he doesn't own around here, he's fighting to get, fighting with any means necessary."

"What are you saying?"

"The other day, I saw Anna riding along the street in front of my place. And I saw Jacob watch her from one end of the street to the other."

"Everyone watches her."

She held up a hand. "I know. But listen. He studied her in a way that makes a woman's skin crawl. He scares me, Philip. Combine that with how he operates around town, and you're in harm's way."

"He may not have any scruples, but I doubt he'd do anyone serious harm."

She narrowed her eyes and nodded toward my bloody shirt on the floor. "He already has."

Leroy stepped around me and looked up into my eyes. "You're going to have to stop him. Don't make me do it for you."

"You two are definitely taking this too far." But I didn't know if I was convincing them or me.

11

Anna was busy when I reached the Johnston house, so Beth took me out back to see her horse, Spink. He was the ugliest beast I'd ever seen.

Beth sighed. "He doesn't even gallop." She crawled onto the split-rail fence.

I touched the horse's shaggy mane. His dirty white coat had definitely seen better days. He nuzzled my stomach and I grimaced in pain but managed a breath. I was determined to tell no one what Jacob had done to me. "I'll bet Spink's a good friend."

"I suppose so." She offered half a smile.

I turned and saw Anna coming toward us. She smiled and for a moment my heart paused. She was beautiful. Her riding boots clicked on the porch before stepping onto the back lawn.

She pressed her lips together then took a deep breath. "There is no better friend than a horse."

I averted my gaze.

As we mounted our horses, I realized I'd forgotten the pain in my back.

She begged to see my herd, so we rode the half hour to

my house. When we passed the small copse where we'd first met, I pointed it out. "Here's Anna's Wood."

My reward was the sound of her laughter.

A cloud blocked the Dakota sun. I looked up and saw a single thick puff of white in an endless sky spread over the grassy plain. From the corner of my eye, I noticed—for the fiftieth time—her riding breeches.

She sighed. "I refuse to ride sidesaddle. And I avoid wagons if I can. Horses are my freedom. That's why I wear pants."

I held up my hands. "No argument from me."

Her voice hardened. "No one tells me what to do other than the Bible. Maybe my father. And probably, possibly, my husband someday . . . if he's right." Her eyes flashed.

I couldn't hold back a laugh. "I get it. You're a woman of principle."

She pointed a finger at me. "And don't you forget it."

Princess let Alita take the lead by a head. A small squeeze from my calves and Princess stepped a bit faster. If she was to be an officer's horse, she had to take command. Yet, over the last few days I had other ideas for her future. She would be a gift for Running Deer if I ever found him. And I now believed I just might.

"Look there." Anna pointed down the ravine.

I grinned. She was viewing my spread.

Anna paused at the lane that dropped into my valley and pointed to the cabin. "Someday I'll live in a house like that." She sighed, leaned forward, and crossed her arms over her saddle horn.

I turned Princess's head down the lane. "Let's go, then."

"Wait. What?"

"This is where I live." I couldn't repress a smile.

As we rode down the lane, a fence on either side, I couldn't help but look at it as if for the first time. To the left, wheat stretched thick and tall from the ground. Ahead stood the cabin, garden, and barn with the James River beyond, a steep hill of green rising from the other bank. On the right, the horses followed a well-worn trail along the inside of the fence.

We paused at the corral and dismounted. Anna immediately reached out to Raven. "Your horses are so beautiful." The other Arabians stood a short distance away, unsure whether or not to trust her.

I watched to see what Anna would do.

She slipped between the rails and reached for the two pregnant mares standing side-by-side.

"That's Desert Sand, and this one is Sheba. Both were named in Egypt."

The horses held back, sniffing her hand, until Sheba, the more social of the two, decided to trust Anna. Then all the horses closed in on her.

They took to Anna like a long-lost friend. My heart beat quickly as I watched them respond to her touch.

A long whinny caught our attention and Anna gasped. "Oh, my. He's huge."

"He's Belgian." Franklin stood at the top of the knoll, looking down on us with disdain, as if such unimportant matters as nuzzling and laughter were beneath him. He lowered his massive head into the grass with no more interest.

As Anna greeted each of the horses, I felt as if I'd brought her home. To stay. It was a dangerous feeling and I tried to swallow it, but the more I held it back the less control I had over my emotions. I knew I was falling in love.

I rode back to town with her, my excuse being that Princess needed more work. We paused near Anna's Wood, found an ancient elm tree where two branches split. Anna snuggled into the nook and I rested on a root, my shoulder against the trunk, listening to her talk and watching the sun ready itself for evening. My back ached, but I didn't care. I had Anna all to myself.

"I wonder what it was like," she said. "I mean, before we came here when it was just Indians. And buffalo."

"Buffalo kept the grass down, I'm sure. And fires helped."

"And the Indians hunted buffalo and slept in their teepees out here on the prairie." She gave a sigh, as if dreaming.

"You'd like that?"

"Yes, I would."

"Well, hunting was a chore for the Sioux." I turned to look up at her. "They didn't care for it. War is what they love." I wondered what Running Deer would think of Anna.

She seemed to choose her next words carefully. "Did you ever sleep in a teepee?"

"No. But I think I might, someday. An Indian, Running Deer . . ." Emotions clouded my mind. "I have to find him, reward him for saving me back when I was a boy." I said it quickly, hoping she would understand how difficult it was to talk about it, and turned away to avoid her gaze. What I suddenly saw in the woods chilled me to my soul. Jeb, Jacob Wilkes's second in command. Knife in hand, he made as if to slash his throat.

Anna was talking. "I'd like to sleep in one. Someday, maybe." Her voice was dreamy.

She touched my shoulder, and I took her hand. I stood. "Let's get back to town. Now."

"Philip?" Alarm showed in her eyes.

"Let's go."

Anna always enjoyed the short walk through the prairie from her house to the mill. Today was no exception. Dew hung heavy on the tall grass as it reflected the morning rays, and she hummed "I'm Redeemed," a new hymn she'd learned with a catchy tune. The smells of clean air and growing plants surrounded her.

She wanted to skip along the dirt path like a little girl. So she did.

The toe of her boot bumped against a root and she stumbled, catching herself just before falling. She laughed, her voice mingling with the birdsongs around her.

Out of breath, she paused.

Oh, it felt good to be falling in love.

She froze. Where had that thought come from?

From her heart. From her soul. Both seemed to be trying to catch her mind up with truths they'd known for days.

She attempted to wiggle her toes, but the pointed end of the boot restricted them. She bent down and loosened the side laces. Before pulling out her foot, she took a look around to make sure she was alone.

She jumped when she saw a hulking beast of a man standing under a lone pine only a stone's throw away, watching her. She laced up her boot quickly.

A voice came from behind her. "Just wait there, while our boss comes to speak with you."

She spun and saw another man, skinny and probably in his forties with white stubble spotting his face.

"Who are you?"

"Pleasure to finally meet you." He took a few steps forward, as did the large man. She was surrounded. "I'm Jeb. This is Ryan. And we work for the most powerful man in Mitchell."

Jacob's men. She shivered. "I'm expected at the mill in just a moment. My father is there. He'll be worried."

Pounding hooves alerted her to a coming rider. Jacob wore a white silk shirt that fluttered in the breeze, pulling tight over his chest to show surprisingly thick muscles across his chest and arms. He jerked the horse's head back as he halted next to her. "I hoped to catch you out this morning," he said, smiling. He stayed on his horse.

"She's in a hurry, boss. Work." Jeb's voice was filled with sarcasm.

"Then I will be brief. Anna, I've decided to court you." He reached into his shirt and pulled out a piece of paper. "I've written the dates that you and I will have dinner." He leaned over with the paper in hand.

Anna tried to speak but couldn't. Did she just hear him correctly? She tried again and finally managed, "I am not free to be courted." She bit her lip as she watched Jeb and Ryan step closer.

"Take the paper," Jeb said. "He's doing you the greatest favor that can be bestowed upon a woman."

She swallowed. "Philip is courting me." Holding her breath, she turned and started for the mill. She refused to look back.

Every tread she made she expected something bad to happen. A knife, or lasso, or a bullet in the back. When the mill came into view, she turned. They were gone.

She sprinted the rest of the way, and her heart leapt into her throat. A black Arabian was tied to the hitching post in front of the mill. Raven.

She burst through the door and saw her father and Philip speaking by the massive round millstone. Both men looked at her.

Philip smiled but seemed to notice her heavy breathing. "Are you okay?"

"Just . . . saw your horse."

The grin on his face warmed her.

"Anna, Philip has asked me if he may court you." Her father raised an eyebrow. "I told him he better ask you." He crossed his arms. "I'm fine with it."

His voice was gruff, but she knew him well enough to see he was pleased. Filled with relief, she threw her arms around her father. "Of course."

After a month of courting Anna, I sat in Caroline's Kitchen, the late afternoon nice and quiet after the normal rush of the noon meal. I was chatting with Leroy and Caroline after my errands, and on my way back to the farm I planned to stop in and see Anna. She'd been sick, and I hoped she was feeling better.

"Marry the girl." Leroy took a drink of leftover coffee, and his wrinkled face puckered. "Should have taken her to the social last night."

"Anna's got a fever, and I didn't feel like going without her."

Caroline returned from taking my empty plate into the kitchen and settled into a chair. "Scott took Becky to the social."

I raised an eyebrow. "He wasn't going to ask her. He thought she'd be too eager."

"He did ask." Leroy slapped the table. "She told him no, she did. That's what'll catch the boy every time."

"She told him no." Caroline leaned forward. "And they both showed up anyway."

A bad feeling shot through my gut right then. It wasn't the food or the company. Just a vague notion I should return home. Something was wrong.

I wished the two good-day and let Raven speed me to the cabin like the wind.

When we reached the overlook above my place, I saw my two pregnant mares down near the corral. As I got closer I could see that Sheba was breathing heavily, and Desert Sand was lying on her side. I dismounted and touched their bellies. I could feel contractions in both.

It was time for them to give birth. But instead of doing it quietly in the middle of the night, standing, both horses were in distress.

12

I burst out of my cabin with a box of matches in hand and just missed running into Anna. Had she followed me from town?

She jumped back and grasped a post that held up the porch overhang. "Running to a fire? Or starting a fire?" She leveled her gaze on my face and sobered. "What's wrong, Philip?"

"I'm out of matches in the barn. Desert Sand, Sheba. They could lose their babies."

She quickly set down the plate of fresh rolls she carried. "What can I do?"

I shook my head. "Go home. It's going to be a late night."

With a huff, she thrust her hands onto her hips. "Now look—"

I couldn't help a quick glance at the corral, where the horses waited.

Anna grasped my arm. Her voice was tender. "Please, Philip, let me help. I'm not sick anymore. I feel fine."

I looked at her soft hand against my arm then studied the pleading in her eyes. My heart melted. "It may not go well."

She bit her lower lip. "I understand."

I led her to the barn and snatched two ropes. I tied a rope into a lariat and handed it to Anna.

Together, we walked over to Sand who allowed us to slip the rope over her neck. "Philip, she shouldn't be down."

"I know." I softened my tone. "We're going to need to see if she'll stand, and we'll get her to the barn."

"Something's wrong with Sheba too."

"Let's get Sand to her feet." I grasped her head and encouraged her to stand. She struggled, rocking back and forth, and finally she stood. Both horses were wheezing.

We led them to separate stalls in the barn.

I tossed forkfuls of hay on the dirt floor. "It's normal for mares to go into labor at the same time." Anna watched what I was doing for a moment then disappeared. I could hear her spreading hay in Sheba's stall. The strong scent of grass filled the barn. I wished I had straw, a softer bed. "Usually they drop their foals at night. I should have checked on them this morning."

Desert Sand settled in the hay.

"How do you know all this?" Anna called.

I rubbed Sand's belly. "Tucker and Princess were easy births. I just woke up one morning and there they were, nursing." I paused and looked over the stall as Anna came close. "I told you I read a lot."

Standing over the mare, I took a deep breath and whispered a quick prayer. I'd actually never done this before.

Anna touched my shoulder. "They'll be all right."

I reached up and grasped her hand, touching her smooth fingers. Her faith gave me hope. "Get blankets from the tack stall near the front. Then light every lantern you can find."

She nodded and jumped to her tasks. My mind desperately searched for what to do.

I lit the forge to warm the barn and set a pot of water on top. The front doors were open, and I could hear crickets calling into the night. The muddy smell from the river behind the barn wafted on the evening breeze.

A guttural scream, deep and penetrating, filled the air.

Anna burst from Sand's stall, a blanket wrapped around her arm. "What was that?"

"Sheba." I raced down the barn's center, past Anna, and skidded to a stop. Sheba was pushing.

"Philip?" Anna motioned toward Sand's stall. Her voice trembled. "Sand's not moving."

My heart stopped. She was lying on her side again. I pointed toward Sheba. "Stay with her." I ran back to Sand's stall.

I settled beside Sand and stroked her forehead, running a finger along the white blaze down the center of her long nose.

I could ride Raven into town to get the vet—Raven could make the journey quickly. But the doctor would take forever, and by the time we made it back, mothers and babies could all be dead.

Sand's belly twitched, and I reached down to feel her warm side quivering.

"Philip, Sheba's in a lot of pain, and she's lying down now, too." Anna called from the other stall. "What do I do?"

"Try to get her up and walk her around the barn."

I could hear Anna grunting as she tried to pull Sheba up. I turned back to Sand. I felt along her belly for the foal's position. The mare started to cough. It was a strange sound coming from a horse, but I knew it meant I was losing her.

Anna's voice came from behind. "I'm walking her." I could hear Sheba's hooves. "How will this help?"

"I think the foals in both mares are turned. Walking may work the baby into birthing position." I frowned. "This one doesn't have the strength to stand."

The book had told me what to do next, but I didn't want to do it. I gritted my teeth. "Anna, is the water boiling on the forge?"

"Uh . . . not yet. No. It's steaming, though."

"The handle's hot, so you may need the smithing gloves. Can you bring it here?"

I heard Anna close the barn doors, and she shuffled into the stall and placed the steaming pot next to me.

"Thanks."

She stripped off the gloves and touched my shoulder. "What's next?"

"I need to reach inside to find out how the foal is situated and then try and turn it if I can."

Since the War Between the States, incredible leaps in medicine had been made, but infection was always a danger. The hot water would cleanse my hands. If infection was a problem with humans, animals were just as likely.

I plunged my hands in the scalding water. Pain shot up my elbows and cleared my mind. I lifted my arms into the air, feeling the heat pass quickly from my fingers.

Anna cringed, her eyebrows crumpled with concern.

I motioned with my chin. "Keep walking Sheba."

She nodded and returned to her work.

Sand coughed. I threw a blanket over her. She didn't move.

I moved from her head to her back legs and pushed her tail aside to slip my hand deep inside her body. Sand grunted and shivered.

"Philip!" Anna cried. "I can see Sheba's baby."

I clenched my jaw and glared at the wall that separated me from Anna. After a deep breath, I shouted. "Great."

"It's not moving, I think it's stuck."

I slowly pushed my hand deeper into the mare. "Pull the foal, Anna. But be careful."

"I can do it. I helped mother give birth to Beth."

"Fine. I'll tell her she gives birth like a horse."

"Philip Anderson . . ."

My arm was in past my elbow now, and I could finally feel the foal. I traced a leg with my fingers.

Anna cried, "It's a girl, a beautiful little girl."

I was afraid I was about to lose both Sand and her foal. "I need you, Anna. Now!"

She hurried into Sand's stall, her sticky hands outstretched.

"Hold her head."

Anna rushed to follow my orders. She settled onto the backs of her boots and cradled the mare's head in her hands. "Her breathing's not good."

PETER LEAVELL

I closed my eyes. "If she dies, I'm pulling the foal as fast as possible. I want you to take it to Sheba right away. Understand?"

Anna tilted her head. "So she'll think she's the baby's mother?"

I nodded and reached deep, until I could feel the tiny hooves in my palm. With all four legs in my grasp, I tried to gently turn the foal. I twisted harder, and Sheba lifted her head and pushed. She had some strength left.

Anna whispered encouragement in the mare's ear.

I rubbed sweat from my eyes with my shoulder, then pulled the hooves until I felt something strange at the side of her uterus.

"What's wrong?" Anna barely whispered.

I'd felt another set of hooves. "Twins." I counted eight hooves again. "They're stuck."

My leg began to cramp and I readjusted my position. Anna looked horrified.

"Ready?" I asked.

She gave me a questioning look.

"I have to try to pull them out with as little damage as possible. Otherwise, they'll die for sure."

Eyes closed, I moved my hand to the first foal's rump, and then moved up its tiny body until I grasped its shoulders and pulled, hard, hoping not to break its neck.

Sheba pushed, and I whispered, "That's right, girl." I helped guide the baby through the birth canal. In less than five seconds, the foal slipped out onto the hay.

I looked up at Anna. "That was easy."

I reached back in and found the second foal, but Sheba had no strength left to push. I tugged at the little body and felt the birth canal tense. The baby didn't move.

"Come on, girl," I pleaded. "You can do it."

I pulled again, my grip firm. If I pulled any harder, it felt like the young horse would come apart. As I pushed the tiny body from side to side, I told Anna to massage the mare's belly. Anna complied. Inch by inch, I felt the baby move along the birth canal. Finally, it slipped from its mother onto the hay.

I examined both foals for damage as they took their first breaths, and they seemed fine. I looked at Anna. "One of each, a colt and a filly."

Sand lifted her head, and I placed the newborns near her nose.

I stood and motioned to Anna. "Let's get out of her way."

We checked on Sheba. Her filly was already nursing.

After Anna and I washed our hands and arms and then washed again, we collapsed across from Sand's stall. The mare had regained her strength and was standing, cleaning her new-borns with her tongue. All three foals stood on shaky legs.

Anna settled next to me, so close I could feel her arm against mine.

We watched for a moment, both mothers caring for their young.

She cleared her throat. "That's disgusting. Why do animals always have to clean with their tongues?"

I laughed. "What else are they going to use?" She giggled and we slumped against the rail. I opened the barn doors again, and under the glow of the lamplight, we tried to catch our breath. The horses seemed healthy.

I looked at Anna. "Are you okay?" I grunted and mentally kicked myself. Perhaps the word was going to stick in my vocabulary.

When she didn't respond, I glanced at her and saw that her eyes were filled with tears.

A wash of feelings I'd been holding back hit me too, and I felt like crying but instead offered her a weak smile. She reached for my hand and held it tight.

The bright light from the roaring furnace cast shadows around the room. The hay shone yellow, reflecting the fire. A gentle night breeze wafted through the doors and I could see a handful of stars. Frogs on the riverbank croaked loudly enough to be heard over the crackling fire.

I took a deep breath and blew tension from my body. I propped my head against the rail and looked up to the loft and rafters. I couldn't remember ever feeling so exhausted. A chill filled the barn, and I shivered.

Anna sighed and settled into the hay. "That was amazing. They're so tiny and helpless. God surely sent his angels down to watch over them. Two fillies and a colt." She elbowed me. "You should be proud."

"I am. I just wish it had been easier on the mares." I stretched my back. "The sire's probably in the pasture sharing a cigar with Franklin."

She smiled. "You were wonderful."

I grunted. As quiet settled on us, I fidgeted with a long piece of dried grass.

After several minutes, Anna grasped my arm. "It's time, you know, Philip. It's time I knew of your past."

The tension I'd been trying to release returned and my mind swirled. I pulled away from her. Now? Did she think because I was emotionally drained tonight I could talk about it?

She faced me. "Philip, I want to help you find your friend, Running Deer." She seemed frustrated. "We're close, after these months of time together," she said. "I won't tell anyone."

"I know you won't tell anyone." I struggled to come up with words to explain. "I would tell you if I knew how." A deep breath. "I've never told anyone what happened to me."

She clasped both my hands in hers. "I'm here. For you. I'm not going anywhere."

A tremor ran up my spine as I studied her earnest face. A loose strand of hair ran along her cheek. On impulse, I reached over to tuck it behind her ear. Her gaze remained locked on me, pleading.

I loved her. I wanted to spend my life with her.

She deserved to know.

Her gaze never wavered.

I brushed hay from my shirtsleeve. "I have no brothers or sisters. Just me. I remember parties at my parents' house. They loved to have friends visit. But my father insisted the West would be our new home." I paused.

Anna nodded encouragement, and I continued.

"We lived in West Virginia. I was maybe ten years old when we crossed the prairie into Dakota Territory." Despite our locked stare and the stirring emotions between us, the wagon returned to my mind. "Mother hated the idea of leaving her home. But my father raced across the prairie to our homestead."

She gripped my hands tight.

"One night, as we camped along the river . . ." I choked out the next words. "We were robbed. Three men. One pulled his gun and shot both of them. I ducked under the wagon and ran away."

Tears filled her eyes again.

My story flowed out of me now. "Indians found me, and I stayed with Running Deer for awhile and learned a lot. Then he took me to an orphanage in Sioux City. I saved money blacksmithing until I had enough to purchase land and a couple horses. I found out orphans were given land at age eighteen under the Homestead Act, so I used the money I'd saved to build the cabin and barn."

"You did a magnificent job." Her smile was gorgeous. "Do you hate them, Philip? The men who killed your parents?"

I lowered my head. "I suppose not. For a long time I did. I wanted to find them and kill them. Now I just wish I could put it to rest."

Her fingers entwined with mine. "So that's how you know so much about Indians."

"I wanted to spend my life with them."

"Why didn't you?"

"Running Deer, the one who spoke English, thought I should be raised by my own people." I looked away as anger coursed through my heart. "Indians saved me. It was white men who butchered my parents."

She laid her head on my shoulder.

I pressed my cheek against her hair. "I would have told you sooner, but I get these funny periods where I'm back there with the killers and my parents' bodies and the burning wagon. It seems so real." I paused, the images returning, threatening to envelope me.

I did my best to pull away from the nightmare. "You were there when I spoke to the Sioux woman."

"I remember."

"Something came back to me as I spoke to her. I remembered a large rock, Devil's Tower, in the background where my parents were murdered. How could I forget something like Devil's Tower?"

She shrugged. "I've read about it."

"Anna, my parents' homestead was in Yankton. We passed right by it and went to the Black Hills. I don't know why."

I looked into her eyes, and she searched mine as if answers lay somewhere in my soul. "The Sioux woman told me where Running Deer is now. Before I met you, I was planning to head to the Black Hills and find him to give him a gift, possibly find some answers. But I was distracted by a troublesome woman."

She frowned and covered her mouth with her hand. "Oh, dear. There's a troublesome woman in your life?"

"Disturbing." I stared at her lips, which seemed to redden. Her smile was inviting in the lamplight.

"What's her name?" She tilted her head and inched closer.

My voice was a throaty whisper. "Anna."

Our lips touched in a long, consuming kiss, coursing through my entire body. I held my breath and pulled away. She slipped her cheek along mine and laid her head on my shoulder again. I stroked her soft hair, the silky strands running through my fingers. I'd wanted to feel her hair since the moment I met her.

She exhaled a happy sigh. "I love you, Philip Anderson."

The sound of mares crunching hay and nursing foals competed with the hammering of my heart.

I wanted to tell Anna the same. I wanted to ask her to spend her life with me. But try as I might, I couldn't tell her what I felt.

My past wasn't to blame. Nor were my overwhelming emotions. I'd lived such a private life, keeping privileged information from others for so long that my love for her was falling into that awful category. I said nothing.

It was the worst mistake of my life.

13

Anna walked alone beside the river. She'd felt alone her entire life. Until she'd met Philip, that is.

She paused at a maple tree and settled to the ground. Her dress flowed around her, and she watched it flutter in the wind.

The brown water of the James River rippled past, reflecting none of the greenery on the opposite bank. A blue sky with high strands of cirrus clouds running through it reminded her of a marble. Of the two, the dark river and bright sky, the water fit her mood.

Nothing could ever make her forget the kiss she and Philip had shared. Just thinking of his lips sent tingles through her body. Their relationship was never stronger—he'd confided in her a past no one else knew. She understood his reason for keeping it a secret. It was as if when he thought of it he turned into a little boy, the memories so painful he could not contain the agony. It made her experiences, while difficult, seem trivial.

She'd seen and heard his deepest emotions that night. However, normally he was like the James River—nothing showed that was deeper than the surface. There was so much more to Philip, but he held it back. For all she knew, it could take a lifetime to discover all his secrets.

The thought warmed her.

The mill wheel slapped noisily at the water, a constant rhythm. Perhaps she should get back to work. She started to rise but decided a few minutes more surely wouldn't hurt.

Telling Philip of her love was a mistake. He hadn't—— maybe couldn't—tell her the same. He did love her, she was sure. The way he looked at her with those piercing gray eyes, as if he would consume her with fiery passion. But then he would reach for her hand, and his touch was gentle.

His hands. How lovely to watch him cinch a saddle or lead a horse or work with his blacksmith tools. His fingers were nimble, quick. Sometimes she couldn't see them as he tied a lasso, they moved so fast. It was magic.

But Philip was strange. While many townspeople respected him and most called him friend, many seemed to fear him. Maybe it was his eyes, more like an animal's than a man's. She herself sensed a volcanic core within, but she couldn't put her finger on what it was. He was kind, generous with his time, eager to please, but it was as if he held a terrible power roiling inside him that could destroy, like a stick of dynamite. He had no desire for revenge or violence of any kind, but it seemed as if he were capable.

Scott rode to the front of the mill, spotted her, and waved. She returned his salute and watched him hurry inside, late from his errand. He'd stopped to see Becky, no doubt.

Scott loved Philip. Would die for him. Their relationship reminded her in a way of David and Jonathan in the Bible. His other close friends, Leroy and Caroline, would probably die for him too.

So would she.

A thought struck her. Maybe he couldn't admit his love to her because being alone—he'd lived that way ever since his parents had died—was all he really wanted. Perhaps a battle raged inside him or he was just set in his ways. There was little she could do to change such a man. Her only hope was to convince him how truly wonderful life could be together.

She dreamed of the cabin, their cabin, and how she would prepare dinner while looking out the window, watching him work with the horses. The sound of a little boy's feet running down the hall filled her head, and she shivered.

Anna grabbed a nearby stick and wrote her name in the dirt. *Anna Jessica Johnston*. She stood, and with her shoe smudged out the surname and replaced it with Anderson. *Anna Jessica Anderson*. Perfect.

She had to know how Philip felt. She must find out if he had the same intentions.

14

Rain splattered on my felt hat and splashed down my oilskin slicker. The gray, oppressive day cut my vision to a quarter mile. Raven's mane was dripping wet. Saddlebags flopped at her sides, the only sound besides the falling rain and sloshing of her feet.

Princess followed behind, her head down, a rope tied to her halter forcing her to keep up with Raven's quick pace.

I wasn't sure if I was crying or if the rain was seeping through my black hat—I'd left my straw hat behind on the kitchen counter. Either way, my cheeks were wet.

The conversation still rang in my ears.

Anna had eaten with me at Caroline's Kitchen, laughing with Leroy and Caroline. And then we'd ridden back to my place. Inside the cabin, she sat in my rocking chair beside the warming fireplace while I prepared coffee. The memory of her soft features, her closed eyes, and her hair draped down over her shoulders and behind the chair brought a lump in my throat.

"Philip, why don't you share your feelings with me?" she'd said.

The coffee pot boiled over and burned my hand. I couldn't hold back an edge in my voice. "It hurts." I stuck my hand in my mouth.

She opened her eyes and sat up. "No, Philip. Really. What do you feel inside?"

She was always one to get right to the point. I wanted to be with her, and she wanted to be with me. Wasn't that enough?

"I feel fine inside."

Her eyebrows furrowed and she stood.

I tried something else. "I mean, I feel like I always do, if that's what you mean."

She set her hands on her hips. "What about *us*? How do you feel about our relationship?"

As I rode my horse, I thought back on the word. *Relationship*. Scott was a buddy. As was Leroy. Although when I thought of Anna, she seemed different somehow. As if she should be allowed a designation of special importance. I did love her, after all. But I couldn't put words to my feelings, and it made me uncomfortable to try.

I knew what she had wanted me to say. At least now, as I rode across the Dakota prairie toward the Black Hills, I understood she had needed to hear me say I loved her.

But the conversation had taken a sudden turn.

She had looked out the front window. I couldn't tell if she was really looking down the lane or contemplating her next words. Finally, she seemed to make up her mind and abruptly turned to me.

"Jacob Wilkes has asked me to dinner."

My muscles tightened and I arched an eyebrow. "Is that so?"

She folded her arms. "What do you think I should tell him?"

I desperately wanted to say, "You are mine—how could you think of such a thing?" But I checked myself. Instead, I heard my own sulky voice. "You should do what you want, of course." I sagged against the table.

"What do I want, Philip?" She turned to me, her eyes

intense, her palms raised, and took a step forward. "I'm giving you a chance to make up my mind for me."

I racked my brain, wondering what she really wanted. Was she really interested in Jacob?

I wanted to hear her words of love, her undying devotion to me. But I couldn't seem to give her the same. If I told her go to dinner with him, maybe she would come back to her senses and ask forgiveness for even considering the idea. "He's a banker's son." I spat the words at her. "He owns half the town. I . . . I'm just a poor farmer. I could never care for you like he could."

I was a fool.

Instantly, tears welled in her eyes and trickled down her cheeks.

She looked at the cabin walls and then glanced at the mantle where my Winchester rifle rested next to my Smith and Wesson. What was she thinking?

I knew I deserved to be shot. As I rode I scratched Raven's withers, and she turned her head to look at me from the corner of her eye.

"What should I have done, girl? You're a woman. How can I fix this?"

Raven snorted and kept her steady pace.

Anna had left, telling me that I might get what I wished for.

The next morning, Sunday, Anna and Jacob had left church together, his face smeared with a contemptuous smile.

Scott had told me any good courtship was worth fighting for. So when I got home from church, as storm clouds moved in on the plains, I jotted down a letter.

> Dearest Anna,
> What a fool I am. I need to tell you how I really feel, not what I think you want me to say. I am sorry. Can you ever forgive me?
> I will say in this letter that life without you means nothing. I would sell my horses for you, everything.
> To give you time, I am leaving for Deadwood to track down Running Deer and repay an old debt.

When I return, perhaps you can find it in your heart to hear what is in the deepest regions of mine, things that are now permanent and will never change. Feelings I should have told you but never did.

With my deepest affection and truly yours,
Philip A.

I had quickly packed supplies in a blanket and stuffed them in the saddlebags, loaded Raven, and left for town, where I stopped at Caroline's for a quick meal. The rain had just begun as I entered. A few people looked up from their tables.

Leroy sat at the usual table, so I slumped in the chair next to him. "I'm leaving for a while."

He rubbed his whiskers. "You look terrible."

"I'm getting away from town for a few days and need to talk to Scott. Do you know where he is?"

"He and Becky are coming in a little while."

Caroline swept a cloth over a nearby table and soon joined us. "Getting busy around here. I may be looking for help soon." She studied my face. "What's wrong?"

"Who said anything's wrong?"

"Your face."

Leroy sucked in a breath. "You and Anna had a fight, I reckon?"

My heart dropped. "Sums it up."

Caroline put a hand on my arm. "Oh, dear. I'm sorry."

I shook off her pity. "I've got business out of town. I'll be back in a few days."

Leroy glanced at the hat I'd laid on the table but didn't say a word.

I snatched my hat and stood. "Look, could you two do me a favor? Can you ask Scott to see after the horses while I'm gone? He knows what to do."

Caroline exchanged glances with Leroy.

"Sure." The old man grimaced. "Sure, we can do that."

"Thanks."

I turned to leave, but Caroline stopped me, her hand on my arm. "Philip, I have a bad feeling about this. Please, be careful."

The soft look in her eyes caused me to pause. I bowed my head. "I just . . . I just need to take care of something and I'll be back. Oh." I reached into my pocket and pulled out the envelope. "Could you see that Anna gets this?"

Caroline grabbed the letter. "Yes." She held it up. "However we can help."

They were silent, and their doleful gazes almost made me laugh. "Look, I'll be fine. I can take care of myself."

Deadwood wasn't the lawless town everyone made it out to be, I hoped.

15

What was my mother's maiden name?

I lay on a lumpy bed in the Overland Hotel in Deadwood, the raucous noise outside keeping me awake.

The journey had been uneventful, and it had taken almost three days to get to the rugged mining town. The stars were bright by the time I'd arrived. I'd set up Raven and Princess at a livery stable then wandered to the hotel and bunked in for the night.

Restless, I rolled out of bed, feeling my linen sleeping pants brush against my legs as I stepped toward the window. The boards beneath my feet creaked. I tiptoed across a small rug. Cool air brushed against my naked chest as I slid the window curtain to the side and looked down on the street.

It was a dizzying three stories down to the road below. Electric lights on the street corners illuminated men wandering from saloon to saloon along the boardwalks. Almost four thousand people called Deadwood home, and most seemed to be staggering off to sleep away their drunkenness.

The thought wandered through my mind again. What was my mother's maiden name? I'd overheard a conversation in the lobby below that sent my mind reeling. A little girl was talking with her mother about her uncle. The girl's discovery that the uncle was her mother's brother was such a revelation to her that she stood open-mouthed for several seconds.

When Running Deer had left me at Sioux City, I'd searched for an Uncle Anderson, assuming he would have my own last name. But what if my uncle had been my mother's brother instead of my father's? He would have had a different surname, and that could be why I never found him.

I needed more information about my family, and I had to find Running Deer.

Sleep wasn't coming, so I dressed, tossed on my hat, and paused as I checked my belt, holster, and gun on the dresser. It was, after all, Deadwood.

It felt good to strap the Smith and Wesson down. I spun the cylinder, counted five shells loaded. The sixth chamber was empty, so the hammer could rest easy. I slipped into the dark hallway as quietly as I could.

Laughter and occasional screams filled the night air outside the hotel. Bright saloon windows and loud pianos dueled for prominence, competing for patronage. I gritted my teeth and headed for the nearest saloon. One bar was as good as another to begin my quest.

I crossed the street and passed a man lying in the rut. A small group on the corner burst into laughter and I flinched, my hand over my gun. Too jumpy. Perhaps this was a bad idea. But the thought of returning to my room was depressing, so I pushed on.

The saloon door swung easily, and lamplight filled my eyes. Tables dotted the interior, sawdust covered the floor, and two wild revelers worked their way between the tables, stumbling past sitting patrons. A handful of men looked up as I stepped inside, but most focused on their card games or the roulette wheel. One man, his arms wrapped around a woman, barely glanced at me before he returned to kissing the girl, her hat ruffled to the side. His hands strayed along her corset.

The bar stretched down one side of the room, and the bartender worked in a fog of cigarette and cigar smoke. His greased hair reflected light from the two lamps and the wide mirror behind him.

I watched him pour a whiskey for a patron, who opened a tiny leather pouch and clumsily spilled a bit of the contents on the sawdust floor. He swore. Then, with shaking hand, he held the bag out to the bartender.

The bartender ran his fingers through his oily hair before he dipped a pinch from the miner's bag then shifted it to his palm and held it out. The miner squinted as he surveyed the man's hand and nodded.

The bartender dropped the dash of gold into something behind the bar. I realized then that gold dust was the currency. But his fingers were still shiny. He ran his fingers through his hair again, removing the excess dust. In the morning if he washed his hair, his basin would be bright with gold dust—far more than if he worked a claim.

The price of that miner's drink was staggering. And the drunken clodpoll didn't seem to notice.

I backed out the door and walked away. Honest answers wouldn't be found in that sordid establishment. Maybe it would be better to just sit and simmer in my room. Was it that I didn't have the sand to hold my own against men of that nature? Or was it that the predominate activities in saloons made me uncomfortable?

A scream caught my attention—not the playful banter I'd heard inside the saloon. Instead, terror edged the cry like a razor. I glanced down the street and saw nothing more than men weaving along the boardwalks.

Another scream rose above the piano music. I hurried to the corner of the building, my boots pounding against the boardwalk. In the moonlight, I could just make out a narrow break between two buildings. Sounds of a struggle came from the darkness.

I stepped into the alley and heard a girl say, "Leave me alone." She grunted.

A man's slurred voice echoed between the walls. "I reckon I can teach you to be a proper whore." I heard a slap, and she screamed again.

I hurried into the darkness between the buildings, and barely made out the shadows of a large man shaking a smaller woman.

The sound of the hammer clicking on a pistol cut through the air. Surprised, I looked at my Smith and Wesson, which I had aimed at the man without thinking. What was I doing? I was no hero.

"Let her go." My voice was calm, commanding.

The man sneered at me. "Get outta here. This ain't any of your business."

"The lady's coming with me. Leave, now."

The man swore. "I paid this whore, and—"

"No. No money." The girl choked out the words. "You didn't give me a dime. And I ain't doing the business no more. I quit."

I took a step to the side, my gun still leveled at his gut. It was odd, pointing the muzzle at a man. "You best let her go."

The girl wrenched herself from his grasp and jumped out of his reach. She blocked my vision, and I stepped to the side to keep the shot clear. The man hadn't moved. I stared at his solid frame. He was furious. What would he do?

I decided not to let him make the next move. "Now, let's talk about the Good Book," I said. "It gives some excellent advice about this sort of thing."

He swore. "Take the girl. She's soiled merchandise."

He shoved past us through the narrow opening and lurched out onto the street, leaving a smell of booze I could almost see.

I eased the hammer back into place and holstered the pistol.

A burst of anger shot through me. I'd just risked my life for a stranger. The taste of death left my nerves on edge.

I turned to the shaking girl. "You and me. Coffee, now."

Her footsteps padded behind me as I marched back up the alley and turned toward the hotel. She paused, as if ready to scurry away.

"Coffee. I'm buying. I deserve a few answers."

She cringed. "I don't owe you anything." Her voice sounded desperate.

"I didn't pull my gun to have you get in any more trouble

tonight. I heard you say you quit. There's going to be changes in your life. Come."

I hurried into the hotel, the girl close on my heels. In the lobby, the grandfather clock read 11:30, but I felt wide awake. The chandelier was lit at all hours, and the clerk remained at his station behind the counter. I gave him a nod as I passed the stairs and walked down the hall into the restaurant.

Several customers in elegant clothing laughed and drank, same as those in the saloons only with more refinement. At least it was quiet enough to talk. I pointed out a table and turned to the girl. I was taken aback. Her disheveled brown hair, dirty face, and torn dress couldn't hide the fact that she was very young.

She gasped.

I frowned. "What's wrong?"

"Your eyes . . ."

"Well," I said, thrown off a bit. "You're a mess, so go clean up. I'll be sitting in here." I tossed her a key. "Room thirty-two. You have five minutes to get back down here. Five minutes."

She paused, looked up at me. "All right, I'll do as you say. Only because I want to. Not because you're ordering me."

I gave a single nod.

"Your name is . . ."

"Philip."

"Philip . . . You're . . . not coming up, are you?"

I didn't care what the other customers thought. I towered over her, feeling heat flush my face. "If you ever ask me anything like that again, I won't save you next time."

She held up her hands. "I'm going. I'm going."

As she left, I plunked down in a chair and a waiter brought two waters to the table. Suddenly thirsty, my nerves got the better of me and I drained the glass before he had the opportunity to leave. He refilled it.

This girl, while pretty, revolted me. Why was I trying to help her? Her lifestyle gave me shivers, and the disgusting filth of what she did for a living made me sick. But Jesus cared for her, and I had to admit, there was some curiosity. Why did she do it? Could she be made to stop?

Maybe I would try. No, I couldn't make her stop. More like coax her to change her life.

Unless she was conning me at that very moment, stealing everything in my room. Maybe sending her up there alone was stupid.

Before I could follow that line of thought, she stepped from the hallway into the dining room. She wore a smile, her hair combed and her face washed. Much better.

But her features turned somber when she sat. "You're not married. So, what is your game?"

"I don't understand."

"No one takes me to dinner."

"What's your name?"

"Rachel."

"Rachel, everyone's human. Everyone needs compassion once in a while." Like Running Deer had shown me.

She looked at me curiously, her skin wrinkling at her forehead.

I leaned forward. "Look. I've never pulled my gun on anyone before. I think I have a right to know a little more about why I did. What happened back there?"

Her jaw clenched. "All right. I grew up in a rich family in Rapid City. My father and I had words. I left for Deadwood, hoping to make him mad. Instead, I ruined what little chance I had at happiness." Her face contorted as if holding back the tears. She looked away, toward the well-dressed men and women. "I didn't mean to get into this business. But a woman on her own . . . I didn't have much choice."

She was silent for a moment, her thin eyebrows creasing. A quarrel seemed to be playing out in her head.

Finally, she reached with a shaking hand to slip the neckline of her dress down her shoulder. Deep gouges and rough patches covered her upper arm and chest. "Bite marks." Her whisper held an angry and bitter hatred. "Men."

I stared in horror.

"My parents will never take me back now." Whatever she was doing to hold her feelings in check failed her, and tears slid down her face. She lowered her head in her hands, as if in shame, but then raised her face. Her eyes showed defiance. "Now leave me alone."

A few patrons in the hotel restaurant glanced our way, but I didn't care. "Rachel, do you read the Bible?"

She looked up at the ceiling and sniffed. "Oh, you would ask that. Do you have any idea how many of my clients read their Bibles?"

I crossed my arms and she leaned back, so I untangled my limbs and tried to sit in a less threatening position. "I don't know if I can help you. I want to. You really can't go back to your family?"

She shook her head.

I sighed. "This may be a long shot, but I have a friend in Mitchell who may need help in their restaurant. Would you like me to ask if they'd be willing to hire you?"

Hope crossed Rachel's face and then faded. "I doubt he'd want me."

"*She* is as kindhearted as any person I've ever known." I opened my hands, palms up. "All I can do is try."

Rachel stared at the ceiling. "I know after . . . him . . . the one you chased away . . ." She struggled for words as she swallowed. "I know I can't go back to that life." Her turmoil played across her features. "No one's ever done what you've done for me. That's why I . . . God, why am I trusting you?" She directed her gaze at me, not God.

I shrugged.

She hiccupped. "He took my money. All of it."

"I'll buy you a room for tonight. Do you have any things?"

"They all belong to the saloon."

This wasn't going to be easy. "Sleep here tonight, and in the morning I'll wire Caroline. You should have your answer by the afternoon."

"I don't deserve your kindness." Her voice was thin and quiet. She hiccupped.

"No. No, you don't. But you left your pride behind a long time ago."

She jerked back and closed her eyes. "I deserved that."

"Are you hungry?"

She looked up, her red eyes swollen and lifeless. "I'm just so very tired."

I sighed, studying her. The last thing I needed now was a ward. "You know why you trust me?" I stood.

She shook her head.

"Because deep down you want to leave all this behind you."

She crossed her arms and gave a small nod.

"Follow me." I headed to the front desk to rent a second room. My journey to Deadwood was turning out to be nothing like I'd envisioned.

16

As I walked the streets the next morning, I felt naked. Everyone wore a gun except me. I bet even the women who walked by had a pistol tucked somewhere on their person. In my mind, I could see my revolver and holster on top of my saddlebag in my room, lonely and forgotten. Where I was headed, I wouldn't need them.

The early sunlight didn't improve Deadwood. Long rows of buildings connected by a common front stretched along the street, which was a muddy mess. I smelled a mixture of vomit and manure.

Deadwood lay in a crescent-shaped valley, the mountains on either side of town either mined or stripped of lumber. As early as it was, I was forced to dodge morning traffic. Men in suits hurried along the boardwalks or rode horses to their businesses. They all had the look of lawyers.

One by one, closed signs in business windows were turned over to reveal *Open for Business.*

Rachel had slept in a room on the first floor, and I didn't disturb her. I'd tossed and turned all night, wishing I'd never met her. But a promise was a promise, so I looked around for a telegraph office.

She was just a child. I figured I was playing a father figure in her life, for why else would she open up to a perfect stranger? I thought back to Anna telling me her troubles when we'd first met.

Maybe I looked like a preacher. Maybe it was my eyes everyone always said were so strange.

The thought of Anna pierced through my heart.

On the end of town the buildings became smaller, more compact. The people wore smooth, colorful clothing and seemed to keep their heads down. This was the Chinese section. The boardwalks were swept, the windows clean, and the buildings freshly painted.

I walked until I found the telegraph office, and at five cents a word, I kept the details of the situation short. Caroline would understand.

A man wearing a green visor tapped out the message.

I told him, "I'm staying at the Overland Hotel. Philip Anderson's the name. Just leave the reply there."

Next stop was to talk to the marshal. If I didn't want to inquire at a saloon, the law was the next best option.

The office was like any other, with its tall, straight facade and thick, heavy door. I pushed it open and was hit by the heady smell of coffee. Two men turned to look at me. One sat behind a desk, his boots hanging over the edge. The second stood near a potbelly stove. Both men's hands hovered near their guns. Their inspection of me took less than a second, starting and ending with my hip.

"Morning." I waved a hand. "I need information."

The man behind the desk lowered his feet and sat up. "Where you from?" His clean-shaven face gave him a youthful look, and his voice was high-pitched and grating.

"Mitchell."

It took me a moment, but I realized they were positioned perfectly so that if a shooter did step into the door, if one of them got shot the other could kill the intruder. A shiver ran down my spine. I'd made the right decision to come unarmed.

I stood in the presence of professionals. These men, even though paid to keep order, were hired killers with badges.

The deputy leaned forward. "I expect you came to see Seth Bullock. He ain't in town."

I'd forgotten Bullock was marshal of Deadwood. His reputation as a gunfighter exceeded even Wyatt Earp's renown, despite Bullock never killing a man.

I took a deep breath. "I'm just hunting information."

The other man set down his coffee mug and straightened his vest. Sunlight streamed through the window and gleamed off his silver badge. His mustache—thick, long, and black—hung over his lip. "What's your name, son?"

"Philip Anderson." I said it too fast. If I didn't get my nerves under control, I'd make a fool of myself. Why was I unnerved by these men? I'd felt the same way about Marshal Stone in Mitchell. Maybe it was their guns or maybe their badges.

With a weathered hand, the mustached man pointed at the deputy. "City Deputy Clark. I'm U.S. Marshal Raymond Hill. What can we do for you?" His voice was kind but firm.

I stuck my hands in my pockets. "I'm looking for an Indian named Running Deer."

Marshal Hill glanced at the deputy. The small man behind the desk sat up. "Why you looking for him?"

"I owe him for something he did a while ago."

Deputy Clark got up and leaned on the edge of the desk. Marshal Hill didn't move. "He kill your brother?"

I looked at him, trying to comprehend his words. "Oh, no. Not that kind of owe. No, more like wages for a kind deed."

Clark rubbed his hands together. "We know Running Deer." He laughed, although he didn't smile. "We run him outta town some time back."

"You ran him out of town?"

Clark looked up at the ceiling as if searching for the right words. "He was . . . trying too hard to be a white man. He placer mined, gold panned, even tried working for one of the big outfits. In the end, old miners remembered being run out and killed by savages. Some took it out on him."

I stared at the deputy.

Marshal Hill cleared his throat. "Thing you got to understand about this town is that it don't care about no one. Hardly a person here who thinks dark-skinned men are human. They think of the Indians as just part of the landscape, like deer or wolves." He took a step forward. "Doesn't make it right. But that's just the way it is."

"So, where is he?"

Clark pointed out the front window. "Big Indian to-do at Devil's Tower. Probably there."

My heart leapt. So the Indian woman was right. He was there. I thanked the men and turned to leave.

"Hold on." Marshal Hill's voice bore through me.

I spun around.

"You're a greenhorn. You won't last a minute out there."

Drawing myself to my full height, I stared at the U.S. marshal. "What do you mean?"

"You aren't even carrying a gun."

"And?"

Hill set down his cup and pointed at the wall. Scattered across the plaster hung yellow sheets of paper with descriptions of wanted men and reward amounts on the bottom. One even had a sketched picture. "The Maxwell Gang will put you six feet under before you have a chance to blink."

"Thanks. I'll watch myself."

He stepped up to me, his weathered face inches from mine. Every word puffed out of his magnificent mustache with the smell of coffee. "I know you, Philip Anderson. You live south of Mitchell and raise Arabian horses. You left home because a girl rejected you, and you're bringing Running Deer a horse because he saved your life as a child. And you don't carry a gun, because you don't know how to use it."

To hide my shock, I crossed the dusty office, stepped up to the potbelly stove, snatched a mug from the wall, and poured myself a cup of coffee. "You're right on all counts but one."

"And that is?"

"Southeast. I live southeast of Mitchell."

The stern look on his face remained, but I heard Clark shift his feet.

I drank the scalding coffee without flinching. "How do you know so much about me?"

"You can't raise Arabians in the Dakota Territory and expect to remain anonymous. And I saw you riding into town. Couldn't tell who was prancing higher, you or them horses. Who would leave his other horses at home, probably pregnant, other than a man who was riled up about something? That's probably why you forgot your gun. That, or you don't know how to use it."

I drained the cup, burning my tongue, and left with my dignity roaming somewhere on the prairie.

That could have gone better.

Back at the hotel, a message from Caroline waited for me already.

Yes STOP send her STOP Caroline

I rapped lightly on Rachel's door, the knock echoing down the long hall. I stared at the blue wallpaper while trying to listen inside. A rustle of sheets and then a groan. Her sleepy voice filtered through the thin wood. "Yes?"

"Message for you."

I heard a sigh then a whoosh of blankets and a whump against the floorboards. "Ouch." The handle jiggled, and the door opened a crack. Rachel's swollen eyelids barely opened as she tried to focus on me. She brushed her messy hair from her face. "Oh, it's you."

"You were expecting someone else?"

"No." She shook her head. "No, never again."

"I've a message for you."

She looked up, surprised, as if she hadn't heard me the first time. With a shaking hand, she pulled open the door. "Come in. I apologize for my appearance. I haven't slept that well for maybe a year."

I stepped inside, and she left the door open, to my relief. The paper had wrinkled in my pocket, but she didn't seem to mind as she read it. Her eyes widened. "So, I have a job?"

"Look. Caroline is my best friend. Like the mother I've never had. If you do her any wrong . . ."

She burst into tears, and I let my words fall away. She held a hand over her parted lips. "I won't. I promise. I just never thought this could happen to me. Not after . . ."

"My friends mean a lot to me. And I protect them." I towered over her. "And I would like to call you a friend."

Her eyes, large and brown, stared up into mine. "Yes, Philip." She seemed to struggle for her next words before she spoke. "You do know there is nothing I can or will give you in return for your kindness. Why did you help me?"

"Pick up a Bible. Read it." I turned to leave but stopped. "There is one thing you can do for me."

"What's that?"

"Make things right with your parents. Then come to Mitchell."

She rubbed the side of her face, which was still wrinkled with sleep. It took a moment, but she finally looked at me. "What you ask is hard. But I'll do it. For you."

"You won't regret it."

She turned and spoke, as if to herself. "I am going to go to Rapid City to see my parents. I'll take the stage. I have money owed me before I leave. Then I'm going to ask my father for money for a train ticket to Mitchell." She turned back to me. "You'll meet me? At the station in Mitchell? If I wire you?"

"I promise."

"It may be a little while."

I shrugged my shoulders.

She clasped her hands together. "I'm counting on you, Philip. You and Caroline. I'm trusting you."

I nodded.

I left to prepare for my journey to meet an old friend and find answers to my past.

17

Devil's Tower rose in the distance like a massive thimble above the rolling hills. All around Raven, Princess, and me pockets of pine trees dotted the landscape. Long stretches of thick grass made the going easy until we reached the Belle Fourche River. A small cliff ran along the edge of the river and finding a place to ford was difficult, but we managed.

On the other side, prairie dogs popped their heads up from their burrows. We picked our way carefully. Didn't want to injure a horse's tendon. Both horses seemed to watch the ground with caution.

Large boulders looked tossed about by giants, and as we progressed the tower loomed higher and the trees thickened. Images of my last night with my parents so long ago tried to replay in my mind, but I pushed them away. Instead, I thought of Anna and her beautiful smile. It almost helped.

The murder scene came to mind again, clearer, until I dismounted and walked beside Raven, hoping that moving my body would clear my head. I topped a ridge, and the sight before me pushed every evil thought away.

Thousands of teepees spread across the plain. Above each

conical, skin-covered home, stripped saplings interlocked to form the frames. A low haze covered the entire camp, blanketing the Indians that mulled about, some in groups, others alone.

In all my travels with Running Deer, I'd never seen an Indian camp. My heartbeat quickened as I watched.

I rubbed Princess's ears, and a stab of regret shot through me. I was going to miss her. After all the hours raising her from a foal, training her to allow a saddle on her back and a bit in her mouth, and feeding and caring for her through the cold winters, she was like a member of my family.

A bush rattled, and I turned to face the muzzle of a rifle. On the other end of the gun stood a boy, an eagle feather tied in his hair. He'd counted coup before, striking an enemy first, and been given this recognition for his bravery. Chances were, he was eager to earn another feather.

With the reins dangling from my fingers, I lifted my hands in the air. Raven snorted.

I'd purposely left my pistols in the saddlebag—no need to upset the Indians unnecessarily. The boy took in the horses and then stepped behind me, motioning with the rifle toward camp. He didn't say a word.

We approached the village. The grass, high and plentiful on the range, was stripped and overgrazed here. As we walked, I mentioned to the boy that I wanted to see Running Deer. In Lakota I told him again and again, until he pointed the rifle at my back.

I quieted.

We weaved around teepees, spaced farther apart than it had seemed from the hill. Several Indians mulled about, as well as white men. The Indians stared at my horses, and the bearded whites looked at me through narrowed eyelids. The smell of sweaty bodies filled my nostrils. Meat roasting on campfires was the only pleasant aroma.

The Indian boy stopped at a teepee painted with a buffalo hunt scene. The teepee flaps hung open, as if the occupant was trying to catch the cool southern breeze.

In the entrance sat Running Deer. His hair had grayed

slightly, and his face was a bit more wrinkled, but he was still the man I remembered.

"*Miya Ca.* You have come." No emotion crossed his face. I smiled. "Running Deer, my friend. I have brought you a gift." I pulled the chestnut mare forward. There was no ceremony like I'd long played out in my mind. Instead, I simply dumped Princess's lead rope into his lap.

He looked up at me while Princess sniffed her new master. "You have come far." He spoke in English. "You are now tall as a pine."

"I promised to repay you for saving my life." I put a hand on Princess. She shook her mane.

Finally, his gaze broke from mine and he looked at the horse. "She is acceptable." He smiled then motioned to a stump nearby. "Come, sit with me. And we will talk."

I tied the horses to another nearby stump and settled on the buffalo robe. While he sat calmly, I could barely contain my excitement. I told him all about the orphanage, Terry Feather and my job as blacksmith, and then I described my homestead and told him all about Anna.

He listened with his head bent toward me, sometimes nodding, sometimes shaking his head as I described Jacob and his control over the town of Mitchell. When I finished my story, he leaned back. "Many bad men. There are good men who live, but it is bad men who make themselves known."

"The deputy in Deadwood said you had trouble there."

He set his hands on his knees. "I have tried to live as a white man, but it is difficult. Always the hunt called for me, but buffalo are scarce. And the horses. To steal a horse is pride in my tribe. But for the white man, the penalty is hanging. It is hard to live so."

I frowned, looked away, and touched the bear claw he'd given me so many years ago that still hung around my neck.

He waved his hand at the settlement. "But this is the return of hope. We come to dance, a ghost dance. The buffalo will return. The white men will leave. It was predicted long ago that we would live next to the white man's gray boxes, and we would starve. In my time the prophecy has come true, and we live in houses like you. Sitting Bull agrees. The only hope is the ghost dance." He waved a hand. "We live as we used to."

I didn't see how a dance could help, but I didn't say anything.

"That is why white men have come to the camp, to keep us from this dance. They know the dance will work and do not want it." Devil's Tower was just beyond the camp. He stared at the tall shaft of stone. "The dance *must* work."

Running Deer insisted I stay the night, and with evening setting in, I reluctantly agreed. Spending the night with these strange people felt intimidating. Once I'd wanted to live with them, to live as them, but now I was too set in my ways. I followed Running Deer around the camp, and he made me comfortable.

The sun set and darkness crept in. Raven and Princess grazed on what little grass remained while food cooked over a small fire in the teepee. Running Deer's mother, an older woman who'd been beaten by the elements, had concocted a strange porridge. Yet the gruel rejuvenated my energy.

Three children—I later learned Running Deer watched these orphans as his own—wandered past us and into the teepee. I glanced at my friend. He smiled and followed them inside, motioning for me to join them. He pointed to a figure under buffalo hide blankets and introduced her as his grandmother.

My mastery of Lakota was taxed as I attempted to follow her stories of Devil's Tower. A bed was prepared for me against the back wall of the teepee. As we lay on our buffalo skins, I could see stars through the opening at the top. The children pleaded with Running Deer to tell stories about Custer.

Running Deer had camped long ago at the Little Bighorn. I listened as he told of the fight, of pushing the cavalry up the hill. He didn't remember Custer being with them and thought the commander might have been killed right away.

The stories quieted, and one by one, breathing throughout the tent evened. Running Deer snored softly.

The fire had died, and the smell of the buffalo hide

mingled with faint whiffs of unwashed bodies in the tent. The opening at the top kept the air moving. I lay on my back and watched the stars.

Anna once said she wanted to sleep in a teepee. Why didn't I tell her I love her? She deserved to know how I felt. I knew she loved me or had at one time. But feelings change, and she may have forgotten me already.

She was probably asleep right now. I wished I could join her, curl my arm around her and bask in her love.

I took a deep breath. Mistakes that teach us can no longer be called mistakes. That's what the old man who taught me to shoot had once said.

It was a good thought. I'd made a big mistake, but I was, after all, raised in an orphanage. If I didn't completely understand the rules and was awkward with women, I had reasons. I had no father to teach me.

Turning on my side, I closed my eyes. This self-pity made me sick. It was time to get some sand, the will to be the man God wanted me to be. I wasn't a leader, had no responsibilities other than the horses, and influenced no one.

It felt as if that was about to change.

18

Anna's hand still stung from the slap she'd given Jacob. He paced across the dining room. He stopped and gripped the back of a chair, the chair Philip had sat in when they'd first had dinner after Sunday services.

Jacob had marched into her house and tried to kiss her. Anna's mother had rushed in when she heard the slap. Jacob's voice was low and controlled, but his red face told a different story. "Anna, you and I are courting." His trembling top lip curled into a thin smile, and it seemed as if it dragged the bottom lip with it. "I'm not leaving."

"Our one dinner was a . . . a mistake."

He curled a fist. "A beginning, you mean." He walked behind her, so that his back was to the front door. She could feel his gaze against the back of her neck. "We'll have a lifetime of beginnings."

She turned her head to look at him. "Never. Leave me. Get out of my life." He grabbed his cane from off the dining room table.

"You can leave now, before my husband comes in." Anna's mother demanded.

Beth had run to get Father.

"I like it here." He took a sniff. "Good food." He looked up the stairs. "Good home my money bought."

Anna clenched her teeth so hard her ears popped.

"Leave," her mother said again.

The door burst open and her father charged in. He saw Jacob and started straight for him, a fist lifting.

"Calvin. I'm glad you're here," Jacob said quickly. "I just came to tell you your loan is due on the mill."

Her father paused, a stricken look across his face.

"And your home." Jacob lifted his cane. "Unless . . ." he raised a perfectly sculpted eyebrow. "Anna, dinner tomorrow night? At the Alexander Mitchell again?"

Anna didn't say a word, and her father was quiet as well.

"Good. Oh, and one last thing. I'll show you out back." He stepped out the door, and they followed. "As you know, Marshall Stone's reelection is coming up. I'm quite sure he won't win, if you get him involved." He rounded the house. "Beth, come too. I want you to see this." He approached the back pasture. "I think Jeb would be a good marshal in Stone's place, don't you?"

Jacob reached into his white vest pocket and pulled out a pistol. He pointed it at Spink and fired. The horse collapsed.

Beth screamed and fell to the ground too.

Anna ran toward Jacob, but her father reached him first. He swung at him with his fist, but Jacob blocked it and punched him hard in the stomach. Her father doubled over, gasping.

"How dare you!" Anna rushed to her father's side while her mother tried to console a sobbing Beth.

"Leave . . . us," her father managed.

Jacob returned his pistol to his pocket and made a gun with his thumb and forefinger. He pointed it at Beth and made a firing sound. He turned to her mother and made the same sound.

Then he walked away.

I awoke before the sun rose. A gray light hovered above the teepee. With great care, I gathered my hat and saddlebags and slipped out. Running Deer sat smoking near the entrance.

He looked up at me. "You sleep long."

The morning sky still held on to a few precious stars. I shivered in the cold mountain air. My breath steamed. "I've gotten lazy."

"Come." He rose, straightened, and pointed with his pipe to my gear. "Leave them."

I eyed him, unsure. I opened the bag, pulled out my holster and belt, then set the bags back in the teepee. I strapped on the gun as we walked silently though camp.

Only a few Indians were up and about.

I walked by his side for nearly half an hour, over a hill and into a small stand of pines. He moved with an easy gait into meadows and past thick, green copses. He talked of changes from when he was a boy.

As the sun appeared, we approached the river shrouded in mist. Running Deer dropped down to the bank and waded across, the water reaching his shoulders. I unhitched my gun belt, lifted it over my head, and crossed with him.

On the other side, I paused by his side to wring out my clothing and tie down my gun.

He looked back across the river, and I followed his gaze. Morning light, red and brilliant, lit Devil's Tower. A shock coursed up my spine as memories returned of that day when our wagon stopped for the night. I knew we were near my parents' graves.

Running Deer headed upriver. I followed, my mind a fog of memories and fear.

He'd stopped talking. The muddy river gurgled beside us, and birds chirped angrily at one another in the bushes. The soft whisper of his moccasins and my heavy boots side by side brought to mind the differences between us. He paused, and without turning to look at me, pointed into a meadow. A tall, thin pine tree rose from the middle of the empty glen.

I realized that here rested my mother and father.

He sat down, legs and arms crossed, with his back to the meadow. He closed his eyes.

I walked toward the lone pine.

Thick buffalo grass covered the grave, the narrow straw stems growing over the rock on which I'd chiseled a cross. With my foot, I parted the vegetation until the rock lay exposed in the pine's shadow. I leaned against the trunk, looking down, a swell of anger building in my chest.

I couldn't hold back the words. "Why, God?" What sense did any of it make?

I looked up at Devil's Tower in the distance. I could almost place myself back in that moment thirteen years earlier.

What had possessed them to come here? This was way beyond their homestead.

There was no answer to my voice except birdsong.

I knelt at their resting place. Rather than ignore the memories and feelings of my past, I let them come. *Why* seemed to be the only thought I could manage. If I could find a reason, surely some of the flashbacks that tormented me would subside.

I found a thick stick and dug at the place where the wagon had burned. An iron wheel ring lay near the surface as well as a scarred piece of wood, the black charcoal remains that had haunted many of my dreams.

Sweat was pouring down the sides of my cheeks where tears had been moments before. Ripping up gravel and red dirt, I found the sod thick but not impossible to cut through. With effort, I made headway. Inches down, I found nails, a rusty hammer, and a few jagged pieces of metal. I also found rotten clothing inside a burned trunk. I tried not to think about my mother wearing the rags.

The sun beat down now, heating the earth, rocks, and grass that spread around me. I paused and surveyed the considerable hole I'd made. Five more minutes was all I'd give myself.

A tiny red, velvet bag lay inside a toolbox. It was faded and weathered. I picked it up with trembling hands. It was knotted closed. I tore at the top, and the rotted fabric ripped easily.

A piece of gold jewelry slipped out and fell to the ground. I flung the bag to the side and eagerly picked up the gilded cylinder. The cool metal was smooth in the palm of my hand. I pressed the button atop the circle, and it flipped open. It was a watch.

Broken glass fell in glittering shards. The hands had stopped at twenty after ten. A shiver coursed through my spine. Was that the moment the wagon crashed in flames?

I looked under the casing. In faded yellow locked against the lid was a tiny picture of my parents. The image of my father's stern glare and Mother's soft, beautiful face swirled around me as the sun seemed to darken. Stars appeared, the wagon stood beside me, and the campfire crackled in the night. Two shadows hunched over the flames, my father reading and my mother cooking. The smell of beans and bacon washed over me.

Mother's voice, sweet and pleasant, called out. "Philip! Supper's almost ready."

Amidst the ruins of the wagon, I relived that night, reality and memories blending into a single moment. Both my parents lifted their heads toward the river, away from me. Voices drifted in the darkness, sounds I couldn't make out. But this time I looked down, saw my Smith and Wesson tied at my hip, and knew this was it. Evil was coming.

Shadows formed at the edge of the fire, then three tall men with sloped hats stepped into view.

They spoke to my father. Tension filled the air. They reached for their guns.

Three quick shots. This time I beat them to the draw. They fell. If only I could go back. I could have saved my parents' lives that night.

I woke from my daydream and saw three new holes in the pine tree ten yards away.

From beside me came a voice. "Revenge is not justice."

I sent the remaining two bullets into the tree before I holstered my pistol. "It feels good to shoot."

Running Deer stepped close, his stern face and straight nose pointed at me. "Revenge is foolish."

I rubbed my forehead and brushed away the memories. "I don't want revenge. I want the memories in my head to go away." I took a deep breath to quell the aching inside me.

"And it matters not whether they have been avenged?"

I waved my hand. "Out there, doing what they did, how long could anyone live? I know they're dead already."

Running Deer thought for a moment. "Yes, you are wise."

I opened the watch and ran a finger along the two faces. "I wish I could have saved them. Too many mysteries to put behind me."

The Indian warrior grunted.

I looked over at the hole I'd made and the remains of our campsite. The stone with the crude cross etched against the face. There was nothing more for me here.

We crossed the river and returned under a blazing sun.

"The worst is that even if I spend my life searching, I'll never understand why."

Running Deer was quick with his reply. "That will not be the case for you, *Miya Ca*. The answers you seek may be long in coming, but you will be satisfied."

The teepees loomed ahead, and we continued through the buffalo-skin village. Very few people wandered in the camp. Strange. On the far end of the settlement, a haze of dust hovered low in the air. We walked closer, and a nervous stir tugged at my heart. I'd left Raven there as well as Princess.

Running Deer seemed to notice something wrong too, and we passed by his empty tent.

The last row of teepees blocked our view, but a thunder of hooves shook the ground and dust choked my throat.

We stepped around the tents and saw a horse track stretched before us in a wide circle. Indians stood along the entire trail, whooping as the horses passed.

The finish line was close by, and a knot of men and women cheered as the horses and riders blurred past and skidded to a halt. The winner sat high with a raised fist.

A new race was already prepared. It took a few chaotic races until I realized they'd created rounds, the winners going on to race again. As they waited, the horses pranced in nervous excitement.

A jumpy, black horse jostled with the rest, a rider clinging to her back. Raven.

I could have let him ride her and then confronted him later. Instead, I charged forward, oblivious of the racers about to start again. I broke through hands that reached for me as I ran out onto the track. Dust filled my mouth, growing thicker the closer I came to the horses.

I called above the whinnies and high-pitched Indian calls. "Get off my horse." Raven's ears pitched forward when she heard my voice.

The Indian turned, spotted me, and wrenched Raven's head around. He dug his moccasins into her flank, and my horse darted out of the small group and charged for me.

He wanted to count coup. Probably not kill me, but strike me with a stick or knock me down in humiliation. I tensed and lowered my body. If he thought I would give Raven up easily, he was mistaken.

Already a large circle formed around us.

Someone from the edge of the crowd tossed the rider a lance, and with shocking skill he twirled the long spear in his hand until the tip pointed directly at me. He didn't want to count coup. He wanted to kill me.

I reached for my gun and then paused. The tree. I'd sent all my bullets into the pine near my parents' grave.

The thunder of Raven's hooves shook the ground.

I whistled, first a low, long pitch, finally ending on a high note. Raven reared into the sky and then twisted, throwing the rider into the dust.

I whistled a single high note, and Raven trotted to my side.

The foam around her mouth showed she'd been mistreated. I wiped it away and stroked her muzzle. "Easy, girl."

The Sioux leapt to his feet, flung the lance aside, and raced for me. From his hip, he produced a long knife.

Running Deer stepped close. "He is an honored—"

The Indian didn't pause. With his forearm, he pushed Running Deer back and pressed on.

The ground under my boots felt slippery as I charged. My hands, steady, reached forward. The dirt crunched beneath me as I puffed for air.

Sunlight gleamed off the knife.

He lunged. I dodged and slapped his arm away.

The knife slashed at my midsection, just missing. The Indian was fast.

I barely caught his wrist, and with brute strength, I held tight.

What he had on me in speed I made up for in muscle. My arms, hardened from farm work, bulged. He swung his elbow against my arm, but I kept his wrist in a tight grasp.

I smashed his jaw with a fist, and he fell.

He wrapped his legs around mine and twisted. I slammed into the dirt, face first. A jolt of fear surged through me. Somewhere behind me was a knife-wielding warrior.

I rolled to the side, just in time. The Indian fell forward, the blade stabbing into the gravel. He was on me in a flash, knife raised. I grasped his arm and managed to hold back the knife just above my face.

I pushed him to the side and scrambled to my feet. Strength won again.

Every breath I took rattled in my head. I knew his speed and weapon would eventually become too much for me. The fight needed to end.

Chirps and calls from the crowd that surrounded us urged him on. He lunged. I stepped to the side and planted a blow to his ear. A look of surprise crossed his face. Before he could react, I clasped my fists together in a vice grip and smashed a blow across his cheek. He flew backward, and the knife landed in the dust.

I rubbed my knuckles and walked over to him, leaving the knife where it fell. Blood trickled from his ear, and he looked up at me with a dazed expression in his eyes.

Running Deer stepped close as the crowd lost interest and turned back to the race. "You fight brave," he said to the Indian. "But no match for *Miya Ca.*"

The defeated fighter turned his head and vomited.

PETER LEAVELL

I whistled for Raven and said to Running Deer, "You can use the same whistle commands for your horse, Princess." I taught him a few more signals I'd trained my horses to recognize. When I glanced back at the Indian I'd fought, he was gone.

Running Deer grasped my arm, a smile on his face. "He is in shame. He will bear it poorly. But bear it he must."

I returned his hold, gripping his arm. "I must go before there is more trouble. I'll miss you, my friend."

A resigned look spread across his face, and his brown eyes seemed amused. "We will see each other. Maybe soon." His grip tightened and he frowned. "Be wary. I feel a coming storm."

I glanced at the cloudless sky. The clear blue dome above us was endless.

"No." With two fingers he touched my heart. "Here."

I released him and grabbed Raven's bridle. "Man is born to trouble, Running Deer."

145

19

B ack in Deadwood the next morning and after a good night's sleep, I had my saddlebags packed and Raven rested, watered, and tacked up. I decided to eat before riding out of the Black Hills. After settling my hotel bill, I chose a small restaurant across the way.

As I sat alone drinking coffee, a hint of guilt washed over me. Why had I hit the Indian so hard? A thought tickled the back of my mind.

He was going to kill you.

Possibly.

You did what you had to do.

There were men in this town who would have killed the Indian without thinking twice. And I was beating myself up over hitting him too hard. Pathetic.

I took a gulp of the hot coffee and felt strength returning.

Wild Bill Hickok had died in Deadwood. The one time he sat with his back to the door, someone nailed him with a bullet to the brain.

Violent town. A quick glance at the other patrons in the

restaurant almost made me spew my coffee. All of us sat where we could watch the front door.

After another gulp of coffee, I sat back and released a long, deep breath. I stared out the window at Raven, waiting patiently for me to finish my meal. Her beautiful dark eyes, much larger than the horses' eyes around her, watched the traffic around her warily.

The Black Hills boasted its own marauders—the Maxwell Gang. They waited for miners to dig the gold. Then they stole it. What kind of force would it take to stop them? Was that why Marshal Hill was in town? He was a U.S. marshal, not someone you see every day. What force would he use? The law? His gun, for sure.

The waitress brought my plate, and I took a bite of potatoes. The food tasted good, so I focused on getting it down. But the weight of the gun on my hip kept pulling my thoughts to violence. If I was being honest with myself, I had to admit it felt good to pit myself against another man and win.

I washed down eggs with the dregs of my coffee. The waitress was there to refill my cup.

I reached down and felt the hammer on my pistol. The leather loop that held the gun in the holster slid off, and I tugged the gun an inch from the leather.

An unsettled feeling touched my heart. What was going on in Mitchell? I needed to get home. I needed to talk to Anna.

I glanced out the window and my fist clenched the gun's handle.

Raven was gone.

Several responses flashed through my mind. Go to the marshal's office. Check the saloons. Go back to the hotel. I shook my head. None made sense. My horse had been there a moment earlier. The thief had to be close. He or she wouldn't just storm out of town. At least, that's what I hoped.

I dropped a coin on the table and raced outside the restaurant door. The street was long and filled with people. Which way? I shielded my eyes to the morning sun rising over the mountain. In the far distance, I thought I could make out Raven's shiny black coat. Someone was riding her.

I took off at a run down the middle of the street, leaping over mud puddles, around wagons and carriages, and bumping past people. A large group of miners crossed the street in front of me, and I pressed through. A handful of insults followed.

The man turned Raven left.

A woman stepped in front of me. I dodged to the side and kept running. I took a left at the corner, passed a tall brick building, and saw the man turn right. I was catching up.

I dashed onto Deadwood's Main Street. A long row of oxen pulling a wagon stretched down one side of the thoroughfare. The dry road gave me better traction as I sprinted past the beasts with their plodding shoes and jingling tack.

We approached the Chinese section of town. Clapboard fronts advertised bathhouses, restaurants, and a laundry. Raven was just a stone's throw away. Her rider, who looked as filthy as a miner and was wearing a tall hat pocked with holes, sat high.

I shouted, "Hey! Get off my horse." My voice was shaky from running, but a few people heard and turned my way. As I drew near, I tried again. "You. You're on my horse."

He kept riding.

I took a second, caught my breath, and finally blurted, "Horse thief!"

This time, the stranger whirled Raven around. He had the reins in one hand, her black mane in the other.

The townspeople stopped and stared at us. Stealing a horse was a serious offense, one worthy of hanging. Even the long trail of oxen was halted nearby.

The man leaned toward me. Up close, his dirty beard and narrow face looked less like a miner and more like a card shark. The clean gun strapped to his side confirmed my suspicion. He was a shooter.

He spit tobacco to the side and faced me. "What was that, boy?" His gravelly voice reverberated between the buildings.

Raven tossed her head nervously. I wanted to yank the dirty man off her back. He was defiling her. "That's my horse, mister. I want her back."

The stranger's bright, gray eyes flashed at me. They almost

149

glowed, and it was unnerving. Is this how people feel when they look into my eyes? Even though I held my gaze on him, I could see the streets clearing around us.

"Ain't your horse, I reckon." He spit again. "Mine."

"You're mistaken." I drew up to my full height. "Or you're stealing."

He swore loud enough to draw people from their businesses. "You got no right to accuse me of stealing."

Hardened resolve coursed through my blood. I looked up and down the street, saw the long shadows above the buildings hanging over us. Birds chirped as they played on signs and woodpiles. Dogs barked in the distance.

I spread my feet wider. "You made a mistake." I lowered my voice. "Get off my horse."

"Why you little . . ." He let the word go. "Can't prove this is your horse."

"Let's look in the saddlebags."

His fist dropped to his side, and he thumbed the loop off his gun. "I ain't dismounting."

A deep voice boomed across the street. "What's going on?" From out of a gunsmith shop marched U.S. Marshal Hill. His wide mustache bristled.

The stranger stared at the marshal, and I took the opportunity to make sure the loop was off my gun. But nothing went unnoticed by the thief. He eyed me and my holster.

I couldn't hold back. "You getting off my horse, or am I making you?"

"Marshal, this boy's trying to steal my horse."

Marshal Hill took a step to the edge of the boardwalk. I could see both Hill and the stranger in one look. A quick glance told me the lawman wasn't wearing a gun. Of course. He was standing outside a gunsmith.

Hill said, "Let's go down to the office to sort this out." The lawman stared at the man on the horse, his stern expression changing to a look of recognition. He glanced at me with concern, and his fingers reached to where his gun should have been.

The stranger's laughter filled the street. "No one's making

me go down to no office. And I ain't getting off this horse."
He looked ready to bolt. Or draw.

I cleared my throat. "Last chance. Get off, or I'll make you
get off."

Hill grunted under his breath. "Take care, boy."

I didn't care. The man was about to ride off with Raven.
She had been one of my closest companions for the past five
years, loyal and uncomplaining. For the second time in as many
days, I curved my lips and blew, first a low-pitched whistle,
then high. With no warning, Raven shot into the air and
twisted, throwing the man off the saddle and into the dust.

He scrambled to his feet, his face red, and he reached for
Raven. She slipped from his grasp and trotted several feet away.

I shouted. "Back off. She's my horse."

The stranger's bearded, red face turned toward me. His
complete attention rested on my gun. "You're going to die for
that."

Hill tried to get the man's attention. "Maxwell. Let's go
down to the office and sort this out."

"How do you propose to do that, with no gun and all?"

A tiny picture crossed my mind. A moonlit night. By the
river. My parents. Why was the vivid memory coming back
now?

From the corner of my eye, I could see Hill stroking his
mustache. His voice was calm and mellow. "Let's not do something stupid here. Boy, why don't you come stand here with
me?"

The stranger laughed. "He ain't moving. Cause he knows
I'm going to kill him."

Hill grunted. "That'll get you hung for sure, Maxwell. Let's
sort this out somewhere else."

I barely registered what was going on around me. There
was no Deadwood, no oxen nearby, no onlookers, no businesses. It was the three of us—Hill on the boardwalk, the
stranger ten feet from where I stood, and me.

Words flew by fast. Hill tried to get the man's attention
away from me. "Leave the boy alone."

"Can't do that, Marshal."

"Killing him won't do you any good."

"You're getting on my nerves, Marshal. I'm shooting him and then you next."

I was in the meadow now, the buffalo grass swaying in the darkness, three thugs walking into camp and threatening my father.

My fingers tingled.

The stranger's cold eyes locked on mine.

"This is between you and me, Maxwell." Hill's voice cracked. "I said, leave the boy alone."

"Wait your turn."

I stood stock-still. I knew the moment. They were about to kill my parents.

"We don't need no shootin'." The marshal screamed. "You can't shoot straight, no how."

The stranger's red face grimaced. "Like h—" He reached for his gun.

I grasped my pistol, cleared leather, and fired. Two shots sounding like one. Both mine.

The man jerked back. He fell into the street, his gun sliding away in the dust. The blasts echoed as the man wailed.

I kept my gun leveled on the stranger. Hill leapt off the boardwalk and sprinted across the street. He snatched up the man's gun and pointed it down at the wriggling man.

Smoke still drifted up from my pistol. The gunpowder and sulfur smell, like in target practice, lingered.

A new smell floated on the soft breeze. Sweet and pungent. Blood.

The man's arms were covered in red.

Hill gripped the back of the stranger's collar and dragged him toward the marshal's office. The trail of blood left a long line in the street.

He turned to me as he passed. "Get off the street, you idiot. What if the rest of the gang is here?"

I holstered my Smith and Wesson and followed, unsure if I was in trouble. I'd never shot a man before. An odd thought passed through my mind. Where did I hit him? Were the wounds mortal? I whistled and Raven came up to my side. Her eyes were wide, and she pranced nervously. She smelled the blood as well.

A small crowd followed.

By the time we reached the office, the stranger had stopped moving, his head drooping to one side. Deputy Clark burst out the door, rifle in hand, a shotgun under his arm, a pistol in a holster, and one tucked in his belt. He paused and looked us over. "What happened?"

"Shut up and get inside." Hill gave a tug, and the stranger's body bumped up over the boardwalk. Clark opened the door, and Hill pulled the wounded man into the office. I tied Raven out front, at first unsure if that was a wise thing to do. But with the growing crowd, I doubted anyone would try to steal her again.

I stepped up on the walk. Clark pointed the shotgun at me. "Stay back."

"Let him in." Hill's voice came from inside. "And you go get a doctor."

Clark gave me a curious look and then without a word rushed out the door.

I stepped inside.

"Lock it."

I bolted the door.

The long hallway had cells on either side. Hill dragged the stranger past the iron bars. I moved to help, but he slung the man onto a cot as if he were a doll.

He straightened, took a breath, and brushed past me. "Come here."

I was in trouble.

He left the hallway to stand in front of the wall covered with wanted posters. He ripped one down. I followed as he returned to the cell and stood over the cot. The stranger wasn't moving other than shallow breathing.

Hill dropped the paper on the thin pillow and grabbed the stranger's beard, pulling his face up. The narrow light that streamed through the window shone on his features.

"Look the same?"

I studied the paper and the man. I crossed my arms.

"That's John Maxwell, leader of the Maxwell gang."

I peered through the bars, staring at the motionless man. "What were you doing, starting a fight with him?"

"He stole my horse."

Hill looked at me from inside the cell. "I told you to stay clear of trouble while you were here." He shook his head. "You're such a greenhorn it makes me sick."

A bolt of anger shot through me. "Greenhorn? You want to talk about a greenhorn?" I shook my head. Suddenly, whether it was a much-needed release or just the joy of surviving, I let go a loud laugh.

"What's so funny?"

I pointed at him. "At least I brought a gun to the fight."

He squinted, and the lines around his eyes creased like old leather. After a quick glance at Maxwell, he left the cell and locked it behind him. He led me to the main room and crossed to the potbelly stove, where he grabbed a tin mug and poured a cup of coffee.

He sighed. "I knew you weren't a greenhorn." He lifted the mug. "You have the look of a killer on you. And a killer can't abide being called a greenhorn."

I picked up a cup, crossed the room, and filled it with coffee too. "You were seeing how riled I'd get by calling me names."

"Something like that."

The doorknob rattled and I jerked. Then someone pounded on the door. "Hey, let me in."

Hill motioned. "It's Deputy Clark."

I slid back the bolt and he rushed in, another man in tow. "Where is he?"

I closed the door behind them. "In a cell."

Clark took the doctor down the hall, but I stopped Hill with a look. "You really thought I was a gunman?"

"You beat Maxwell on the draw. Where were you aiming?"

I felt my cheeks redden in embarrassment. "Shoulders. Didn't want to kill him."

We followed the doctor back to the cell, where he leaned

over the patient and carefully removed Maxwell's shirt. One enormous hole with pooling blood punctuated each shoulder. Hill took a deep breath. "That's good shooting."

I'd hit where I aimed.

The U.S. marshal's eyes flashed. "I'd say you'd best become a fighter. The Maxwell Gang. They'll be after you now."

Deputy Clark grabbed his hat from his head and slapped it across his thigh.

"Would someone tell me what's going on?"

Marshal Hill started back toward the front office. He paused and turned, offering a bemused smile. "We just witnessed the birth of a gunman."

20

The train car rocked back and forth on the uneven tracks, rattling my mind.

The monotonous landscape and long stretches of vast prairie broken only by small towns where the train paused for a passenger or water soon lost my attention. Every so often, at the edge of a field, cottonwoods or elm trees had been planted to break the wind. The rest of the plains were a sea of lush grasses—prairie bulrush, Indian ricegrass, and more buffalo grass. Yellow flowers lined the railbed, but I had no clue to their name. Horses didn't eat the flowers.

My mind spun as I considered my future. What would life be like now that I'd shot a man?

Marshal Hill had handed me the wanted poster. "There's a reason Maxwell had a five-hundred-dollar price on his head." He'd reached into a safe and pulled out a wad of bills. With quick fingers, he separated a few from the pack, returned the stash, and closed the safe. He sat behind the desk and wrote out a receipt for me to sign. "He's robbed and murdered miners, settlers, Indians, you name it. He's the scourge of the Dakota Territory."

The money looked wrong in his calloused hands, as if it were too base, too dishonorable to deal with. He handed it to me. "I feel it my duty to warn you. Life for you will change. I can keep the news from the papers for only a short time, like you requested. But the nation will hear of it in about a week. And the gang is going to hear of it. I can't say what they'll do. Could come after you or just break up without their leader. Hard to say."

"I understand." I put the money in my shirt pocket.

Hill had leaned back. "You're a good kid. I can tell by how you hold yourself. I don't want to see you dead. Be careful."

I hadn't known how to respond to that.

He kept talking. "I was in town to capture Maxwell. Those were my only orders. I'll be heading back now, so I can't protect you."

"Should I check in with Marshal Stone when I get back to Mitchell?"

"I'd feel better if you did."

His features had been etched with concern, and his lips were taut. The man was old enough to be my father, and his concern had felt beyond the call of duty.

The train jolted sharply, and my head bumped the window.

I rubbed the spot and wondered how Raven was faring in the horse car.

It was best to spend the money—blood money—fast, so I spent twelve dollars on the train ticket. That was high because Raven came with me. But out of five hundred, it felt like nothing.

I dreaded Anna knowing what I'd done. Even though Maxwell was a wanted man, she would hate me for sure, or at the very least, fear me. No, she couldn't find out in the newspapers. I needed to tell her myself eventually. That's why I'd left the office out the back door and Marshal Hill handled the news reporters out front.

I thumbed the hammer on the Smith and Wesson and kept my eye out for train robbers, although I saw nothing for a hundred miles any direction. I'd once thought this land was tame, that law controlled every corner. But between the fight at Running Deer's camp and shooting Maxwell, I now knew better. The gun would stay with me.

We approached the Missouri River. Trusses held the bridge that spanned the wide expanse of water. Below the bridge, smoke from the engine settled over the water, which flowed as if it didn't have a care.

I shifted in my seat and checked the sun's position. It was around three or four in the afternoon. At this rate, we'd pull into Mitchell at dusk.

My stomach rumbled. I'd have a meal at Caroline's Kitchen, talk with Caroline if she had time, and maybe Leroy. After that, I'd stop by Scott's house for a few minutes to see how he did taking care of my herd and inquire about Anna. Then I'd hurry home to feed the horses from my own hand and read by the fire. It would be good to sleep in my bed again.

As we pulled into Mitchell, the brilliant ball of orange cast long shadows from the station across the railroad tracks. I pulled Raven from her car, noted she needed a good rubdown, and sensed she was as ready for her pasture as I was ready for home. Steam billowed from the train as we weaved through a mass of carts, horses, and small clusters of travelers talking.

Mitchell was quiet and peaceful after Deadwood. Children snatched a few more moments outdoors before dark. Frogs croaked near the river.

But the city felt different. And I knew why.

I was now a gunman, alert to whatever danger might be lurking around the next corner or in a nearby doorway.

Humid air pressed down on me, oppressive compared to the mountains. The night crept around corners of buildings, every nook, every crevice. I took in the stark and cracked wood planking of the restaurant, the red sign, and the windows that shimmered from the lights inside.

I dropped from my saddle and wrapped the reins around the hitching post. Patrons leaving Caroline's glanced at me and hurried by. The door squeaked as it closed behind me.

I recognized the two families who were eating on the

other side of the room and nodded. They just stared at me. Had they heard about the gunfight already?

Leroy must have gone home after his twentieth cup of coffee, since his usual table near the kitchen was empty. I tossed my hat on the table. Caroline strolled from the kitchen, a plate in each hand. A warm glow swelled within me at the sight of her plump, round face.

She spotted me and turned pale. "Philip. You shouldn't be here."

I held out a hand to steady her. "Are you feeling all right?"

She shook her head.

The door burst open, and she screamed.

I spun to see a vast silhouette in the doorway and the shadow of a shotgun pointed at my head. I would have pulled my gun if I hadn't caught the glint of a star on his chest.

"Hands high." The man's deep voice boomed through the dining room.

My heart raced. I slowly lifted my arms.

The two families threw their chairs back and ducked under the table. I heard Caroline's plates crash to the ground and her sharp intake of breath.

The man stepped forward, and in the lamplight I could see Marshal Stone's red, sweaty, bulldog face. Two deputies flanked him, weapons drawn. The marshal said, "Take his gun."

The deputies sidestepped toward me, their pistols aimed at my chest.

Stone motioned to me. "Step back."

"Why, what's going on?" I didn't move.

He lifted his shotgun to his shoulder. "Take a step back, or I'll kill you."

The earnest look in his face gave me reason to step back. Or perhaps it was the way his finger hovered over the trigger.

I felt the weight on my hip lighten and hands searching my vest as the deputies investigated for weapons.

"He's clean," said one.

Stone moved closer. "Philip Anderson, you are under arrest for robbery and murder."

21

Darkness filled the jail cell. A draft of cold air filtered through the barred opening above my head and chilled me to the bone. Rain spattered through onto the cot, which was five inches too short for me and smelled of mildew. One end was soaked.

I banged on the bars and called down the empty hallway, the vacant cells echoing my voice. But Marshal Stone didn't answer. I couldn't stick my head far enough into the corridor to see the front office. But I knew he was there, because every once in a while I heard a shuffle.

And I knew when he locked the door for the night and left me to pace the tiny room like a caged animal. I fought against the walls closing in on me and almost won. Finally, a warm glow filled the hallway, and the sound of the potbelly stove's door shutting told me it was morning and he was back.

For years I'd passed the marshal's office, glancing up at the tiny windows on the side and wondering what it was like to be in a cell. Now, as the gray morning light contrasted the dull black of the iron bars, I feared this would be my last home.

I grabbed the cold bars and kicked the door with my boot

heel, more frustrated than I'd ever been before. I tried not to think of Anna out there with Jacob. And me locked up . . . alone.

I heard the front door of the marshal's office open, and a man's voice drifted past the empty cells. Then Marshal Stone replied, sounding angry. But whoever was out there wouldn't back down, and the pitch of their argument rose.

Soon I heard the sound of shuffling feet down the hall. Scott and Leroy appeared. My heart leapt into my throat, and I had to swallow the sudden urge to cry out. My friends had come. I wanted to hug them both.

Marshal Stone stepped into my line of sight. "Keep it quiet. And when I say it's time to go, you go."

Scott threw the lawman a salute. "Yes, sir."

Stone glared at him and then left.

"Scott. Leroy." It was so good to see them my legs went weak. I sat on the cot. "What's happening? No one's telling me anything."

Leroy looked subdued. He chewed at his bottom lip.

Scott cleared his throat, and I noticed he kept away from the bars. "Maybe it would be best if you tell us what happened."

I stood. "What?"

"Caroline told us you were arrested last night, but the marshal wouldn't let us see you until this morning."

"You're dodging the question." I grabbed the bars. "What's happening?"

Scott studied me for a moment. "This ain't no time to play dumb, Philip."

"Don't do this to me."

The old veteran frowned. "You really don't know, do you?"

Finally, Scott jutted his chin toward First Street. "The Wilkes's bank was robbed, and a guard was murdered. The clerk was shot in the arm, but he escaped."

I gripped the bars. "And they think because I was out of town, I did it." I threw my hands into the air.

"There's more, Philip. The man who did it was about your

size. He wore your hat and clothes. That straw hat everybody knows you own."

I groaned. I'd left my hat on the table at my cabin when I left for Deadwood.

Scott leaned close and whispered, "I went to your house but didn't see your hat anywhere."

"Are my horses still there?"

He shrugged. "They're fine. I check on them every day. The babies are doing well following their mamas around. And the marshal's got Raven."

I glanced at Leroy. His face was pale, and he looked ill. "You okay, Leroy?" I had to stop saying *okay*.

"No, I ain't. I told 'em you was out of town, at Deadwood, and they didn't believe me. I'm sorry, Philip. I done the best I could. Maybe he don't believe us 'cause we're your friends."

Scott ran his fingers through his hair, messing it up. He threw his hands to the side. "I don't understand why the marshal isn't working harder to get the facts."

The sound of the front door opening caught our attention, and we all looked in that direction. After a hushed conversation, Caroline appeared, a basket in her hands.

She rolled her eyes. "Marshal Stone dug through this basket as if I'd put a file in it." She put her hand to her mouth. "Oh, Philip. You look terrible. I won't ask how you slept last night. I couldn't close my eyes for a moment." She brought her hand to her heart. "What can we do for you?"

The smell of cornbread and hash wafted into the cell, and my stomach rumbled. "Been a while since I've eaten."

She lifted her basket. "Here you are, my boy." She passed everything through the narrow spaces between the bars. Eventually her basket was empty, and she handed me a wooden spoon. "Marshal took my fork."

I bowed my head to thank God for my food and took an extra moment to wonder if He knew what He was doing. I sure couldn't figure it out. I placed the bowls on the bed and sat down to eat.

We talked as the food calmed my hunger and cleared my brain. "I have an alibi in Deadwood. Someone can wire

Marshal Hill, and he'll fire back a telegram confirming I was there."

My mood lightened. If all went well, I saw myself reading beside my fire tonight. And with any luck, no one would ever know the trouble I'd gotten myself into there.

Caroline reached into her basket and pulled out a newspaper. "Read this."

I took the paper, spread it out across the cot with one hand, and shoveled food in with the other hand.

Robber Villain Found!

In a desperate arrest attempt, this June 3, 1887, one Philip Anderson was put behind bars after resisting. He was found in Caroline's Kitchen, heavily armed and ready to fight.

Authorities at the railroad station recognized this killer as he boldly stepped off the train. They immediately alerted Marshal Stone's office. Stone and Deputies Boothe and Stiles rushed to his favorite hideout, where they found him with a revolver at his side. Deputies were forced to disarm him and were able to wrestle him to jail where he awaits trial.

Citizens are both relieved and shocked. "We don't need this kind of trouble here," said one concerned citizen. "Why did he wear a gun? If he wasn't guilty, he wouldn't need one."

Marshal Stone was unavailable for comment but one thing is definite, the jail is under heavy security while this high-profile murderer awaits trial. With the evidence readily available and the court dockets being cleared of lesser cases, trial will start tomorrow, June 5.

The verdict of guilty will result in hanging.

Wednesday, Philip Anderson walked into the Wilkes Bank and Loan, pistol in hand—

I crushed the paper into a ball. "They've hung me before the trial."

Scott leveled his gaze. "Most in town feel this way."

"How can they do that?"

Scott pointed at me. "I told you to get rid of that stupid hat."

Silence bounced off the stone walls for several moments. Leroy shuffled his weight from one foot to the other. "There's a bounty on your head. Fifty."

I choked. "Only fifty?" Maxwell was worth so much more.

"Oh, please, Philip." Caroline put a hand over her heart again. "Don't joke like that."

I looked at the concern etched on her face, and a lump swelled in my throat. Did she really feel responsible for me, as a mother would?

I took a deep breath to clear my thoughts. "All right. Let's get to work then. I have something all of you can do."

Leroy raised his eyebrows. "Even me?"

"Leroy, your assignment is the most important." I leaned close and lowered my voice. "I need you to send a telegram to Marshal Hill in Deadwood. Ask him to confirm the dates I was there. His response will immediately clear up this matter." I tapped a finger on a bar and looked at Scott. "Let's play by the rules. Scott, can you find me a lawyer? Any will do. I've plenty of money, but it's tied up right now in my wallet, which is with the marshal."

"What can I do?" Caroline's dark eyes shone in the dim light.

"Keep feeding me. And keep a running total. I'm depending on you for meals."

She shook her head, her jowls quivering. "On the house."

They stood near the bars, unmoving and not saying anything.

I snorted. "You three act as if you're at a funeral. I'll be fine. We're almost home free."

Leroy shook his head.

A sense of dread washed over me. "What? What aren't you telling me?"

Scott groaned. "You're forgetting something." He sighed and dropped his shoulders. "Someone is out to get you."

Leroy grasped the bars. In the growing light, I could barely see his wrinkled face and stubbled chin. "If you didn't do it, someone else did. Someone's a murderer," he hissed. "He wants you dead, and I think that someone is Jacob."

22

The walls of my cell were rotting around the edges. Perhaps I could break through. If I did, what life could I live? Anna and the horses were everything to me.

I leaned back on the cot and let my brain wander.

Why would Jacob go to such great lengths to put me away? The games played here were life and death not love and hate. Was Jacob capable of murder?

That evening, Scott visited again. Becky was with him this time, clinging to his arm. He got right to the point. "No one will represent you, Philip."

"What?"

"Not a single lawyer in town is willing to take your case."

"But I have a right to a defense."

"You do." Scott glanced at Becky. "But there's pressure on legal counsel in town." He lowered his voice. "Jacob, I'm sure of it. Everyone's afraid of him."

I clenched my teeth and gripped the bars.

"Philip." Scott's eyes flashed in earnest. "I'll represent you."

"You?"

"It's me or Leroy. We're the only friends you have left in this town. You can't defend yourself."

My heart sunk. I turned and looked out the window. All I could see was the tops of the buildings of downtown Mitchell. What was going on out there? "Yes, Scott, please represent me." I paused. "Leroy was in earlier. He waited all day at the telegraph office, but no one sent a message back. I was hoping Hill would still be in Deadwood."

Scott shook his head. "It doesn't look good."

"Can you stall the trial? Until Marshal Hill gets back to us?"

He stuck his thumbs in his belt and lowered his chin. His voice deepened, echoing around my cell. "Your honor, I'd like to go over the exact movements of every person in the Dakota Territory." He lifted his chin. "Am I *ever* short on words?"

Becky giggled.

I heard the main door open and close. While I would welcome a true lawyer, Scott's devotion made me want to hug him. I was the most hated person in town, yet he defied everyone to help me.

Caroline shuffled down the hallway, tray in hand. She handed me a bowl of stew between the bars plus a chunk of bread. I bowed my head, took a bite, and gave her a thumbs up.

She smiled. "Glad you like it."

I winked at her.

She set the tray down on the floor and crossed her arms. "Leroy's still at the telegraph office. I think he's going to sleep there tonight."

Caroline's eyes were red-rimmed and swollen. Scott's face showed determination, Becky's concern. And Leroy was standing at his post in hopes of hearing the dots and dashes that would vindicate me. I had good friends.

That night I tossed and turned on the cot.

I prayed for forgiveness. The violence of Deadwood had led to this punishment, no doubt, God's poetic justice doled out for my sins. Turn the other cheek. And I had defended myself, defended Raven with violence. Should I have just let her go? I pulled the thin blanket over my shoulders. Was God trying to tell me my possessions belonged to others? I didn't care about most of my possessions, but my horses were different. I loved them.

Rain splattered through the open window again, filling the cell with a damp chill. I shivered.

Sometime during the night I must have slept.

Voices drifted down the hall, and I awoke to a warm glow at the edge of my cell.

Marshal Stone clanged the bars with a pot. I sat straight up. "You got a visitor."

In the middle of the night?

He set the lamp in a nook on the other side of the hallway and marched back to the office, grumbling as he went.

A form in a dark cloak appeared, the face covered by a hood. Whoever it was paused in the dim light, a sinister, menacing shadow. Had Jacob sent an assassin? I stepped back, prepared to duck if I saw a gun.

Two hands appeared, white in the lamplight. I tensed. The hands reached up and slid the dark cloth back.

I gasped. "Anna."

Her black hair spilled out of her hood, and her eyes were barely visible in the lamp's soft glow. She wasn't smiling. Please God, help me make her smile.

She lifted her chin. "Philip." She seemed to want to say more, but her voice failed her.

I reached through the bars to touch her arm, but she drew back. Her shoulders drooped, and she looked away. "No, Philip."

I swallowed the growing fear. "Did you get my note?"

She shuddered. "He's going to kill you."

"Who?"

"You know who."

"Anna, what happened?"

"He's going to kill you, and it's all my fault." A sob escaped her lips.

I touched her back, and this time she didn't pull away. "I have an alibi. I am innocent."

She seemed to digest that information for a moment. With a tremor, she shook her head. "It has nothing to do with that. He's still going to kill you."

"Jacob?"

Her body stiffened. "I despise that name."

Silence filled the hall as I tried to memorize every curve of her silhouette, her smell of flowers and rain. I needed to remember it forever.

"Did you get my note?"

She shook her head. "Scott gave it to Beth, but she said he took it from her."

I clenched my fists. Jacob knew of my feelings and couldn't allow a rival for Anna's love. That had to be why he'd gone to such incredible lengths to put me away. "I love you, Anna. Love you more than my own life. Please, I can't imagine life without you. Marry me, Anna. When I leave this jail, marry me. We'll never part again."

My outburst seemed to shake her. She turned toward me, despair filling her eyes. "I've come to ask you never speak to me again."

I stared at her. "Why? I've just asked you to spend your life with me."

"Look where you are. This is because of our love. Yours and mine. I would marry you if I could." She drew herself to her full height, nearly six inches shorter than mine. "He will kill you if you show any interest in me. He has an uncanny ability to control others."

I took a breath, looked down at my hands, and flexed my fingers. "I can protect us."

"No, Philip. This is good-bye."

"You don't understand."

"No, *you* don't understand. If he killed you, I'd never forgive myself. I was selfish enough to try to make you jealous, and now I must pay the price."

"I need to know—did Jacob commit the robbery?"

"I . . . I don't know. He's behind it, I'm sure of that."

The chemistry between us seemed to ignite the air.

I tapped the bar, and a metal ping reverberated through

the cell. "Anything you can tell me will help. I can't defend you or me if I don't know everything there is to know about Jacob Wilkes."

She frowned. "I can defend myself, Philip Anderson. It's you I can't protect, or my family, unless you leave me alone. I heard him tell his men to put your foals' heads on spikes."

A wave of revulsion passed through me, but I shoved the gory thought from my head. "He'll go after me, whether I leave you alone or not." He killed the guard at the bank. He could kill again. Drawing away from her, I paced the tiny cell. "You love me?"

"That's why I'm here. I love you, and I want to protect you."

"You trust me?"

"I want to."

"Will you ever stop loving me?"

"Even if I have to marry Jacob and . . ." She grimaced. "Even if I carried his children, I would still love you."

Jacob needed to know of my gun fighting abilities, and perhaps he would think twice about playing these games with me. "I have a plan. But you need to trust that I can defend myself."

She looked at me, a ray of hope in her eyes. "I just can't think of a way. He's put so much pressure on the people of this town, on me. Business is awful at the mill, and Jacob wants to foreclose on us. I can't let my father's business fail. Jacob won't let me live my life, won't let me go anywhere or see anyone. And there's nothing my father can do. He's already threatened to throw him in jail if he defaults on his loan."

"We must wait, Anna, if we can. Jacob will sooner or later make a mistake, and we can use it. But until then, can you endure?"

"I . . . I don't know." Her resolve seemed fragile, and she leaned against the bars. "You remember Beth's horse, Spink? He . . . he shot him, right in front of her. As a threat. I didn't want to tell you, but you don't seem to understand what he's capable of."

I unclenched my fists and reached through, touched the

back of her head, feeling her thick, silky hair. Her eyes, large and sad, gazed at my face. I drew her close, and I searched for her lips with mine. She seemed hesitant, but I stroked her hair, and after a moment she eagerly returned the kiss.

"I wish I could break you from jail." Her voice was soft. I felt her breath against my cheek.

"When I'm free, we'll find a way to stop him from threatening you."

"And my family? He says Jeb is watching Beth, will do horrible things to her if I step out of line. If any in my family don't do as he says."

I wanted to break the bars and go after Jacob with my Smith and Wesson.

"I love you, Philip, more than you'll ever know."

After she left, the horror of what Jacob was capable of sank in, and I knew this wouldn't be as easy as marching up to him with my revolver.

I slept fitfully after Anna's visit until shouting outside the window woke me up.

"An example. Hang him. We don't need this kind of trouble in town."

"Citizens, unite to destroy evil."

The men's angry voices grew closer.

"Punish evildoers."

"God demands justice."

Shadows flickered on the ceiling.

I glanced out the window to see a large crowd marching around the jail, a few with torches in their hands, others with lamps.

"Bank first, our businesses next."

"Protect our children."

I saw a rock flying toward the window and ducked. A bottle crashed against the bars and bottle glass rained on my head and shoulders. I crawled under the cot.

And then a shotgun blast shattered the night. Marshal

Stone's voice filled the silence that followed. "Disperse. Every one of you, go home. Trial's tomorrow. There'll be plenty of justice then."

"You got a prisoner in there, and we want him."

"Buckshot in the behind is what you'll get unless you disperse. And I'll tell your wives why you're spending the night in jail." He coughed. "You're pioneers, not a lynch mob. Go home."

To my amazement, his words must have worked because the night quieted. I crawled onto the cot and peeked out a corner of the window. The crowd was muttering and wandering down the dark street, kerosene lamps swinging at the men's sides, men who were once my friends and associates.

Marshal Stone stepped in the building and stood outside my cell door. "You all right?"

"Thanks for what you did out there."

He grunted. "This town ain't got any guts. Doesn't take much."

"They hate me that much? They really think I did it?"

He spun on a heel and called over his shoulder. "They all *know* you did it."

23

The night left fog in my brain. I rubbed my tired eyes and gazed at the place Anna had stood just a few hours earlier. Maybe it was a dream. But her words echoed in my mind. She loved me, and that was all that mattered. I brushed glass from my hair.

I took my shirt off and shook it out, wishing I could have a clean one for the trial. Marshal Stone stepped into view as I was buttoning up again. An empty pair of handcuffs dangled from his hand, and shotgun-toting deputies stood on either side of him.

The streets were crowded with onlookers who lined the path to the courthouse. They fell silent when we drew near. Women wearing bonnets, men in suspenders and bolo ties, and children with faces washed and their hair slicked back stared at me like I was Satan himself. The only sound was the clinking of my cuffs and ankle chains.

Many of the businesses we passed were closed. I pressed my lips together. Evidently this was a special day. It wasn't often that a supposed murderer walked amongst them.

The four of us made our way to the marble pillars that

supported City Hall's shallow portico. The round dome towered high over the entire town. I felt lightheaded, as if this couldn't really be happening.

We made our way to a back entrance. Several onlookers hissed and some booed. Most were quiet.

Someone called my name, and I saw Pastor Humphrey waving at me. He held up his Bible. "Prayers, lad."

I nodded his way. My close friends, and at least the pastor, were kind faces in the turbulent crowd.

We entered the building in the back and made our way down a long passage with a marble floor. Paintings of the Dakota Territory stretched along the wall. We passed through an oak door and into the courtroom.

Townspeople sat shoulder to shoulder on pews like the ones at church. In fact, I recognized many of them from church. Men stood three rows deep in the back of the courtroom and along the walls, all vying for position. Others stood outside the open windows, looking in. All the spectators turned in unison as we entered the room.

I ignored them and focused on Scott, who sat at a table on one side of the courtroom. His puffy eyes, rumpled red hair, and disheveled shirt suggested he'd had a long night. But he flashed a grin when our eyes met.

The deputies led me to Scott's side. He quickly cleared a stack of law books from a chair.

I settled next to him and looked around. No judge or jury yet.

He leaned close. "You ready for this?"

I took a long breath and released it.

He pursed his lips. "Yeah, I know what you mean."

Across from us sat the prosecution and Mr. Wilkes, Jacob's father. The lawyers wore suits that rivaled any I'd seen in *The Gentleman's Quarterly* at Jed's barbershop. Black jackets, long mustaches, silver hair slicked back—they looked the very part of justice. I glanced at Scott, who saw what I was looking at. He tucked in his shirt and smoothed out his hair. "You and me, eh, buddy?"

I shifted and spoke slowly. "Sure, you and me."

The deputies sat behind us. Marshal Stone made his way to a chair near the witness box and dais where the judge would sit.

Jacob and Anna sat together behind the prosecution's table. He glared at me and put an arm around Anna. She looked down.

"Scott." I couldn't keep the growl from my voice.

"Yeah."

"We've got to beat these guys."

"I'll do my best."

"We need to do this for Anna."

He took a deep breath through his nose and blew it out. "For Anna. And for you."

I glanced back at Mr. Wilkes. His hands rested on his large belly, fingers interlaced, thumbs tapping each other. His frown and furrowed brow showed deep thought. Did he know I was innocent?

Marshal Stone reached into his vest pocket and pulled out a watch. "All rise."

A whooshing sound filled the room as everyone rose and conversations died. The side door opened, and a large man with thick graying hair and bushy sideburns stepped through, his black robes swishing. He sat, picked up a pair of spectacles, and set them on his bulbous nose.

Marshal Stone stepped forward and motioned to the audience. "Be seated."

The sound of my handcuffs slapping the table when I sat caught the lawman's attention. He swiveled, hand on his gun.

I swallowed. Everyone was jumpy.

Thirteen men, dressed in their Sunday finest, filed into the room and sat in chairs alongside the judge's box.

We all watched the judge read court documents. Although no one spoke, the tension seemed to heighten with every page he turned.

I tried to study the jury members, but they looked away every time I made eye contact. I knew none of them.

The judge's baritone voice broke through the silence. "Both legal representatives, please approach the bench."

Scott leapt up and rushed before the judge, while three of the prosecution's lawyers took their time. All four listened to the whispers of the large man, and finally, after Scott made a hushed comment, they all returned to their seats.

"Everything's fine." He patted my shoulder.

The judge shuffled papers. The crowd seemed to hold their breath. "The plea entered is not guilty. The prosecution is ready with a case, and the defense has been denied postponement."

A quick murmur, and then silence filled the room again. Scott leaned back in his chair. I wondered how much he'd learned from the law books last night. Asking to postpone the trial—smart idea.

"Ladies and gentlemen of the jury," the judge continued. "We have in our midst lawyers on the prosecution who maintain their bar. On the defense, however, is a less-experienced lawyer without the same credentials. I have carefully examined his knowledge and abilities, and I request you treat his defense as if he has the full credentials of a practicing attorney."

Several on the jury nodded their heads.

"I will run a relaxed court." His voice deepened. "If I feel this atmosphere favors the prosecution or defense in any way, I will maintain discipline." He leaned over the table and looked down at both the prosecution and Scott, his glasses low on his nose. "If either side abuses my willingness to work with them, my patience will end and strict rules will be enforced. All laws of civility will be adhered to. I do not allow cursing, alcohol, or animals in this courtroom."

Scott leaned over. "But he let Leroy in."

I choked.

He looked up and raised his voice. "I do not allow crowd participation. Silence must be maintained. We are not here for entertainment. I will deal out contempt of court and jail to anyone who breaks this rule."

No one in the courtroom moved.

"Since we would like to finish this trial today, we'll proceed immediately. Opening arguments will begin with the prosecution. Mr. Adams, please proceed."

A thin lawyer with gray hair and a narrow mustache stood. "Ladies and gentleman of the jury, my name is Daniel Adams. I've been practicing law for decades now, and in my experience, no case has been as clear-cut as this. We will prove to you that the defendant, Philip Anderson—strapped for cash to support a fancy lifestyle—walked into a bank, the Wilkes Bank and Loan, and proceeded to rob the teller. In the course of events, he killed a guard and wounded the clerk, as well as made off with ten thousand dollars."

He stepped from behind the table and approached the jury box. "This crime was premeditated by a spurned lover seeking revenge. Combined with a need for money and the reckless use of a gun, Philip Anderson committed a callous crime, the cold-blooded murder of one of Mitchell's own upstanding citizens, Mr. William Hansen." The lawyer pointed his finger at me. "This man is a dangerous killer who must be hanged."

He spun on his heels, returned to his seat, and sat down.

The crowd murmured, until the judge cleared his throat. Silence ensued.

All attention now focused on Scott, who pretended to work on a document, scribbling nonsense, from what I could see, on official-looking papers.

Finally, the judge said, "Mr. Ladd?"

Scott stood and approached the jury.

He opened his hand and pointed toward me. "Philip Anderson was not in town when this crime was committed, so the charges are false. Terrible as false charges are, I'm even more appalled by the character debasement the prosecution is pulling from the clouds." Scott indicated the audience. "The whole town knows Philip is a man of considerable reputation. They also know how much work he's put into his horses and land and how much he loves both."

Scott droned on, painting a picture of me taking a horse to a friend in the Black Hills. He wasn't boring, but people began to fidget. I had a feeling everyone wanted him to get on with it. The looks on the jurors' faces proved it.

Somehow, Scott managed to gobble up nearly an hour of

court time. After he concluded his opening statement, he calmly settled into the chair next to mine.

The prosecution was then allowed to call their first witness. Mr. Adams stood and called for the clerk from the bank.

A short, balding man I recognized from the bank hobbled to the witness chair. He set his left arm, which was supported by a sling, on a Bible and lifted his right hand. In a soft voice, he repeated the marshal's words and mumbled his oath.

Mr. Adams adjusted his jacket. "Matthew Dow is your name, correct?"

"Yes, that is correct."

"Mr. Dow, do you possess a good memory?"

The clerk fidgeted, and his voice was taut and high-p itched. "That's partially why Mr. Wilkes employs me. My head for numbers and memorization."

"Any other reasons?"

"Oh, yes. My attention to detail. Nothing gets by me."

Mr. Adams stepped from around the table and approached the witness chair. "So you can remember the last conversation you had with the defendant before he robbed the bank and murdered the guard?"

Scott leapt to his feet. "Objection!" His voice carried through the courtroom like a trumpet. "Prosecution treats it as a fact that my client is a murderer, and it hasn't been proven."

The judge glanced down. "Mr. Ladd, please lower your voice. No shouting is necessary." He turned to Mr. Adams. "Objection sustained. Prosecution, you know better."

Scott sat and leaned over to whisper. "Testing me to see if I know what I'm doing."

"Glad you do."

Mr. Adams reached a finger through his greased hair and scratched. "Mr. Dow, tell me about your last conversation with the defendant."

"The last time Philip was in the bank, he asked if I felt safe. He asked if the bars could really stop a robber, and he asked when the last robbery in the bank took place."

"Which was?"

"Never. The bank's never been robbed." The clerk's narrow face turned sullen. "Until last week."

The lawyer leaned against the bar in front of the witness chair. "Tell me about Philip Anderson. Do you like him?"

"Of course. He's a good customer. Always friendly. I had no issues with him."

"When he visited the bank, what did he usually wear?"

"Normally, he wore work coveralls, sometimes blue jeans, and a cotton shirt. But what most sticks in the mind is his straw hat. Always wore it. Straw hat and coveralls, usually."

"Would you be able to identify them?"

"The coveralls I might, but the straw hat—there are no two alike in the county. It's seen better days. Yes, I can identify it."

Mr. Adams walked to a table where several items were laid out. He picked up a hat—my hat—and coveralls. "Take a close look at these. Was the robber wearing them?"

The clerk glanced at them. "No doubt about it. Those were what the robber wore."

"Can you point to the person you've seen wear these items before?"

"Sure can. Right there." He pointed a white, bony finger directly at me.

Doom settled onto my shoulders. Did I think he would point at someone else? I leaned over and whispered, "Scott?"

He patted my shoulder again. "I know, buddy. I'll do my best."

Mr. Adams handed the clothing to Marshal Stone, who set it back on the table. Subdued murmurs filled the courthouse as the lawyer shuffled papers. He turned back to the witness. "Does it surprise you that a robber would wear the same clothing in a heist that he wore daily?"

The clerk pondered the question for a moment. "No." He glanced at me. "It's little details people miss when they're nervous or excited. I see it in people's paperwork and accounting all the time. But he wore a red mask up over his nose, covering his face."

Mr. Adams nodded and returned to the table. "This mask?"

"That's the one."

He handed the mask to Marshal Stone and thrust his thumbs into his vest pockets. "I'm thinking about something, and I'd like you to do the same. Because it seems odd for him to wear the same hat he wears daily, a hat everyone would recognize, and yet mask his face. But think back on events, if you will."

"Objection." This time Scott didn't look up from his paperwork, as if objecting was a normal occurrence.

"Sustained. Questions, Mr. Adams."

The lawyer glanced at Scott and then to the bank clerk. "If you were to rob a bank, would you be scared?"

Scott looked as if he were about to say something, but kept his mouth shut. Instead, he leaned back and watched.

Mr. Dow nodded. "Mighty scared. I'd be afraid of getting shot. Or caught."

"Any number of things may go wrong." The lawyer swung his arms wide. "You could be shot or have to shoot someone. Or get holed up in the bank. There's a lot to think about."

Scott slammed a fist on the desk and stood. "I object."

The judge pounded his gavel. "Approach the bench, both of you."

Scott moved around the table and stood before the judge, looking small compared to the imposing lawyer. I couldn't see Scott's face, but Mr. Adams scowled.

Scott returned to his seat with a look of grim determination.

The lawyer went on with his questions. "When the robber walked in, was he carrying a gun?"

"Yes."

"Tell us what happened next."

"He walked up to the counter, stuck the revolver through the bars, and pointed it at me. Then he handed me a bag and told me to fill it with money."

"What time was this?"

"About seven thirty in the morning. Mr. Wilkes wasn't there yet. No one was but me."

"Did you fill the bag with money?"

"Mr. Wilkes had always said the law is on our side, that if we were robbed to give up the money, and the law would get it back."

"Just answer the question."

"Yes, I filled it with money, about ten thousand in cash. And some in gold."

"You had that in your till?"

"No, in the safe. I opened the safe and got him the money."

The lawyer leaned closer to the clerk. "So what happened next?"

"I handed him the bag. But I heard whistling and knew the security guard was coming through the side door." The clerk's voice started to tremble. "I held on to the bag. The robber pointed the gun at my heart. The security guard walked through the door beside me. I pulled on the bag, and the robber fired through the bars, hitting me in the shoulder. I let go of the bag as I fell, then heard another shot. That was the one that killed Mr. Hansen."

"Anything else?"

"After he left, I managed to make my way to Hansen. He was dead." The clerk lowered his head and wiped his eyes.

Tension in the room pressed in around us. I closed my eyes for a moment. When I opened them, the lawyer was gripping the bar. "Do you know where the hat, mask, and coveralls were found?"

"I heard they were found in a weed pile behind the bank."

The lawyer glanced at Scott. "I need to ask you about motive, Mr. Dow. Something that can be a bit speculative."

The witness nodded. "I understand."

"Where does the defendant live?"

"South of Mitchell."

"Does everyone know this?"

"Many. It's not a secret."

"Sod farm?"

"Log cabin. One hundred and fifty or sixty acres. A barn."

The lawyer scratched his head. "Does he farm the land?"

"Mostly horses."

"He raises horses to till the land?"

"No, not that I know of. He rides them into town, Arabian horses. Everyone talks about them."

"What kind of deposits does the defendant make? Big ones?"

"Usually five dollars here, ten there. And then he withdraws big chunks after it adds up."

"But never deposits large enough to afford, say, another horse?"

"Never."

"To pay for logs to be shipped from the Black Hills to build a home?"

"No."

"A barn?"

"No."

"Hay for the winter?"

"That's possible. Or he might grow his own."

The lawyer stuck his hands in his pocket. "How much would a person need, in your opinion, to start a ranch like that?"

"A lot. Probably a thousand."

The lawyer paused and then put emphasis on the next question. "Do you know anything of the defendant's past?"

The clerk thought for a moment. "No, I guess I don't."

"No more questions." Mr. Adams turned and sat behind his table.

Scott wrote on his paper for nearly three minutes, the silence in the room growing awkward.

"Mr. Ladd." The judge broke through the quiet. "You may question the witness."

Scott continued to write, nodding. I glanced at the paper, saw *Mary had a little lamb* written over and over again, and I tried to hold back a smile.

Without looking up, Scott sighed. "How long have you known Philip Anderson?"

"About four years."

Scott glanced at the man. "Five. He's been banking at

Wilkes's bank for five. I thought you were good with details."
He stood, approached the evidence table, and snatched a
document. "The land is his, deeded through the Homestead
Act. Says here he received the land at age eighteen because he's
an orphan. You didn't know that?"
"No."
"Anything in those five years that would have given you a
clue he would rob a bank?"
"No, but that last conversation about the bars—"
"Anything before then?"
The clerk shook his head.
Scott took his hand out of his pocket and wiped his lips.
His fingers trembled.
"The land was free because Philip Anderson worked it for
five years. Free and clear. So you're saying he robbed a bank to
support his habit of raising Arabian horses?"
I smiled.
"If he needed the money, maybe."
"Did you know Philip Anderson is a blacksmith? That's
where he makes most of his money?"
"I'd heard."
Scott's face was growing red. "Let me ask you if this
sounds like the Philip Anderson we all know. An Indian
woman shopping at a local grocery store was out of money, so
he came to her defense and paid for her flour." Scott's voice
rose. "He cared enough to speak in her native tongue." He
turned to the clerk and yelled, "Does that sound like a man
who would pull the trigger on another person?"
I cringed.
The bank clerk was equally angry. "If he was willing to give
money to Indians, then surely he must rob banks!"
Scott pointed a finger at him. "You said he wore a mask."
"Yes."
"And a hat."
"That straw-ugly hat."
"Tell me about the eyes of the thief."
"The eyes?"
Scott shouted, "Can't you hear me? The eyes!"

"I object!" Mr. Adams stood. "The defense is bullying the witness in an uncivilized manner."

The judge grunted. "He has every right to do so. Overruled."

Scott took a breath. "I must have gotten a bit excited. I apologize. But I would like to know if you've ever seen eyes like Philip Anderson's."

"Not that I know of."

"Take a closer look. Is there anyone in the world with eyes like that?"

"Hard to say."

"If the thief was wearing a hat and mask, surely he wasn't wearing something over his eyes. You would have said so. You must have noticed how piercing they are and the unusual light color."

The clerk looked exasperated. "He held a gun. That's all I noticed."

Scott turned to the evidence table, set down the deed, and picked up the hat. He held it high and looked as if he was going to ask a question. "Nothing more." He set it down and walked towards his seat, mumbling loud enough for all to hear. "Just thought you would have noticed his eyes, that's all."

The prosecution remained behind his table. "Did you notice his clothing?"

"Yes."

"And does anyone in the whole Dakota Territory, to your knowledge, own such a hat?"

"No."

"And again, you're sure it belongs to the defendant?"

"No doubt."

"No further questions."

The lawyer looked down at his document then stood. "I'd like to call Leroy Jenkins to the stand."

I turned to see Leroy rise from the back row and limp to the witness stand, a hand on his back. He nodded at me.

"Mr. Jenkins, you're a fixture in this town. You know everyone, and everyone knows you."

He smiled. "Thanks."

"Does anyone own that straw hat?"

"It's Philip's. It were stolen."

"Ah, stolen. Yes, I'm sure you have proof." He gave a patronizing look. "But let me ask you, did the defendant tell you where he was going?"

"No, but—"

"You're good friends, aren't you? If he goes to Caroline's Kitchen, he always eats with you, is that right?"

"Yes, I love the boy, but—"

"No more questions."

"But—"

"No more questions." He motioned to Scott. "All yours."

Scott didn't look up from his paper. "No questions."

The courtroom buzzed.

I grabbed his arm and whispered, "What?"

"Trust me. He's too close to you."

The judge dismissed Leroy. The war veteran made it to his feet and hobbled forward, looking at me sadly, as if he'd personally tightened the noose around my neck.

The prosecution called several more witnesses, mostly people I'd done business with in town. Each one confirmed the straw hat and coveralls. Scott tried to draw statements from them that I wasn't capable of anything remotely violent.

Memories of Deadwood filled me with guilt. If word of my gun battle reached Mitchell before the trial ended, I would be hanged for sure.

The noon meal was called and court dismissed. I was led back to my cell. Caroline came soon after with a large plate of food. "I'm to be called next to the witness stand. I'm scared." Her hands shook as she passed the small bowl through the bars.

"You'll be fine. Thanks for dinner."

She leaned closer. "I'll say anything you want, Philip. Anything that would help."

I touched her hand. "Tell the truth."

She hurried away, and I ate in silence.

No telegram came from Deadwood.

24

Caroline filled the entire witness chair. Her breath came in raspy gasps and sweat stained her blouse.

I wiped the moisture off my brow. In the afternoon heat, everyone suffered.

The prosecutor walked toward her, his hair freshly oiled, his smile fake and gestures wide and exaggerated. "The defendant eats at your establishment regularly, does he not?"

She nodded.

"Is that a yes?"

"Yes." She glanced at me.

The lawyer followed her gaze and stared directly at me. "You have feelings for the defendant."

"I was married. My husband and son died ten years ago in a railway accident." She took a deep breath and put a hand over her heart. "My boy would be Philip's age."

"So you would say he is like a son?"

"Yes."

"He was in your restaurant when he was arrested?"

"Yes."

The lawyer wandered to the edge of the jury box and

leaned against the rail, hands on his hips. He turned back to Caroline. "Describe his attire on that day."

She looked at the crafted ceiling as if remembering. "Dark blue shirt, blue pants, and a wide-brimmed black hat."

"Anything else?" His face turned red.

Caroline obviously wasn't telling him what he wanted.

"He wore boots."

The lawyer rushed across the room in a whirlwind. His fingers curled into fists and he waved passionately. "Guns! Did he have any guns?"

The crowd gasped.

She shrunk back in horror, shaking. "I . . . think so."

I had to hold myself back. He was trying to show she was too sympathetic to me, might even lie for me.

He screamed in her face. "You think so? How many guns come into your place? Is it a common occurrence?"

Scott growled. "Object. This tone isn't needed."

"He can use any tone he wants." The judge sounded as if he wanted to agree with Scott.

Adams stood close to Caroline. "Do you run a den for outlaws? A gambling parlor? How many guns?"

"I don't know."

"One gun? Philip Anderson's gun?"

Caroline nodded, her breath coming in gasps.

"Perhaps you were harboring a criminal that day." The lawyer set his hands on his hips. "Perhaps you were in on the robbery!"

Caroline's head tipped forward, and her body curled. She slammed onto the floor.

Marshal Stone and several others rushed to her side.

Scott and I jumped up at the same time. The crowd erupted. I heard cries of "Hang him!" as well as "Leave her alone!"

I turned to the lawyer and tried to yell above the commotion. "Leave her alone. Save it for me, coward."

Scott pulled me back.

A fight started in the crowd. I glanced back, saw Jacob and Anna slip through the crowd and out the door.

The brawl was growing despite the judge pounding the gavel over and over. Marshal Stone stepped between the two tables and pointed his shotgun over the crowd. "Quiet!"

No one listened.

I saw him switch cartridges, point the gun in the air, and fire. He used a blank.

The crowd quieted. Marshal Stone stepped through the townsfolk. "You. You, you, you, and you." He pointed with his shotgun. "Outside, now."

People returned to their seats as Doc Wilson revived Caroline. The marshal led the men he'd cornered to the back, where his deputies waited.

The judge remained seated, but fire blazed in his eyes. "If an outburst like that happens again, this trial will continue behind closed doors. And I will send the entire town to jail."

Not a sound came from the crowd. The moment reminded me of an angry schoolteacher scolding his wayward students.

The judge turned to the attorney. "Mr. Adams, are you finished questioning this witness?"

"No, your honor."

"Mrs. Hynes." He looked down at Caroline. Her head wobbled and her face was white. "Will you be able to continue after a short recess?"

She closed her eyes, and the doctor glanced up at the judge and shook his head. "She'd better rest. That was quite a shock." He glared at the lawyer.

Her voice was barely audible. "My heart hurts when he yells like that."

The judge rubbed his chin, a disappointed look on his face. "Prosecution, are you finished with this witness? Can she stand down?"

Adams's jaw was clenched. "I have more questions for her."

"Fine. Court adjourned until tomorrow at seven. Those in attendance will do well to remember their manners." He pounded the gavel. "Both counsels, meet in my chambers."

Scott's face glowed, and he slapped my back. I breathed a sigh of relief. Another day was a gift from God.

The room cleared, and I was nearly the last person out, led by Stone himself. I turned to see Caroline sitting alone in the courtroom, crying.

"I'm so sorry." Caroline stood on the other side of the bars of my cell. Her eyes were swollen and red, her face and neck splotched with a rash.

Scott sauntered down the hall, stopped in front of my cell, and patted her arm. "Good work, gal. You bought us a whole extra day." He picked a drumstick from the burlap sack of fried chicken she'd brought. "You might have saved Philip's life."

Her eyes widened. "You think so?"

He nodded and took a bite. "Where's Leroy?"

I reached through the bars and snatched a wing. "Telegraph office. His dedication is inspiring."

"Excellent." Scott stood tall, his bearing confident. "I mentioned to the judge we might have some late evidence to submit. He said it would be permissible."

I chuckled. "Listen to you. You're starting to sound like a lawyer."

"I love my work. I think the judge is favoring us. There's really no reason why he should have postponed the trial like that."

Caroline flashed a sly grin. "You should have seen Becky's face when you got angry. Oh, she likes you, Scott."

Scott's face blushed.

Between bites I said, "I had a visitor last night."

They looked at me.

"Anna."

Scott raised an eyebrow.

"She said Jacob was behind this. That he's dangerous."

Caroline huffed. "No surprise." A shout from the front office jarred us all to attention, and soon a small group of people walked down the hall followed by the deputies who opened cells and ushered in the men the marshal had pointed out at the courthouse.

Leroy shoved his way through the confusion, his face white and chest heaving. He paused in front of the cell and bent over, hands on his knees, trying to catch his breath.

Scott grabbed Leroy's shoulder. "Did it come? The telegram?"

Leroy shook his head. "Jeb was in there." He coughed. "Jacob's second. I heard him talking from outside the window. 'You haven't sent none of their wires, right?' I hear him say. And the operator says, 'Not a one.'"

I looked at Scott. "No help's coming."

Leroy's eyes were wide. "We may be in trouble."

25

Anticipation wound through the spectators packed into tight rows, the men in the jury box, and across the judge's face. Despite the open windows, heat and humidity hung low in the room.

Fights had broken out the previous night all over town. I could hear most of them from my cell. Some believed I was guilty, and those I counted as friends came to my defense.

My own tension ran deeper. If no telegram had been sent, no help would be coming. We'd discussed riding to another town to send the telegram, but chances were that Jacob and his men were keeping an eye on the roads. We'd be too late anyway.

Should I escape? Run? Even if I could manage it, would it be worth living on the lam and restarting my life somewhere else? The thought of leaving Anna with Jacob was insufferable. I had to risk it. Stay and stand up for myself.

Caroline sat in the witness chair again, her jaw set and her eyes narrowed in a determined gaze.

Mr. Adams stood. "No further questions for Mrs. Haynes."

Caroline gasped. "What?"

The judge showed no reaction. "Defense."

Caroline put a hand on her chest. "He put me through all that to dismiss me without another question? Doesn't that seem wrong to you, Your Honor?"

The judge frowned at her. "It's not up to me to decide. Defense, your witness."

Scott stood. "Had Philip ever worn a gun into the restaurant before the night he was arrested?"

"No, he hadn't."

Scott rubbed his chin. Dark circles under his eyes made him look older. The pressure of coming up with a suitable defense with no alibi seemed to be weighing on him. "You've known Philip for five years?"

"That's correct."

"How did you first meet?"

"He came into my place and got to talking with Leroy, and then I joined them. Been chatting ever since."

"You said earlier that Philip never wore a gun. Why do you think he carried one on that specific day?"

"He'd just gotten back from Deadwood. It's a dangerous town, so he wore one."

Scott tapped a finger on his desk and looked up at the ceiling. His confidence seemed to slip. We'd talked earlier about introducing my telegram to Caroline from Deadwood, but the defense would counter with the idea that I paid someone to send it for me. Chances were, Jacob would hire someone to claim they sent it.

"Thank you, Caroline. No more questions." He sat. The wind seemed to be knocked from his sails.

The judge turned to Mr. Adams who said, "No questions." The attorney seemed disinterested.

The judge rubbed his forehead. "Next witness."

Adams leaned forward. "I'd like to call Anna Johnston to the stand."

The crowd murmured. I turned to look at her. She had a horrified expression on her face.

When she didn't move, the judge cleared his throat. "Anna Johnston, are you in the courtroom?"

She rose slowly.

"Please come take the stand."

She swallowed and clutched her red dress. "I don't wish to be a witness."

"Mr. Adams. Is her testimony vital to this hearing?"

"It is, Your Honor. For motive."

"Miss Johnston." The judge turned his attention to Anna. "I can issue a subpoena, hand it to Marshal Stone, and he will escort you to the box."

She held her head high. "And if I refuse to speak?"

"You will be escorted to jail unless, of course, your words could incriminate you for wrongdoing."

A glimmer of hope crossed her face.

Jacob grasped her hand, pulled her down, and burrowed his face in her black hair. I wanted to strangle him. While he whispered, she looked at me. Terror mixed with pain passed from her heart into my soul. She stood again, her face pale. As if in a trance, she walked to the witness box and sat down.

She glared at the prosecutor as Marshal Stone brought a Bible forward.

"Miss Johnston." The judge's voice was stern. "Please put your left hand on the Bible and raise your right hand."

Anna continued to look over the marshal's shoulder at the lawyer.

"Miss Johnston. May I remind you of the implications of perjury? Jail time, as well as reputation—"

Her eyes widened as she turned to the judge, and her words came in a short, crisp burst. "I'm fully aware of the implications, Your Honor." She crossed her arms.

My heart beat quickly. He shouldn't have spoken of her reputation. Oh, how I loved her.

"Take the oath."

A cough erupted from the crowd. I recognized Jacob's tenor in the sound.

Anna hesitated then took the vow.

"Very good." Mr. Adams smiled, a sweet, sickening smile. "Miss Johnston, what is your relationship with the defendant?"

"Fifth amendment."

The lawyer laughed. "Are you saying the answer would incriminate you? Or Philip?"

"Me."

"I can deduce you were involved in the robbery then?"

If Anna owned a pistol, it would be pointed at the lawyer's head. "Friends. Philip and I were friends."

"And now?"

"We've had a falling out."

My insides churned.

The lawyer paced in front of the witness box, and Anna's eyes followed him like prey watching a predator. The jury leaned forward, hanging onto every word.

"Is Mr. Anderson . . . Do you like Mr. Anderson?"

"Yes."

"Are you aware of his reputation around town?"

"I'm new to Mitchell."

The wind brought the soft sound of a train whistle, and I imagined myself in the passenger car rolling gently along the rails away from this town forever.

"Would you agree that he's well respected, well liked, and wouldn't hurt a soul?"

Her eyes were cautious. "I would agree with that."

"Did he ever speak to you about his dealings with Indians? That he speaks Sioux?"

Anna shifted. "He speaks Lakota. But I know French and—"

"It's a well-established fact that dealings with Indians are usually shady, wouldn't you say?"

"No, not in—"

"And that someone who knows the language usually runs guns and whiskey? Do you know of the James-Younger Gang, Miss Johnston?"

"I do, but Philip isn't—"

"Notorious gang that robs trains, banks, people."

The train whistle was too loud to speak over as it pulled into the station down the street. Adams paused. After the blast of escaping steam ended, he continued. "Jessie James was a killer. Do you know what he did near the end of his career?"

Anna shook her head.

"He was an upstanding citizen, Miss Johnston. He helped those around him, was a good man, worked in a church. But he lived a double life. Do you believe we have the same case here?"

"No!" She looked close to tears.

The crowd mumbled, and the judge pounded his gavel. The spectators quickly quieted.

"The key that kept Jesse James in check was that he loved a woman and a woman loved him. Do you love Philip Anderson, Miss Johnston?"

She opened her mouth, but no sound came. Her forehead wrinkled as if she were in pain. I glanced at Jacob. He held his chin high, an arrogant, victorious look in his eyes.

If she told the truth, what would he do to her? Or to her family? If she lied it would be before God, and she would have to live with the denial of our love the rest of her life.

I wished she would look at me so that I could assure her that a lie would not affect our love—at least not on my part.

Anna shut her mouth then opened it again.

"I take it by your silence that you are in love with him. And thus we can deduce that the relationship is strong enough for Mr. Anderson to take the game of love into dangerous territory, robbery, and murder."

A loud slam at the back of the room caused everyone to turn their heads.

Anna's face paled, and she brought a hand to her mouth.

I tore my gaze off her and looked toward the commotion. In the doorway, highlighted by a ray of light streaming through the upper windows, stood a gunman. His thin, weathered, enormously-mustached lip brought a smile to my face. Two guns swung low on his hips and light gleamed off his polished badge.

For a moment there was silence, and then everyone was talking at once. His spurs chinked as he stepped forward as the judge pounded his gavel.

U.S. Marshal Raymond Hill slid into the chair next to Scott and nodded at me.

I was free.

With everyone's attention on Marshal Hill, I glanced at Anna. She returned the gaze, and I winked.

Scott handed me a piece of paper with his tiny handwriting scrawled across it. I leaned close to read it. *Who is this man sitting next to me?*

"My alibi."

He smirked, sat back, and put his hands behind his head. "Your Honor, may I approach the bench?"

The judge gave Hill a smart nod and then took a deep breath. "Both councils, approach the bench."

Scott nearly skipped to the front. When Adams joined him, my friend put a hand on the prosecutor in a friendly gesture as he explained what had just happened. It seemed Anna could hear the conversation, for a smile crossed her face.

Adams shrugged off Scott's hand and started into a whispered tirade. His hands gesticulated wildly as if disconnected. Laughter from the crowd must have reached the judge's ears, but he did nothing.

Finally, Adams stared at Hill for a moment, as if deep in thought. "No more questions." Then he sat and added quickly, "Prosecution rests."

"Does the defense wish to cross-examine the witness?"

"No, your honor."

Anna slipped from the witness stand and returned to her seat, her face unreadable.

Scott turned and lifted a hand, like a preacher. "I'd like to call Marshal . . ." He frowned and looked toward the bench. The judge whispered. Scott straightened. "Marshal Raymond Hill to the stand."

The marshal stood, stretched his back, and sauntered to the witness chair, giving Marshal Stone a nod. He took his oath and sat down.

Scott rubbed his chin, and I knew he wondered where to start.

"Have you gotten any telegrams from Philip Anderson the past three days?" he asked.

Hill looked surprised. "No, I have not."

Scott nodded, and he gave me a knowing look. Then he

turned and contemplated the marshal. I hoped Scott would not attack Jacob by pressing the telegraph inquiry. We just needed freedom. We could take care of the rest later.

"Marshal Hill, did you see the defendant in Deadwood?"

"I did."

"Can you tell us how he caught your attention? Was it his eyes? Is that how you remember him?"

He grunted. "Those gray, wolf eyes would be memorable enough. But that gunplay in Deadwood will be remembered forever in the Dakota Territory."

Scott's head jerked up. The crowd murmured and the judge leaned forward, apparently forgetting to use his gavel to silence the crowd. Scott rested an arm against the rail in front of the jury. "Gunplay?"

"Oh, surely you read about it in the paper. I promised Philip I would keep the press quiet, but I couldn't hold them back forever. You know how they are. Every town in the Dakota Territory was wired the story."

Scott growled. "Our telegraph system has been unreliable as of late."

Mr. Adams stood. "Objection. The telegraph office is not on trial here."

"Sustained."

Scott took a few steps toward the prosecution table and glared down at them. "To those of us who were not granted access to the information, Marshal Hill, please enlighten us. What happened?"

The marshal sat back and settled in as if to tell a good story over a campfire. "I was getting my guns cleaned at the gunsmith and heard a ruckus outside on the street. I stepped out, saw John Maxwell on Philip Anderson's horse. You ever seen that animal, Raven, she's named? Once you see her you always remember."

"Please refresh the memories of those who don't know who John Maxwell is."

"Who hasn't heard of him? Leader of the Maxwell Gang in the Black Hills. I was sent by the U.S. government to track him down and bring him to justice."

"Did you?"

As Hill spoke, I turned to check on the crowd. They were mesmerized by the slow Texas drawl of the lawman. Anna was no exception. I cringed at what she would hear next.

The marshal smoothed his mustache. "Like I said, I stepped out on the boardwalk, no gun in hand. The busy street was clearing fast. Maxwell had been thrown off that horse of Anderson's, and he was going to kill someone; he didn't care who. He'd killed men before for less than Anderson claiming the horse was stolen, and many he'd shot in the back. Others he outdrew. Maxwell's hand hovered over his gun, and Anderson just kind of stood there, as if in a daze. I knew I couldn't go back for my gun in time, so I was out of this gunbattle. Maxwell's hand went for his gun so fast, it was a blur."

He paused. Complete silence filled the room.

Hill turned to Marshal Stone. "Travis, did you bring Philip in at gunpoint?"

The city marshal nodded. "Shotgun."

"Did you have the hammer back?"

"No."

"Then if he'd had his gun and was really a criminal, you were a dead man. Philip is so fast with a gun, he could have dropped six men in the time it takes to pull the hammer."

The crowd burst into chatter. Scott turned to me with a proud I-knew-that look. I stole a glance at Anna. Her eyes were turned toward the window in a far-off gaze, and a slight smile played on her lips.

Now you know I can protect you.

Scott ambled over to the defense table and leaned against it. "So the defendant did shoot and kill a man, only not in Mitchell."

"Two problems with that. The first is Philip. He's too soft-hearted to kill a man. I've ridden with some names—Hickok, Bullock, Carson, Cody, and many other quick draws. Philip's better'n 'em all. But he didn't kill Maxwell." He held up two fingers. "Shot him in each shoulder, two shots before Maxwell could even clear leather."

Scott blinked. This wasn't the lawyer Scott anymore. This

was the fellow I ate and shot target practice with. "He's that fast?"

Hill laughed, as if enjoying the conversation. "When the first bullet hit Maxwell's shoulder it should have spun him instantly, momentum twisting him. But Philip hit him in both shoulders and knocked him straight back. That's so fast, the bullets had to be in the air at the same time. I checked Philip's gun. He'd fired twice. Both bullets were his." He smiled at Marshal Stone. "This man's no criminal, Travis."

A bead of sweat trickled down the city marshal's bulldog face. He swallowed.

Scott took a deep breath, as if to collect his thoughts. He let the buzzing crowd quiet down. "You said there were two problems."

"Yep. The first is that Philip hasn't killed anyone. The second is that Philip left Deadwood for a short time, long enough to take a train to Mitchell, rob the bank, and return."

Scott looked confused. "I don't understand. He still could have robbed the bank? And why are you smiling?"

"Because he has an alibi for those two days. I just don't know where the alibi is."

There was a moment of silence.

Hill removed his hat and scratched his matted hair. "You know what it's like riding on a train car with half a dozen Indians? They never sit. Walk this way and that." He pointed his hat in the direction of the train station. "Most of the passengers look the Indians over, especially the ones dressed in their war bonnets, thinking they're going to sack the train."

Scott stared at him. "What are you talking about?"

"Stuck on a train for hours when the normal roof over your head is stars? I don't blame them for needing a minute before they come to this crowded building. Now, I need to warn you about the Sioux. They aren't liars. Never would tell a fib, even if their life depended on it." He set his hat on his head and pointed. "There we are, right there. This will clear Philip Anderson's good name."

Everyone turned. In the doorway, festooned in feathers, makeup, and a vest covered with beads, stood Running Deer.

26

I stared into the flames and listened to the talk as the campfire burned a stone's throw from my cabin.

Scott and Becky chatted about his stint as a lawyer. Becky tried to get an idea into his head. "If you hadn't put up such a stirring defense, I'm sure the prosecution wouldn't have dropped the charges."

"Maybe. Maybe." His voice was soft and contemplative.

For the position I was in, he'd done a fine job. I owed him more than I could ever repay.

The logs shifted as they burned. Sparks shot up into the sky, bright enough to shine like stars in the waning light. Thick steaks purchased from Hans, my neighbor, revolved slowly as I turned the spit handle. The meat threw a shadow against my cabin.

Across the way, just out of earshot, U.S. Marshal Hill and City Marshal Stone argued. Running Deer sat nearby with a handful of Sioux closer to the river, talking to each other and glancing at the horses in the pasture.

I missed Anna. She would have loved this—the Indians,

the outdoor cooking, the celebration of a victory. It felt good to be free, but what was it without her?

What did she think of me now?

I looked up and saw the marshal watching me. He nodded at Stone, stood, and came over. He patted my shoulder. "Lucky break."

"Glad you made it in time."

"Learned of your arrest over the wires and knew you'd need an alibi for those two days, so I found Running Deer and hightailed it here."

I checked the meat, still dripping red, so I kept turning. Almost ready. "Will you stay for a while?"

He grunted. "Leaving tonight. Midnight train. Have an important prisoner and a gang still on the loose. Couldn't resist doing you the favor of saving your life, though. Since you saved mine." He lowered his voice. "I telegraphed you I was coming. Looks like your little town has a few problems."

"Seems like."

"I'll help you with it after we get Maxwell hanged and his gang dispersed."

I studied his eyes for a moment and saw genuine concern. "I'd say I could handle it, but I'm not so sure."

"Well, I'll do what I can."

I nodded and stared into the fire again.

He sniffed and brushed at his mustache. "I know how you're feeling right now. Kind of empty. Hollow after winning your trial. You know why that is?"

I shook my head.

"Because not one thing has changed from before the trial. You've changed, inside, but no one knows it. And nothing can be done about it. 'Cause the change in you isn't good."

"No, no it's not." I stared at the ground around my feet.

"You aren't just a homesteader or rancher any more. That was my fault, having to drag your story into the open. You've gone from a quiet horse trainer to a gun-toting shooter out to defend everything he loves."

"How do you know so much about it?"

He patted my shoulder again, and I welcomed the gesture.

"Been there, Philip. One day you define yourself one way, the next you're a different man. I'll give you a tip."

"I could use one."

"Stop thinking about yourself. Don't ever think about yourself. Just think of others, their troubles. Act on that, and you'll be fine."

"I didn't want to be this. To be a gunman. To be a hero."

"I know. But you're thinking about yourself again." Hill blew out a breath. "Think on others. Here's something to think about. Running Deer's agreed to be my deputy."

I tilted my head. "Oh, yeah?"

He smiled. "I need help. And he's caught between two worlds."

Running Deer as a law officer? I glanced over Hill's shoulder to study the Sioux. I wondered what would happen to the children he watched. But yes, it fit well.

I noticed that while I was thinking about my friend, I'd stopped dwelling on myself, which felt good.

Scott stretched and said, "I have a meeting with the judge tomorrow."

I pulled the steaks from the fire. "Why? More to do with the trial?"

He shrugged. "I have no idea. My guess is he plans to give me a severe reprimand over my conduct in court."

I smiled. I doubted that would happen.

We ate, and afterward said our good-byes. In the glow of the red-hot embers, Running Deer put a hand on my shoulder. "We will meet again."

Conversation with my Indian friend had been brief, and I hoped that someday there would be time to learn more about my childhood savior. Marshal Hill mounted his horse and saluted. Scott and Becky followed. As they rode away, they became shadows and finally disappeared into the darkness.

Only Marshal Stone remained.

I took a bucket, scooped up hot coals, and hauled them to the cabin. The marshal tagged along, carrying a large bag.

"Coffee?"

He nodded, and we stepped up on the front porch and

entered the house. I dumped the coals into the fireplace and lit lamps until the room glowed. Soon I had a pot of coffee brewing on the fire.

The marshal sat in a rope chair in the corner with the bag by his side while I sat in my rocker.

He dropped his hat on his knee. "I didn't expect things to work out so well for you."

I tapped the arm of the rocker with a finger and tried to read his face, but I couldn't. "Seemed like you were itchin' to pull the hangman's lever."

He rested his elbows on his knees. "My job."

"So, now you have a killer on the loose. What are you doing to find him?"

"We're in a bit of a ticklish situation here." He let out a big breath in a steady stream. "On one side I've got law and justice, and on the other elections are coming up. I can't help if I'm not elected."

The coffee boiled. I filled two mugs and handed one to him, taking mine to my seat. "You're still talking riddles." I knew what he was saying, but I wanted to make him uncomfortable, to hear him say it.

He put a hand on his knee and squinted. The wrinkles around his eyes attested to a hard life and years of experience upholding the law. "If you want to live long, you're going to have to let this crime go."

"Why do you say that?"

"Look, I can't say for sure who robbed the bank. For all intents and purposes, evidence still points to you. If it wasn't for that alibi, everybody would still think you're guilty."

I started to speak.

He held up a hand. "You're innocent. The townsfolk now believe you're innocent. But if you or I start pointing fingers without some iron-clad proof, we're never going to find the killer."

I wondered if Jeb or Ryan—Jacob's minions—committed the crime, or if Jacob had the guts to shoot a man himself.

The marshal sipped from his mug. "Good. I can tell by your face you're getting my point. If I'm a loose cannon I lose my job, and a new sheriff's not going to help you. That's a guarantee."

"All right. So you want me to keep my mouth shut for now. Fine, I can do that."

The worry lines on Stone's brow relaxed. "Raymond Hill and I were talking. We think it's best you stay put on this here ranch for a couple weeks. Or leave town."

"What?" The absurd suggestion made me fumble for words. I grabbed at the first thing that came to mind. "Not even go to church?"

He rubbed his chin, his face ruddy in the lamplight. "Can you go without trouble, without talking to people? Just get right back here?"

"I can do that, I suppose." I thought of Anna. She was still under Jacob's thumb, and he was just as powerful as ever. I stood and pointed a finger at him. "But if it comes to it, I will defend myself."

Marshal Stone reached for the cloth bag in front of him. He unbuttoned the flap and pulled out familiar tools. My guns.

"Here." He held out the belt with my Smith and Wesson. "Wear this. It must be on your hip every moment of the day and night. Your life is in danger. Between the Maxwell Gang and the problems you have around here, you've gotten yourself in a passel of trouble."

"Why ask me to stay alone on the ranch then?"

"Or leave. Make it several months. I'm hoping if you're out of sight you're out of Jacob's mind."

I set the gun on the nearby table. Something in Stone's face turned sour, and for the first time a swear word was uttered under my roof. He clenched his fist and slammed the armrest with a dull smack.

"What?"

"You don't understand. Put it on. Now. Go on."

I was confused, but I followed his orders.

"Hill claims you're fast," the marshal said. "Fastest in the territory. Great. Sign up for a shooting contest. You've got enemies who don't give a fig you're fast. These guys only pull a gun when odds are so stacked in their favor they can never lose. Like when you turn your back. Your little secret's out. There's going to be some bad guys who want to test themselves against you."

He took a deep breath and slowed down. "Your life is all but taken already." He motioned to the bag. "You've got plenty of money in there. I'm guessing it was a reward?"

I nodded and then paced in front of the fire. "Fine. I'll stay on my farm. I'll wear a gun. I'll watch my back. I might even skip church. But one thing—what if I want my girl back?"

Stone drank his coffee in one gulp and set his hat on his head. He stood. "If I were you and I wanted to live . . . best to get used to the idea of Jacob Wilkes marryin' Anna Johnston."

27

C offee at night—never a good idea. I worried and fretted, tossed and turned. I was in my own bed, but Stone's warning reverberated through my head. *Stay on the farm. Or leave. Make it several months.*

What worried me most was protecting my horses. Inside my log cabin, I was fairly safe. Shuttering the windows and barring the door made my cabin a fortress. I didn't care about the blacksmith equipment in the barn or even the barn itself. Replaceable. But I couldn't protect my horses. They were in the pasture right now and could easily be gunned down, knifed, or stolen. First thing in the morning, I'd have to lock them in the barn.

I sat up in bed and ran a hand through my hair. I was too emotional. I loved my horses, but they were also a commodity. My financial future was bound to selling them one day. I knew that if the horses were killed or stolen my investment was gone. The reward money would probably last me a few months, but if I couldn't blacksmith or train horses, I'd be stuck after that. I needed to turn Tucker, who was almost fully trained, into more cash. If the worst happened after that and Jacob got to my horses I'd have enough if I combined what I got from the sale with the reward money to start over if I had to. Marshal Stone would be happier if I left anyway.

Once I had a plan, I slept.

Before the sun rose, I brought Franklin, my stallion, the yearlings, and the mares with their foals into the barn, then packed my bags and settled them on Raven's back. I tied Tucker behind and strapped on my Smith and Wesson. As a precaution, I put the Colt revolver in my saddlebag for backup.

A damp chill had settled on the morning. Dew tipped the long blades of grass along the lane. As I started up the rise from the valley, I turned and saw the thriving wheat, the green pasture, my cabin bathed in fog, the barn rising from the mist. I would be gone for a single day. I prayed my small herd would be fine without me for that short amount of time.

Raven let loose a long whinny. I clicked my tongue. "C'mon, let's go."

We turned left, southeast toward the Missouri River and Fort Randall, in the opposite direction of Mitchell.

As noon approached I ate several pieces of deer jerky as I rode. Soon a wide ribbon of water blocked our way. The Missouri. From what I'd heard, very good fishing could be had in this river.

We followed the Missouri south until the terrain changed from a grassy plain broken by thick groves to a wasteland. Not a blade of grass or a tree broke the desolation. Fort Randall lay in the distance. I'd heard the soldiers had stripped the land for fuels.

The hot, humid wind swirled around us in a miniature tornado.

We continued, Raven dropping her head and snorting. She didn't care for this desert, but Tucker pranced alongside us without a worry.

Ahead, cavalry regulars rode along a worn pathway until coming across the practice jumping fences of the training grounds. Their horses soared over the long poles, which were stretched horizontally. Sometimes the riders held tight, and other times they crashed to the ground. I couldn't help but smile. A firing range nearby was put to good use, soldiers with rifles testing their skills, sharpening their aim. A cheer rose from the shooters—someone had made a bull's-eye. Raven, Tucker, and I steered wide of them.

I rode into the fort. Two long buildings stretched parallel to each other, with two small buildings capping each end, creating a rectangle. A large drill area with a United States flag flapping in the breeze filled the center. The sun beat down on the grassy patch under the flagpole, where soldiers milled about in slow motion. Humidity could drain even the best of men.

Soldiers looked at us as we crossed the courtyard. Some faces showed a mixture of contempt for me and a lust for my horses. Others looked at us as if we didn't belong. I glanced at the gravel below, checking for hoof prints to make sure riding in the fort's center square was acceptable. There were marks everywhere.

I noticed a group of officers leaning against a horse rail before a smaller, gray building at the end of the fort. I stopped Raven in front of the porch and dismounted, trying not to groan. It had been a long ride.

The insignia on their uniforms came into view as I neared. A sergeant was chatting with several lieutenants. As I stepped onto the porch, a whistle erupted from the group. One of the officers broke away and sauntered toward Raven, while the knot of men moved closer, laughing.

"Them are purty horses, mister." He paused near the hitched pair and studied me, his gaze landing on my revolver. I knew what he saw—a tall, lean man with his duster and denims, a black hat, two days' stubble, and bright, piercing gray eyes.

I looked like a killer, and I did nothing to dissuade him of the idea.

After nodding, I turned toward the door.

"For sale?"

He had a hand on Raven's rump. Her tail flicked back and forth as flies circled.

The man's complexion was pockmarked, probably from childhood smallpox. His large ears drew more attention than the two bars on his uniform.

"How much?" he asked.

I continued to gaze at him, and he locked his eyes with mine. I held the look, and after a moment he twitched and looked away.

"Chestnut is five hundred."

The other soldiers whistled.

The two-barred soldier shook his head, laughing. "You're crazy, mister." He motioned at Raven. "How much for blacky?"

"Not for sale."

He looked at his fellow soldiers and puffed up his chest. "What do you say we take these horses and send this boy back to his mamma?"

A few in the group laughed, but the sound died quickly.

I took a few steps forward, close enough to see a bead of sweat trickling down the side of his face. I kept my voice low. "You need to understand, this horse has a way of being stolen and coming back to me. Only, the thief ends up . . . hurt. Bad."

The officer's face puckered. Before he could say another word, he clamped his mouth shut. I heard the door open behind me. "Stand down, Jackson."

I turned and saw an officer. His bars boasted the rank of captain, and I figured he was probably in charge of the fort. His white hair and pencil mustache, as well as his smooth gait and calm steady hands, gave me the impression of a man who was an officer first and a gentleman second.

He paused at the end of the shaded porch and looked at me. "What do you want?"

"To sell you a horse."

"We have horses. And suppliers." His tone was weary. "If you'd like to set up a contract to supply us with horses, see our quartermaster."

I stood my ground. "I want to sell *you* a horse."

The man placed his hands behind his back and lifted up on his heels. "Now, why would I need a horse?"

I stepped closer to him. "The chestnut is called Tucker. Comes from a long lineage that stretched back to the stables of Solomon. Bedouins and knights, as you may well know, have always preferred the Arabian for war." I leaned closer. "George Washington rode an Arabian. This is an officer's horse."

He smirked.

I continued. "Tucker comes with training. My name is Philip Anderson, and I'd be honored to demonstrate, if you'd like."

"Training." He grunted and ran a gloved hand along the porch's railing. "Fine. A ride around the flagpole is in order. Carry on."

As I transferred Raven's saddle to Tucker and tied her to the hitching post, I knew I had to do something to catch this man's attention. I pulled the Colt out of Raven's saddlebags and thrust it into my belt next to the Smith and Wesson.

I leapt into the saddle and turned to the officers. "Meet me at the training grounds." With that, I made a kissing sound to Tucker, and in a flash he nimbly left the soldiers behind.

From the corner of my eye, I saw the officers running behind, trying to keep up. Even the captain made his way toward the training grounds.

Despite the long walk across the prairie, the young gelding seemed eager to work. His spirit, always high, seemed higher today with an audience. It flashed through my head how much I'd changed. I never would have stood up to those men like that only a few short months ago. Shooting a man did that to you, I guessed.

Soldiers lined the edges of the first obstacle in the course. I turned Tucker into a wide circle. The ground was a blur beneath us, the ride smooth, like sitting on a cloud.

The first section was about a quarter mile long, a straight shot. Tucker lowered his head and raced faster than Quarter horses and Morgans. And while he wasn't as fast as a thoroughbred, to these men who rode only mass-bred animals, Tucker was a once-in-a-lifetime show. Several hundred men hurried from the fort and lined up along the course.

I slowed Tucker as we approached the barrels and this, I knew, was where he would shine. With nimble legs at speeds that surprised even me, we wove around the obstacles. My knee bumped one, and it rocked but didn't fall.

I looked ahead to the jumps and tried to swallow my nerves so Tucker wouldn't sense them. We hadn't worked much on jumping, and the timing had to be perfect.

We vaulted over a two-foot-high pile of stones. Next, a long hole stretched in front of us, and with a little more speed we sailed over. His hooves landed squarely on the ground and continued to churn across the field.

Before us, several log fence jumps were lined up in a row. I checked Tucker, slowing him momentarily so he could collect his balance. Height and correct placement were needed here, and I watched in dismay as several soldiers added an extra rail to the last jump, making it as high as my chest.

We cleared the first, and the second was close. I let him take his time as we approached the last, but then I took complete control with a firm hand on the reins and tight pressure with my knees. The fence loomed before us.

Tucker leapt through the air, threw his front legs over the bar, and I sensed his midsection barely clearing the pole. He tucked his hind legs close to his body. His hooves thudded into the soft gravel on the other side.

I heard the soldiers burst into cheers. Some near the firing range shot rifles into the air. We thundered past long rows of men so fast their uniforms looked like a blur. Tucker's feet barely touched the ground. I bent low to whisper in his ear. "C'mon, boy." I relaxed my legs and continued to move with the horse.

Our last ride together.

I followed the narrow trail that passed by a long row of glass bottles thrust onto poles, a small hill just behind them. Soldiers ran from the area, and when I pulled the Smith and Wesson, they sprinted. I turned in the saddle, lifted the revolver, and released the reins.

A picture of the robbers entering our camp flashed through my mind.

Tucker and I were almost to the bottles.

The outlaws moved in on our little camp, and I prepared to aim. But then the image faded, and I was in Deadwood standing before Maxwell. He was shouting at Marshal Hill. All the while, his trigger finger twitched above the butt of his gun. He was about to pull it on me.

My mind went to my parents' camp again. The men reached for their guns. My father did nothing.

I was even with the bottles, almost too late to fire. I fanned the hammer fast. Five bottles exploded. The sixth chamber was empty.

I holstered the gun and pulled the Colt from my belt. Five more bottles exploded as we passed. Two left. I whipped out the Winchester from the scabbard with one hand as I thrust the Colt back in my belt with the other hand.

With the rifle tucked close to my shoulder, I pulled the trigger. It felt like a wild shot, but the bottle vaporized. The final bottle was set back slightly, and I misjudged the distance. The bullet fell short and ricocheted into the glass. It shattered into a million golden pieces.

Tucker slid to a halt directly in front of the captain. The roar of the soldiers was almost deafening as they crowded around me.

I couldn't catch my breath.

The captain saluted and gave me a wry smile. "Are you trying to sell a horse or a man?" He adjusted his hat. "What did you say your name is?"

"Philip Anderson." I dismounted and stood in front of him.

He looked into my eyes. Was that a look of recognition? Or was it my wolf eyes that unsettled him?

The captain thrust his thumbs into his belt. "Come back to my office. We'll talk."

I patted Tucker's neck. "There's one last thing about this horse you need to know." I lowered my voice. "Is there a soldier here who needs humbled?"

Captain Smith's eyes glinted. He lifted his chin and called out, "Jackson!"

The redheaded soldier who was sulking at the edge of the building took several steps forward. "Yes, sir."

Smith looked at me expectedly.

I turned to the young officer. "Think you can ride him?"

"I can ride any horse." His chest puffed out. "They're just like women. Have to show 'em who's boss."

An image of Anna flashed through my mind and how she'd respond to the comment. That soothed my conscience for what was coming.

Without another word, he leapt onto Tucker from behind and dug his heels into the horse's sides.

I whistled, first low, then high. Tucker reared back and gave a wicked twist.

Jackson slammed into the dust. Laughter filled the air.

Captain Smith chuckled. "That might come in handy."

"I used that trick recently on a horse thief."

Cries from the soldiers caught my attention and I spun. Jackson was running for Tucker, a thick stick in his hand. I gave a high-pitched whistle, and Tucker reared, his front hooves aimed at Jackson's head. The officer swung and hit the horse on his shoulder, a glancing blow. I gave two short whistles and Tucker dropped to the ground, lowered his head, and charged into Jackson. The soldier flew through the air and crashed onto the gravel.

Tucker didn't stop like I'd trained him to do. He reared again, momentarily hovering over Jackson before he plunged his hooves downward, just missing the officer's head. I gave a low whistle, afraid Tucker would kill the man.

The horse spun and trotted back to my side.

Captain Smith touched the shoulder Jackson had hit, concern in his eyes. I knew he wanted the horse. "Spirited. I like that in a horse." He aimed his chin at the fort. "Sergeant Bennett, take him to the livery stable. My men will cool him down."

The commander stepped over to Jackson, who still lay on the ground and who looked as if he'd just escaped death. "You're confined to quarters."

The captain looked at his men. "Dismissed." As the men dispersed, I removed the saddle from Tucker's back and cinched it on Raven.

A melancholy feeling washed over me. From birth to breaking to now, this horse had become more than a friend.

He was like my child. I patted Tucker's chestnut muzzle, and I left him.

I pulled an envelope from the saddlebag and stepped onto the porch. When I opened the door, I saw Captain Smith's office immediately to the left.

He sat behind a sparse desk. Beside him was an equally empty bookshelf holding only a few war manuals. A houseplant stood beside two windows that overlooked the parade grounds, the sign of a woman's touch.

The captain stood. "Care for a drink?"

I nodded. "Water, if you have some. Dusty trails."

He reached for a pitcher and two glasses that sat on top of a cabinet. "Word gets around, Philip Anderson. I'd heard you raised Arabians." He poured water into both glasses. "And I read about your little trick in Deadwood. Where did you learn to shoot like that?"

"Not in the cavalry."

"Your rifle aim could use some practice though."

I smiled but kept silent.

He took a sip of water at the same time I did. The water wet my parched tongue.

The captain set his glass down. "We all need a little luck, or as some would say, help from the Almighty, now and then. Like you got with your rifle shot. But as a soldier, one finds that God is simply a fleeting idea to cling to in times of danger."

I sighed. "And luck is so much more."

He gave a genuine laugh and sat down. He held out his hand toward a seat. "I think I'll buy your horse." He paused and pursed his lips. "Philip, I don't know how to tell you this, so I'm just going to say it." He leaned forward and folded his hands, a serious expression on his face. "It's time for you to know anyway."

I stared at him.

"I've kept an eye on you for five years now."

What was he talking about?

The captain ran a hand through his peppered hair. He opened his mouth and paused. Finally, he looked straight at me. "I knew your parents."

28

"Y ou knew my parents?" I stood up. "And you knew where I was all this time?"

A sad look crossed his face. "Yes. I didn't feel the need to introduce myself. Until now. You were happy doing what you do, raising horses and making a living on the few inches of soil afforded to men in the West."

The answer was completely unsatisfactory. Even though I'd been orphaned years ago, I was still desperate to know more about my parents. "Would've been nice to know."

His tone sharpened as he leaned forward. "Sit down, Philip. You're lucky I'm telling you now." He spoke as if I was one of his unruly soldiers. His face softened, something I was sure his soldiers would never see. "You weren't ready. Now you are. Now you need to be ready."

I shook my head. "That doesn't make sense." This man apparently knew my family and was close enough to my parents to care about me.

He must have seen my thoughts play out on my face. "I want what's best for you, Philip."

"Why?"

"Because I was there when you were born."

I took a calming breath and sat down. "How did you know my parents?"

"I met your father in West Virginia before you were born. During the War Between the States, your father had black-smithing contracts with the military. I was a quartermaster then, on my way to becoming a general, if the war had continued. But—"

"What was he like?" I couldn't help interrupting him.

"He was a decent fellow." Smith took a drink. "Kept to himself. Like you. Although you're not much like him in appearance. Your smile is his. And dark skin, like your father. But that's all."

Many a night I'd tossed and turned, replaying every memory I could muster of my mother and father. Now the answers were coming, and I could barely contain my swirling thoughts, excitement, and apprehension. What if I learned something I'd be better off not knowing?

"Your mother . . ." He stared at the desk. "She was the life of West Virginia. Her parties, her flair . . . She was beautiful." He sucked in a long breath and released it.

The captain looked out the window as if it were a portrait of the past. "She made every person at those parties feel like her own personal guest. From grand affairs and military balls to a few friends attending her famous teas." He laughed. "She loved her tea."

"Teas?"

"She was from England. Did you know that?"

I shook my head. "I didn't."

He looked thoughtful. "Her parents, your grandparents, were from England and immigrated when she was a very young girl. She tried so hard to destroy that wonderful accent of hers but couldn't quite do it. It only added to her charm."

It was as if my parents' lives, what I'd known of them, had been chipped into stone inside my head. And now this man was recarving the rock. It hurt.

He couldn't stop talking about my mother. "Constance had high cheek bones, like yours. You don't have a gap in your teeth like she did, but you have her eyes." He sighed. "Glory, those eyes."

I cleared my throat. "Did you . . . love my mother?"

His broad grin made me feel comfortable, as if he was starting to like me. "My boy, that's my entire point. Everyone loved her. Deeply. She was an amazing woman." He frowned. "I like to think I was a close friend, almost a godfather to you." He chuckled. "You were a spunky little tyke. Intense. You could spend hours playing with the same toy." His forehead creased. "Good with your hands."

I wished I could remember the captain, but I didn't. "Do you know how they died?"

"I tried to send letters to their homestead, but they were returned. I made inquiries that came back without answers. The rumor mill said some thieves were caught and all but one killed. Before he was hanged, he asked forgiveness for killing a couple in the Dakota Territory, one of his many transgressions. He described a beautiful English woman and a boy who got away. Since I hadn't heard a word from your parents, I figured it was your family."

I took a few deep breaths.

"I tried to find you. One day I heard your name, as a new homesteader in the territory, and today we cross paths." He smiled. "Your eyes gave you away before you even told me who you were."

The man fell silent, and we sat for a moment. It was as if he knew I had to process everything he told me. "Tell me more."

"Your mother was a fine cook, a devoted wife and mother, and she loved horses. She didn't want to go West. In fact, she was emphatically against it. But in the end, well, sometimes your father had ways to get her to do things."

"Did he beat her?"

"No, he didn't have to. Your mother needed love and attention like a soldier needs his canteen. He would withhold his love from her. Without conversation and kindness, she would shrivel. Terrible crime. So many men eager to pour affection on her, and the one man she was devoted to refused what she needed." He looked out the window again, as if remembering. "I am happily married. Was then, too. But if your mother—" He bit back his words, as if he'd said too much.

I ignored the comment. "My parents were killed near Devil's Tower. But their homestead was closer to this area. Do you know why they traveled past it?"

His brow furrowed. "That doesn't make sense." He tapped a thumb on his desk. "No sense at all."

"Do you know my mother's maiden name? I seem to remember I have an uncle."

His body sagged. "You don't know?" He cringed. "I thought you knew."

"Tell me."

"Philip, your mother's maiden name was Maxwell. And she has a brother in the Dakota Territory."

"You mean . . . he's still living?"

"Yes, he's alive, for now." The captain's eyes glinted. "His name is John, John Maxwell. The man you shot in Deadwood is your uncle."

I fought the tightness in my chest. It took several seconds before I could speak. "No. No, that's not right. It's not him."

Smith just looked at me, sympathy etched on his features.

The truth began to sink in. I was unable to speak.

"His eyes, Philip. What color were they?"

I closed my own eyes, not wanting to believe what I was hearing.

Captain Smith leaned back and set his elbows on the desk. "Two extraordinary men on opposite sides of the law. Of course you had to meet eventually."

"I'm no one special."

"From what I read and what I just saw, you're the best gun in the territory. He was a close second."

"He's just a simple horse thief who took the opportunity to steal the best horse in Deadwood. That's all."

The officer bared his perfectly white teeth, and his voice lowered. "You are the opposite of Maxwell in so many ways. But he's your uncle, nonetheless."

I pictured Maxwell. Without a beard, he could look like

me. He had no accent like his sister other than a gravelly American one. But his eyes. I remembered looking into his eyes. We had the same eyes, my mother's eyes. I reached into my pocket, pulled the watch out, and opened it. My mother's extraordinary face looked back at me.

I stood. "I need to go."

"Philip." Captain Smith's voice was calm and understanding. "You still going to sell me that horse?"

"Sure." I shrugged.

"How much do you want for him?"

"How about four hundred?"

"That's a lot of money. Three fifty?"

"Fine."

He grinned. "You're welcome to stay the night here. You can rest up and return home tomorrow."

"I need to get back to look after my horses."

He stood. "What do you mean?"

"I've got myself some trouble in Mitchell. Nothing I can't take care of."

He walked to a safe that was set against a wall and started working the combination. "If there's anything I can do to help…"

"I'll let you know."

He opened the door, reached inside, and counted out loud. After a moment, he closed the safe and crossed his office to hand me the money. "I'm invited to a political party at the end of this year in Yankton, and I'd like for you to go with me. Your parents would've been there." He grinned."After enjoying so many of your mother's wonderful parties, it's almost poetic to think of the two of us attending together."

Poetic for him, but not for me. "I'll think about it." I couldn't hide the pain in my voice. "I need to get on my way."

With one last pat on his rump, I left Tucker at the livery. Raven and I pushed for home, sometimes at a trot or lope, sometimes at a walk. The sun was down by the time we made it. I was relieved to see that my horses were still alive.

I needed to prepare for a return trip to Deadwood. I had

questions for John Maxwell, like how did my sweet mother's brother become the biggest outlaw in the territory.

At my front door, I found a note thrust between the door and the frame. I slid open the envelope.

It was a telegram.

Will be there 9AM tomorrow STOP Thursday STOP Rachel

I'd forgotten about the young girl from Deadwood.

29

I should have been feeling kind and charitable as I rode into Mitchell. After all, I was trying to help a girl get a fresh start in life. But I was in a hurry to get to Deadwood to talk with my uncle. Instead, I had to pick up Rachel and deliver her to Caroline's.

And I knew Marshal Stone wouldn't be happy to see me in town after asking me to stay away.

I dismounted near the train station and adjusted my gun belt. I pictured Marshal Hill's expression when he learned I was related to John Maxwell. His mustache might turn white.

"Mr. Anderson?"

I spun and put a hand on my revolver.

Beth, Anna's sister, was walking toward me.

My heart was beating fast, and my hand shook. I'd almost drawn on a little girl. I came close to unbuckling my belt and shoving it in Raven's saddlebag.

Beth stepped onto the boardwalk, her hands behind her back. The morning sun played against her blue bonnet. Her cheeks were rosy and she looked pleased to see me.

Her gaze settled on my gun. "Mr. Anderson, can you shoot Jacob?"

I choked and leaned closer. This was one conversation that didn't need to be overheard. I glanced at the real estate office behind her and up and down the street. This close to the train station, there was an abundance of people. While many looked on since I was famous now, no one seemed interested in our conversation.

"It's a little more complicated than that." But the thought had passed through my mind.

"He shot my horse." She screwed up her face. "He's mean to us, Anna most of all."

I wanted to charge into Jacob's office and beat his smug face. "What does your father say about it?"

"He's too nice to Jacob."

I straightened and patted Raven's forehead. "I'm sure there are reasons."

"Yeah, Daddy owes Jacob a lot of money. A lot. There's a grate on my floor, in my bedroom. I heard Mommy and Daddy talking about . . ." Her face crumpled. "Jacob will put Daddy in prison if he doesn't pay him soon."

My growing apprehension turned to dread. Anna was being held hostage. If I were a father, would I let my daughter court such a man?

But I knew the situation had gone way beyond courtship. The entire family was being held hostage, with any number of threats against everyone.

She pointed at my hip. "Was that the gun you used?"

I knew she was talking about when I shot Maxwell. "I guess it was, yes."

"Anna said you were wonderful when you were in Deadwood. She said she learned about it in the courtroom. And that you have fascinating friends."

Anna must have said exactly those words, because Beth could barely get the word *fascinating* out.

At least Anna didn't despise me for what I'd done.

The train's whistle shrieked, and Beth held both hands over her ears.

"Thanks for talking to me, Elizabeth. I hope we'll talk again soon."

She smiled and nodded then skipped to a nearby store.

I bit back tears and looked into the sky. *God, I'm so sorry.* I'd almost pulled my gun on her. Was I turning into a monster? I needed someone to talk to, to help me sort through the questions that pressed deeply on my brain. How did my faith in God, my reliance on Him for my safety, fit with the gun on my side? How do I turn the other cheek for my enemies?

I looked around and saw Ryan, Jacob's paid hand, across the street. He was watching Beth. I groaned. He'd seen our conversation. He mounted his horse and rode back into town. Dear God, they were even following a little girl.

I had to help Anna and her family.

But first I had to tend to Rachel. The train squealed into the station shrouded with billows of steam and smoke. Workers ran along the tracks to unload the train as a dozen carts lined the road, waiting for goods. Horses neighed nervously as the train screeched to a stop. Almost before the train halted, people stepped down out of the cars.

I felt stupid when I realized there was no way I would be able to haul Rachel's life possessions all the way to Caroline's place. I glanced around and spotted an empty horse-pulled cart with a dirty man I recognized sitting beside it. "Joe, you got a job?"

"Huh-uh."

"Can you haul my passenger?"

He nodded. I tied Raven to the hitching post before I headed for the train and stepped onto the platform to scan the disembarking passengers.

I almost didn't recognize her. Wearing a brown dress with long sleeves, a hat that was as nondescript as the dress, and a look of reserved patience, Rachel blended in with the other passengers.

I smiled and waved. The change in her was real.

Rachel saw me. A few steps and we met. She stood in front of me, her head down, hat covering her face from my view.

I decided to get right down to business. "How did your parents take the news?"

She peered from under her hat. "Good. They said I could stay with them, but . . ."

"You need to make it on your own. Understandable. Good."

She smiled, the lines on her face and her wary expression a testament to hard living.

"Where are your bags?"

"Just one crate, there."

A conductor hauled the huge case from the baggage car. "There you are, ma'am." He wiped sweat from his brow.

She handed him a dime and he smiled. "Thank you, kindly, miss."

I stared down at the crate.

"Philip, is it true?" she asked. "The things the papers say about you?"

"You mean capturing Maxwell? Yep." I grabbed both handles, lifted, and barely got the crate off the ground. With a deep breath, I hefted it to my chest. "Let's go." I started toward the platform stairs.

"You're a hero."

"That's what I hear." But other than the eyes of every Mitchell resident on me, I didn't feel like much of a hero. In fact, I was feeling pretty low at the moment. I couldn't go to Deadwood to question my uncle because of a former prostitute, and I couldn't talk with the woman I loved because of a maniacal fiend who thought the world was his possession. On top of all that, I missed Tucker and Princess. My only solace was that Captain Smith seemed to be a kind man, and Running Deer was good to horses. Both would have good lives.

I managed to make it to the cart and load the crate onto it, but by the time I got there my knees shook and I couldn't feel my arms. Joe, who watched us from his perch on the wagon's seat, looked Rachel over but didn't say anything. I helped her climb up beside him, and he flicked the reins.

Joe's old horse could barely budge the cart, but we slowly made our way to Caroline's with me following on Raven.

We stepped inside as lunch was on, all twelve tables full. I saw Caroline hurrying to the kitchen, but when she passed Leroy at his usual table, she reached out. He grabbed her hand, and the touch lingered.

As Leroy watched her leave, I approached his table. "There something you want to tell me, buddy?"

"Nope." He grinned. "Nary a blessed thing."

I patted his shoulder.

Caroline bustled from the kitchen with dishes in each hand and three plates balanced on her forearms. "Oh, Philip. Goodness. How are you?" Her face glowed with perspiration, but she looked happy. She glanced over my shoulder. "Are you Rachel?"

The girl stepped around me, reached up, and took the plates from Caroline. "I am."

The two locked eyes for a moment, and I saw unspoken communication between them. Caroline pointed. "Tables one through six here, seven to eleven on this side. Leroy is the name of this table." She set down the dishes and squeezed his shoulder. "In the kitchen are two full plates for table eight."

Rachel beamed.

Turning toward the kitchen again, Caroline spoke over her shoulder. "You can stay at my place until you find your own."

Rachel gave a nod and Caroline disappeared behind the kitchen doors. I waved at Leroy and stepped outside. I took a breath. Done. Rachel and Caroline would be fine.

I felt an arm wrap around me, and if it weren't for the brown cloth of Rachel's sleeve, I would have gone for my gun. She gave me a quick kiss on the cheek.

A tear trickled down the side of her face. "Being free from Deadwood is more than anything I could ever ask for. Thank you."

I tried to smile, and as Rachel returned to the tables, I wiped my cheek with my sleeve.

She had a lot to learn.

I adjusted my saddle, threw my leg over Raven, and looked around. Jeb stood in the middle of the street, watching.

He'd seen Rachel kiss me.

30

My heart ached for Anna as I spoke to Pastor Humphrey. But what was I willing to do to win her back?

The preacher's enormous body reclined comfortably in the church's front row. I sat next to him and tried to explain what I'd had to do to defend myself. My voice reverberated around the empty building. "I'm not proud of shooting a man. I just want to help Anna and her family."

He nodded. "You and Anna are the perfect couple. But Jacob holds this town by the throat, as he does you."

The light from the stained-glass windows cast a colorful glow on my hands.

"Of course turning to prayer and the scriptures is the first thing we do." There was no conviction in his voice.

I closed my eyes and took a deep breath. "Hard to do when a man has a gun pointed at you."

"Prayer and Bible reading are practice. Hide the Word in your heart so when a gun is pulled you'll know right from wrong." He sniffed and rubbed his nose. "You've done that."

"Is self defense right? Jesus died without defending Himself."

"Pull your gun to defend yourself and others. And let God decide who is right and who is dead."

For some strange reason, the meeting with Pastor Humphrey left me feeling more like a gunfighter and less like a church member.

I stopped at Scott's tiny, one-bedroom shack, hoping to get some news about Anna. But I had to admit I also wanted to mope and feel sorry for myself. I hitched Raven out front and knocked on his door.

"Come in."

I was surprised to find Becky sitting at his table, helping Scott pore over law books. "What's this?"

Scott beamed. "Brown, Stone, and Thompson have agreed to let me study law under them. The judge arranged it so now I'm studying to pass the bar exam."

Becky's gleaming eyes told me all I needed to know regarding how she felt about courting a lawyer. She smiled. "Since he lost his job at the mill, this has been such a blessing."

I looked at Scott. "They fired you?"

He shrugged. "Business was awful. And honestly, Jacob's got Mr. Johnston's throat in a vice. It's bad, Philip. Very bad."

I sat on the edge of his bed. "What did Anna ever see in Jacob? Why did she agree to have dinner with him in the first place?"

Becky sighed and reached over to pat my arm. "It was the argument you two had that sent her to him. I think she wanted to make you a little jealous."

I got up to leave, feeling more discouraged than ever. As I left, Scott stepped outside with me. "You're depressed because your life's changing. It's unsettling, but God will guide you through."

Still, I wished I wasn't becoming a gunman.

I had one last bit of business before I left town. I needed to close my account at the Wilkes bank.

When I stepped inside the clerk who testified against me stared at my gun. His arm was still in a sling. A guard immediately came forward and escorted me to the bars. When I explained what I wanted the clerk made some notations on a ledger, counted out bills from his drawer, and handed me an envelope. He winced as he moved his arm. "Your account balance minus the appropriate fees."

With a quick tear I opened the envelope, saw an invoice with the fees listed, and some cash. One dollar and fifty cents. "Satisfactory. Good day."

"Philip." The clerk's eyes held an earnest look. "I really thought it was you. I'm sorry."

I gripped the envelope in my hand and gave him a nod.

I was relieved I didn't see Jacob or his father. Did his father know Jacob had been behind the robbery?

I deposited the cash in First National Bank on Main Street, a new bank struggling because of Jacob Wilkes, and headed home. The afternoon gave way to early evening as I rode. I felt very lonely but didn't know what to do about it. The wind drifted across the prairie and rustled the trees in Anna's Woods. I stopped and took a moment to remember the night I'd saved her.

But I didn't linger. I had to keep moving. "Let's go, girl." Raven took off just as I felt something slip over my shoulders and pin my arms to my sides.

The rope burned into my arms as I flew out of the saddle and slammed onto the ground. I'd been lassoed.

I heard the air escape from my lungs, but I scrambled to stand and reach for my gun at the same time. A figure loomed over me, and a knee snapped upward into my gut. Before I collapsed, I felt a hand at my holster and the revolver's weight disappeared.

I gripped the grass that ran down the middle of the road, trying to catch my breath. A man towered over me. Ryan, one of Jacob's henchmen. The man who had seen me talking with Beth. I was tall, but he was nearly a head taller. From my vantage point, he was a giant. His boots, close to my face, looked like canoes.

I searched for Raven. She'd gotten caught in some brush just off the road. From the corner of my eye, I saw three men with rifles coming down the road. One came and stood next to Ryan. It was Jeb, Jacob's second.

"He's looking too healthy to talk to the boss," Jeb said. "Ryan, take the pride out of him."

Ryan reached for me, and I aimed a punch at his knee. It connected, and the big man roared in pain. He grabbed my shirt and picked me up to slap my face with his free hand. The sting sent sharp barbs through my skin. He doubled his fist and threw a punch into my stomach. Any air I'd managed to collect expired into the prairie. I fell in a heap at his feet.

"Ryan does a fine job, wouldn't you reckon, Anderson?" I could see Jeb's thin face glaring down at me. "There's more of that coming in a moment, but first, a word from the man who backed this little enterprise."

Hooves thudded, and I looked up to see eight men surrounding me. One rider came near. The horse stopped, and Jacob, dressed entirely in white, slid from the saddle. He reached into the rifle scabbard and pulled out his cane.

Not the cane. My back still ached from the last time.

Jacob looked at me like I was a worm he was about to pulverize. I was powerless to take him down. My stomach cramped.

He spoke one name. "Beth Johnston."

I winced. "What about her?"

His voice was calm. "Don't talk to the kid."

I managed to catch my breath. "Free country."

"She's the sister of my love. My territory."

"You only love money."

Jacob nodded to Ryan, and his boot connected with my chest. I doubled over again.

"When you speak with Beth or Anna, you're only hurting them." He settled on his heels next to me. "My job is to protect them. My options are unlimited."

"This isn't the way."

"Since you only spoke to Beth, your life is spared. For the moment." He stood and reached into his pocket. "But a lesson must be learned." He drew out a pistol and pulled back the hammer with a loud click. He leveled the gun and aimed at Raven.

"No!"

He smiled. "You should have stayed away from them."

I sucked a deep breath, the pain coming in spasms, and whistled a low tone. Raven jerked back, pulled away from the bush, and galloped into the prairie just as Jacob fired.

He missed.

"Throw me a rifle."

One of his men tossed him a gun, and he lifted it to his cheek. Still lying on the road, I twisted myself toward his legs, knocking him to the ground. His shot slammed into one of his men, whipping the unfortunate man to the ground. He held his bloody arm. While Jacob was still down, I managed one solid punch at his face.

The men rushed in and held me down.

Jacob picked up his cane and laughed. "You've lost Anna." He turned to his men. "Do what you want with him. Just don't kill him. Yet."

Ryan's fists felt like hammers. Jeb's boots pummeled my back, and I felt repeated blows against my kidneys until I couldn't feel my back anymore. I could taste blood as they beat me, and I saw red drops fall onto the ground.

After what seemed like hours, my body was numb and my brain foggy. The world spun and my feeble attempt to defend myself ended when a wicked kick to my temple caused the edges of the world to darken. My right eye was swollen shut. I rolled over onto my stomach.

"Stop." Jacob's voice sounded muffled, probably because of my puffy ears. He stood over me. "Lesson about to be learned."

I heard a whistle and felt a slap against my back. He swung again, then again, over and over. I could feel my enflamed skin tearing.

With a growl, he gave one last swing that slashed the back of my legs. "I will kill Beth, and then I will kill you if you continue to tread on my territory. And I will tell the town of your liaison with Rachel Fulton."

I was slipping into the blackness that threatened to overtake me, but that's what Jacob wanted. I kept telling myself over and over to stay awake, stay awake.

"Jacob . . ." I could barely move my cracked lips. "Someday that cane will be the end of you."

Jacob laughed a hideous mix of hatred and pleasure. He and the other tormentors rode toward Mitchell in a thunder of hooves.

Nightfall was chilling me. I forced my eyes open, looking through tiny slits into the darkness. Had I passed out?

I felt a cold nuzzle on the back of my neck, familiar and comforting. Raven's soft nicker helped arouse me. With all my strength, I pushed myself onto my side.

I gasped. Bearing pain was part of being a man, but I'd never felt anything like this before. My back screamed. My head spun, and I was glad I hadn't eaten supper.

Raven dipped her muzzle, and the reins slipped over her head. I reached up, grabbed them with my left hand, and tried to pull myself to a sitting position.

Surely someone would come by. But I couldn't wait. I needed to get home before I passed out again.

I crawled across the road, using Raven's reins for support until I was in the deep grass. Blood trickled down my face. Almost blind, I groped around, hoping to find my Smith and Wesson.

I had watched where it landed, and thankfully, I was in the right spot. I grasped the barrel. If Jacob had been smart, he would have broken my hand and kept my gun.

With the reins and gun clutched in my hands, I pulled up to my knees and leaned against Raven's leg. She was still, as if understanding. I grabbed the stirrup and stood with a groan.

I tried to lift my leg, but my back and thighs screamed in protest. My muscles cramped and refused to move. "Oh God, please help." I managed to put the stirrup around my boot and pull my entire weight up onto the saddle. The stirrup slipped and I lost my balance and toppled back, crashing onto the ground.

Blackness edged the corner of my mind, and the pain seemed to lessen. Sleepiness settled over me. I wanted to curl into a ball and sleep as the Dakota prairie consumed me.

I used the strange absence of pain to stand again, ignoring

the cramping and blackness that pressed in. I lifted myself into the saddle again, leaned forward, buried my face in Raven's mane, and managed, "Home."

Every step she took was torture. Sometimes the pangs rushed me like an angry bull; other times I felt a strange energy wash over me. But the desire to sleep was getting stronger.

The fenders of my saddle were wet with blood. As Raven trotted, the slash across my thigh seemed to open. I could barely hold on to the horn.

I needed to get home before I blacked out again. Raven's neck became my lifeline. I gripped tight.

I thought I felt Raven turn onto my lane and drop into my valley, and my split-rail fences lined the edge of my vision. Raven finally halted, and I fell to the ground. I looked up, saw my cabin, and pulled myself onto the porch.

I could hear my horse happily munching on the grass.

Despite being home, I was going to die at my front door.

31

My own screaming woke me. Burning agony pummeled my body. Strong hands held me down. Jacob's men? I thought I saw Scott. I fought against them until blackness washed over me again.

Johnston's Mill was shrouded in fog. The waterwheel slapped a steady rhythm. I could see Anna before me in a white linen gown that revealed the curves of her well-turned figure. I wanted desperately to hold her, to run my fingers through her hair as I pressed her body against mine.

But she turned away, and her soft features faded into a villainous grin. Where had her sweet smile gone? Jacob moved close to her, wrapped one arm around her, and set his other hand on her hip, massaging the curve. He pulled her close. She kissed him.

I lay on my back with earthen walls towering on either side of me. Scott, Becky, Leroy, Caroline, and even Rachel looked down on my body. Anna and Jacob watched over the edge of my grave as well, and he whispered something into her ear. She laughed.

Pastor Humphrey stood, and with Bible in hand, shook his head. "He should not have tried to be a hero."

Rachel reached down, picked up a handful of dirt, and sprinkled it on my face.

Gradually, I felt my mind clearing. The grave had been a dream. I could make it go away if I opened my eyes.

I forced them open and saw that I lay on my back in my own bed. Through the blur, I saw a dog. It was black and white with ginger spots. He sat next to me, watching me.

I reached up to pet him, but the fire stabbing my back stopped me.

The dog wagged his tail and ducked his head under my hand. I grasped his soft fur and tried to speak, but my mouth was dry.

It took a staggering effort, but I managed to sit up. I looked down. Bandages covered my chest, one shoulder, arms, and legs. I felt my forehead, which was also wrapped with gauze. I started to shake my head to push the cobwebs away but then thought better of it.

I managed to form a few words. "Where'd you come from, puppy?" It didn't quite sound like English through my swollen lips, but the dog seemed delighted.

I stood and grabbed the post of my bed to steady myself. Excruciating.

Running my hand along the course log walls, I made it to my bedroom door. I looked down, saw that a linen robe was draped over the door's handle. I slipped it on and stepped into the hall. The dog rushed past me into the front room. I followed.

Morning light streamed through the open windows. Scott was reading by the fire.

He looked at me and his eyes widened. "What are you doing up?" He leapt to his feet. "You need to be in bed."

I motioned toward my chair.

"Are you sure?"

I shrugged, and he helped me settle. A groan escaped my lips.

"Here, let's put a blanket behind you."

It helped.

He thrust a mug into my hands. "You've got to drink some water, buddy."

I sipped, the water passing through fat lips and down my parched throat.

I worked my jaw. "What happened?"

Scott leaned close to me. "I was hoping you could tell us."

"Jacob."

He jumped up and slapped a fist into his palm. "I knew it. I told Marshal Stone, but he didn't want to listen." He turned to me. "Two days ago, your neighbor Hans found Raven wandering around without a rider and blood on the saddle, so he brought her home. You were unconscious on your porch. He ran for a doctor and then got me too."

"Thanks." The word was hard to form, but I needed to say it.

"You woke while the doctor was stitching you up." He pulled the small mirror from my wall and handed it to me. "Your chest is black and blue under those bandages. And your back took some stitches, but it's mostly a pulpy mess."

The image that stared back at me was black, yellow, torn, and unrecognizable.

"We've all taken turns watching you. Oh, and this is your dog. I named him Trevor. Hans gave him to you."

I couldn't process the information. Instead, I looked at my redheaded friend. "Thank you, Scott."

"When you're better, we're going to go downtown and show Jacob a thing or two. You with your—"

A knock rattled the front door. "Open up." A man's voice called.

Scott looked at me, his eyebrows raised. "Who is it?"

"Marshal Stone. Open up this instant."

Scott moved close to the door. "I would like to remind you, Marshal Stone, that as Philip Anderson's lawyer, the following conversation will be recorded on triplicate—"

It sounded like Stone kicked the door. "Scott, you little . . . You better open this door right now or I'll break it down."

Scott slid the bar and opened the door.

The marshal took several steps into the house, saw me, and for the second time a curse word was uttered under my roof.

Scott closed the door. "Jacob did it. Go arrest him. Throw him in jail."

The marshal frowned. He looked down at me. "Philip Anderson, I'm arresting you for assaulting Jacob Wilkes."

32

"Not funny, marshal," I mumbled.

Stone settled into Scott's seat and rested his elbows on his knees. "Jacob's got a black eye. Says it came from you." He swore again. "You look half dead."

"Got me from behind."

"Told you to watch yourself. To stay home."

I shifted, and fire washed down my back. "I know."

He shook his head. "I thought about arresting you to maybe get some sympathy on your side, but you'd probably die if I brought you in. Maybe I *should* arrest Jacob."

"We're not going to do anything." I wished we could, but there was nothing that could be done. Jacob was king of Mitchell. Like Pastor Humphrey said, he had me by the throat. I knew he would hurt Anna and her family if I pressed charges. "I don't want to give him the satisfaction."

Scott shook his head. "We've got to arrest him."

Marshal Stone didn't take his eyes off me as he spoke. "I have two deputies. Jacob's got a dozen paid guns. Philip's right. There's nothing we can do right now." He stood. "I don't like it, but I can see what's going on here. I'll check with the county sheriff to see if he can spare a man to keep an eye out on your place."

I nodded, and my head throbbed.

The marshal stood, stretched, and turned toward the front door. He pulled at a suspender and nodded at Scott.

I swallowed, trying to moisten my mouth. "Marshal. I've stayed clear of Anna. And he still almost killed me."

He swore again.

It seemed I would never get to Deadwood and see my uncle. I didn't know how he was faring with his gunshot wounds. I tried to make peace with the idea of my uncle being the head of the Maxwell gang, but it festered like a sore. Unable to do anything else, I simmered in the juices I had created. Somehow I'd gone from being a simple farmer and rancher to a gunman. Anna's family was being held hostage. Her father would lose his business. And I'd been beaten up, all because I had fallen in love with Anna.

No, that wasn't true. All because I wouldn't just tell her I loved her. I was a coward to try to tell her in a note. A note Jacob had intercepted.

As I watched Scott bend over a pail running my clothes up and down a washboard, I decided Jacob wasn't just dangerous. He was insane.

And it was time to let blame lie where it belonged, on the shoulders of the one who had caused all the violence. Jacob.

I would defend myself and let God decide what would happen. I only had one cheek to turn. And he'd hit them both.

Days went by, and I still could barely move. At night I would dream of Anna. And in the light I thought of Jacob Wilkes as I watched my horses out the window.

The moment I could whistle again, I started Trevor's training. I taught him to follow hand commands as well as whistles. It was fun to see how eager he was to please, and the dog was nearly as intelligent as my horses.

Many times Scott would greet Becky on the front porch with a kiss, and she would cook and care for me. I didn't mind her being there. I heard them talking about how Scott would survive without a job, and I pressed one hundred dollars into his hand. He didn't want to take it—I could see it in his eyes. But in the end he did. He was a true friend, and no one would hire him because of that fact. Jacob made sure of it. And Scott had much to learn before he would be useful enough to the law firm to actually get paid.

Rachel took a day off from Caroline's to care for me. With her past, I was uncomfortable, but I couldn't be picky about my nurses.

"Even though your eyes are swollen, I can see you don't trust me." Rachel had finished scrubbing the entire house, and as I sat on the edge of my chair she unrolled the bandages around my chest and back. I wore pants but still felt naked and exposed.

She let the bandages fall into a small, blood-stained pile.

With a cool hand, she pressed several bruised areas on my abdomen. "Does it still hurt?"

I winced.

She took a can of salve and basted my skin. The burning was unbearable.

"I'm sorry, Philip, but this is for your own good. You helped me, saved me, and now I'm returning the favor."

She touched a particularly deep gash and I drew back. Without a word, she continued to work. "You've taught me so much about courage and doin' the right thing. Helping you now isn't just about being nice to you because you were nice to me. It's the least I can do."

"Rachel, your life is in danger." I swallowed. "He knows you're helping me. He will hurt you to get to me."

She pretended as if she didn't hear. Instead, she kept talking and I listened. She talked about Caroline and Leroy having a strange relationship—they held hands but didn't kiss. She talked about hating men, but I didn't count since I was like a brother. And about how you can't trust gunfighters, although she could trust me. She had lived in a town full of them, after all.

When she was done I was exhausted and curled up with Trevor on my bed. I'd almost drifted off to sleep when I heard a scream.

Trevor leapt up and barked furiously. Rachel ran into the bedroom and gripped my arm. "There was a man looking in the window!" Her shrill voice was filled with panic.

I grabbed my pistol, and she helped me to my feet. We made it to the front room where she pointed toward the kitchen window. "He was a big man. There. He stared at me for a moment and then left." She still clung to my arm, and I could feel her shaking.

I peered out the window. Only weeds overtaking my garden.

There was no porch on this side of the house, so the person looking in the window would have had to be a giant. Ryan?

Rachel helped me out onto the front porch, but we saw no one. I patted Trevor as he sniffed the breeze. Nothing.

She held a hand to her chest and started to cry. "He scared me."

"Let's get inside." I stopped in my tracks. "Rachel, what happened to my wheat field?" Where tall shoots of grain had stretched to the sky, only stubble remained. The heads lay scattered on the ground. A sense of despair filled me.

She clasped my arm and pulled me inside. "A hail storm came when you were unconscious. Scott fixed the shingles on the roof that broke." She looked up at me with sad eyes. "I'm sorry."

I sighed. What else could go wrong?

As soon as my back scabbed over, I began caring for the horses. I rubbed Raven and noticed a gash on her back. Scott nodded. "Looks like she was grazed by a bullet or something. Been putting salve on it."

"Thanks, Scott."

Even though I felt weak and the sun's glare made my head ache, Scott and I walked through the horse-cropped oat grass to the firing range. I needed to keep my skills intact now more than ever. I was still working out my memories, and everything seemed mixed up between my parents and Maxwell. I would let them sort out in my mind as I fired at the target.

I gave a low whistle, and Trevor loped behind us. He veered into the field and barked at the growing foals, frolicking back and forth. The sight warmed my heart. I couldn't wait to start training the babies when they got older.

A wagon rolled down the lane and approached my cabin. Scott stopped shooting. "Your ride's here."

"Ride?"

"Becky and I want to take you to Caroline's. Our treat. She and Leroy want to see you."

"I'm supposed to stay on the farm."

Scott lifted a hand. "Nonsense. You're going crazy. And besides . . ." He hesitated. "Business hasn't been so good for her. People aren't eating there like they used to."

"Wouldn't me going there hurt her business more?"

Scott pulled me toward the wagon. "Any damage to Caroline's reputation, you did already. Let's go."

The bumpy ride was tortuous, but the company at the end was good for me. I sat next to Leroy, and Scott and Becky sat across from us. Caroline settled into a chair at the end of the table. Rachel served us, a wide grin on her face.

"Caroline, are you feeling okay?" I huffed. Perhaps I would always say *okay* now.

She nodded. "Between worryin' about you and the restaurant here, I've been feeling tired lately. Rachel suggested I take the day off tomorrow."

Rachel filled our glasses with water. "I demanded it."

"Good." I took a sip. Caroline's eyes were swollen, and her face pale. I had an idea. "Why don't you take the rest of today off, too? I can cook."

They all burst into laughter.

I frowned. "So, no?"

After a brief silence Leroy said, "Don't let her go." His

abrupt change of subject made everyone jump. "You and Anna had a good thing. Don't let her go."

I flinched. "I know, Leroy. I'm trying to get her back."

"'Cause when I was in the war, I left someone I loved here in Mitchell. Firesteel it was called back then."

Even Rachel paused to listen. Caroline leaned forward.

"Honor, glory, all that horse manure . . . I joined the infantry to impress a girl named Charity. I was sixteen. While I was gone I got hit in the leg and back, and everybody thought I was dead when I didn't come home right away. So my brother married her. When I got home, I wouldn't talk to him or her." He cleared his throat. "She died giving birth to a baby. The baby died too."

Caroline took his hand.

He sucked in a deep breath. "I don't go to church 'cause my brother's your preacher."

"Pastor Humphrey is your brother?" For a moment I forgot my aching body.

Leroy nodded. "He don't go by our last name. It's Jenkins. I told him he ain't fit to be a Jenkins, and he honored what I mouthed off to him. I'm tellin' you that because you and Anna had a good thing. Don't give up on her."

I glanced at Scott. "Someone once told me love is worth fighting for. And I'm going to do just that."

After another week I felt well enough to weed the garden. I was wearing a linen shirt. The wind whipped the cloth against my bandaged skin and throbbing muscles.

I was relieved when the hoe slid easily through the soil and the weeds toppled quickly. I didn't have the strength to chop through crusted dirt. My satisfaction at doing a job, any job, kept me whistling. Trevor looked up from where he played near the river, saw I wasn't calling him, and returned to his play. A bird chattered at me from the corner of my house, and I tried to return his song.

The garden was a mess. Corn, squash, and beans that had

been damaged by the hail storm should have been harvested by now.

Working with a gun belt strapped around my waist was awkward, but I'd never be caught by surprise again. Ever. I knew next time it would be more than a beating. Probably a bullet. I kept moving as I worked the garden. I bent low, making myself a hard target for a rifle to hit.

A movement caught my eye. I looked toward the river at the thicket to see if the sapling would shake again but saw nothing. I glanced at Trevor, who leapt high into the air to snatch a butterfly and missed.

Maybe I was too jumpy. I turned back to my hoe and weeds and worked on a particularly tough thistle. Out of the corner of my eye, I saw movement again, and this time I whistled for Trevor. When he looked my way, I flashed an *L* with my thumb and pointed a finger, telling him to move to the left. I'd not used his training for anything but play, so I was interested to see how he'd do now.

I slipped the loop off my revolver's hammer.

The dog trotted fifty feet to my left and kept pace as I moved forward. His nose remained high in the air, sniffing. The wind was still, so I doubted he'd pick up a scent.

I made my way over to the sapling, and saw no one. The grass was bent as if someone had been lying down, but with so much foliage, there was no way of seeing tracks. A county sheriff guarding me, perhaps?

I called Trevor and we pushed through the bramble, thorns catching at my shirt and Trevor's fur. We reached the riverbank. Trevor sniffed tracks in the mud following the river, and I leaned over to study them. The footprints were small, the boots delicate. A woman.

We followed her trail to a small clearing where I guessed a horse had been tied. There was a pile of manure, not spread around as if a horse was passing through. I dropped to a knee and traced a clear track with a finger. No two horses made the same print. Horse shoes always played differently against the dirt depending on the horse's gait. This track belonged to Alita. There was no doubt.

Anna had been watching me.

I looked up to the top of the ravine and saw a rider gallop around a bend, disappearing from sight.

My heart warmed and then ached.

33

For the first time since I'd been hurt the ride into town felt good. Morning sun warmed my back and calmed its healing itch. My bruises were yellowing as the color drained from them. Best of all, the swelling was gone, so I looked more human than I had in weeks.

Raven was spoiling for a run and I didn't care to be caught by surprise on the ride into Mitchell, so we galloped all the way to town. I wanted to tell my friends I was returning to Deadwood tomorrow.

It was easy to forget Marshal Stone's warning not to come to town. The last visit to Caroline's had gone without incident.

As I entered Mitchell, we hurried past Wilkes's bank. I had as much right to travel the main thoroughfare as any other citizen, but I wasn't going to push it.

I turned the corner. As we did, Raven and I nearly knocked Anna off her feet. She stopped, her eyes wide as I hauled back on the reins.

Her beauty wasn't marred by the dark circles around her eyes or the frown on her face. My eyes didn't leave hers as I quickly dismounted.

"Anna." I was surprised at the catch in my voice.

"Philip, I can't speak to you." While her words were harsh, the haunted look in her eyes seemed to ask me to take her into my arms.

I wanted to lift her onto the back of my horse and ride away with her. But then Jacob's words slammed into my brain. *I will kill Beth.* I scanned the streets. A handful of people visited on the opposite corner, and a woman with two children crossed the street. No sign of Jacob's men, but that didn't mean they weren't there. Watching me.

I knew I couldn't touch Anna, couldn't speak to her. I quietly uttered, "I love you, Anna."

"Philip . . ." Her voice was deep and throaty. "I love you, too." She touched my face. "Look at what they've done to you." Her eyes were moist. She traced a scar along my cheek. "I'm so sorry, so sorry about Caroline."

I stiffened. "What do you mean? What about Caroline?"

Anna held a hand to her mouth. "Philip, ride to the restaurant. Quickly, please." She stepped close. "Be careful. He's asked me to marry him . . ." She stepped past me and hurried around the corner.

I longed to follow her, but worry drove me and I let Raven take me to Caroline's Kitchen. We came close to running down a man crossing the street. He looked up at me annoyed, but his protest was cut off. Being the town gunman came with privileges.

As I neared the restaurant, I saw Scott on his horse. He saw me and stopped, alighted, and tied the reins to the hitching post. I dismounted before Raven halted. "What happened?"

Scott's eyes were puffy and red. "Caroline died last night." He brought a hand to his head. "I was on my way to tell you."

I grasped the rail.

Scott rattled on about how Rachel found Caroline lying on the kitchen floor that morning, how the doctor said her heart gave out, how the restaurant belonged to Rachel now. But those were mere words. I wanted to pull my gun and kill something. To make everything right. Now. No more waiting.

"Talk to Rachel, Philip. She thinks going back to Deadwood

is her only option. She won't believe us about the restaurant being hers."

"Where is she?"

"In the house."

I followed Scott into the restaurant, empty now except for Becky who sat on a stool, quietly weeping. Scott sat down beside her and placed an arm around her. I went through the kitchen, out the back door, and across the alley to Caroline's house. I knocked on the door. All I heard from inside was crying, so I opened the door.

Rachel's hair was undone, her face blotchy. She sat at Caroline's desk, a handkerchief in her hands, staring at the floorboards.

She looked up at me. "No, no. You can't make me go back. I won't go. I will die first."

"Rachel, no one wants you to go back."

A new round of sobs. She threw herself into my arms. "Please don't let them come and take me back. I won't go. Please, Philip."

"No one's going to take you, Rachel. Get ahold of yourself." The shock was wearing away, and the full weight of Caroline's death replaced the numb feeling inside me. She had been like a mother to me.

Rachel pulled away and wiped her nose. She sat back in the chair. "I can't do this, Philip. I can't stay and try to fill her shoes. But I can't go back, either."

"Rachel, look at me. Here's what's going to happen. You'll be closed for a few days after the funeral. And then you'll open back up. The restaurant is yours. Caroline has no family and would've wanted it this way. You'll stay here and you'll succeed. No one's going to take you back to Deadwood."

"I don't think I can do it." She put a fist against her forehead.

"With God's help you can."

She took several breaths, each one slower than the last. Finally, she nodded.

"Let's go back to the restaurant. The best thing we can do now is spend time with friends." I stood. "I think Leroy is going to need us."

Caroline had once told me she felt sorry for her pallbearers, because they wouldn't be able to lift the casket. But when Scott, Leroy, a few loyal patrons, and I lowered her body into the grave, she didn't seem all that heavy.

Pastor Humphrey talked about Caroline for a few moments, explaining that she believed in the Lord but didn't attend church because she wanted to give the town a good place to eat after the service.

A gentle breeze rustled the cottonwoods, and the sun warmed my hair. The dew was almost gone, but the fresh morning remained. I looked up into the sky and knew Caroline was in heaven. I would see her again, but I would miss her on this earth.

I glanced at her tombstone. *Died September, 1887. Heaven enjoys her company and her cooking.*

When Pastor Humphrey and Leroy hugged, I swiped at my eyes.

On the way home I stopped at my new bank, the last vestige of finance in town that dared compete with the Wilkes establishment. I pulled ten dollars from my account and then stopped at Jon Pole's Saddlery.

"I need new reins for Franklin, Jon. I've cut my last ones, and I'm ready to clear more land."

He rubbed his stained hands on his canvas apron. "Philip, you know how much I like you. By golly, the whole town respects you and is proud of you. But, you see, I've got a family. And debts . . ."

"Jon, say what you've got to say."

"I can't sell nothing to you, Philip. Or my loan will come due. And—"

I slammed the door on my way out.

I focused on rubbing Raven down after I finally made it home. The rest of the herd grazed in the field. I didn't notice the riders approaching my barn. It was not until they rode across my yard toward the corral that I saw Jacob flanked by six of his men.

Behind him, dark clouds roiled. A thunderstorm was brewing.

His spotless, expensive-looking suit sported a bulge near the breast, undoubtedly a pistol. Mine sat on my hip. I could shoot him now. And four of his men.

"Jacob, you're going to get caught in the storm." He didn't belong on my dirt farm and was not welcome near my horses or my dog.

"Philip." He dismounted lightly, any hint of a limp gone. Both hands rested on his cane. He leaned over it, studying me. "Is there somewhere we can talk?" he asked. "Perhaps a cool drink is in order?"

"I'm fine right here."

The fake smile never left his face. "I came to discuss the differences we might have and how we might set them aside."

"On your terms or mine?"

"Perhaps we can come to a mutual understanding that would be advantageous to both."

"A business arrangement, you mean."

Jacob picked up his cane and studied the end. He twisted the shaft so that the handle seemed to reflect the clouds. "Philip, I think you understand I enjoy the finer things in life. I also enjoy rewarding those around me with worldly possessions. The people of Mitchell deserve to prosper, so I have made it my life's purpose to procure businesses, make money, and to dispense wealth throughout the city in the interest of upgrading the lives of those who share my vision.

"Mitchell is preparing for major change, both economic and political. You're not inept, Philip. You understand these things. You've created a name for yourself not only in Mitchell but in all the Dakota Territory—and soon the entire United States—bringing attention to our humble town. Both you and I possess the skills to take Mitchell to new heights, to lead the town and its people to unfathomable riches as the state capitol and railroad hub."

He paused.

I said nothing. Instead, I set down the curry brush and took a step forward. The smell of Jacob's cologne hovered in the stiff breeze.

"I have contacted the railroad, and they plan on adding rails from Yankton to Mitchell. We've been working together to make our fair city the center of trade and commerce for the territory. I have been chosen by the people to lead them into this new era through my natural gifts. I need support from lesser leaders, such as yourself, to realize this dream for a greater Mitchell."

I'd never heard him talk this much, like he was making a speech.

I set my boot on a short bench. "You want my support?"

"You know of the men I hire to help with chores around the city." He indicated the men around him with both hands.

"They were there for our little meeting outside the woods." I heard a distant rumble of thunder.

Jacob waved his hand. "I'm willing to let bygones be bygones. Those men protect my interests, and those who might hurt Mitchell are reminded of the greater good. My men are paid handsomely for their loyalty. Jeb is intelligent, Ryan has brawn, and the rest are average men. But you, Philip, you embody all those qualities in one man. I'm offering you a job. Come work for me."

I straightened. "You want to hire me?"

"I pay well. Eighty dollars a month plus incentives for work well done. That is more than Marshal Stone makes. Imagine it, Philip. You could live here, and with the money I pay you could expand this tiny farm into a ranch stocked full of Arabians. I can make you marshal of Mitchell, if that's what you want. Either way, it's an opportunity you can ill afford to pass up."

"Your cane, I think, made my decision for me long ago."

"Like I said, let's let bygones be bygones."

Incredible. I could control Jacob's empire with my gun, perhaps even wrestle it from his hands. It would be possible to keep a close eye on Anna and have more opportunities to speak with her.

"And Anna?"

"She is mine. She has chosen me, and the sooner you understand that fact the easier life will be for you."

I chuckled. "No. You give Anna to me, and I might consider working for you." It disturbed me to speak of Anna as a possession that could be passed back and forth, but I would speak his language.

His brow lowered. "I think you should take this offer, Anderson. You don't know all the powers that can work against you."

"What powers are those, Wilkes? You're just a bully who gets his thrills from stomping on people. No, I won't work for you."

Jacob's face reddened and he spun on a heel, his limp returning. He turned to stab his finger at me. "Your vision is obviously limited by your lack of education. In the future, remember I offered you an escape from the possible trouble that may come your way. Now I can no longer protect you." He mounted his horse. "I've given you too many opportunities, Anderson. No more." He lifted his chin. "I need to get back to town. I have an important dinner engagement with a beautiful woman. Her soft kisses await. And after I take that woman home, I'll spend the evening with Anna."

He spurred his horse and joined his riders. I crossed my arms and gripped my biceps to keep from pulling my gun.

I didn't move until he was well out of range.

Lightning ripped across the sky. Unfortunately, it didn't strike Jacob Wilkes.

34

I couldn't keep Jacob's strange proposal from spinning in my mind. Who tries to kill a man and then invites him to join his posse?

I stood by my earlier observations. Jacob was insane.

Trevor growled and I jerked out of bed. My senses switched to high alert. With stealthy movements, I slipped a shirt over my head, pulled on my trousers, and strapped on my gun belt.

I made Trevor stay in the bedroom, and I hurried into the dark front room to peer out the window. Through the moonless September night, I thought I saw movement on the lane that led to my house. I jogged down the hallway and left by the back door without a sound. Trevor whimpered inside.

Cold air goose-bumped my skin as I crept around the perimeter of the house. I felt open and exposed. The brilliant stars seemed brighter than I'd ever seen. A thick band of white stretched through part of the sky.

I passed by the corral and settled into a depression by the lane. Moisture seeped from the ground into my skin.

Four riders, their outlines just barely visible, approached. I pulled my gun.

Their voices drifted over the quiet night air. The smell of fresh rain still permeated the darkness. In the East, clouds lit up with lightning.

"Don't know why you're doin' it this way."

"Shut up." This voice was deep and powerful, one I thought I recognized. "You're not good enough. Besides, he has a personal interest in the matter."

"I don't like it, neither."

I let them ride past, just inches from me. Their horses were skittish and could surely see or smell me. Without a sound, I climbed onto the road. "Hands in the air."

The men swore.

A voice boomed. "That you, Anderson?"

"Marshal Hill? Are you coming to arrest me?"

"Got a guilty conscious or something?" I could barely make out his shadow, but I saw him lower his hands. "We need to talk. Not a lot of time."

"Coffee?"

"Always time for coffee."

I led them to the front porch where they dismounted. Hill turned to the others. "Keep a sharp lookout."

"Yes, sir."

I stepped inside, Hill behind me. I let my dog out of the bedroom, and he approached the marshal growling. I motioned with my palm flat, and he calmed and sniffed Hill who settled into a chair.

I started up the fire.

Hill leaned forward. "You heard us?"

I glanced at Hill. "Barnum's Circus out there." His handsome mustache was surrounded by unshaven stubble. I smelled the outdoors on him. "How long have you been on the trail?"

"Week or so. Look, Anderson, you're coming with us. We're trailing the Maxwell Gang, and they've split. A handful broke from the main pack and headed your direction. We broke trail and came to warn you."

"How do you know they're after me?"

He stood and grabbed the pitcher of water from me. "Get packed, and I'll tell you on the road."

"I can't go."

"Important business?"

"I haven't made coffee yet."

He pointed toward the fireplace. "I'll take care of coffee. Get moving."

I started for my bedroom. The edge in his voice was sharp enough to convey something was serious.

"I can't protect you and hunt the gang if you're here. But you've got to hurry."

I did as he asked, and while I threw a few items in my bedroll, he talked.

"The Maxwell Gang robbed a bank in Rapid City."

I paused. "It wasn't me."

He smirked. "After the robbery, the gang split. So the posse divided up. Your old friend Running Deer is heading to the hills after the main group. I followed this band to Mitchell."

I threw a few extra changes of clothes into my saddlebags. But then the look on the marshal's face gave me reason to stop.

"We found a note, Philip, partially burnt. The gang is being paid by someone in Mitchell to do a job here. I'm guessing we both know who's paying them and what the job is. I'd arrest him but I can't prove he wrote the letter, and so far he hasn't done anything wrong until he actually kills you."

I considered telling him about Jacob's offer to join him yesterday, but he didn't need to know. It struck me as typical Jacob Wilkes—get me comfortable and then kill me. Hire the gang whose leader I put behind bars. My death would look like revenge. It was smart.

I shoved all the ammunition I owned into another saddlebag. "Marshal, you think if we can connect Jacob to the gang he could go to jail?"

"That's the idea." He felt the pot. "Lukewarm, but it'll have to do." He poured the coffee into two mugs. "There's one part you might disagree with."

I rolled up the bedroll and tied it. "What's that?"

"You may have to shoot people."

"Already done that."

"No, that's not the part. I can't let you keep shooting people as a citizen. Too much paperwork. I'm going to have to deputize you." He tossed a piece of metal through the air. "Here you go."

I caught the star midair.

"There are eight we're up against, Philip. We'll follow these guys until reinforcements arrive or we meet up with Running Deer."

"Of course I'm coming. One condition—"

"I'll pay you a dollar a day, food's my expense."

"No, not money. When it comes time to interrogate, let me be there."

He smiled and drank his coffee. "Now you're talking."

I took a quick vow to protect the Constitution—a document I'd only read once—and hauled my gear outside.

"Your horses are going to town. Can they be led or do we need to drive them?"

"We can lead them. I'll be riding Raven."

"Marshal Stone owes you a few favors. So I'm betting he'll find a safe place for them along with your dog."

It was an easy matter to lasso the horses and pull them to town. The foals trailed their mothers. But it was difficult to say good-bye to Trevor. I'd grown attached to the pup. Marshal Stone promised to care for him and the horses.

As morning light grayed at our backs, Hill returned to the trail. Eight outlaws left a wide track—easy to follow. We followed the tracks again just outside of town, heading straight back to my farm. We looked over the ravine and saw nothing. No horses, no killers, no movement.

The front door of my house was now open.

The other men split off to check the barn and outhouse. I entered my cabin, gun at the ready, and noticed several knives missing from the kitchen. I rushed to my bedroom, looked under my bed for my red box from my parents' wagon. It was still there.

My Bible lay on the mantle. I hadn't packed it. Scolding myself, I grabbed it.

I closed the door as I left, and with a sigh, glanced at Hill. He shook his head. He was right. The gang had been after me.

"They're gone," I said.

I leaned on a pole that supported the porch roof. "We're close. We'll get them."

His horse pranced for a moment, unsettled by our nerves. He calmed him and looked at me. "We're going to track them down, but nothing stupid. We can't take in eight men."

I tapped a foot against the floor boards, thinking. This wasn't going to be easy. I mounted Raven, and her energy pulsed through my body. She was as ready as I was to get moving.

The tracks skirted the now-empty pasture. We followed the fence along the edge of the ravine until it turned left, and the trail headed straight for the copse of trees. I pulled my revolver, unsure if the outlaws were hiding in wait. The others, taking my cue, did the same.

We rode into the small clearing in the center of the trees. The grass had been worn down to dirt from the constant vigil of Jacob's men. I'd spied them in the area before, and they had made no attempt to hide. They simply camped here on my property.

I scanned the ground and spotted something. "Stop."

The others instantly paused. I slid off Raven and holstered my gun. I took a few steps forward and dropped to a knee to check the track. I traced it with my finger, thinking.

I could tell someone heavy had mounted the horse and ridden off with the bunch, the impressions sinking deep in the dirt. I walked closer to the marshal, dread filling me. "Alita's been here. I know one of these tracks are hers."

"Alita?"

"They have Anna's horse. I hope they don't have Anna."

35

M arshal, I'm riding back to town to find Anna."
He looked away, tipped back his hat, and swore. "That's
a mistake. Time's important here. The gang will be heading
back to the Black Hills. We've got to follow."

"I have to know if they've got Anna." I mounted Raven.
"It'll eat me up. You know that."

He clenched his teeth and shook his head. "All right."

I squeezed Raven's sides with my legs.

She flew up the ravine and across the prairie.

I slowed her as we rode through Mitchell. First, we
stopped at Scott's house. I knocked on his door, and he
answered wearing a pair of linen pants. He ran fingers through
disheveled hair. "Philip? Isn't a bit early?"

"Maybe for you lawyers. Look, I need to know if Anna's
in town. Can you check her house and the mill?"

He looked confused for a moment but then nodded.
"What's happening?" He reached behind the door, grabbed a
shirt, and slipped it on.

"The Maxwell Gang's after me. A posse is tracking them,
but I need to make sure Anna's here and not with them."

He nodded. "Give me five minutes and I'll join you."

I stepped inside and lowered my head. "You can't go with me. I just need you to check on Anna." My friends were so eager to get involved, so keen to help.

"You aren't leaving me behind on this one."

"You need to stay." I struggled for excuses. "I'm afraid Jacob will go after Rachel or Anna, maybe even Becky, just to get at me. Please stay here and protect them. Please."

He kicked a chair, and it flew across the room. "Why, Philip? Why's all this have to happen? None of it's fair. Especially not to you."

I had no answer.

Scott gripped the back of the other chair, his knuckles white.

I took a deep breath. His loyalty was weakening me, but I needed to be logical. "You make this easier for me by staying. Thanks, buddy."

"I hate it. I want to pull my rifle out and shoot people." He looked at me and must have seen concern on my face. He stammered. "I mean I want to shoot bad people. Ones that deserve it. Not just anyone." He rubbed his forehead. "Well, maybe one person, in the arm."

"You can go on the next posse. I promise. Will you check on Anna?"

He took a deep breath. "Right away."

It took him ten minutes, which felt like an eternity while I waited in his tiny shack.

He returned.

"Anna?"

"At home. I made an excuse to talk to Mr. Johnston and saw her inside."

Relief swept across my soul. I mounted Raven. "Scott, protect them. I don't know how long I'll be gone."

"Don't do anything I wouldn't do."

I tipped my hat. "Like killing people?"

He smiled, and I thundered off to catch up with Hill and the posse. I was sure Anna didn't even know Alita was missing.

The outlaws' trail led straight for the Black Hills. We rode all day and into the blazing sunset.

I turned to Hill, slumped in the saddle. "What makes a man want to be a marshal?"

The excitement of the morning had turned to the dull monotony of tracking. All day, I'd stared at the tracks on the ground. Where they went, I would go.

Marshal Hill shifted in his saddle. "Kit Carson talked me into it. I worked the Pinkerton Agency for a time, but Carson told me there was more good to be done as a U.S. marshal, and I listened. Never looked back."

"What was Carson like?"

"Good man. Honest with people but even better with himself. 'Fessed up when he made a mistake, like hating on certain Indians. Some deserve hating, like any men, but not all. And he saw that he was doing just that, hating all of them." Hill set both hands on the saddle horn. "I respected that."

"He kept his calm when the lead started flying?"

The marshal smiled. "There's some men that seem a cut above the rest in a fight, as if the world slows down for them and they can move quickly, making the right decisions, out-guessing the enemy."

I pointed toward the setting sun, the direction we were heading. "Too bad none of these men are like Carson."

He lowered his hat to block out the sun. "They'll kill you faster than a rattlesnake bites." He gave me a sideways glance.

"Then why do you seem so confident?"

He chuckled. "Because they're not as dangerous as you."

36

Raven crossed the endless plains without complaint. I knew when a horse was ready to stop and rest. But my jet mare, with her watchful dark eyes, did everything I asked of her and more.

It was the men I rode with that slowed us down. Raven was as eager to push through the night as I was. Marshal Hill would do it. But the other three were played out. So we lost time.

The next day was the same, and on the third day late in the afternoon dark hills finally rose on the horizon. The grass became scarce, and we followed the trail into the Badlands. Dust choked the canyon walls, the steep cliffs holding in the suffocating powder. I pulled a bandana from my saddlebag and tied it around my face.

The Badlands received very little rain, but when it did rain water came in heavy torrents. Cliffs had been eroded away so that dry gorges ran up the sides of the canyon walls, acting as funnels for the downpours and creating arms that reached into the canyon. Watermarks and erosion made it obvious.

I took off my hat and rubbed sweat from my brow. Above

the desert ravines blue sky stretched from canyon top to canyon top.

The walls, as high as the hotel I stayed at in Deadwood, were streaked with white and red lines layered on top of each other to create magnificent patterns. Some walls reached a pinnacle, while others stretched into flatlands above us. I turned to Hill. "You know, I read there are dinosaur bones in the Badlands."

Hill's mustache pushed his bandana out. "I doubt the Maxwell Gang is sightseeing. Keep a sharp lookout. I've got a bad feeling."

I took a swig from my canteen. The metallic water was warm, but it quenched my thirst. In the distance I could see a wavy mirage that looked as if water was rushing toward us. I studied the declining ridges that ended in the canyon. They would be perfect for an ambush.

The deputy next to me guzzled from his canteen then wiped his mouth. What was his name? Pat.

I heard a sickening *thwack*. Pat dropped his canteen, curled in the saddle, and slipped off the side of his horse. He slammed onto the canyon floor.

Gunfire echoed against the steep walls. Puffs of dust rose before us followed by more gunshots.

Raven reared, but I held on tightly to the saddle.

The others turned and galloped the way we came, leaving the squirming deputy on the ground. Dust from the horses engulfed us, making it hard for the enemy to see us. But the gunfire continued.

"Easy, girl." I pulled Raven's head to one side until she stopped, her training overtaking her instinct to flee. I jumped from her back, grabbed the deputy, and with a grunt threw him over the saddle. Then I seized Raven's reins and sprinted for a ravine, creating natural protection. Bullets sprayed around us, and I fought the panic rising in my heart.

We darted into the crevice. There was just enough room for Raven, and I hid behind the thick stone shelf. I slipped the deputy from the saddle. Blood streamed from his belly and he shook violently.

It was only a matter of time for the man.

I tied Raven to a gnarled log and pulled my rifle from its scabbard. Before I tended Pat, I checked the knot on Raven's reins one last time. It wouldn't take much for her slip back to the canyon and take a bullet. She tugged at the reins, her natural urge to run as powerful as mine.

The deputy's eyes rolled backward, and I crawled to his side. "Hold on, fellow. We'll take these guys and then get help. But you have to hang on." His breath came in short gasps, and his eyes closed.

I moved to the edge of our shelter and peeked out. The dust cleared, and I could see more ravines like the one I hid in further down the canyon. Two small flashes of light caught my eye before bullets slammed into the rocks in front of me. I ducked and covered my head.

"Philip!" I heard Marshal Hill's voice from behind me. "How many do you make out?"

I shouted backed. "Two, on the left."

"We see two on the right."

Four. Better than all eight.

"How's Pat?"

I glanced at the deputy again. His breathing was even, but he was slipping away. "Not good. Gut shot."

Crawling along the dusty gravel, I repositioned myself along the ravine wall and pointed the Winchester forward.

The marshal kept talking. "How are you fixed?"

"Pinned down."

A man rose from his position and darted ahead. I fired, and he leapt back to cover. Perhaps I should have brought Scott along, after all.

"God help us." My whisper came without thinking.

I noticed the ravine I was in wound up the canyon, but it wasn't as steep as the others. A plan formed in my mind.

"Marshal." I lowered my voice. "Can you hear me?"

"Yep."

"I'm flanking. Don't shoot me."

I heard his voice, and then he and the two deputies began a barrage of steady fire.

Raven whinnied as I scrambled to my feet. A quick check on the deputy told me no change. First I'd take care of the outlaws, and then I could help him.

I reloaded my rifle, took off my bandana and hat, and started up the gully. I crawled through the cover and tried not to raise any dust. Dead brush tickled my skin as I went, and then even those plants disappeared. Sweat poured into my eyes, and I had to stop and wipe it away. I heard the gunbattle continue behind me.

I edged over the top, and a blessed breeze ruffled my hair and cooled my wet skin. The smells of sulphur and dust faded and the fresh scents of prairie returned. It took a moment to scout the outlaws' position. I realized I could run across the narrow ridge without being seen.

My apprehension grew as I pressed forward over small tufts of brown grass and gravel. The falling sun streaked across the white rock, and I shielded my eyes from the glare.

I approached the enemy's ravine and stopped in the shadow of a tall, chimney-shaped rock.

About twenty feet away an outlaw stepped out onto the crest, saw me, and lifted the muzzle of his rifle. I dropped to one knee as he shot from the hip. The bullet passed overhead. When he stopped to work the bolt, I lifted my rifle and I fired.

The bullet smacked his chest. He fell backward and didn't move.

I cocked the rifle's lever, and the bullet jammed. I looked at the chamber—caked in dust. There was no time to clean it.

I tossed it aside as I sprinted forward and grasped for the dead man's gun, but the stock had snapped from the man's fall, his body smashing the weapon.

My Smith and Wesson was the last option.

The dead man had tried flanking us, as I was about to do to his comrades. Would they be watching? I saw his hat on the ground beside him and grabbed it.

Hopefully they'd just glance at me, see the hat, and think I was one of them.

I edged along.

The outlaws returned Marshal Hill's fire from behind the

natural benches. One was stationed below me, another two across the way.

A strange sensation struck me as I climbed down the ravine. I could see my shadow descending onto the canyon floor, and I pictured a tall, muscular man with slate-gray eyes and dark hair, a brown vest with a star over a denim shirt, a pistol strapped to his hips. My boots crunched on blanched gravel, the sound smothered by gunfire. When I got behind the outlaw, I pulled my revolver and fanned the hammer back. "Throw down your rifle."

He lifted his head, looked at me, and carefully raised his hands. Still crouched, he let the rifle slip from his fingers. But then he reached for his pistol.

I fired. The bullet ripped into his chest. He hit the dirt wall then slowly sagged to the ground.

I'd killed my second man in two minutes. My hands should have been trembling, but as I pulled the spent cartridge and dropped in two bullets so that my pistol carried six shots, my movements were steady.

I stepped into the center of the canyon floor and crossed the short expanse to the other side. Marshal Hill and the others stopped firing. The two outlaws continued shooting. They apparently hadn't noticed their fellow bandits were dead.

Pistol in one hand, I tossed the outlaw's hat I'd borrowed between the two men. They spun, eyes wide.

"Drop your guns. The fight's over."

They glanced at my eyes first and then the badge.

"Yeah, I'm the one you're after, the one who put Maxwell in jail. And you're going to join him. Unbuckle your holsters and come with me."

Both men had long, greasy hair and tangled beards. Their clothes were covered in dirt.

One man spat, and they both reached for their weapons.

I fanned the hammer with my left hand and fired with my right. In an instant, I sent all six shots into their filthy bodies.

They dropped to the ground.

I stood and watched them die.

Marshal Hill came running, but I held my revolver on the

two dead men. I searched for remorse and found none, shocked by the ease at which I'd just killed four men.

Hill kicked one of the outlaws with the toe of his boot. "You can lower your gun. They're no threat now."

I reloaded, thumbing one shell at a time as I continued to search my soul for feelings. I scanned the area for their horses and saw them tied to an old stump down the canyon. No Alita.

The other deputies raced around the corner in a cloud of dust. They looked at me and then at the bodies. "What in tarnation happened?" asked one of them.

"How's Pat?"

The other deputy waved his hand. "Gone."

I walked away, Marshal Hill close behind.

I could see the deputy's body before we got to him. I kicked a small rock across the floor of the canyon. "Those lamebrained idiots." I turned back to look at the deputies.

Was I angry because I had killed men or because Pat died? I decided it didn't matter. "I'm going to scout ahead. Why don't you come with me?"

He gave a sad smile. "I better take care of the bodies. You ride on ahead and find a good camp."

"What? Why are you grinning?"

The marshal lowered his head. "These men picked the wrong man to deal with."

I passed the two deputies as they rifled through the outlaws' pockets. It took a moment to find my hat and jammed rifle, then I pressed on, alone.

I was relieved when the canyon opened up and Raven and I rode across prairie again. With a wary eye on the trail, I caught a glimpse of Alita's prints every now and again mixed in with the other horses the outlaws were riding.

How had my life come to this, I wondered. One moment I was about to marry the woman of my dreams, and the next I was a lone gunman. How could God have turned my life in this direction?

The men I killed had murdered Pat, and if I hadn't stopped them, they would have killed the rest of us. They needed to die. I just hated being the instrument that did the killing. It was one thing to think about taking a life and quite another to actually do it.

Did God want me to kill those men?

I needed to protect the innocent. Anna and Beth.

What had Pastor Humphrey said? *Draw. Let God decide who is alive and who is dead.* I would need to think more on that.

The trail continued toward the Black Hills, and after a short stretch of prairie, rose into the mountains. It was strange how quickly the mountains popped up from the flatlands.

If the remaining gang turned around, from their vantage point above me they would see a single rider on their trail.

I didn't care. There were only four of them now.

37

The morning mountain air seeped into my bedroll. I shivered.

I heard movement in the camp but refused to open my eyes. It was Marshal Hill rolling out of bed.

I dreamed of Anna, her bonnet as bright blue as the sky. Thoughts of death and blood tried to break through the vision, but I held on to her image. I lay back and she leaned over me and smiled.

Something moved close to my bedroll, and I opened my eyes. Instead of Anna, Marshal Hill hovered above me, his black mustache enormous and his beady eyes sharp. "Time to ride."

I pushed him away. "Too close to me."

His eyes held amusement. "I bet you let that little woman close to you."

Anna's passionate kiss flashed through my mind. I sat up and rubbed my head. "Yeah, but she's a better shot than you. So if she wants to get close, I let her."

Marshal Hill grunted and turned toward a small pile of wood. "That's the great secret." He leaned down with a match and struck it on a nearby rock. "We don't allow women in a posse because the outlaws would never stand a chance." He lit the kindling. "Women are natural killers."

I stretched, grabbed my boots, and turned them over. Empty, no snakes. "That I believe." I slipped on a boot. "Can you imagine a whole posse of women on your trail?"

The marshal grunted. "Don't know if I'd keep running or let them catch me."

The fire snapped and popped in the tiny alcove I'd found the night before. Trees stretched high above us, and the smoke from the fire wafted up through the pines. I rubbed my sore backside.

The coffee was hot before the other two began to stir. Marshal Hill pointed his cup at them. "I'm sending them to Rapid City with the bodies. There's a reward for every member of the gang. But mostly I want to get them out of the fight. They're no good."

I took a cup from my saddlebag and filled it with coffee. I sampled the black drink. "This is horrible."

"Took me fifty years of practice to make it that bad." He took a careful swallow. "Just how I like it."

I motioned with my thumb at the bodies. "You suppose we can keep my part in this quiet?"

He grunted again. "With those two around? There's no possible way. You're going to have to own up to this as well."

"I want this goose chase to end."

"Yep, I'm with you on that. We're to meet Running Deer in Hill City around dusk."

After a quick breakfast of warmed bacon and beans, the marshal fired a few instructions to the two deputies and they rode away. I fixed the jam in my rifle while the marshal kept a keen lookout.

We broke from the outlaws' trail and rode for Hill City. The path we followed wound through the mountains, up and down hills, past mines and shacks, and along a low cliff. After the desert, this felt like Eden.

Around midday Marshal Hill headed toward a sod house. A creek wrapped around the tiny home, and I wondered what it would be like to live in such an idyllic setting. A few drops of rain splattered against my hat, and I looked up. A large, dark cloud hung overhead. The distant sound of thunder echoed against the cliff that rose on the other side of the creek.

Marshal Hill dismounted. "Hello? Anyone home?" He stepped up and pounded on the door.

No sound.

He pulled his horse into a small lean-to and motioned for me to do the same.

"I'm going to make some coffee." He slung his saddlebag over his shoulder. "Running Deer should be here in a bit."

"I'll make the coffee this time."

The sod house was a single room and small, but the bed and utensils fit neatly around the walls.

Marshal Hill looked up from the tiny potbelly stove. "He won't mind us using his house while he's gone. I'll leave a dollar."

"You know him?"

The marshal shook his head and struck a match.

I sat on the end of the bed. Rain pelted the grass roof and thunder shook the ground. I looked down at my hands. How could I have killed those men?

Hill grunted. "I know that look."

I swallowed and tried to force a smile.

He crossed his arms. "Sometimes we've got to do the thing we hate most. Almost preordained. God seems to enjoy making sure there's something we have to do that makes us uncomfortable."

I cocked my head. He didn't make any sense.

He took a step closer. "Look, some men are begging to be killed, and no amount of teaching in jail or Bible thumping in church is gonna change 'em. It becomes a matter of getting them before they kill too many. Who knows how many lives you saved yesterday?"

I leaned back and watched as he opened the door and held the coffee pot out to collect rainwater running off the roof. "After I lost the need for revenge for my parents' murder, the idea of using my guns as anything other than sport was detestable. But I know those boys deserved killing. It was us or them."

I forced myself to dig into the real problem. "I think I made gunplay sacred in my head as a boy. I know I'm fast and accurate. But it's an art, and . . ." I looked up at the sod ceiling supported by rough rafters. "And I just used it in the most debase way."

"I can shoot holes in that idea easy enough. What are you really thinking?"

I couldn't help but grin. "All right. I'm just wondering why God gave me this skill—good at killing."

The marshal set the pot on the stove and whistled. "Profound, Anderson."

I scowled.

"I'm no expert on the Bible, but you're thoughtful enough about your actions that I know you read it. God used plenty of people in the Bible to dole out justice. Stop thinking about the philosophical reasoning behind everything and do your job." He poured coffee into my mug.

I chuckled and took the cup from him and enjoyed my coffee. Thankfully, he changed subjects and started talking about mining in Hill City. The gold in the creek was played out, but the shafts still produced enough tailings to keep miners interested in the area.

The rain stopped and we both stepped outside. A new sound, almost like thunder, filled the air. Coming around the bend and through a bank of fog appeared over a dozen riders. I recognized Running Deer in the lead. The thundering horses resounded off the cliff wall behind us.

Beside me, Marshal Hill's weathered face showed signs of the trails he'd ridden over the years. The gun battles and the savage country had taken their toll on the man. The men riding toward us looked his equal. Every one of them could serve as a fearsome marshal somewhere.

When they stepped into a saloon, I knew they were instantly branded bounty hunters or outlaws. The tools of their trade hung by their sides and off their saddles. Each man had one hand holding his reins, the other hovering close to a weapon. And the horses were just as fearsome as the men who rode them.

Death's black hand followed these men wherever they rode. I swallowed. These were men of my kind.

They fanned out into a long row and slowed as they approached. Running Deer was still in the lead. He'd cut his hair and donned white man's clothing.

The others scanned the camp, looking first at the marshal then me. Their eyes assessed me as I would a killer. Many glanced at Raven. They stopped, their horses huffing. Their eyes continually scanned the area for threats.

Running Deer nodded toward me. I returned the salute. I couldn't control the tension in my muscles, and I stuck my thumbs in my belt to keep from fidgeting.

Marshal Hill stood just outside the door and addressed the men. "Anderson killed four back there in the Badlands. That still leaves fifteen, maybe twenty in their hideout. But we need at least one alive so Anderson can interrogate. And don't shoot horses unless you have to. Anderson has interest in one in particular. You know their cabin, the layout, and what we need to do. By the time we get there, it'll be dark."

"Sounds like it's Anderson's War."

A few men chuckled.

Hill lifted a hand. "Let's ride."

While he talked, I memorized their faces, so I could recognize them in a fight. They all wore badges, and as I glanced down to make sure mine was on, Hill called out. "Pair up!"

I mounted Raven and we broke into a column of twos. I found myself next to a lanky man about my age.

He stood on his stirrups and stretched. "Name's Time Jackson, but everyone calls me Jack." I could hear his Western drawl.

"Philip Anderson, but everyone calls me Philip."

Jack smirked.

We started into the mountains.

Jack pulled his gloves tight over his knuckles. "Is it true you hit Maxwell in the shoulders?"

I gave a single nod.

"And you just killed four more?"

I didn't respond.

Jack tipped his hat back. "Why didn't you kill Maxwell when you had the chance?"

I started to say "Because he's my uncle" but knew I'd regret it if I did. And I hadn't known he was my uncle at the time. Privileged information.

Jack said he was the one who found the cabin the Maxwell gang now occupied and reported to Running Deer.

Darkness began to cloak the pines and towering rocks.

We crested the ridge and the black gave way to a tiny sliver of moonlight. Below, a cabin twice as large as my home lay nestled in the arms of two hills. Windows glowed with lamplight, and shadows could be seen inside. A small corral nearby held horses—more than a dozen. I took a deep breath. At least that many men, maybe more. Surprise was vital.

The door opened and cast light from the cabin onto the front yard. A shadow appeared, and I watched a man look around, a rifle cradled in his arms. He turned, taking his time, and returned to the cabin and closed the door.

Marshal Hill flashed a hand in the air, a preset signal to split up and find our positions. Everyone dismounted and led their horses through the woods. As we passed the marshal, he motioned to us. "Hoot when you get around back." I could barely hear him.

Our horses thudded as they walked on pine needles, but we were far enough from the cabin I was sure the sound didn't reach them.

Twenty minutes later, we had the hideout surrounded. Our horses were picketed some distance away. Jack and I found a rotting log lying parallel to the back wall and settled behind one end. Others passed us and found trees to hide behind near the cabin's corner.

Two large, curtained windows dominated the back wall.

Jack gathered a deep breath and let out a hoot that sounded half coyote, half buffalo. Curtains on the cabin windows parted, and the outlaws peered through, alarm on their faces. One man motioned and the lights went out.

I pulled my revolver. "You call that an owl?"

Jack shrugged.

Marshal Hill's voice carried through the night. "Burn them." Several torches flared and fiery streaks filled the night as the torches were flung at the cabin. The dry shingles immediately sparked and flames shot into the darkness.

"You're surrounded." Marshal Hill's voice penetrated the crackling fire. "Come out, hands on your heads. Leave your weapons behind."

The windows burst in a flash of gunfire, and I ducked behind the log. One shot smacked a tree just behind me.

I peered over the log, pointed my revolver at one of the cabin's windows, and fired at the same time as Jack. We peppered the opening, firing at flashes. Our revolvers offered tiny explosions as well, pinpointing our positions. A bullet smacked the log in front of me. I ducked down, praying the log was thick enough to protect us.

Echoes of gunshots filled the night. Men's screams came from inside.

A massive plume of smoke filled the window, and a blast ripped through the night. I ducked as a double-barrel load of shotgun pellets hit the log. I rose in time to see a man leap through the window. Jack and I fired, and the man crumpled to the ground.

Another man followed, and I fired. The hammer fell on an empty chamber. Jack's shot went wide.

The outlaw fired back and I ducked. He scrambled for the corral, a bullet smacking the wood just above his head, leapt on a horse, and sped away.

I jumped to my feet and holstered my gun. "I'm going after him."

The sprint to Raven took precious seconds. I mounted and dug my heels into her sides. She hit full speed in three bounds.

Branches and brush seemed to speed by us. Just in time, I ducked under a low bough. The sounds of gunfire diminished as the cool night breeze brushed against my skin. The chase invigorated Raven. She darted ahead, and I could make out the outlaw's shadow racing up the opposite hill. Raven's powerful legs made up the distance, but not as quickly as I would have hoped. The man had picked a fast horse.

We gained on him as he reached the top of the hill. He sprinted down the other side, pausing only to cross a rocky stream. He turned and saw me, then spurred his horse to a full gallop.

Raven and I approached the stream, and I could feel her gather herself like a spring to leap over the rocks. Her hindquarters propelled us through the air. We settled on the other side as softly as a skipped rock across water.

The outlaw turned to the right, and Raven easily matched the move. Her body strained in pursuit, her muscles rippling beneath my legs. He climbed a sharp cliff and reached the top, and we followed. The ground leveled out, broken only by jutting rocks and thick pines. Just ahead, the man pressed on, and I realized he had to be riding Alita.

Raven was winded but she gained ground on the even surface. Her wide nostrils were perfect for long sprints, taking in air in massive gulps. We rounded a boulder and the outlaw turned, pistol in hand. He fired and missed. I turned Raven just as he fired again. The bullet smacked a nearby tree.

I pressed Raven hard until we matched his pace, running side-by-side, fifteen feet apart. He aimed at me and I pulled my gun. It was empty, but the outlaw panicked and fired a snap shot that missed me. His next shot dry-clicked, and he swore. He flung the gun at us, and it bounced against Raven's withers.

Then he veered to the left. Raven matched the move. Both horses worked hard, clods of dirt flying high. Their hooves pounded steadily and their breaths were short and fast. Raven closed in, and I could just make out the man's hair flying in the wind.

I yanked my right foot from the stirrup, propped my leg against the saddle, and with a mighty thrust, flew through the air. I plowed into the rider. His body crumpled under the blow, and we tumbled to the forest floor in a knot.

I slammed my elbow into his stomach and heard the air whoosh from his body. Without giving the man a chance to recover, I balled both fists and slammed them across his temple. He fell back and didn't move.

Now, perhaps, we could get some answers.

It was time to prove that Jacob Wilkes hired the Maxwell Gang to kill me. Time to end Anderson's War.

38

A half hour later, with the unconscious man slung over
Alita's saddle, I returned to the cabin on Raven, Alita's
reins in my hand. In the distance, an orange blaze rose like a
beacon against the star-filled sky. Smoke rolled into the night.
There was no gunfire to be heard.

I was tired and hurt as I rode into the clearing. Lawmen
lifted the bodies scattered around the burning cabin and laid
them out in a single row, a ghastly scene that seared itself into
my mind. I rode toward the cabin until I felt the tension in
Raven. She would go no closer to the smell of death.

I tied her to a bush, Alita next to her, and then grasped the
gangman by the collar and threw him on the ground.

All eyes were directed at me.

Marshal Hill stepped close. "They're all dead."

I glared at him. They were to keep at least one alive. "I
captured one."

The others broke from their work and wandered close. I
braved the heat from the cabin fire to pull away a bucket from
the porch. A bit of dirty water sloshed at the bottom, and I

dumped the contents over the man. He sputtered and tried to rise but dropped back down in the dirt.

I rolled up my sleeves and loosened my collar without taking my eyes off him. With feet planted wide and muscles flexing, I stood over him. Sweat trickled down my cheek, the burning cabin behind me.

Marshal Hill came toward me, but I held up a hand. He stopped and took a step back.

I pulled my gun.

Even in the firelight, the criminal's face shone pale. He glanced at his dead friends, at the burning cabin, then back at me.

With unshaking hands, I opened the Smith and Wesson and let the spent cartridges fall on his body. His breath quickened.

"You can make this easy. Or hard. Your choice." I looked at him and flashed a wicked grin. "I prefer the hard way."

One by one, I pulled a cartridge from my belt and shoved it into the chamber. I needed this man to think I was as crooked as he was and would do anything to get information, and I allowed every bloodthirsty thought I'd ever had spill from me.

He leaned back on his elbows. Enough light shone from the cabin that I could see defiance in his eyes. "You're Anderson."

I offered a single nod.

The deputies circled us, surrounding the prey.

He sputtered. "I could tell by your eyes. Wolf's eyes. They say you was raised by wolves. That you're only half human."

My jaw clenched. I snapped my gun closed, took a deep breath, and fired a shot into the ground next to his ear.

I pulled the hammer back, aimed again and fired, the bullet just missing his thumb and forefinger. The man jerked back.

"Who hired you?" I pulled the hammer back again, the click easily heard over the crackle of the fire.

"I . . . I don't know."

"Wrong answer." I fired at his other hand.

"No, please." He inched backward.

I raised my voice. "Would any of you men complain if this man lost a body part tonight?"

Marshal Hill's voice was somber and quiet. "Do what you have to do."

I was a shadow, a demon from hell, standing over this man. But he could see my eyes, probably glowing.

I growled, "Who hired you?" and pointed the gun at his leg.

"He offered us money to do a job."

"What was the job?"

"I . . . I can't say."

I spun the gun on my finger and pointed it at his head.

He held up both hands. "To kill you. Good money. Really good money."

"Why did you take the horse?"

"One of ours was played out. We needed one. We demanded it as first payment." His breath came in heavy gasps. "Yours were gone when . . ."

"Who hired you?"

He shook his head.

"Name." I lowered the revolver and fired just below his crotch.

"If I give you a name, you won't hang me, right?"

I turned to Hill. "Marshal?"

Marshal Hill drew his gun, aimed past me, and pulled the trigger.

I turned to see the bandit lying twisted in the dirt. Blood covered his chest, and a knife lay near his hand. He'd almost reached it while my back was turned. I dropped and grabbed his shoulder. "Talk. Talk to me. Give me a name."

But he was dead.

I closed my eyes. This couldn't be happening. We were so close. I stared at the glint of steel near the man's hand. The knife had a wicked curve, and its polished surface reflected the fire. The man was going to kill me. Marshal Hill saved my life.

I watched the body, hoping he would wake up and I could prove the connection between Jacob and the gang.

The marshal holstered his gun. "Strange sense of honor.

Guess he figured a bullet from you or I or any of these men would be better than hanging."

The men took his body and stacked it with the rest. I stood at the edge of the clearing and stared into the darkness, the heat from the burning cabin behind me fueling my rage. Maybe I wasn't so different from my uncle after all.

I felt a hand on my shoulder. "I'm sorry, Philip." There was honest regret in Marshal Hill's voice.

"Yeah." It was all I could manage.

He patted my shoulder and went back to the bodies.

All this killing. For nothing.

Was this justice?

Not for me.

39

Deadwood buzzed with news of the Maxwell Gang's demise.

Men shook my hand, paid for my meals, and women huddled in groups and pointed at me. From what I gathered, most felt I took down the entire Maxwell Gang by myself.

The newspapers agreed with public sentiment.

Anderson has found his calling—sending men to the afterlife for eternal judgment.

I bided my time until Marshal Hill let me see John Maxwell. The leader of the gang was still rotting in jail because the judge had decided he might be valuable in stopping his fellow gang members. But now that the gang was dead, Maxwell was scheduled to hang. I sat in my hotel room and stewed. Finally, a knock came at the door, and I pulled my gun. "Come in."

Hill stepped in and glanced down at the revolver. "Bit edgy?"

I lowered the gun. "Did you send it?"

The marshal removed his hat and ran his fingers through his graying hair. "Yes."

"I had to know. Thank you."

He stepped inside and closed the door behind him. "Instant reply. No banks robbed in Mitchell. No murders. Your horses are fine."

I settled into the chair and sighed. "Means a lot. Thank you."

The marshal stood there, hat in hand. He shifted his feet.

I took the hint. "You look like you've got something on your mind."

"All the boys are back at the office having a little party. They're dividing up the reward money as well. Come on down. Remember Deputy Clark? He's been asking for you. And Jack. He took a shining to you."

"I want to go home, Marshal."

"I know. But a senate committee is coming to town, and they'll want to talk to you. There was a lot of killing, and it all revolved around you. They'll have questions. You're lucky they're sending aides instead of making you go to Washington."

I lowered my head in my hands and rubbed my forehead.

"Philip, you've got something on your mind. Tell me. Maybe I can help."

"Let me see Maxwell."

"When you tell me why."

I stared at the floor under my boots. "My mother's maiden name was Maxwell. He's my uncle." I didn't want to tell him, but I needed to see my uncle. He was scheduled to hang tomorrow.

Marshal Hill looked down at me for a moment, rubbing his mustache. "I'm sorry to hear that."

I pursed my lips. "Only family I've got, from all accounts." I gripped the back of a chair behind a small writing desk. "Don't let the press get wind of that."

The marshal walked to the window and looked down. "You are the most complicated . . ." He grunted.

I unpinned the badge and handed it to him.

He shook his head. "Keep it. This isn't over yet." He

turned to me, and I saw the concern etched in his eyes. "I'll let you speak to Maxwell. You'll give me your guns first. I hope you find what you're searching for. Life's not been kind to you."

I repinned the badge and took a deep breath. Life hadn't turned out anything like I planned. *God made you a gunslinger. The sooner you get ahold of the idea, the better.*

Packed in the sheriff's office, laughing and eating, were a dozen lawmen. I nodded toward Running Deer.

"Hey, look who's here! Loverboy himself." Jack came up and slapped me on the back. "Heard the story. Now all we need to do is ride into Mitchell and clean that little town up."

A tiny glimmer of hope flickered within me until Marshal Hill stepped in. "No."

I turned to him. "Why not?"

"Because it's Marshal Stone's territory. And because your nemesis hasn't done anything we can prove yet."

"You mean no one will testify against him."

He gave a small shrug, the gesture as helpless as I felt.

I suffered through several minutes of the chatter about the night's events. They wanted to hear about the chase so I told them.

Finally, Marshal Hill wandered over again. "He's in the same cell as before. Go on back." He held out a hand. "Give me your gun."

I placed it into his outstretched hand and slipped down the hallway. The noise behind me muffled, and the silence of the wall of cells enveloped me as I pressed on. I reached Maxwell's cell and stopped.

The bearded man lay on his cot. He glanced up. His eyes, cold and gray like my own, studied me. "Come to view your handiwork?"

I'd been waiting for this moment for weeks. I searched for the right words, digging into my soul. "You okay?" I grimaced.

He grunted and sat up. "What do you care?" He ran a hand through his hair.

I tried to look at him as my mother's brother. The

resemblance—I saw it now. The narrow nose, dark hair, strong bone structure with pointed chin, all features I had as well.

"What made you do it? The murdering and robbing. Your family loved you."

He gave a chuckle and crossed one foot over the other as he leaned back against the wall.

I watched him sitting there in silence. What could I say to change this man's heart?

"Can't lift my arms above my shoulders, thanks to you. Then again, you don't have to lift them to hang. You just gotta wriggle and die."

The man was the last of my family, and when he died I'd be truly alone.

He sat on the edge of the cot, a look of confusion on his face as he stared at me. His voice softened. "You really don't want me to hang."

"Just wonderin', what's it like on that side of the law? Using your gun to get things you didn't earn?"

He waved a hand. "It's living by faith, faith that the next person you rob has what you need."

"Do you have any family?"

He stared at his feet. "They're all dead."

I tried not to look eager. "What happened?"

"Look, I'm tired of answering your nonsense questions. Why don't you head on—" He froze.

I jerked around, but the hallway was empty. I looked back at him.

He rose to his feet and took a tentative step forward, looking at me. "Philip Anderson."

I didn't move, afraid even to breathe.

"My sister married an Anderson."

"I know."

He lifted his hands then let them fall. After a moment, he rubbed his chest. His chin quivered. "My sister . . . was the only family I had."

"No, she wasn't." I kept my voice firm.

He covered his face with his hands, and then with a deep breath brought them away. "It stands to reason we'd have to face off one day. Our skills with guns and all. And you bested me."

Captain Smith had told me the same. "It didn't have to be that way."

He looked up. "Yeah. Well . . ." He stood up straight and puffed out his chest. "Here I am. Your uncle."

"What was she like, my mother?"

A tenderness filled his eyes. "Smart, beautiful. Everyone loved her. Except for the man she married. All he loved was money."

"Is that why he went out West?"

Maxwell crossed his arms and turned away. For some reason, that was the wrong question. Silence reigned.

I waited.

Finally, he sighed. "Was in West Virginia when I received word. The Army had come across a burnt wagon with blacksmithing material on it. The bodies had already been buried." It was strange to see this hardened criminal overcome with sadness. "I thought you died with them."

"I survived. Ran."

"Where did you learn to shoot like that?"

I shoved my hands in my pockets. "Wanted revenge, but then I lost the feeling."

He nodded. "I always thought if I had been with them that night, I could have saved them."

"So why did you turn to crime?"

His answer came quickly. "You become what you hate."

"Uncle." I tried the word, and unfortunately, it sounded good. But this man would hang. "You stole my horse."

"It was a job. Easy work for an amazing horse. Good taste, nephew." Coming from him, the familial word sounded forced and awkward.

I stepped close to the bars. "Who gave you the job?"

"I don't know."

I grasped the metal cell door. "You don't understand. I must know. Any information you're holding back, uncle or not, I will get it."

He whistled. "You are your mother's son. Nothing would

stop her either. Except your father." He sighed and adjusted a suspender. "I received an anonymous wire that described your horse. 'Steal it,' it said. And one hundred dollars would be waiting for me at the saloon two days later." He rubbed his beard. "If there was more, I would tell you."

"Your gang was contacted by a man in Mitchell to kill me. Did you receive a wire about that?"

He shook his head.

My voice rose. "What good are you to me?"

He stood. "I'm your uncle. You better show me some respect, boy."

"Respect? I shot you because you were stealing my horse!"

"You got lucky."

This wasn't working. It felt wrong, uncomfortable. "Look, you're going to hang. It's my fault, and I understand you hate me for it." I searched for the right words. "I could have killed you."

The thought seemed to sober him. "You saved me so I could hang."

"And this is the thanks I get." I offered a sarcastic smile.

"What's really bugging you, boy? Uncle, yes I am. A law-breaker, yeah. Your mother I loved, but I hated your father. You're alive, but you're sending me to the gallows. What's really eating you?"

"My parents passed over their homestead and headed west for the Black Hills. Why?"

He whistled again and sat down slowly. "If you don't know why, I'm not going to tell you."

I paused, a thought forming. "Come to think of it, why did *you* pick the Black Hills?"

He squinted but he kept silent.

My anger burst through my composure and I kicked the bars. "Why?"

"Taking the reason to my grave, boy. It's the least I can do for you." He lifted a hand and pointed east. "Go home. Live your life. Marry a fat girl, have kids, die happy."

My mind still worked the problem. "What if I told you my parents were killed *beyond* the Black Hills?"

His eyes opened wide, and he stumbled for words. After a few moments, he clamped his mouth shut.

"Please. Were they looking for something?"

He wandered up to the bars, close to me. "Kid, I don't know you. Figure it best not to get to know you. You seem likable. But there's a secret that died with your parents. And I'm going to die with it as well. Because frankly, someone in this family deserves to die in bed. And this secret will kill you, Philip." He pointed at me. "Will kill you."

He turned back to his cot and lay down. With a sigh, he covered his head with a blanket.

The next day, I watched him hang.

40

I spent the following days with Jack. His company wasn't so bad, but when I learned the Senate aides would not need to speak to me when they arrived after all, I left. It seemed Marshal Hill had some sway in the government.

Since leaving my house in the dead of night I'd acquired a tall stack of reward money, a list of kills, and a badge. Marshal Hill patted me on the back as I climbed onto the train in Rapid City. A feeling of dread washed over me. "Get home," Hill said. "Something bad's happening. I can feel it. You can feel it. I'll be there when I can, but I've got to go to that blasted party in a few days."

The train whistled, and the conductor called for boarding. "What party?"

"That statehood party in Yankton. Wish you could go. Could sure use you there. A friend would be nice to talk to. Going to be a lot of politicians mostly."

The train car lurched, and we moved forward. Hill was already several feet behind. "Why would I go to a party like that?"

"Because Jacob and Anna are on the guest list." He

pointed at me as we pulled away from the station and yelled, "Philip. Stop being the reluctant hero. Just be who you are."

I found my seat. A crushing weight of depression settled on me as I watched through the window. Being the fastest gun in the territory had bought me the worst days of my life. *Hero.* The word tasted like hot iron.

The problem with being a hero is that it's impossible to sleep. People in the car recognized me. The front page of the Deadwood newspapers had featured a drawing of the burning cabin and me standing over all the bodies. The drawing and the story spread across the country. Chances were, today the Mitchell papers would run it too, and Jacob would know his scheme had failed.

The gun at my side felt heavy. I didn't like being a hero.

My old teacher had been right. Guns were an existence, a lifestyle.

The wide Missouri river stretched below us in a shimmer of blue, and a few hours later Mitchell loomed in the distance.

If the story ran today in the Mitchell newspaper, Jacob would be on the alert. He would have to do something, if for no other reason than the possibility I might have connected him with the Maxwell Gang.

My dread grew. Something was happening. I could feel it. I pressed my cheek against the window and stared as far down the track as I could at Mitchell. The train slowed as we skirted the town. I could make out the darkening streets at dusk and saw Marshall Stone running along the boardwalk with a shotgun in his hand. He rounded the corner and ran straight for Caroline's Kitchen.

I pulled out the deputy marshal badge and pinned it to my thick cotton pocket as I marched down the aisle. Passengers looked up as I walked by, but I ignored them. The conductor at the doorway stood. "Mr. Anderson, sir, please take your seat. We'll be arriving in just a moment."

"I'm jumping now." I tapped the badge and brushed by him. "Leave my horses at the station for me." I opened the door. The massive couplings below jostled under the strain connecting the heavy cars. I stepped down the passenger step and without hesitating I leapt off the train and hit the ground at a run.

I left the tracks and sprinted toward Caroline's. The door to the restaurant was open, so I stepped inside. I could hear screaming from the kitchen, and through the double doors I could see Leroy and Becky.

I tore through the empty front room, my boots thumping, and rushed into the kitchen. Fresh blood was splattered against the table, the walls, and across the floor. A group of men huddled around a form on the floor.

Marshal Stone's face, his brows furrowed and jaw set, looked up at mine. He swore. "You're the last person I need right now."

I stepped closer. Surrounded by Stone's deputies, Rachel lay on the plank floor. Deep slashes riddled her face and arms. Her clothing was soaked in blood and her raspy breath filled the room. She clung to Becky's dress as loosely as she clung to life, yet she spotted me. "Philip . . . Jeb . . . tried to . . ." She lay back and moaned.

I leaned down and grasped her cold hand. She'd lost too much blood. I heard a strange gurgling sound every time she breathed and saw that several slashes crossed near her heart. Her lung had probably been pierced. One deputy turned and vomited. Another put his palm over the hole.

Marshal Stone said something to Leroy, and the older man slipped out the back of the kitchen.

I stared at Rachel in horror. "This is my fault." The attack was against me, against someone I cared for. She was my friend. I watched as life ebbed from her body. "Where's Doc Wilson?"

"On his way."

I saw in my mind Jacob ordering Jeb to thrash her. They knew I was coming back. I stood, a reluctant gunman no longer. I would kill Jeb and then Jacob.

Rachel slipped into unconsciousness. There was nothing I could do for her. I strode out of the kitchen, brushing past the doctor who was just entering.

As I stepped into the cool night, I heard Marshal Stone's voice behind me. "Anderson."

I walked into the street.

"Anderson, stop right there or I will be forced to shoot you."

I spun. "You wouldn't dare."

"You leave this to me. This isn't your fight."

"The devil, it's not." I pointed back to the restaurant. "She was my friend, my ward. This is my battle, Marshal, and no one else is getting hurt because of me."

Stone came so close he was inches from my face. "You've no right to go after him."

I pulled the badge forward. "I have every right. In fact, as deputy U.S. marshal, I outrank you."

"Not in this town or county. You take orders from me. Now, march down to the jailhouse. You're under arrest."

"I'm going nowhere. Get out of my way." I pushed him.

He balled a fist and leaned back. I prepared to return the blow.

"Stop this!"

Only one voice could give me pause. I looked at the figure running toward us.

"Anna."

Marshal Stone took a step back onto the restaurant's portico.

"Stop, Philip. Stop it now."

"Anna, what are you doing here?"

Breathing hard, she moved close. "Leroy came for me. You need to calm down."

I pointed toward the kitchen. "Have you any idea what it looks like in there? It's a slaughterhouse." Anger welled inside, threatening to choke me. "See what Jeb's done?" I looked at the fresh blood on my hands. Rachel's blood. "God, this ends now. I've waited too long. I'm killing Jacob and Jeb and Ryan now. All of them."

She stepped close enough that I could feel the warmth of her body. "And then what?" She glanced at Caroline's. "Take his place?"

My hands curled into fists. Rage slithered like a viper inside my head, my guns the venom.

PETER LEAVELL

"Together we triggered something hideous in Jacob." The
nearby kerosene lamp brightened the street and reflected her
tears. "We have to live with our decisions. But we can't make
it worse."

I shook my head. "I want to spend my life with you and
not have to wonder who Jacob's next kill will be."

She unpinned the badge from my chest and placed it in my
left hand. Curling her fingers around mine, she said, "You're
changing, Philip. You're not the man I knew a few months ago.
You'll fight for this love we have. I know that. And I will help
you. But tonight, this battle is not yours or mine." She leaned
close.

I whispered in her ear. "You understand who I've
become?"

I let my cheek settle against the side of her head and I
closed my eyes. She kissed my cheek, then slid her lips along
my jaw and kissed my lips.

Her breath tickled my ear. "You're still my Philip." Her
lips touched my cheek again. "But please, Philip. Promise me
you'll go home."

I pulled away, the angry fire still burning deep inside me.
"Anna, Alita's at the train station."

She jerked back. "You have her?"

"The Maxwell Gang had her. Jacob gave her—"

Someone was charging toward us, and we both turned. A
young man ran up to the marshal. "Somebody done try to kill
your horses."

Marshal Stone glanced at me and then at the boy. "Did
you stop them?"

"They got a colt, but the rest are alive. Trevor was the one
who saved the rest by barking."

Anna grasped my hand, and I saw her look at me.

The marshal called for Becky. She hurried out. "I need you
to get Scott. Tell him to bring his rifle and meet me at the jail.
You'll stay the night there as well. Leroy will too. And a few
more men in this town who've not been bought." He pointed
to me. "Ride out to your house. Take a quick look around for
any possessions you want to keep, in case they burn your place.

305

Then hightail it back to my office. You have any other friends I need to know about?"

Becky's face turned white, and she held her hands to her mouth. "Scott is at your place, Philip. He wanted to watch it, just in case." She put a hand on her forehead. "Please . . ."

I glanced at Anna. She nodded.

I sprinted for the train station. It was nearly half a mile, but I'm sure it took me less than three minutes.

The horses were already unloaded, and I ran past the man checking them out and leapt onto Raven's bare back. I heard him call for me as I sped away, riding my horse bareback like I'd ridden so many years ago with Running Deer.

My horse's muscles churned as we raced through the night. She thundered along the road as I anticipated her every move, becoming one with my friend Raven. The trees seemed to fly as fast as my memories. The cottonwood tree where Anna and I talked of Indians, the ground I crawled on after my beating, the trail I took on my first trip to Deadwood, and every tree and rock I memorized in five years of riding the road. Even in the darkness, they stood stark and recognizable.

At the top of the ridge, I looked down and my heart stopped.

My cabin was engulfed in flames. Much like the cabin in the Black Hills I'd helped burn.

Raven couldn't run down the ravine fast enough. "Come on, girl!"

Great bursts of flame licked up from the roof and windows. Raven barely slowed as I jumped from her back and ran up on the porch. "Scott!"

I reached for the door but paused as a touch of hot flames licked at my skin. The heat brought a picture of the burning wagon I'd entered as a child back to my mind, and I couldn't move. "Scott!"

I thought I heard a cry from inside.

The memories flooded my mind, but I pushed them away and kicked the burning door. Flames roared throughout the house. The heat was intense. "Scott!"

I heard a pounding and then a weak voice. "Help!"

The heat singed the hairs on my arms, but I ran into the flames. Through the front room and into the hallway I hurried, breathing smoke.

I tried the bedroom doorknob, burning my hand, but it was locked and the key was gone. Taking a step back, I lowered my shoulder and slammed against the door with a grunt. It didn't budge.

Why did I build this place so well?

The back of the house crashed into a burning ruin, sparks showering over me. The house was about to come down on us.

I stole across the way and grabbed a hammer from the storage room. With a solid grip, I slammed it against the knob. It didn't move. I swung again, harder this time. Nothing.

With all my strength I swung, and the wood around the knob splintered. I tossed the hammer aside and raced into the room.

Scott lay dazed under the bed, smoke whirling above him in deadly curls. His hands were tied behind his back.

I lifted him to his feet. He coughed. With a grunt, I hauled him over my shoulder and hurried through the living room. Falling embers showered on us. My lungs filled with more smoke.

The opening was engulfed in flames but I pressed through into the open night and set him down.

Coughs racked his body, but I ran back inside. The kitchen collapsed. I rolled out of the way, the rafter just missing me. I dove for the bedroom, grabbed my family's treasure box, and turned for the door.

The front caved in, and exploding sparks surrounded me. Heat singed my skin.

A massive burning log now hung where the door had been. My last hope was the window. I picked up a chair, shoved it through the glass, and the roof above collapsed.

I jumped out the window as my house crashed to the ground in ruins.

I tried to inhale and went into a coughing fit. I crawled to Scott, who lay on his side. "You dead, Scott?"

"Can't catch my breath."

"Take it slow." But I needed him to recover quickly. Who knew who was watching? We had to get out of there.

I untied his hands, and he tried to stand.

Scott hacked. "I was thinking of taking up smoking." He took an unsteady step. "We better get back to town. I heard them say Jeb was going to hit Caroline's Kitchen. Rachel's there."

I whistled for Raven.

As she trotted close, I turned and watched the cinders of my life blow into the river.

41

I kept my grief in check until I held the dead colt in my arms. The other horses stood nearby, except Sand who paced frantically. It sent a stab straight through me. She didn't know why her baby didn't move.

With care, I set the colt down and patted Trevor. His tail wagged happily. I felt better when I petted his soft fur, so I lifted him in an embrace.

When I regained my composure, I returned through the back door of Marshal Stone's office. I glanced at the cell where I'd spent too many long days when I'd been suspected of murder and robbing a bank. I kicked the bars.

I'd lost so much. Rachel barely clung to life, my house and possessions were gone, Anna was hostage to a fiend, and Scott sat in the marshal's chair, trying not to cough up a lung.

Black soot streaked his face, and he scrubbed a rag against his skin. "That was close."

I sat on the other side of the desk. "I'm sorry, Scott. You okay?"

"It wasn't you who torched your house." He leaned close.

"It was Jeb who tied me up. But I'm sure I heard Jacob and Ryan's voice."

A shiver went down my spine. "You almost died."

"That's right. Now they've made this Irish boy angry." The determination on his blackened face remained steady. "No one tries to kill me and gets away with it."

"We'll get them. Soon as the marshal gets back, we'll go after them."

The door opened and Marshal Stone lumbered inside. "You're not going after them. I'm not either."

Scott scrambled to his feet. "That's absolute blamed nonsense."

The marshal walked over to a gun rack and pulled down a shotgun. "Philip, I'm going to ask you to do one of the hardest things you could possibly do."

"What's that?"

"Go to the party in Yankton."

I stood alongside Scott. "Are you out of your mind?" Mr. Wilkes had wanted me to go too. And Marshal Hill. "What is this party about, anyway?"

"Statehood. Perhaps the presidency after that, with our electoral votes. I am going to get some help to clear this mess up, but I can't spare a man to watch Anna. She's going to Yankton with Jacob. With you there, his attention will be focused on you, not causing more problems in town. Jeb and Ryan don't dare show their faces here, since a Territory judge says I can now shoot them on sight, so I doubt they'll cause more problems without orders."

I shook my head. "I need to be here."

"Marshal Hill will be at that party. I need him here. Ask him to come back. Tell him what's happened. He should come."

Scott roared and swiped a hand across the desk, sending papers and utensils flying across the room. "No! We go after them now. Becky may be next." He doubled over into another coughing fit.

"She's at the doctor's office with Rachel." The marshal's voice remained calm, and he ignored Scott's tantrum. "My two deputies are guarding her. But I need a deputy to watch the horses here." He stepped over a heap of papers and reached into a desk drawer. He pulled out a star and slammed it on the desk. "You get the job. Can you shoot?"

Scott looked up and lifted an eyebrow. "Uh, with a rifle, and I can come close with a pistol."

"Hired. Put it on. Twenty-five cents a day. Plus food if you're working guard duty in the office."

He straightened, and after a few small coughs, a smile crept up one side of Scott's face. "Deputy. All right." He nodded. "All right, yes."

"I'm going to get Doc Wilson to listen to those lungs of yours. But first, clean up this mess."

Scott looked at the strewn papers.

I crossed my arms and leaned against the side of the desk.

The marshal hitched up his pants. "Look, Philip, without the Maxwell Gang or Jeb and Ryan, Wilkes is going to have to start doing his deeds himself. Go to Yankton. The train leaves at three. And when you get there, buy some party clothes. You set for money?"

I flashed a smirk and reached into my pocket. The massive wad of cash could carry me for years. "Reward money. I got about one quarter of it for taking out a quarter of the gang myself." I peeled off a fifty-dollar note and set it on the desk. "For you, Scott. Payment for watching my place."

He opened his mouth to speak but paused and looked at the roll of bills in my hand. The single greenback I'd handed him looked like a tiny fraction of them, and that seemed to decide him. "Thanks, Philip. Be careful."

On the way to the train station, I visited Rachel, who was being tended at the doctor's house where several rooms were set aside for the sick.

The room smelled of illness and blood. The windows and shades were closed, and a single lantern lit the area around her bed. A thin sheet covered her bandaged body. If it weren't for her chest rising every few seconds, I would have guessed she was dead.

"She needs rest." The doctor kept his voice low. "Don't wake her."

I reached into my pocket, pulled out fifty more dollars and handed it to him. "Make sure she has everything she needs."

He nodded and slipped from the room.

I looked down on my dependent. Her struggle for life was in its most harrowing hours, and I wished I could infuse strength into her so that she might heal. "Dear God . . . please." I couldn't say more as tears threatened to form.

Her eyelids fluttered. "Philip?" She sounded as if her tongue was swollen.

I held her hand. "Lay still. Just rest."

She closed her eyes. "Jeb . . ."

"They're looking for him."

She was silent for several moments, and I thought she'd gone back to sleep. She tried to take a deep breath and grimaced. "So sorry, Philip."

"Oh, Rachel, whatever for? This is my fault. I'm the one who's sorry."

"If I hadn't come to Mitchell . . ."

I dropped to one knee and gripped her hand tighter. "Caroline would have died alone."

"Yes . . ." She mumbled a few unintelligible words but then fell asleep.

I didn't like the way everyone looked at me on the train, so I veered away from the station and found that the stagecoach was about to leave. I boarded, adjusted the saddlebag under my feet that held my entire household possessions, and pulled out the box from my childhood youth. Inside was my Bible.

I read it, the only comfort I could cling to.

The elderly couple riding with me fell asleep. I'd not slept the night before, so I decided to do the same.

I closed my eyes. Jacob's face appeared in my head, and I knew that soon I would have to kill him.

The reluctant hero was almost eager now.

42

Anna couldn't close her eyes. Each time she tried, dreams of blood washed over her like the ocean . . . Rachel's blood.

She sat up and pulled her warm robe around her, felt its caress against her skin. With a sigh, she lit the candlestick beside her bed, lighting her way to the stairwell. She walked quietly downstairs, her left hand holding the light, her right hand sliding along the smooth, wooden banister. The living room fireplace still glowed with hot embers and cast warmth at the bottom of the stairs. She walked through the kitchen and into her private reading room.

She dreaded the carriage ride with Jacob tomorrow. His hired driver was more a guard than a chauffeur. She hated the way the guard looked at her, as if she were . . . she refused to think the word. Her stomach churned.

The candle lit the tiny room, and she settled into her soft chair and wrapped her robe tightly around her.

How could Jacob be so evil? Rachel was almost dead, Philip had lost his home, and her father his business. If he refused to work for Jacob at the mill, he would be sent to jail.

She'd learned Jacob's history, knew his shrewd investments in the railroad and real estate had given him power. But for him, it wasn't just the rents, stocks, and bonds that satisfied. It was controlling people's lives.

She let thoughts of Philip brush away the bad thoughts. Her family had long talks about him, and she cherished every word, every memory. Every time he looked at her, his eyes told her everything she needed to know. They burned with a passion so deep it consumed her. And she wanted to be consumed.

She blamed herself, even though she understood she couldn't control Jacob's actions. If it weren't for her, things may have worked out differently. She thought back to the *Count of Monte Cristo*, how Edmond Dantès learned from his mistakes. She would do the same.

"Oh, Philip." Her whisper seemed to make him more real.

She'd wanted to comfort him when Caroline died, but he seemed accustomed to dealing with grief. Of course. He was no stranger to tragedy. And now his cabin was gone. If she could only comfort him when the bad dreams came at night, and the demons of the past haunted him even during his waking hours.

What scared her most about Jacob was his unpredictability. No one knew what he was thinking. He was quiet, his words usually reserved for threats or business dealings. He'd never actually said he loved her. He never touched her. Not once. She was grateful for that, at least.

She held her head. These thoughts were driving her to insanity. She stood and glanced through the bookshelves and pulled out a blue book, *Names and Their Meanings*, and settled back into the chair.

She flipped open the book and scanned through names of people she didn't know. Tired of it, she tried names she knew.

She looked up *Alita. Noble, winged.* Alita was both. When she galloped, it was as if she had wings. It was good to have her back, thanks to Philip.

She found *Anna. God has favored me.* Did He really favor her? To dangle a life she wanted in front of her but make it impossible to ever have? She supposed that's where faith took over, that God knew better than she did about what was best.

Faith wasn't easy.

She wondered about Philip's dog. What was his name? Beth would know. Wait, Trevor. Oh, she wanted to just nuzzle the dog's jowls. She spun through the pages and found the *T* section. *Prudent.* Well, that certainly told her a little something about Trevor.

Perhaps it was time to find Jacob. She turned to the right page on the first try. Jacob. *Held by the heel.* If it weren't for Philip holding Jacob's heel, the town would belong to him. Instead, the money mogul had to address his unrelenting rival.

She tapped the book's spine for a moment. Why hadn't she looked up Philip's name before? She didn't think of it when they were courting. And after, she didn't want to.

Her family usually looked up names together for entertainment. Somehow their meanings could always be connected to the person's choices or character. It was so much fun. But Jacob's domination had taken all their minds from the simple joy.

Her hands were clumsy because of the cold, she told herself. But the closer she came to *P*, the more they faltered. Her fingers traced the dark type, the gentle curves in his name. And then she read the meaning.

She held a hand against her heart and felt it beating rapidly.

She didn't know how it would happen, but she would hold on to her faith. In that moment, she knew she could never marry Jacob. She needed to be with Philip.

After a deep breath, she looked at the name again. Philip. *Lover of Horses.*

43

After a hotel room in Yankton was secured, I decided it best to check in with the local law. From their point of view, it was unnerving to have a U.S. deputy marshal showing up in your town unannounced. It would make me nervous if I were the local marshal.

The late September morning was almost chilly. I strapped on my gun, pulled an oilskin trench coat over my shoulders, and put on my hat as I closed the hotel door behind me.

Yankton's streets reminded me of the days I could walk the streets of Mitchell without being on full alert. Even here, I kept a sharp lookout for trouble. Wagons rolled by, and people scurried along the boardwalks, probably on party or government business. I shook my head. Presidential electorate. Statehood did touch a sense of my pride, and I understood the need to drum up support for Mitchell to become the capital if the Dakota Territory was broken up into two separate states, but I had other things to worry about.

A tall façade with wide lettering above the door indicated I'd found the marshal's office. I crossed the street and took a deep breath before entering. I was law now and needed to act appropriately. I pulled out my badge and opened the door.

The office was a single room with two jail cells in the corner. Almost a dozen men milled around in deep discussion. Some glanced up, but most kept talking.

The fellow closest to me nodded, and I lifted my badge. "Philip Anderson. Is the marshal in?"

The room quieted and all eyes turned to me.

An older man crossed the room with hand extended. "Sam is my name, and I'm the marshal. We've heard of you."

"It seems trouble follows me. I wanted to let you know I'm in town, so you can prepare for it."

Sam glanced at the other men. "These are all deputies we're using for the statehood party tonight. Shouldn't be any trouble."

They looked like farmers with guns. While I trusted farmers more than gunmen, we would probably need a few killers—killers of men, not snakes and badgers.

The door opened behind me and in stepped Marshal Hill.

Relief flooded through me. The candid surprise and pleasure on his face warmed me.

He held out a hand, and as we shook he grasped my shoulder with his other. "Good to see you, Philip. I hope all is well?"

I shook my head. "Jacob's taken matters into his own hands. Rachel was stabbed over a dozen times, but she's still alive, and my house was burned down. Scott was inside, and I was just able to pull him out before it collapsed." I took off my hat and ran my fingers through my hair. "Oh, and a horse of mine was shot and killed. Plus, no one will sell me anything in Mitchell."

Sam set a hand on his hip, just over his gun. "I'm thinking you should probably leave town."

I glanced at Marshal Hill, who looked amused. He walked to the center of the quiet room. Everyone watched. "Did Jacob bring Anna with him?"

"That's why I'm here. Marshal Stone sent me to watch them."

Marshal Hill nodded at Sam. "You've got real trouble

descending on your town . . . You have a right to be worried. Cancel the party."

"Now wait a minute, Hill. You can't just cancel an important party that's been in preparation for months. This party will go on."

"But with Jacob and Philip both here, trouble may be brewing."

"That's why one of them is leaving. I don't care which."

I was the tallest man in the room, the youngest, and probably the most seasoned killer other than the two marshals. With slow fingers, I unbuttoned my trench coat, pulled it off, and set a boot on a chair so the Smith and Wesson swung wide. "Jacob, then."

Hill took his coat off as well and tossed it to the side. "Sam, I understand how you feel. But there's no getting around this. Yes, there may be trouble, and yes, it's your town. But chances are Jacob won't do anything in public. So only Philip will get hurt."

I couldn't hold back a smirk.

Sam shifted his weight from one foot to the other. "Well, all right then. I just don't want trouble, that's all. Won't be any guns allowed inside. If you have words with him, take them outside."

No guns? I gritted my teeth. "I'll make sure not to kill too many people."

As I purchased clothes for the night and a seamstress pinned the hem on the legs and sleeves, I couldn't control my growing frustration. I wanted to get out of the tiny tailor's room and find Anna. Had she arrived in town yet with Jacob?

The clothes took all day, and by the time I made it back to my hotel room, my stomach growled. A quick glance at the clock showed an hour until the party.

I washed, shaved, and put on the white shirt with ruffles along the front. The small white tie fit easily around my neck, and I managed to knot it on the first attempt. The black pants felt soft and smooth compared to the jeans and cottons I always wore. The black jacket fit squarely over my muscled shoulders.

From gunman to dandy. I felt foolish in the clothes. Until I stepped in front of the mirror. I stared. The black cloth accentuated my dark hair. The two combined made my steel-gray eyes even more noticeable. I barely recognized the man looking back at me.

Tonight was a big night. Jacob would be working to build his popularity among the politicians while I . . . did what?

I pictured Anna in a red dress cut around her shoulders, her hair falling past her soft skin and down her back. And then I saw Jacob by her side.

A burst of rage shot through me. I picked up the water pitcher and flung it against the wall, shattering it. Jacob had won.

I looked out the window toward the sky, the moon already on the rise. "God, I don't know how You're going to fix this, but I need some help."

There was a token I'd saved from the fire inside the family box. I would give it to Anna tonight. I resolved to walk out with Anna or not walk out at all.

I pulled out the trinket and slipped it into my waistcoat pocket.

Enormous pillars held up the building's overhanging porch. A giant outdoor electric chandelier lit the entrance.

A butler at the open door nodded, and with a gloved hand, motioned toward the inside. "Welcome, sir. Please see the attendant."

I stepped into a large foyer, where cherry wood molding topped the shoulder-high red velvet wall covering. Rich brocade wallpaper rose from the molding to the high ceiling. A man in a three-piece suit with tails stood behind a book the size of a saddle that rested on a podium. I waited until two ladies in front of me were signed in and then I moved to the podium. Their dresses swished as they left.

The attendant looked over my dark coat and white tie ending at my top hat before he made eye contact. His bald head and large hooked nose amplified his air of superiority. He raised an eyebrow. "Ah, sir, I'm unacquainted with you. Would you please state your name?"

"Philip Anderson."

"Ah, I see your name here." A look of respect crossed his face. "Welcome to the party. I trust you are not carrying firearms?" He tapped the side of his nose, as if he knew my reputation.

"I left my guns in the hotel room."

"Excellent. Leave your hat with the attendant, and enjoy the party."

I did as he asked and was directed toward a hallway.

The long entrance was lit with electric lighting that played against mirrors with gilted frames. Between the mirrors hung large oil landscapes illustrating the various regions in the Dakota Territory, from rivers to plains to wheat fields to mountains. Busts of famous men such as Abraham Lincoln rested on stands every dozen feet. I nearly stumbled over the colorful Oriental rug that stretched the entire length of the floor.

A painting of dogs surrounding a man in a red suit caught my eye, reminding me of Trevor, and I paused to enjoy the rich colors. I took a deep breath, surprised at how relaxed I felt. Maybe giving it to God had helped.

I kept moving down the hall, noticed a painting of the Badlands, and kept going. I didn't need reminders of that place.

At the end of the passage, an attendant stood behind another podium. "Sir, may I have the pleasure of announcing you?"

"I'd rather you not."

He gave a stern look. "It is custom."

I thought to give a fake name but decided against it. "Philip Anderson."

"Ladies and gentlemen, announcing Philip Anderson."

Conversations hushed and people turned my way. Ignoring their murmured exclamations, I stepped into the ballroom and surveyed the crowd. Where was Anna?

44

I wove through clusters of chatting guests and crossed the carpeted floor to reach the food tables that stretched along the far wall. It was difficult to judge how many people were in the ballroom. The mirror-covered walls reflected the revelers and seemingly enlarged the space. Massive gold chandeliers warmed the perfumed air. Before long, the room would be stifling.

I turned as more guests were announced. One politician after another, their names I'd read in newspaper articles. Businessmen and their wives, all in suits or fancy dresses, crossed the floor and visited with others. Making connections, business deals, things I didn't need. As a gunman I was dangerous, not in their coalitions. But they came for a good cause, to support the Dakota Territory's statehood.

A short man wearing spectacles stepped close. His keen smile and energetic handshake caught my attention. "Mr. Anderson." His voice was high and sharp.

"Yes."

"I'm writing a book about the winning of the American

West, and I would love to interview you in the coming weeks."
He rocked on the balls of his feet, forward and back.

I spotted Marshal Hill walking in from a separate entrance
on the other side of the ballroom. I wanted to go over to him,
a friendly face. "A written interview?"

"If you like." He followed my gaze to where I was looking.
"I'll get you the questions soon. You live in Mitchell, correct?"

"Yes." I wanted to speak with Marshal Hill. He started my
way. I released an audible sigh.

"That's bully, thank you." The man held out a hand, and
I shook it again. He left and wandered to the other end of the
tables, talking with others as he went.

To my surprise, someone else I recognized stepped up.
Captain Smith from Fort Randall was dressed in a dark blue
dress uniform that highlighted his white hair.

Both Hill and Smith arrived at my side at the same time. I
reached out to shake the marshal's hand. "Marshal Hill, I'd like
you to meet Captain Smith. He purchased one of my horses.
Captain Smith, this is U.S. Marshal Hill."

After the normal pleasantries were passed, I motioned
toward the man who asked for the interview. "Who is that?"

Smith raised an eyebrow. "Theodore Roosevelt. Lives
north of the Badlands, about two hundred miles."

I shook my head. "Can't decide if I like him or not."

The captain smiled. "People either love him or hate him.
There's no middle ground with Roosevelt. Give it time."

"How is your wife?" I directed the question to Captain
Smith.

"Ill, unfortunately. But she sends her regards."

I turned to Hill and realized I didn't know if he was married. "Do you have a family, Marshal?"

His gaze landed on something just behind me, where the
drinks were being served. "I have a wife and two children back
east."

"Do you see them often?" Captain Smith also saw the
drinks, and it seemed as if they worked quickly through the
conversation to get to the bar sooner. Perhaps that was how
they endured parties like this.

"I don't."

A burst of light flashed near the middle of the room, and all three of us spun to see a small cloud of smoke lifting up from a photographer, whose camera was pointed at us.

I noticed that both officers had reached for the guns they didn't carry. My hand hovered near my hip.

The announcer called out more names, and the room filled quickly. Finally, he announced the names I hated to hear in the same breath. "Announcing Jacob Wilkes and Anna Johnston."

A blue dress curved over her shoulders and swung gently down to her hips, where the fabric cascaded to the floor and trailed behind her. Her hair was arranged in a tight bun, revealing her long, white neck. She looked up, noticed people looking at her, and self-consciously touched the side of her hair with a gloved hand.

I realized my mouth was hanging open and quickly closed it. Jealousy stabbed my heart. I wanted to be the one with Anna, to call her mine. I felt like an animal wanting to own her, keep her. I pushed away the thought and focused on how to protect her.

Captain Smith and Marshal Hill both brushed their mustaches.

The captain put a hand on his sword hilt. "It appears Aphrodite has come to Earth and joined our party."

The marshal grunted. "She is quite the woman. About half our age, though, wouldn't you say?"

"She's taken."

Both men looked at me.

Marshal Hill reached over and snatched a piece of cheese. "And how would you know that? She's got a different name than that boy she's with."

I gave a cold stare. I almost said *she's mine* but stopped myself. It would sound like Jacob. "That's her."

"Wait, you don't mean . . ." The marshal popped the cheese into his mouth and spoke around it. "This is the girl who started Anderson's War? Our Helen of Troy?"

I watched her scan the room. "Yes, she is." I hoped she was looking for me.

He gave a short whistle and looked at Captain Smith. "You know of Philip's troubles?"

"Not much. Only what I read in the papers."

"There's a war in Mitchell. She's the prize the two boys are fighting over."

"She's not simply a prize. She's the world to me."

The captain sighed. "Oh, to be young again."

Marshal Hill cleared his throat. "I'm going to meet her." He gave us a half-bow and walked in her direction before I could object.

He approached her, and Anna must have recognized him from the trial because she beamed, honestly happy to see him. Jacob's ire was palpable.

"Anderson?"

A voice behind me caught my attention. I turned and saw a small group of plump men in dark suits. They all held cigars, and their gold watch chains hung low.

One man offered his hand. "Louis Church. I'm governor of the Territory."

I shook his hand. "Pleasure." It was a lie. I didn't care.

Some of the men stood with one hand in their pocket, others were holding their drinks.

The governor, short but full of passion in his eyes, shook his head. "I've followed what you've done for this territory, sir, and if this party had a guest of honor, I would nominate you."

"Thank you." My interest in him grew.

Marshal Hill stepped by my side and clapped me on the shoulder. "If it weren't for Anderson, we wouldn't have the Maxwell Gang bottled up."

I noticed Jacob closed in as well and stood near the politicians, part of a larger circle surrounding me.

"True. Very true." The governor pursed his lips. "Many a sleepless night I wondered how to stop them. Our new state will owe you a debt of gratitude."

I couldn't help but glance toward Jacob as I said, "My service is nothing compared to what this land has given me, Governor Church. Too many people look to control our citizens' lives. I want to free them."

Jacob's composure never faltered as he said, "Perhaps it is possible to do both." He held out a hand to the governor. "Jacob Wilkes, from Mitchell."

The governor shook it. "You're a banker, am I right?"

"We're opening another bank right here in Yankton. That will give us three."

"Quite the growing enterprise."

Jacob smiled. "Just getting started."

The governor glanced at his fellow politicians. "That kind of thinking costs money."

Jacob straightened his white jacket and leaned on his cane. He was a picture of perfection. He'd even purchased a new cane for the occasion—probably couldn't get my blood off the old one.

He smiled. "There's plenty of money in the territory . . . for those who know how to use it."

Governor Church gave Jacob a nod. "Perhaps we can talk later, young man. For the moment, I need to freshen my drink. Philip, would you join me?"

"Of course."

He broke away and I walked by his side. "Philip, everyone is talking about you. Yet you won't talk to the press."

As soon as I put a stop to Jacob, I would talk to a reporter. I'd promised myself that consolation while in Deadwood. There was a misconception about Philip Anderson, and I wanted to set the record straight.

The governor continued. "I'd like you to give a short speech tonight. Nothing big, just a few words about what being a Dakotan means to you. And why you put your life on the line to protect her."

Anna was the reason, but I guessed he was looking for something more political.

He patted my shoulder. "I'll let you know when to come up to the dais." He picked up a drink and returned to the small group.

A speech. I picked up a handful of dried peas and popped them in my mouth. I'd never before given a speech, unless school recitations counted.

I noticed that Jacob was still hobnobbing with the politicians. That meant Anna was alone. I searched the crowd for her.

Music filled the room, and I turned to see a small band on the stage. Violins, cellos, flutes, and trumpets all combined to play a pleasant tune. I paused to listen.

Governor Church stepped onto the stage and the music quieted. Two violinists continued to play, although almost too quietly to hear.

The governor lifted his hands. "Thank you for coming tonight. We're here to celebrate the Dakota Territory. But it will be the last time we do, because soon we'll be celebrating South Dakota's statehood."

The crowd applauded. I joined in.

"I'm Governor Church, and I would like to thank several people who have joined us tonight." He mentioned names, most I'd read about in newspapers or heard in idle chatter between Mitchell's residents.

The clapping was warm and generous.

"Tonight, we also have a young hero with us, one who singlehandedly captured John Maxwell in a gun battle and returned to help put the Maxwell Gang's reign of terror to an end. Philip Anderson, please come up here." He motioned to me.

The sound of applause swelled.

As I walked toward the stage, the crowd opened for me to pass. I saw Jacob leaning on his cane, staring at me. His look of hatred penetrated my soul, and I knew tonight he would try to kill me. I needed to find Anna and get back to Mitchell.

Instead, I stepped onto the stage.

The governor patted me on the back. "He's too humble to talk to the press, but tonight he agreed to talk with you about what makes this land special. Give another round of applause for Philip Anderson."

The governor stepped off the stage as he clapped, turned, and looked up at me.

I opened my mouth but nothing came out. All I could think about was three hundred people watching me, waiting for something brilliant. Finally, I saw Anna near the hallway opposite the main entrance. She was smiling. She looked as if she was pleased with me and that she knew I could do this.

I couldn't speak to hundreds of people, but I could speak to her.

"Hello, are you all okay?" That was a dumb way to start. I felt like kicking myself for using that word.

But several people remarked "Yes!" from the crowd.

I let a few more words go. It felt like I was opening my hand and throwing butterflies into the sky. "I'm more comfortable standing in front of a runaway stagecoach than a crowd, I guess."

I heard some laughter.

"About all the Maxwell Gang stuff the governor was talking about, I have to tell you it's not about just one person strapping on a gun. It's about a group of men and women coming together to do what needs to be done."

I was starting to find a rhythm. "It took great people to make our wonderful country. Farmers, investors, transportation builders, they all came together to do something marvelous. They lived their lives, daily trying to make the world around them a better place. And you know what? It worked."

I paced along the stage, raising my arms to emphasize points. "It's no secret why the Republicans want to split the territory and create two states. They'll have more power, more seats in Congress. More electoral votes.

"But forget what the politicians want. What do the people want? They want statehood. They've lived on the land, built farms and ranches, much like myself. They've gone before, done the work, and now they cry out to create a state. They want, no, they *need* representation in this government.

"Because there are men in this territory, even in my town of Mitchell, who are scheming to control and destroy what our citizens have created. I will no longer sit by and watch it happen. We will work together to stop these evil men.

"So politicians, it is your task—no, it is your duty to make this territory a state. If you fail, all the toil and suffering over the years has been for naught. This party tonight is not for us, but for the thousands who have gone before us, who are crying out for us to join the greatest country in the world, the United States of America."

Applause tore through the room. I stepped off the stage and walked directly to Governor Church. I knew what needed to be done.

I realized it wasn't just Mitchell Jacob wanted to control. If we were a state, Jacob could influence, coerce, or buy representatives.

The governor smiled and held out a hand. "You speak well, my friend."

"Thank you." I stepped close, and as I did I saw Jacob's scowl. I had to get Anna away from him. I had to beat him back to Mitchell. "Governor, could you do me a favor? I need you to speak with Jacob Wilkes about your plans. Make it as long as you can. As a favor to me. I may even vote for you."

The ovation began to die down.

The governor tilted his head, a bemused expression on his face. "I can do that for you, but first I need to give a speech as well."

"Please." I gripped his arm. "I beg of you, start the dancing now and speak later. I desperately need for you to talk with Wilkes right this moment."

He looked around and finally nodded. "All right." He stepped on stage, and as I made my way through the crowd to Anna, several people patted me on the back. Others tried to stop me to talk with me, but I pressed by them. Behind me, the governor announced the dancing, and the band began to play a waltz.

Marshal Hill grabbed my arm. "That was amazing. And foolish. Jacob's mad enough to find you after the party and kill you. He knows full well that was directed at him."

"I'm going to get Anna now. We've got to run back to Mitchell and get her family out of there."

He gave a grim nod. "Meet me in Rapid City. We'll find some place to protect you there. But I can't arrest him, Philip. You're on your own."

I passed a knot of people and came into full view of Anna

who stood alone in a corner, a downcast expression on her face. She brightened when she saw me walking toward her. Then her eyes widened, as she looked around for Jacob.

I grabbed her hand. "Come with me."

"But Jacob!" Even as she objected she tried to keep up with me as I pulled her away.

We left behind the band, the dancing, and the conversations and entered the quiet of the narrow hallway. Her dress swished as we hurried away from the ballroom.

"What's going on?"

"We've got to get out of here."

"We can't leave. Jacob will—"

I found an open door on the left, and I pulled her into it, closing the door behind us.

Bookshelves lined the walls, while the fire that blazed in the hearth lit the room. Red curtains were draped over the windows.

She grabbed my hands. "What are you doing? This is dangerous."

"We need to leave, Anna. Together. Now. We have to get back to Mitchell to load up your family and my friends and all of us flee to Rapid City."

She clutched her heart. "Why now?" Despite her objection, a smile crossed her lips.

"Because Jacob is not in Mitchell right now. And right now I hold the attention and adoration of every person here, which Jacob can't stand. I will die tonight if I stay. Marshal Hill agrees. So I'm running. It's either that or kill him. Come with me."

Her eyes were full of terror.

"I've got money. We'll get your family and run. Together."

I watched the battle play out on her face, the turmoil of passion and fear. "Philip, I'm not so sure."

"Look. I didn't want to be a hero. But my faith in God has taught me one thing. Follow Him and hope for the best. I'll go back to the hotel, get my guns, and hire a wagon to take us home."

She winced.

I took her hands. "Please, Anna. I will do my best to protect you and your family. God will take care of us."

"Philip . . ." Her voice trailed, wavering.

I leaned down and pressed my lips against hers, and for a moment the dangers of our love were trumped by our passion for each other. Her warmth and hungry energy passed into me. I longed to make the moment last.

We pulled away at the same time.

I took her hand. "Will you come with me?"

"Oh, Philip, you know I will."

I pulled her toward the door and reached for the knob. I pulled.

Locked.

My heart jumped. I looked at Anna, whose mouth gaped in horror.

I hurried to the massive windows, reached up, and pulled back the red curtain.

She screamed.

Ryan stood on the other side of the window.

The darkness behind him left only the firelight to reflect the man's menacing presence. Jacob must have seen us come into the room.

Ryan snarled and slammed the rifle's butt against the window. Glass flew, and I covered Anna as the shards fell.

We backed deeper into the room. Ryan aimed the rifle at us. "Hands up."

From outside came the sound of laughter.

Jacob stepped from outside the window into view. He shook his head. "That orchestra is hideous. Remind me to kill them next."

Anna clutched my hand. "Leave us alone, Jacob. You can't control us anymore."

He feigned a sad smile. "That's why I have to kill you. Thankfully, that excuse they call music will cover the sound of two rifle shots."

I released Anna's hand. If I lunged for Ryan, she might be able to escape past them through the window. I would take a few bullets, but she could get Marshal Hill.

He growled, "I obviously haven't instilled enough fear in either of you, and that is my fault." He shook his head. "I hate to do this. You've taught me so much. I haven't run into someone of your caliber for so long. Ever, actually. You should have taken me up on my generous offer, but it's too late now."

He aimed his chin at Ryan. "Shoot him."

I heard a rustle, and saw both men turn to Anna. I turned too. She held a small Derringer, which was pointed at Jacob. "If you shoot Philip, Jacob dies."

The room was silent for a moment. Then Jacob's slow laugh filled the room. He clapped. "See why I love her?" He held a hand to his heart. "She's a feisty one." His face contorted and he tapped his cane on the carpeted floor. "She won't fire. Kill him."

Ryan lifted the rifle.

The blast was deafening.

45

Ryan spun backward. His head slammed into the window frame and he crashed to the ground. His hulking form didn't move.

"Anna, Anna." Jacob clicked his tongue. "You wasted your shot on Ryan. Now I'm going to have to punish you as well."

I started to back up, toward the fire, Anna beside me.

Jacob lifted his cane and held it in both hands. With a quick tug, he separated the cane into two parts, one a sheath, the other a sword.

I thought of my guns in the hotel.

I snatched a poker from the fireplace and hissed, "Anna, when he moves, run, get help."

Anna darted for the open window.

Jacob picked up the wooden globe and flung it at her. The heavy orb slammed against her skull and she fell like a rock, unmoving.

Inside me an old feeling I never thought would return came unbidden and pure. Revenge.

I wanted to kill Jacob Wilkes.

Although the feeling was strong, I was stronger now, and I found purpose in the feeling. Watching Jacob, I leaned down and felt Anna's neck, just above the necklace. Her heartbeat was strong.

Jacob took the opportunity to rush me. He brought his sword down in a wicked slice.

I lifted the iron. Sparks flew as the sword deflected to the side. I leapt up, just in time to stop a second slash.

Jacob was fast. No sign of a limp now, probably a faked affliction for sympathy or to throw off his enemies. He lunged straight at me. I slapped the sword aside and thrust. The edge of the iron nicked his elbow. He slashed again, and the sword tip sliced through my jacket.

Scott had said I had the fastest hands he'd ever seen. I needed them now. And a quick-moving body.

I jumped back before he could make good my defenseless position. "Jacob, you ruin more of my suits."

Without responding, he swung for my head, and I ducked. I thought to hit his legs, but his attack came so fast I could only deflect his weapon. Sparks rained down on the carpet as the onslaught forced me back toward the hearth. The fire's red glow reflected off the glimmering steel sword.

He pressed. I stayed on the defensive, my blacksmith's strength seemed adept at wielding the heavy iron. Jacob, though, seemed to be warming to his work. One slash nicked my shoulder, and I felt blood trickle down my arm.

Sweat dripped down the side of my face, but there was no time to wipe it away. He lunged, this time to finish me, and I caught the move by leaping to the side and snagging the sword in the iron's hook. His weapon caught for just a moment, I stepped in and elbowed his face. He stumbled backward, tripped over Ryan, and fell out the window.

I hoped to press the advantage and followed him into the night. But he was already standing and prepared to attack.

Jacob was a master with the blade. He would find a way through my defenses soon. I needed to end this fast.

In the darkness, the sparks flew like shooting stars. Every clash of iron to steel echoed against the building as we battled back and forth. Sometimes I had the advantage; sometimes he pushed me back.

I hated retreating.

The weapon I had was for defense only. I could do little damage other than serious bruising unless I was able to stab him with the blunt end or use the hook against his skull. He wasn't about to let me swing back far enough to get the momentum I needed.

The only way to stop him was to get in close. I tried using the hook to grab the sword on every attack, but he was too quick.

Across hard-packed gravel we fought, circling each other like hungry wolves. I'd back away then push. He would deflect and attack. I needed something, anything to change the balance of power.

Jacob slapped my iron high, and I brought it down on the sword. He spun with a side slash, and again I found the iron too high. He thrust straight at my heart.

I brought the poker down as quickly as I could and hit the sword, dropping the tip. The force sent the blade deep into my thigh.

White-hot pain surged through me, but I saw an opening. Instead of backing away, I sent an upper-cut into Jacob's jaw.

As he fell, the sword pulled from my leg. I couldn't hold back a roar.

I swung the iron at his sword and snagged the hilt with the hook. I yanked it from his hand and it fell at my feet.

Before he could lunge for the sword, I grabbed it and pointed it at him.

Breathing hard, I growled, "It's over, Jacob."

He glared up at me. "It's only begun, Anderson."

I narrowed my eyes. "You can't go back to Mitchell. I'll hunt you down. We'll prove you robbed your own bank. You've already lost."

There was a look of mild interest on his face. He shrugged, rose to his feet, and sprinted into the darkness.

I tried to chase him but collapsed when I put weight on my leg. Using the poker for support, I walked back to Anna.

Long before I could see inside, her frantic voice drifted into the night. "Philip's out there with Jacob. Go help him, please."

"I'm here." I lifted my leg over the sill and Ryan's still-unconscious form, and I ducked inside.

"Philip!" Anna jumped up but fell back to the couch where she'd been sitting next to Marshal Hill. The marshal was looking at the cut on her head. Several other men looked as if they were about to follow her orders.

She sat up, and the marshal steadied her.

She reached out for me. "You're bleeding!" She gasped as I came close. "Bleeding bad!"

"Just a scratch. Are you okay?"

"My head hurts. But Philip, you've got to hear what Marshal Stone has to say."

"Marshal Stone?" She wasn't making sense. Maybe it was the head injury. "Isn't he in Mitchell?"

I heard a chuckle and Stone stepped near. His red bulldog face actually held a smile as he helped me to the couch. "Came as soon as I could."

Marshall Hill stood so I could sit by Anna. I gave him a grateful smile.

"I'm going to wrap a bandage around that leg," Stone said. "But I want you to see this first." He handed me a burnt stick with a knob at the end.

I studied it for a moment. "Jacob's cane."

Roosevelt, the writer I'd just met, walked in with a medical bag. "Doctor was too slow, so I took his bag." He saw me and flashed a smile.

Marshal Stone grabbed the bag and pulled out a long strip of cloth. "We found that cane at your house. It's the evidence we needed to get a subpoena to search Jacob's father's house and the bank. We found records of a house that Jacob owned but didn't live in just outside of Mitchell. Inside, we found the missing ten thousand dollars from the bank." He wrapped the bandage around my pants leg and pulled it tight. "We'll get a doc to clean this later."

"I think you'll find Jacob at his hotel room right now," I said, putting weight on my leg. It hurt, but I could walk.

Roosevelt reached into his breast pocket and pulled out a small pistol. He tossed me the gun. "Let's go."

I caught the pistol. It felt good to have a weapon in my hand again. "You brought a gun?"

"Never could abide doing things by the rules," he said with a smile.

Marshal Hill pulled his own gun. "Anna, what hotel is Jacob staying at? Do you know his room number?"

She nodded. "It's the one on Douglas by the river. His room is number twenty-seven."

I looked at Yankton's marshal, Sam. "Where are those deputies of yours?"

"Out front."

"Better keep them protecting the party." I pointed the gun to the unconscious Ryan. "And keep him quiet."

My leg was stiff, but a few minutes later as Roosevelt and I along with Captain Smith, Marshals Hill and Stone, and a few deputies closed in on the hotel, I looked at Roosevelt again. I couldn't help but like the man after all. He had inner strength and infectious energy.

Captain Smith suggested we split up. Some men covered the back of the hotel and others hurried inside.

Roosevelt and Marshal Stone stepped into the hotel with me. I had my badge in hand and flashed it at the lobby clerk.

I turned to the marshal. "Any use questioning him?"

Stone leaned toward the clerk. "A man came in here and threatened that if you told anyone he was here, he'd kill you. Am I correct?"

The clerk looked both ways and gave a quick nod.

Marshal Stone marched up the stairs. Roosevelt and I followed close behind. With guns drawn, we crossed the second floor.

I pictured a long, drawn-out siege with Jacob locked in his room. He would call out demands and threaten people with their lives.

I also pictured Jacob dead with a bullet in his heart.

Marshal Stone stepped up to the door.

Glass shattered on the other side.

Stone kicked the door in, and we rushed inside the small hotel room. Empty.

The marshal rushed to the window, aimed his gun, and fired. A few more gunshots sounded and then silence.

I crossed the room to look out.

Stone holstered his gun and sighed. "I don't think we got him."

Marshal Hill came into view below and looked up. His thick mustache looked like a bandana covering the lower half of his face. "Wilkes had a horse waiting down here," he yelled. "He shot a deputy in the shoulder. Got away."

Marshal Stone's bulldog face turned sour. He swore.

I looked at Roosevelt. He clacked his teeth together. "Let's go get him. You and me. Right now."

Everything in me wanted to take him up on his offer. Fire coursed through my leg, and I collapsed. "I may have to stand by and watch this turn."

Marshal Stone kicked the bed. "Well, at least we've got him on the run now. And a warrant will be issued for his arrest. I'll go after him tonight." He pointed at Roosevelt. "You have to stay here."

Roosevelt placed both hands on his hips. "That's bully, I suppose." He frowned and looked like a child who was told he couldn't go to the circus. "I'll stay and protect Philip and Anna."

46

Anna's hair blew from her face as she walked toward me. The morning sun lit her bright eyes, and her smile lit my heart. We had fought hard for this moment. I would drink in her presence all the way from Yankton to Mitchell, savoring every moment.

Roosevelt held her trunk over one shoulder. Something he said made her laugh. They approached the stagecoach, and he loaded the crate in the back. Then he leaned over and gave Anna a kiss on the cheek. "You remind me of my dear Alice."

Anna raised her eyebrows. "Alice?"

"My wife died some years ago. You remind me of her."

Anna smiled, but she didn't say anything.

I patted him on the back. "You don't panic in a scrap. I like that."

"You run into any more adventures, come find me. That was most invigorating." He inhaled deeply through his nose, as if preparing for a swim. "I plan to exit ranching. Winters are devastating my herd. One more hard winter, I won't know what to do. Perhaps politics are again in my future."

I looked at Anna. "Maybe life will settle down now that Jacob is on the run."

The stagecoach driver hitched our horses to the back of the carriage.

Marshal Hill and Captain Smith stepped from the town's small hospital and came over to us. Hill crossed his arms. "How's your head?"

Anna reached up and touched the bandage. "Better. Thank you."

"Philip." The captain lowered his voice. "Before you leave, I remembered something else that might be important. Would you like to talk about it in private?"

I'd learned my lesson about privileged information. I needed to be more open with my friends. "Everyone here is trustworthy."

His expression was grave. "Of the others in your parents' confidence, some are of importance. But your mother and father spent a good deal of time with one person you may have heard of."

"Who?"

"George Custer."

A picture I'd seen of the man in a newspaper flashed in my mind, along with the article about his death.

And then another image hit me.

I was fifteen or so, target practicing with the old man. The grassy field made a perfect place to practice. Almost every day, I took out my revenge on a massive stump.

A man came into view. Instead of riding along the road, he headed toward us. He wore a cavalry officer's uniform and his hat was smashed on top of golden curls of hair.

I suddenly realized who the man had been. Perhaps Custer? If he knew my parents, had he stopped to check on me?

Before I could recall the conversation word for word, I felt a hand brush against mine, and fingers intertwine with my own. "What's wrong?" Anna asked.

I looked at her face. "I . . . remember something from when I was a kid."

She squeezed my hand.

"I think I met Custer. Before he died."

Captain Smith pressed his palms together. "Did he say anything?"

"I can't remember." I rubbed my fingers against my forehead. It had been a long time since I told a lie. I didn't like it, but something felt wrong about sharing the conversation I had with him.

"I'm going back to the fort," Smith said. "If you need anything else, you know where I am."

Marshal Hill patted my shoulder. "You rest that leg. I'll be in Mitchell in a couple days. We've got some things to discuss with the governor while we're here." He brushed his mustache. "And Philip, now that Jacob is on the run . . ." he paused. "There's an opening for a new gang in the territory. I'm afraid he'll probably take the job. Keep the badge and gun handy."

47

"A nna, I have to do this."

Fire shone in her eyes. "Don't expect me to go in there with you. Or to like it."

I looked up to the second-story window of Wilkes Bank and Loan. "Any information I can get from him will help me understand why all this happened. And what he might do next."

"I'll be right here."

I unstrapped my gun and handed it to her.

As I stepped inside the bank, the guard let me pass. I was expected. I climbed the stairs and knocked on the door. *Jacob could use your calming influence.* His father had spoken those words months ago. How far we'd come since then.

"Come in."

I opened the door and saw the rotund man staring down at the street. He didn't turn to look at me, only stood staring out the window with both arms clasped behind his back. "She's beautiful. One of the most beautiful women I've seen. You can't blame Jacob for trying."

I stood near the desk, waiting.

"You turned down my offer to watch over my son, Philip." He faced me. "And well you should have. I thought Anna could make him a family man." He rested his hands on the back of his chair. "They stood, right where you stand now, and I planned a wedding for them."

I kept silent.

"You don't know what it's like, Philip." He held out a hand, palm up. "I raised Jacob on a knife's edge. Good on one side, bad on the other. Business walks that line, sometimes teetering one direction or the other. He fell off that razor's edge."

I nodded.

"He has no mother. I was married to my business. He showed ambition, so I financed it." He shrugged. "I didn't pay enough attention. And you paid the price."

After a moment, he sighed. "I'll tell you what I'll do for you, Philip. I'm going to rebuild your house, bigger and better. My expense."

I stared at him. It wasn't to be nice that he offered to do this. The man was making a business decision. Chances were, he was making a penance so the town would sympathize with him, the poor father abandoned by his son and left to clean up the mess.

I turned to go.

"Something you should know, Philip." The senior Wilkes cracked a knuckle. "Jacob amassed quite a sum of money, over two-hundred-fifty thousand dollars. He withdrew it all last night."

I winced, tipped my hat, and left.

Outside, Anna stood smiling in the bright sunshine.

She reached for my arm and interlocked it with hers. "Can I have my handsome knight all to myself now? I want to spend some time with the good guys and check on Rachel."

"That's what I was thinking." I took her hand. "They're going to be surprised when they see you."

We stopped by Doc Wilson's house. He said Rachel's recovery was going well and she was resting at what had been Caroline's home.

"It's Rachel's home, now," I told him.

The walk was beautiful, the afternoon sunlight reflecting off the leaves that boasted reds, oranges, and greens. At the door, Anna waited out of view.

I knocked, and Becky opened it up. "Philip, you're home!"

Scott popped his head into view. "Hey, buddy! You're limping."

I stepped inside and saw Leroy beside the bed, a wide grin on his face.

And best of all, Rachel was sitting up. She looked horrible but alive. "Philip." Tears sprang to her eyes.

"I have a surprise for you." I couldn't hold back a laugh. "I just wanted to be sure you were well enough that you wouldn't be too shocked."

Anna walked through the door.

Becky squealed and threw her arms around her.

Laughter filled the room.

Scott ran his fingers through his red hair. "She here to stay? What happened in Yankton?"

Anna broke her hug with Becky and sat beside Rachel's bed, taking her hand. "Oh, do we have a story for you. But let me tell you, Philip getting stabbed by a sword isn't the half of it."

Later that afternoon I visited the charred remains of my homestead. Mr. Wilkes promised to rebuild the cabin, but for now the barn would have to do for my temporary living quarters. I stoked the blacksmithing forge and prepared to climb into the hayloft and settle down for the night. Anna loved me. If I ever doubted it before, I didn't now. Her gentle goodnight kiss still lingered on my lips, and I couldn't help smiling.

Trevor barked, jumped, and ripped at a leather ball I'd made for him.

"Not this time, boy," I said.

I took the trinket from my pocket, the necklace I'd meant to give Anna. The jewelry had surprised me when I'd first opened the box as the wagon burned next to my parents' bodies. As a boy, I hadn't known its value. The right time hadn't come to give the necklace to Anna. I had wanted the moment to be perfect. It felt like the diamonds and emeralds, encased in gold, would cheapen all we'd been through. As if we could make our feelings stronger with pretty rocks.

I put it back in the family box and set it on the shelf with my blacksmith tools. It would make a beautiful wedding gift.

Trevor growled and shook the ball back and forth until it flung from his jaws. It flew towards the shelf and hit my family's treasure box. The red box smashed to the ground.

I rushed over to pick up the pieces. "That's a bad dog." Trevor backed away, tail between his legs.

"Oh, all right, come here." He ran to my side and I patted his head. Then I dropped to my knees. The necklace was unharmed. I picked up the box and tried to decide what to do with it. The battered lid was completely destroyed and torn from the hinges.

I cocked my head, seeing what looked like a yellowed piece of paper protruding from inside the cloth lining of the lid. With a quick snap, I broke the lid into two pieces and the paper fell to the ground. I picked it up. Unable to make it out, I walked closer to the fire.

It was a note, but the paper was so old I couldn't quite make out the words. It seemed to be written in a foreign language. I turned the paper over. I could make out a sketch of mountains, a cave, and an *X*. Near the center was a tall column. Beside it was written in pencil *Devil's Tower*.

I traced the paper with my finger and shuddered. A map. A stupid treasure map. This was what my parents were following when they died—and what Maxwell didn't tell me.

I sat holding my head in my hands, pushing away the disgust. I wanted to talk to Anna in the morning. Whatever the map pointed to, the item had left a wide swath of death and destruction.

I held the map over the forge. Burn it, I told myself. Let it go. Maxwell wouldn't tell me for a reason. Said it would be for my own good.

I hesitated. But what if the treasure was something

important, a piece of history perhaps, or something belonging to my family?

I folded the paper and tucked it away on the shelf.

I closed my eyes and remembered the question George Armstrong Custer had asked me when he visited Sioux City as I was target practicing as a boy.

"You didn't happen upon a map, did you?"

Historical Note

Reading a novel penned by Peter Leavell means one thing—history.

I've spent my life researching American history. Of the hundreds of gunplay accounts in the Wild West, each starts with the phrase *gunfights were rare.* Then the violence is written or portrayed in vivid detail. To pull a gun then was similar to car wrecks today. You only hear about the deadly ones.

In the *Dakota Sunrise* series, the setting is as historical as I can make it. Mitchell is real. The desire for statehood is real. Struggles for power and the political structures are all accurate. Characters with names you might recognize, like Theodore Roosevelt and Governor Church, are real.

The Maxwell Gang is fictional, although groups of outlaws committing crimes were commonplace. Marshall Hill is fictional as well, but his style and abilities make for a case study of a mixture of men. Anna Johnston, Scott Ladd, Leroy Jenkins, and the rest are fictional. Philip Anderson, however, is a character I created when I read the diary of a young man who wanted to raise horses in the Dakota Territory. "You won't make a go of it," he was told. So the boy became a cowpoke in Texas. Philip Anderson, as a fictional character, decided not to listen and made his dreams come true.

About the Author

Peter Leavell, a 2007 graduate of Boise State University with a degree in history, was the 2011 winner of the Christian Writers Guild's Operation First Novel contest and 2013 Christian Retailing's Best Award for First-Time Authors. Peter and his family live in Boise, Idaho. For entertainment, he reads historical books where he finds ideas for new novels. Whenever he has a chance, he takes his wife and two homeschooled children on crazy but fun research trips. Learn more about Peter's books, research, and family adventures at his website:
www.peterleavell.com

Discussion Guide
(Warning: Includes spoilers!)

1. Anna trusted Philip with her secret. Why? What was it about Philip that made her comfortable enough to share her story? Is there someone similar in your life? Are you the kind of person people tell their troubles to?

2. Philip hates his eyes. But people are drawn to him because of their unique beauty. Do you have features you hate but people seem to like?

3. Everything Philip Anderson does seems to be successful, even swordfighting, which may have more to do with strength than skill. Do you know someone who is good at everything? Do they take it for granted? Are you like that?

4. If love is worth fighting for, as Scott says, why do you think there are so many divorcing today?

5. Sometimes an emotionally charged event, like Anna's incident in the woods, draws people together more quickly than dinner dates and movies. Philip and Anna didn't spend much time together before they fell in love. Have you ever been a part of an event where you felt strangely close to those who were involved with you?

6. Philip doesn't see himself as a hero. Do you see him as a hero? Does protecting others make a person a hero? Or are all forms of violence wrong, no matter the reason?

7. Do you agree with Pastor Humphreys' opinion about violence?

8. Orphans in the mid-to-late 1800s were abundant. A provision in the Homestead Act allowed for orphans to work land at age eighteen. What would you do if you were orphaned in the 1870s?

9. Anna Johnston doesn't conform to social norms, although she doesn't simply defy them for insolent's sake. She just wants to be comfortable. But the pressures for social conformity were even more powerful in her day than they are today, especially for women. Would you wear riding pants when 99% of the town's women wore dresses?

10. How could Philip better come to terms with the trauma he suffered as a child?

11. Becky turned down Scott's offer to go to a social. It drove him into a frenzy to know her better. Do you think playing hard to get works?

12. Is Jacob Wilkes bluffing when he says he'll kill Beth Johnston?

13. Philip's recollections of his parents are different than everyone else's memories. Is there something in your life that you remember differently than others? Perhaps regrets that shouldn't be regrets at all?

14. Are there secrets you've discovered in your family that you'd like to know more about?

15. Is Anna Johnston someone you'd like to become friends with? Why?

16. At the end of the story Philip uncovers a map and is tempted to burn it. Would you destroy it? Or would you savor the mystery?

Visit the Mountainview Books, LLC website for news on
all our books:

www.mountainviewbooks.com

CPSIA information can be obtained at www.ICGtesting.com
Printed in the USA
LVOW06s1449010415

432905LV00009B/1239/P

ML   L - / 5